WHITE
SLAVES

Fifteen Years a Barbary Slave

Other novels by the author

Playing Rudolf Hess

An Absolute Secret

Shipwrecked Lives

Remembrance Man

WHITE SLAVES

Fifteen Years a Barbary Slave

NICHOLAS KINSEY

First Printing: May 2023
ISBN 978-0-9952921-8-5

Cinegrafica Films & Publishing
820 Rougemont
Quebec, QC G1X 2M5
Canada
Tel. 418-652-3345

In memory of my mother
Winifred Mary Pryce

CONTENTS

AUTHOR'S NOTE

The sack of Baltimore is one of the most extraordinary stories of corsair piracy of the 17th century and is well documented. This novel is an imaginative re-creation of the true story of the 109 Baltimore men, women and children: their capture by corsairs in the summer of 1631, their 38-day voyage down the coast of France and Spain, their brutal separation at the Algiers Slave market and their new lives as slaves in a foreign land. It is closely based on the historical record. The events, dates and even the names of the characters are accurate.

Solid historical research went into writing this novel, which was inspired by several remarkable books: Des Eskin's *The Stolen Village*, Joseph Pitts' *Encountering Islam, An English Slave in 17th century Algiers and Mecca*, and Adrian Tinniswood's *Pirates of Barbary*. Of course, when the facts are not available, the writer's job is to invent. This novel remains a work of historical fiction.

Nicholas Kinsey
March 20, 2023

PROLOGUE

"All, all asleep within each roof along that rocky street,
And these must be the lover's friends, with gently guiding feet
A stifled gasp! A dreamy noise! The roof is in a flame!
From out their beds, and to their doors, rush maid and sire and dame.
And meet, upon the threshold stone, the gleaming sabres fall,
And o'er each black and bearded face the white and crimson shawl,
The yell of 'Allah' breaks above the prayer and shriek and roar,
O, blessed God! The Algerine is Lord of Baltimore."
The Sack of Baltimore, Thomas Osborne Davis

Baltimore is a tiny village in the southwest corner of Ireland settled by English colonists in the early 17th century. The village is protected from the violent Atlantic storms that strike the coast by Sherkin Island, Cape Clear and Fastnet Rock with its lighthouse built in 1854. This is the most southerly point on the Irish mainland and was known as "Ireland's Teardrop" in the 19th century when it was the last part of Ireland that emigrants saw as they sailed west to America.

The warm winds of the Gulf Stream collide with the cold Arctic air that blows along the west coast of Ireland, creating stupendous seas. The winds howl around Roaring Water Bay, which offers shelter against the furious Atlantic storms. Baltimore sits at the mouth of the Ilen River with the breakwater of Sherkin Island in front and the hills behind. In the early days, Baltimore was known as Dún na Séad or the Fortress of Jewels. The castle, built in 1215, still stands today.

The O'Driscoll clan, the Gaelic lords of Carbery, ran a successful racket of piracy, smuggling and extortion for centuries around Baltimore and along the coast from Kinsale to Kenmare. The English victory in 1601 at Kinsale against the Irish and Spanish invasion force put an end to Irish resistance and destroyed the old order of Gaelic lords. The impoverished Irish rover, Sir Fineen O'Driscoll, was a shrewd diplomat and hastened to exchange his Irish titles for a knighthood after an audience with Queen Elizabeth I. He realized that his best bet was to collaborate with the English and so he entered into an agreement with Sir Thomas Crooke, an eminent theologian and English politician from Northamptonshire, to lease the impoverished town of Baltimore to the Calvinists for the establishment of an English colony. Crooke planned to install West country fishermen in the town and use Cornish processing techniques.

Crooke was a leader among a group of Calvinist radicals who thought the elite hierarchy of bishops in the Church of England should be replaced by a system where every man was his own priest. Their egalitarian views were subversive and rejected by many in the English Protestant Establishment. The radicals wanted to be free to worship as they saw fit and to do away with the ritual and vestments of high-church Anglicanism.

James I, the new king after the death of the Queen, liked the idea of ridding the English mainland of Protestant radicals and having a strong English presence in West Cork. He granted full recognition to the town as a borough and gave the colonists the right to return two members to the Irish parliament. The Baltimore settlers worked hard and the pilchard fishery grew prosperous.

In the summer, boys would stand on the cliffs looking for the telltale shimmer of shoals of fish out at sea. When a shoal was spotted, a cry would go up and the men would run down to their boats in the cove below Baltimore. They would work in teams with a crew of eight in the seine boat and half a dozen in follower boats. The fishermen were directed by huers who could track the movement of the shoal from the high ground. Seine nets were often a quarter of a mile long and up to sixty feet deep, with cork floats on the surface.

At the signal, the crew would drop the net and row as hard as they could, one going clockwise and the other going counterclockwise to draw in the net and trap the writhing silvery pilchards. Using wicker baskets, they would load them onto their boats and take them to the storehouse in the cove called a 'palace' (from the word *palis* for enclosure) where they would be salted and placed layer upon layer in piles. After three weeks, they would be rinsed in fresh water, tightly packed in casks, and pressed down by weights to squeeze out the valuable oil. The town of Baltimore revolved around the pilchard industry. It sustained the fishermen and their families, but also coopers, carpenters, shipwrights and a dozen other artisans and merchants. Lots of women worked in the fish palaces and press houses. A good catch could produce six hundred barrels of pilchards, including a large quantity of oil used in oil lamps.

While other freethinkers were emigrating at great risk to Holland and the New World to establish Puritan or Pilgrim settlements, Crooke's West Country Calvinists thrived and prospered in Baltimore and helped secure an English presence in Ireland.

MAP OF IRELAND

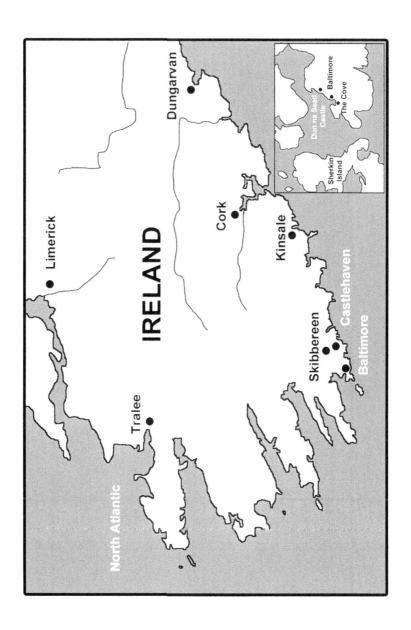

MAP OF FRANCE & SPAIN

MAP OF NORTH AFRICA

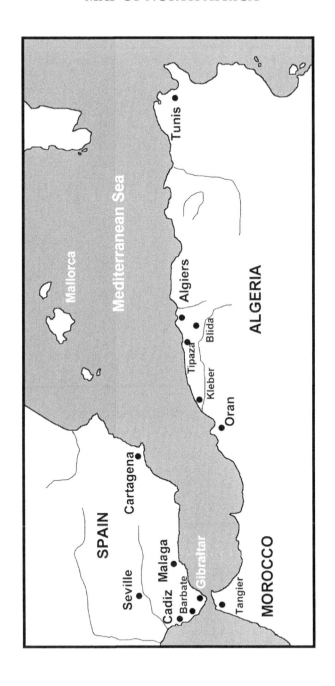

PART ONE

KIDNAPPED

One

June 20, 1631
Baltimore, West Cork, Ireland

Malcolm woke up just before dawn broke over the cove. He heard a loud crash and climbed out of bed. He sniffed the air and smelled smoke. He was barely six years old, but he knew something bad was happening. He ran to his parents.

"Da, wake up. I can smell smoke."

Stephen Broadbrook woke instantly at the sound of his son's voice.

"Help your mother," he ordered, throwing on his clothes.

Malcolm crossed to his mother's side and tugged at her arm. Joane, five months pregnant with child, looked tired and worn as she slipped out of bed. Her husband went out through the back door while Joane tried to wake young Liam. Moments later, they heard a knock at the front door and Malcolm went to open it. Standing on the threshold was a fierce-looking Turkish janissary wearing a long red tunic and a traditional *bork* with a jewelled ornament affixed to the forehead, brandishing a curved yatagan sabre. The big man smiled at the awestruck boy, who remained frozen in place, too scared to move. As the boy called his mother, the man grabbed him and entered the cottage in a flash of movement.

"Malcolm, the roof is burning," screamed Joane beside herself with fear. "Where are you, darling?"

She ran out of the bedroom with Liam, aged four, only to stop dead in her tracks at the sight of the janissary, holding young Malcolm under his arm. He stared at Joane for a moment as they heard the crackling sound of burning thatch above their heads. The janissary quickly herded mother and son out through the front door while he followed with young Malcolm. The house was already

3

becoming an inferno, with burning thatch falling from the eaves.

As they emerged from the house on the sandy shore, they were amazed by the large crowd of men, women and children in their nightclothes huddled together and surrounded by Turkish janissaries with raised sabres and muskets. A janissary was supervising the burning of the row of cottages arranged three deep in an arc around the cove. The fires lit up the night sky.

Stephen Broadbrook cursed his own stupidity. He should have looked to his own family first. Instead, he had smelled the smoke and run blindly to the shed for a water bucket. A moment later, as he returned with the bucket, he was astonished to see Turkish soldiers hauling his neighbours out of their burning cottages. Stephen had heard vague rumours of Turkish corsairs marauding Ireland's southern coast and had dismissed them as fantasy. Now he knew they were true.

His heart plummeted at the sight of Joane and the boys as a huge soldier dragged them along the beach to join the others. The raiders had been intent on setting fire to the cottages and somehow Stephen had escaped their attention, but that would not last. He hid in the underbrush for a moment to observe what was happening before he ran off to alert the main village of Baltimore.

Joane and the two boys were pushed into a ring of villagers held captive by the janissaries. Some of the men were attempting to fight back, but they were unarmed and no match for their adversaries. Most were dragged out and clubbed to the ground. Timothy Curlew was making a big show of pushing and shoving and hurling insults as they forced him out of his home with his young wife. He was the village loudmouth and it was natural for him to react this way. Few people liked the man, but he was putting up an admirable fight against the raiders. A red-bearded janissary tired of his antics, lifted his yatagan sabre and with one frightening swing beheaded young Tim in front of his wife. A cry of despair and desolation was heard from his wife and the neighbours.

The men knew they had no chance against so many armed soldiers. Their yatagan blades were wicked weapons, short infantry sabres used for slashing and thrusting strikes against their enemies. The yatagan had a curved, single-edged blade about two feet long with a sharp point and was light enough for single-handed use. Even the strongest fishermen, Richard Meade and John Ryder among them, could do nothing against the janissaries, but try to comfort their wives and children as best they could. They were hardy fishermen who worked long hours in the fish palace lifting wooden barrels of salted pilchards, but they were cowed by the slaughter of their neighbour.

Only one other man showed any sign of resistance in the face of such odds. John Davis lunged at a janissary with a filleting knife, but the man simply stepped aside and in one fluid movement disembowelled him in front of his family. The fight quickly went out of the villagers and was replaced by a prolonged wail of despair.

Sally Gunter sat on the sand in a state of shock, surrounded by her seven sons and their nanny. Richard Lorye tried to comfort his distraught wife and sister, along with their four weeping children. Corent Croffine's wife and daughter were inconsolable as they sat on the sand with their male servants near the family of Thomas Payne, whose son had been burned by the falling thatch. His wife was attempting to comfort the boy as the daughter cried out in despair. Bessie Flood hung on to her son as a janissary holding a sabre ordered them to the boats.

Watching all this from a distance stood a short, bearded man in a buff coat and turban with a commanding presence. Murad Reis was sixty years old and a Dutch corsair whose real name was Jan Janszoon van Harlem. He had meticulously planned the raid on Baltimore. Near him stood John Hackett, an Irish fisherman in dirty overalls and a flat cap.

"*Attaccar, attaccar collina*," ordered Murad in Sabir, the lingua franca of the janissaries.

Suddenly, a good half of the Turkish soldiers on the beach abandoned their positions and took off running up the hill towards the village, followed by Murad and Hackett.

"Mister Hackett, these people are speaking English?" asked Murad, in his accented English.

"Course, they are, captain. They're bleedin' anabaptists."

Murad looked at Hackett with surprise.

"They are Anglicans, then."

"They are damned heathens from Cornwall. We've been tryin' to kick their arses out of Ireland for over twenty years after the English king gave them this land."

"They seem to be very prosperous from the size of the settlement."

"Baltimore is a right good place for pilchards, sir. They catch them in the bay with their nets and salt them at the fish palace in the cove."

"Yes, but I wonder why you and Fawlett brought me here. Aren't there any Irish people on this coast?"

As the Turkish force approached the modest houses in the village, they noticed the doors were wide open and most of the occupants had fled into the night. The janissaries went from house to house, seizing anyone who hadn't already tried to save themselves. Several old and infirm people were escorted from their homes.

They were interrupted by the sound of musket fire coming from above the village. Unbeknownst to Murad, an older man, William Harris, had escaped the attack at the cove and was already moving among the cottages up near Dunasead Castle, imparting news of the attack. He had fired his musket to awaken the people to their plight.

Murad stopped for a moment to listen to the gunshots and the sound of a drumbeat — a military tattoo calling men to arms. The sound reminded him of another place time out of mind when an armed confrontation with the local authorities had killed many of his men.

"Mister Hackett, pray tell what you make of that sound?" asked Murad.

"Beg parding, sir."

"Nobody told me there would be a detachment of soldiers in this village."

"Ain't nothin' to worry 'bout, sir. Just a bunch of drunks firing off their muskets."

"You told me you knew this place," said Murad, shaking his head in frustration.

"I do, sir. Don't worry, it ain't nothing."

They listened to the drumbeat starting up again, and then Murad made his decision. He refused to take any chances with the success of his mission. He shouted an order.

"*Ritornar, ritornar —*"

What Murad didn't know was that the nearest contingent of soldiers was over fifty miles away in the coastal town of Kinsale. The military tattoo was being performed by a neighbour on his drum as Harris loaded up his musket for another shot. Murad waved his men back, and they marched down the hill to the cove, pushing their captives before them.

The dawn light was just coming up as a heavily laden boat containing the male captives and their armed janissaries headed out of the cove to the corsair ships moored in the outer bay. On the shore, the janissaries were busy herding the women and children towards a large rowboat. A wailing sound could be heard coming from the weeping women and children.

"Go on with you, Giles," said Jenny. "Come along, Cecil."

The Gunter nanny was a tiny black woman with bird-like features who was helping put one of the Gunter boys into the boat. She wore a nightcap and was sick with fear. She turned to Sally, holding baby Walter in her arms.

"I cain't go with you, Missus Gunter. My daddy will never forgive me if I go."

"Just get in the boat, love," said Sally, taking the baby from her. "If you don't, them Turkish bastards will kill you."

"But my daddy will beat me black and blue."

After the seven Gunter boys were installed in the boat, Sally took a moment to wrap the diminutive nanny in her strong arms and to whisper reassuring words in her ear. Jenny was the daughter of a popular Jamaican barman in Roaring Water Bay, a village a short distance north of Baltimore.

Murad, Hackett and the janissary force arrived from behind the burning cottages and descended to the beach.

"Hackett, how'd it go?" asked the English captain, Edward Fawlett, who was watching the loading of the women and children.

"We're not taking the town, Fawlett. The commandant was spooked by a few musket shots."

"Well, if it ain't that papist bastard hisself, John Hackett," yelled Sally Gunter, who didn't suffer fools gladly. Hackett was well known in Baltimore and always had an axe to grind again English Protestants.

"Damn your blood, Sally."

"You brought these men to our shores, Hackett. You're an Irish spy. I swear by God's blood, the devil will fetch your ugly black-poxed carcass."

"Irish filth," snarled the raw-boned, red-faced Croffine woman, standing near the boat. "I spit on you, you papist bastard."

Hackett backed up as the angry woman spat on him.

"I curse you by fire, by water, by the food you eat, Hackett. I curse your children—"

Her voice rose as profane shouts from the womenfolk joined with hers wishing evil spirits on Hackett.

"—may they die in agony and the worms of the underworld gnaw on their bones."

Hackett stepped forward to strike the woman but was held back by a stout Spaniard with a menacing look.

"Don't," murmured the man under his breath at Hackett. "You want to hit this woman? You can hit me. I'm bigger than her."

Hackett moved to confront the janissary, but quickly gave up as the man waved his sabre at him.

In the boat, Felix Gunter, aged fifteen, appeared calm and serene as he put his arms around his frightened younger brothers Giles, Geoffrey, and Cecil. He believed they were all going on a trip together and wondered what his dad would say when he came home and found the house burned to the ground and the roof gone.

Sitting across from his brothers Caleb and Lionel, there was Ciara, the Evans' maid with her dark hair, green eyes and alabaster skin. Felix had a terrible crush on Ciara, who was going on twenty and a Roman Catholic. She was a beauty to behold and already she had the attention of most of the Turkish soldiers. She came from Castlehaven, a small coastal town not far from Baltimore. She sat next to Mrs. Evans and her son Amos opposite their cook. She was an intelligent girl and spoke good English for an Irish person.

Sally swung herself up into the boat and sat down with Jenny and her sons across from Felix and the boys. Blonde Joane Broadbrook stepped into the cold water in a white shift carrying young Liam who she passed to a stout Spanish janissary who put the child in the boat.

"*Por favor, madre,*" said the man, lacing his hands together to provide Joane with a foothold to climb into the boat. She hesitated at the sight of the dark Spanish janissary, but finally accepted his help and stepped into the boat next to Liam. Next, Malcolm pulled himself up and climbed over the gunwale to sit next to his mother.

The last person to get into the boat was a pretty redhead, Besse Peeters, who was alone and sat by herself. She was a thin, pale-skinned girl barely sixteen years old whose parents were away visiting friends when the attack came. As soon as the women and children were installed, the janissaries pushed off, rowing out into the bay.

Two

Ten Days Earlier
English Channel

Captain Murad was very fond of his 300-ton Dutch-built xebec. She had a narrow hull and was fitted with oars like the corsair galleys of the Mediterranean. She was perfect for raiding — her shallow draught allowed her to get in close to shore and her long prow was ideal for boarding enemy ships. With her lateen sails, she could sail half a point closer to the wind than any square-rigged ship. Her foremast was raked forward while her main and mizzen masts were straight. When the wind died, her oarsmen could take over and move the ship in short bursts of up to seven knots. She could mount attacks on becalmed vessels or escape from enemy ships by moving to windward or hiding in shallow coves. But when she had the wind, it was almost impossible to catch her as she raced away at twelve knots or more.

Xebecs were found everywhere in the Mediterranean, but were considered unsuitable for sailing in the Atlantic Ocean, where rough weather could easily swamp them because of their low freeboard.

Another weakness was that xebecs could not withstand enemy broadsides due to their light construction materials. They were not built with the heavy oak timber used in a man of war.

With a contingent of two hundred and thirty soldiers at his disposal, Murad knew he had an almost irresistible force when he unleashed them on an unsuspecting enemy. He could attack and hold practically any village or small town along the coast for several days at a time while he plundered and captured local people. The ship's twenty-four pieces of ordnance included twelve-pound bow- and stern-chasers that could easily bring down the sails and mast of many a merchantman, leaving them defenceless in an attack.

Sailing in the lee of his ship was a small two-masted xebec with eight-pound bow- and stern-chasers commanded by Arturo Khalil, a Lebanese corsair. Murad used Khalil and his xebec for foraging and intelligence gathering along the coast. Khalil's xebec held some eighty janissary soldiers and allowed Murad to attack unsuspecting ships from two opposing directions.

Murad was getting old for this kind of caper. He was a Dutch *renegado* who had 'turned Turk' (converted to Islam) before prospering as a Muslim corsair. He had taken part in numerous raids along the coast of Spain, Portugal, France, and Italy for the Republic of Salé on the Atlantic shore of Morocco. He had been elected President and Grand Admiral of the Salé fleet in 1624 but tired of his responsibilities and in 1627 moved his operations to Algiers.

Slaving and plundering expeditions were hit-and-miss. You could spend half the day trying to corner a fishing boat to board it and find nothing of value, but a wizened old man, a teenage boy, and a bit of spare change. Two male captives hardly paid for your time. It meant constantly being vigilant and trying to spot the right targets. Furthermore, your small army of janissaries and captives had to eat and drink, so you had to organize regular foraging expeditions for food and water on land. Stealing cattle and sheep from farmers was easy enough, but slaughtering and dressing the meat took time, as did netting, preparing and salting fish. Weeks could go by with very little return for one's efforts.

His focus on this trip was plunder. Slaves were a good business, and the demand remained high for galley slaves and fair-haired young women from Northern Europe, but on this trip, he hoped to seize an English or Dutch merchantman returning from the Far East or the West Indies. The risks were high, but the potential reward would dwarf that of even the most successful slaving raid.

Huge fortunes were being made by traders in spices, and he wanted a share in those riches. He knew all about the British East India Company and its Dutch rival, the VOC, the *Vereenigde Oostindische Compagnie*. The profits from the sugar, coffee and spice trade in the markets of London and Amsterdam were phenomenal. Spices like cinnamon, cassia, cardamom, ginger, pepper, saffron, and turmeric were in high demand all over Europe.

The British and the Dutch used huge merchant ships called Indiamen. Witnesses described them as "great houses of five storeys rising from the middle of the sea." One such ship was the *Madre de Dios*, a Portuguese carrack, which was captured in the Azores in 1592. It was an 1800-ton monster that was so big it couldn't be brought into London because the Thames River wasn't deep enough. Instead, it had to be sailed to Dartmouth to unload.

Murad had hatched a plan for cutting out a returning Indiaman near Ushant on the French coast before it sailed east into the English Channel. They would seize the ship and sail it to La Rochelle where it would be offloaded with the help of a protestant merchant. He would make a huge profit from the sale of the cargo in France and avoid the cost and the risk of sailing the ship all the way back to Algiers. The Dey of Algiers, Pasha Hussein, was a partner in the enterprise and supplied all the janissary soldiers, who were paid a fixed salary of twenty pounds per annum plus a small bonus from the profits of the voyage.

Murad knew the conditions would have to be just right to make his plan work. It would have to be a nighttime operation with a calm, windless night, and it would require the combined action of both of his ships and a great deal of stealth. His janissaries would climb the sides of the tall ship and board the vessel before the crew knew what was happening. He didn't fear the heavy guns on these merchantmen because they were mainly there for appearances' sake, and the crews were not trained to fire them effectively.

The plan was a good one, but after a week of sailing about in the English Channel, he had absolutely nothing to show for it. On his first day, he had run into a convoy of Indiamen heading east, accompanied by several British Navy ships of the line. Frustrated, Murad had sailed north towards Lyme Regis, looking for worthy prey along the Devon coast, but found nothing to match the Indiamen. He would have enjoyed attacking a town or a village, but he didn't want to alert the English navy to his location. He worked his way southwest and then sailed west along the coast of Cornwall before leaving Land's End and heading out into the St. George Channel.

The busy passage between England and Ireland was full of ships of all kinds and, on the 17th of June, Captain Murad spotted a promising English merchantman on its way to Ireland. He glanced at the Dutch flag flying from his mainmast and knew that his ship would easily pass for a Dutch *fluyt* or flyboat in these waters. His partner, Captain Khalil, sailed the smaller xebec in the lee of the merchantman and waved to the captain as he got closer.

The English captain waved back. It was a tactic that Murad had used dozens of times to cut out a ship. Make an unthreatening approach on the lee side before you launch an attack from the windward. Khalil sailed closer to the merchantman, engaging the captain with grand gestures and friendly waves. On the windward side, Murad waited, ready to launch an attack if the merchantman tried to make a run for it.

At the last moment, the merchantman swung hard to starboard hoping to escape, but Murad's ship cut him off while Khalil made the approach to board the vessel. He yelled an order to his janissaries to prepare for boarding and called to the boatswain to open the rowers' hatch. The oars came out, and the oarsmen got to work closing the gap. There was no escape possible. The smaller xebec quickly rowed towards the cargo vessel and boarded it. A horde of janissaries in their red tunics with pistols and sabres jumped easily from the prow of the xebec onto the main deck and seized the ship. The captain, Edward Fawlett, gave up and reduced sail as the soldiers took control of his vessel. The janissaries ordered the crew and captain into a line on the deck and started searching them one at a time.

Barbary corsairs liked to make an example and often beat their prisoners into submission. They grabbed the first mate, an older man with white hair, and tied his legs to the mast with rope before throwing him over the side of the boat. He couldn't swim and bobbed up and down in the waves, gasping for air. The Devon men were appalled by such barbarous treatment. As the poor man dangled from the boat, the janissaries emptied the pockets of the crew and worked their way below deck, seizing food, cash, and any goods of value. Then they went to work dismantling the ship for spare parts. They piled everything on the deck, ready for removal to the xebec. The attack and the stripping of the merchantman happened very quickly and, within an hour, Fawlett's ship was sinking to the bottom of the channel as the raiders sailed west.

The Old Head of Kinsale is a massive headland that sticks some three miles out into the sea and is topped by a castle built by Milo De Courcy in 1223. It's a major landmark on the Irish coast. John Hackett of Dungarvan was fishing close to shore in his twelve-ton fishing skiff when he ran into a Morad's xebec coming around the headland. He waved to the Dutchman and continued dragging his lines until a second, smaller xebec detached itself from the first and raced towards him. Hackett had no time to escape or to try to defend himself.

A dozen janissaries jumped from the prow of the xebec directly into the skiff and seized the vessel. The five sailors on board gave up when they saw the yatagan blades appear in the hands of the invaders. The skiff was soon tied to the gunwale of the xebec ready for inspection. Captain Khalil ordered the fishermen out of the skiff and lined them up on the deck of the xebec to be searched for coins and other valuables.

Meanwhile, Khalil's cook in a turban and wearing a dirty apron appeared on deck and went over to examine the catch. The skiff had a full load of codfish and was greasy with fish heads and guts. There were already several barrels of salted fish lining the gunwale. The cook ordered the janissaries to haul the salted fish onto the xebec.

As the men stood in a line on the deck, a man's head suddenly appeared in the shadow of the hold and called to Hackett.

"Hey John, a gràdh. They catch you too?"

"Tom, cully. Where's your feckin' boat?"

Thomas Carew dropped back down into the hold as a janissary struck him on the head with the flat side of his sabre.

"Look behind you, cully," said Carew from the shadows.

Hackett turned and saw Carew's skiff tied to the larger xebec as it approached. He waited his turn in the line-up and wondered whether he might find a way to negotiate an exit from his predicament.

After a short time, Hackett was taken to the command xebec while his disconsolate crew waited on the deck of the companion vessel to hear of their fate. Hackett was led into the captain's cabin on the poop deck, where he sat down on silk cushions near a low table. Opposite him sat Captain Murad in dark robes and Captain Edward Fawlett. A servant brought in a hot pot of Turkish coffee and served it in tiny cups.

"My men tell me you are the captain of the skiff. What's your name?"

"John Hackett, sir, from Dungarvan."

"You're Irish, so I presume you know this coast well."

"Yes, sir."

"You speak English, Mister Hackett. A lot of Irish don't know English, so I suppose you must have some education."

"A wee bit, sir."

"You don't know my friend here, Captain Fawlett. He's an Englishman, and he lost his ship on his way here."

Hackett nodded at Fawlett.

"Do you know the life of a galley slave, Mister Hackett?"

Hackett shook his head.

"I will have my men show you exactly how low a man can sink when he becomes a galley slave."

Murad drank his coffee and observed the two men, who were appalled by the threat of slavery in North Africa. Hackett smiled at Fawlett, confident he could negotiate his way out of this dilemma.

"Mister Hackett, what can you tell me about Kinsale?"

"It's a large town, sir, on the river Bandon."

"You think it can be attacked?"

"Well—," attempted Hackett before he was interrupted.

"No, sir," said Fawlett. "It is defended by a fort on the larboard side as you go in. They have twelve pounders and an English man of war sits in the port with ten six- and eighteen-pounders."

"You are very knowledgeable, captain."

"It's well known, sir," said Fawlett. "I have been there many times."

"Thank you. What about you, Mister Hackett?"

"No codding, Fawlett," said Hackett to his English colleague with a sarcastic air. "What does a cove like you know about Kinsale?"

Fawlett grinned at the Irish fisherman and continued.

"I know me ports on the south coast. Been there many a time."

"You have, have you?" demanded Hackett, peeved to be stood up by the Englishman.

"A Spanish fleet tried to take Kinsale from the English back in 1601," continued Fawlett with a smile. "They failed."

Three

In the outer bay, the male captives were quickly unloaded on Captain Khalil's xebec and the boat returned to the cove. On the deck, the red-bearded captain in his white turban silently observed the captives as they were lined up in their nightshirts. The Baltimore men were a scruffy lot, cowed with the fear of God in their hearts. They were simple men who knew their situation was hopeless. They were going to be sent below decks to join the other captives, but first, the captain needed to strip them of their valuables and remove any troublemakers. He pulled a young fish plant worker with a scraggly beard out of the line. The man looked scared to death and was as good a choice as any to serve as an example. Khalil kicked the legs out from under the man, forcing him to his knees. Another janissary pulled the shirt off his back and started to beat him with a stick.

Khalil waved for the first man to come forward. A smith named John Amble stepped forward, and the captain noticed the burn marks on his face and arms. He nodded at the man and sent him away. A second man stepped forward, pulling some coins from a pocket that he tossed on the ground in front of the captain. He was excused. The beating of the youth continued as the men presented themselves, one after the other.

A skiff loaded with women and children came around the headland and sailed into view in the outer bay. They were taken to the command vessel where a janissary force was waiting to receive them. On the companion xebec, the Baltimore men were descending a ladder into the dark hold of the vessel, where they would spend the rest of the voyage. As they moved towards the ladder, they could see their women and children arriving on the command vessel a hundred yards away. They waved and shouted words of encouragement before they disappeared from view.

Suddenly, three captives surged up the ladder, pushing the Baltimore men aside. The first, a lithe Portuguese man, sprinted for the rail and in a blink of the eye was over the side before the surprised janissaries could react. The other two stumbled onto the deck, heading for the railing, but were too slow. They were emaciated Frenchmen, who were weak from captivity. Khalil calmly pulled a pistol from his belt and shot the first man in the back while the janissaries set upon the second with their sabres. The poor wretch collapsed in a bloody heap hacked to death.

The Baltimore men standing in line looked on in horror as the janissaries scanned the water for the first runner. The Portuguese man was already some fifty feet from the ship and making for the shore when a janissary took up his musket and shot him dead. His body floated in the water for some time as a reminder to the captives of what awaited them if they tried to escape.

The spectacle was too much for the Baltimore women and children on the other ship who broke into an uninterrupted wail at the sight of the slaughter and the dead man floating in the water. It had happened so fast that the women and children were terrorized. They had no idea who the men were. For all they knew, they could have just witnessed the death of a husband, father, or brother.

The janissaries on the command vessel ignored the outcry, pushing and cajoling the distraught women and children into line for inspection. Aga Santos, the janissary commandant, stood at the head of the line in his jewelled *bork* and red tunic, watching the women come forward and hand over their valuables to the young janissary standing before them. The man held a bag open in front of him as one by one the women approached and dropped their rings and jewellery into it.

"It's for safekeeping," he repeated in a friendly tone each time a woman threw something into the bag.

The line moved forward slowly. As the women and children were released, they were sent below. A janissary helped them down the ladder into the cargo hold. Not all the women, however, were willing to give up their family heirlooms to the Turkish raiders. The Harris family maid, Ellen Hawkins, stood at the head of the line and with an imperious air refused to give up her gold wedding ring.

"I ain't givin' it up," said Ellen, glaring at Aga Santos. "It's mine. I ain't givin' it to no Turk."

Ellen had only recently been married to a young Baltimore man, and it was just too much for her to abandon all hope of returning to her beloved. A janissary grabbed the short round woman and hauled her out of the line to the masthead. He seized her hand with the ring and slapped it up against a wooden upright. He held it fast as a second man readied his sabre. But Ellen was having nothing of it and, blind with rage, she fought the men like a crazed animal. She was strong for her age and easily knocked one man to the ground as the other struggled to hold on to her. They soon slapped her hand back on the upright and got ready with the sabre when they heard a command from the first mate.

"Stop," yelled Marcellus, "the captain is coming."

Murad appeared on deck, walking the line of women. He stopped in front of Joane and smiled at her children.

"These are your children, milady?"

"Yes, sir," said Joane.

Murad looked down at young Liam, who was terrified by the events he had witnessed.

"What is your name, child?"

Liam looked up at the big man, but couldn't utter a single word. Joane stepped forward.

"His name is Liam, sir. He's four years old."

The captain picked up the boy as the women and children watched silently. Murad walked over to the lateen sail and lifted the boy's hand so he could touch it. He then put the boy back down near his mother and gave an order to Marcellus in Sabir. Commands rang out and Marcellus led Ellen forward to the captain's cabin. Murad moved on and stopped when he saw young Ciara standing alone.

"Well, well. Aren't you a lovely thing? How old are you, my dear?"

"I'm almost twenty, sir."

"Good. I'm sure you will do well where you're going."

Murad moved on and stopped near Emma, a handsome, dark-haired woman in her early thirties with three young girls.

"Hello, what is your name?"

"Emma Pierse, sir, and these are my girls."

Murad noticed an older woman standing behind Emma and the girls.

"And who is this lady?"

"She's my mother, sir."

"Well, you've got a large family. Don't worry, we're going to take very good care of you."

He continued on, stopping in front of Rosamond Ryder and her two children.

"And your names are?"

Murad continued chatting amiably with the women until they calmed down. They had seen terrible things, but now he was going to make it right. He smiled at the women and stepped back to make an announcement.

"We are weighing anchor in a very short time and will be on our way. You will be safe in the hold and a meal will be served. You will be well taken care of."

He ordered his men to continue their search for valuables and returned to his cabin. The line moved forward again and the women and children were led off to the hold.

Murad entered the cabin and found Fawlett and Hackett waiting for him while a janissary guarded young Ellen with the gold ring. The two men stood up.

"Well, it looks like no one in Baltimore cares much about our captives," said Murad. "Should we wait to ransom a few or should we go?"

"They are simple folk, sir," said Hackett. "They ain't got no money for ransoms."

"This one didn't want to give up her wedding ring," said Murad with a laugh.

In the corner, Ellen glared at the captain.

"I'm sure she will eventually," said Fawlett. "Just give her some time to think about it."

Murad smiled at Fawlett.

"We don't worry about a missing finger or two on our women, Fawlett," said Murad. "We'll be leaving shortly. I want to thank you both."

Hackett nodded and stood up. He made to follow Fawlett out of the cabin when the captain pulled him aside.

"You can take your man with you."

"Thank you, sir."

On the deck, Hackett's friend Carew was waiting for him. The three men climbed into Hackett's skiff and Carew raised the sail. The women were still descending into the cargo hold as Hackett's skiff towing Carew's boat disappeared in an easterly direction.

It was dark in the hold, with only a few rays of sunlight penetrating the gloom. There was a quiet keening and weeping going on among the women, punctuated by sudden outcries from young children. There were grandmothers, mothers, servants, maids, sons and daughters, all suffering from seasickness and fear of the unknown.

At fifteen, Felix was the oldest of the Gunter children. He was a strong, good-looking boy with blond hair, a nascent moustache and an unnaturally calm disposition. He had started working in the fish palace when he was only eight and had been out on the boats not long after. Young Felix had been caught several times in the bay in dangerous storms that had reduced his friends to tears, so not much scared him.

This time, it was different. He was afraid for his mother, his six younger brothers, and their maid, Jenny. His father had been away on a trip on the night of the raid, so his mother was alone to look after her large family. She looked ill from seasickness and worry, and Felix felt she wouldn't be able to offer much comfort to his brothers. The boys had cried on the beach when they realized they might never see their father again. The hold was jammed with weeping women and children, all of whom were having similar thoughts. Felix did not see how any of this could end well.

The families were gathered in groups around the perimeter of the hold. There were some thirty women and more than fifty children, many of whom were still in a state of shock and suffering from seasickness. The hold stank of vomit and human waste, which came from the head installed at the far end of the wooden cage.

An order was heard from the main deck and there was the sound of footsteps as the crew scrambled about, getting ready to sail. Sails were loosened and raised, followed by the grinding sound of a windlass. The women and children looked up with increasing apprehension. There was a high keening sound as the women lamented their departure from Baltimore for an unknown destination.

They could hear the waves slapping against the hull and then the ship heeled on its port side and took off at a fast clip, close-hauled to the wind.

In the back of their minds, every captive hoped that a British warship would come to their aid and deliver them from the Turks, but the sounds from the deck were routine and quietly efficient. There were no shouts from above to suggest any sign of pursuit. Sally listened carefully and hoped for a sign of divine intervention, but nothing came as she sat in a corner holding baby Walter in her arms. She had installed young Cecil in the hammock and he was already fast asleep, exhausted from the long day. The xebec sailed on, crossing the Celtic Sea to the coast of France.

True to his word, the captain provided food for the captives. The trap opened and a large food tray descended into the gloom before it was rescued by Felix and his brother Caleb. It contained a large quantity of boiled codfish, heads and all. The Gunter boys put it down on the floor and waited while a second tray descended to them. Sally handed the baby to Jenny and stood up, feeling out of sorts and nauseous. She told Caleb to put the two trays in the middle of the hold so that everyone could partake.

"Good Lord, we have food," said Sally in a loud voice. "Let's proceed in a clockwork fashion. All those on my left pray avail yourselves of the food first, one family at a time."

The older Gunter boys took pieces of cod and withdrew to let the Chimor family have access to the food. Only one boy stood up to take some fish, while the others stayed put, too seasick to eat.

"Damn your eyes, Sally," shrieked Emma Pierse, storming over. "You ain't runnin' the show no more."

Sally hardly blinked an eye as Emma shoved her away.

"Ain't nobody put you in charge down here," said Emma, standing near the ladder with her hands on her hips.

It had always been a natural thing for Sally to take charge. The Gunters were pillars of the Baltimore community and ran the fish palace, where loads of pilchards were salted in wooden barrels every year. Sally had handpicked her employees and managed the fish oil production for most of her working life as her husband William handled the sales. The Gunters were terrible penny pinchers and drove a hard bargain. They were admired only because they were prosperous and their seven boys looked like a smiling staircase when they were lined up one next to the other.

"You smoke it, Sally? This time we're gonna do it my way," said Emma.

Back in Baltimore, Sally would never have tolerated such disrespect from an employee, but lost in the hold of a pirate ship, other rules prevailed. Sally turned away and went back to Jenny and the baby, leaving Emma to distribute the food. Felix was so surprised by his mother's behaviour that he did nothing. All eyes were on him as the oldest son. He felt flushed with embarrassment as he realized most of the women — including the beautiful Ciara — had expected him to stand up for his mother and the Gunter clan. That moment had passed, and now Emma Pierse had hers as she gestured everyone to the food trays.

Emma had hated the Gunters ever since they had sacked her husband for being a troublemaker and talking back to his superiors. Emma and Hugh had spent a hard winter ignominiously begging for food in the village — or rather, Emma had. Hugh had taken to drink wherever he could get it, and it was not until the spring before the Gunters relented and took him on again. Emma had never forgiven them, but her pathetic victory degenerated into a jostling free for all as people crowded around to take whatever food they could get before it was all gone.

Four

June 20, 1631
Baltimore, this present Monday morning.
Right Worshipful Sir,
This my letter to let you understand that this last night, a little before day, came two Turk men of war of about 300 tons, and another of about 150, with a loose boat to set their men ashore, and they have carried away of our townspeople, men, women and children, one hundred and eleven, and two more are slain; the ships are at present going westward.

I thought presently to give your Worship intelligence, and have sent a messenger apurpose, and I pray to give him content for his pains, and I am doubtful that they will put in about Leamcon or Crookhaven. I pray give intelligence westward. This with my service remembered.

I rest, etc.
Joseph Carter, Mayor of Baltimore

Castlehaven, West Cork

Myles was the fastest runner in Baltimore and all the surrounding parishes. It was said in Skibbereen that on hearing the winnowing sounds of a snipe a mile away, young Myles could run fast enough to sweep up the snipe in one hand and a partridge or a pheasant in the other. He was running down the muddy track near the pub when he saw two working men with a wheelbarrow repairing the washed-out road. They had laid a plank or two over the creek bed and turned just in time to see Myles racing towards them.

"*Dia dhuit ar Maidin,*" mumbled the greybeard, wishing God be with the young man this lovely summer morning. Myles was in a hurry and hardly noticed the men. They watched as he jumped the creek and ran off to the pub just down the road.

"That lad," said the greybeard, "must be mighty thirsty."

The men chuckled and went back to work. Long minutes passed and then they heard angry and profane shouts as the crowd of early morning drinkers stumbled out the door and set off towards the harbour. The two workers exchanged quizzical looks and hurried down the road to the pub to find out what was going on.

Myles' news of the attack on Baltimore spread like wildfire through the town. Would Castlehaven be next? The question was on everyone's mind. There was anger in the hearts of the crowd as they converged on a merchant vessel at the dock. They were ready to take on the Turks themselves and hoped an attack was imminent. They demanded that the captain of the cargo ship go after the raiders and bring back the hostages, but the captain was having none of it. As the angry crowd yelled obscenities at the crew, Edward Fawlett climbed onto the dock behind the protesters. John Hackett's gaff-rigged fishing boat had just arrived at the dock and was now shoving off, towing Carew's boat behind it.

Hackett and Carew felt very conspicuous around the sullen crowd. It was obvious to anyone that they had not been fishing. Their boats were riding too high in the water after Murad Reis had seized their catch. On the dock, several local fishermen were watching them as they beat a hasty retreat out into the bay.

"Hey, John, that Fawlett cove better keep his mouth shut," said Carew, holding the tiller as Hackett raised the sails to catch the westerly wind. "There's gonna be a hellish row when the story comes out."

"Ah, Tom, cully, no worries. There ain't a single witness left in Baltimore. We'll be in the clear in Dungarvan."

The wind came up, and they sailed around Bunnaglanna Foreland into the Atlantic swell, heading east.

Celtic Sea

The conditions of the male captives were far worse than those of the women. They were in the smaller companion vessel that trailed Murad's xebec on the port side. The ships ran fast and easily managed bursts of twelve knots. Down in steerage, the captives moved about, trying to stay dry from the sloshing bilge water. There were no hammocks and little comfort for the men. To get any rest, they had to lay their arms and legs over cables, blocks and sails, and when the ship heeled, they had to get up to avoid the splash of bilge water. It was a stinking dirty hole with around seventy men packed in like herrings along with rats, lice and fleas.

The twenty Baltimore men were a tough bunch of hardscrabble Englishmen used to living rough, but this was the worst they had ever encountered. They sat in tight circles around the lowest part of the hold, trying to stay dry. The best places in steerage were taken up by fifteen Frenchmen and twelve Portuguese who had been captured weeks ago and by the twenty-four Devon and Irish fisherman captured in the last few days. The French and Portuguese were in poor health, constantly scratching themselves and some showing open sores.

A Frenchman invited John Amble and his group to join him in the chain locker away from the bilge water. Amble, Payne, Meade and Ryder moved there while their friends pushed their way into drier space near the Portuguese.

"*Depuis combien de temps êtes-vous là, monsieur?*" asked Amble, who had spent his early life in France with a French mother and a Cornish father.

"*Trois semaines.* I speak some English, sir," said Jacques, an older man with red-rimmed eyes and a pale countenance.

"We were taken this morning," said Amble.

"Where?" asked Jacques.

"West of Ireland."

"*Mais vous êtes anglais, n'est-ce pas?*"

"*Oui,*" replied Amble. "We're from Baltimore on the west coast."

The Frenchman nodded, having vaguely heard of the English Protestants and their fishery on the west coast. He closed his eyes, thinking about his two friends who had just escaped.

"Did you see my friends?" asked Jacques.

"No, but I heard them running and then the shot," said Amble.

"I saw it all," ventured Richard Meade, a hard-muscled fisherman with blue eyes and tousled blond hair. "They didn't stand a chance against those Turkish bastards."

"They were from my village," said Jacques. "They were desperate to get out."

"I'm sorry to hear it, *monsieur,*" said Amble.

Thomas Payne, a fisherman from Baltimore, moved closer to hear the conversation. He was a big man, but quiet with an intelligent air. He expressed himself with difficulty, so people often took him for a half-wit.

"What is our destination, *monsieur*?" asked Payne.

"They're taking us to Algiers," said Jacques. "That is, if we survive."

"We're goin' east, maybe southeast?" asked Amble.

"Yes, sir. We're returning to France."

"This ship is fast," said Payne. "We'll be there in a day or two."

In the dim light, the English captives hadn't noticed the man rocking gently in the bilge water with his eyes closed.

"Is he dead?" asked Payne.

"*Oui, monsieur*. He died yesterday."

The Englishmen shrank away from the dead man, and a feeling of absolute hopelessness overtook them.

"We'll be dead in a week," Jacques gestured at the corpse. "Some of us before then."

Baltimore, West Cork

Stephen Broadbrook walked slowly along the shore, examining the remains of the burned-out cottages. He looked haggard in his dirty clothes and felt emotionally drained. He had strong feelings of guilt. He had not protected his family in their moment of need, yet here he was revisiting the site of his failure. The cottage was his only remaining connection to Joane and the boys, and the child Joane carried in her womb. He arrived at the third cottage near the end. The door was ajar and banging in the wind. Most of the roof was gone, and the interior was full of charred timber, the thatch and wattle reduced to ash. *We were so happy here,* he thought. *What would become of them now?*

Stephen stepped inside and had a look around the kitchen. There was little to save, but he had to save what he could or he would go mad. Somehow, the kitchen table had survived. He brushed away the thick layer of ash that covered its surface, then collected an iron pot, a few cups, several knives and forks, one of Liam's favourite toys, and other odds and ends. He had just placed them reverently on the table when a sliver of memory drew his eye to the fireplace.

Last year, Malcolm had lost his first tooth and run home from school, clutching it proudly in his hand. Joane had made a great fuss over the lad when Stephen had told him he must throw the tooth into the fire, lest a witch use it to gain power over him. The same evening, father and son had stood together facing the hearth and recited the words of Saint Peter (5-8-9):

"Be sober, be vigilant; because your adversary, the devil prowls around like a roaring lion looking for someone to devour. Resist him, steadfast in the faith, knowing that the same afflictions are suffered by your brethren in the world."

Stephen had followed this with the Lord's prayer and Malcolm had glanced up at his father before throwing the precious bit of enamel into the fire. For a moment, nothing happened and then suddenly there was a small explosion within the flames, its sudden report causing Malcolm to jump with surprise. It had been a small moment, but Stephen could still remember the loving smile on Joane's face as she reassured Malcolm with a gentle hug. For days afterward, the lad remained convinced he had witnessed a miracle.

Stephen wanted to relive that moment again and again, but reluctantly he felt himself returning to the present. He went into the bedroom, each step disturbing the ash that was all that remained of the straw bed and furniture. He did not know what made him look down, but the metallic glint that caught his eye was a miracle all its own.

It was Joane's gold wedding ring. She hadn't worn it on the night of the attack because her fingers were often too swollen during her pregnancy. She must have forgotten it, or maybe she dropped it on purpose to prevent the Turks from getting it. He touched his lips to the ring and thought about his lovely wife when he was startled by a loud knock on the door. Stephen put the ring in his pocket and tried to compose himself before venturing out of the room.

Given the condition of the cottage, it seemed oddly formal that the man had knocked at all, but Stephen was grateful that he had. William Gunter was a big fireplug of a man in his fifties. He and his wife Sally had owned and run the fish palace that so many in Baltimore had depended on for their livelihoods. All of that had changed now, but he had not lost his natural air of authority.

"I saw you come in, Broadbrook," he said. "I'm sorry for your loss.

How are you keeping?"

There was no truthful answer to such a question since Stephen did not know himself. Gunter nodded amiably and tried again.

"I would like to help."

Stephen looked lost and said nothing.

"This is a terrible time for all of us, Broadbrook. The Christian thing to do—"

"I don't need your help," said Stephen, interrupting.

"Where will you go? You can't stay here moping around. You need to get on with your life."

"This was my life, Gunter. I have heard talk that Captain Hooke in Kinsale will be going after them. The *Fifth Whelp* is a well-armed ship."

"The corsairs are long gone, Broadbrook. Don't expect Francis Hooke or anyone else to be of help. I hear Hooke can't even get out of the port for lack of supplies. It's an intolerable situation."

Stephen stared at the older man, not wanting to believe a word of it. He had pinned his last shred of hope on the rumour that Hooke was setting off in pursuit, but he knew enough about William Gunter to realize that the man was well informed. Lashing out at him would do no good.

"I'm sorry about your wife and those wonderful boys of yours, Gunter. You've lost your family, just as I have."

Gunter looked away for a moment, then nodded his thanks.

"Is there nothing we can do?" asked Stephen.

"I doubt our own Richard Boyle, the Earl of Cork, will do anything to help us," said Gunter. "Boyle and his people don't care a whit about the people of Baltimore and won't lift a finger for us."

"There must be something," Stephen persisted.

"Our only chance is to ransom our families."

"Ransom them with what?" Stephen asked, exasperated. "I have nothing. I don't have two pennies to rub together."

"It's our only chance, Broadbrook. We must appeal directly to Parliament in London to ransom our families."

Five

"Qui voit Molène voit sa peine
Qui voit Ouessant voit son sang
Qui voit Sein voit sa fin
Qui voit Groix voit sa croix."
Old Breton proverb

("Who sees Molène sees his penalty, Who sees Ushant sees his blood, Who sees Sein sees his end, Who sees Groix sees his cross.")

Celtic Sea

The corsair ships sailed southeast at twelve knots with a strong, westerly wind. The mastheads flew the Dutch ensign and there was not a single Turkish janissary visible on either deck. The men were below decks, catching up with their sleep. Captain Murad stood on the deck with his first mate holding an astrolabe and a cross staff. Murad measured the angle of the sun with the astrolabe to determine their latitude. He wanted to sail as close as possible to Ushant Island on the French coast. He knew he needed to sail exactly three degrees south from Baltimore to make it to Ushant at 48.46 degrees latitude if he didn't want to miss the island completely. If he went too far north, he would end up in the channel heading for Saint-Malo and too far south he would end up in a particularly dangerous area called the Brest roadstead. He checked the ship's compass near the tillerman and gave an order to sail further south on a south-south-east heading.

It would not be long before they caught sight of the French coast. An officer appeared on the poop deck with Ellen Hawkins in tow and led her to the below decks, where the oarsmen sat in rows. They scurried along under the oars until they reached the crew quarters at the other end. Sleeping men were installed in hammocks along the wall and woke up at the sound of the officer's voice.

"*Viens, ma jolie*," said a Frenchman waving to Ellen as a Spaniard intoned "*Ven aquí, querida*" with a laugh. The men got up to have a better look at the woman. Ellen screamed as a man jumped her and threw her down on his sea chest. The gang rape went on for a good hour before they let her go.

The officer returned to collect Ellen and took her back up on deck, where Aga Santos waited to supervise the removal of the ring. After her violent treatment below deck, Ellen had no fight left in her. A janissary seized her hand and did it so quickly that Ellen had no time to react. She was even surprised when she saw him holding up her severed ring finger.

It was time for the evening meal in the women's hold. There were several trays of boiled fish and crusts of bread on a makeshift table near the ladder. A dark gruel was being doled out into tin cups by Emma Pierse, Bessie Flood and Emma's three girls. The girls fanned out, bringing the gruel to the nearest children and their mothers, and then going deeper. One of the girls carried a goatskin of water.

Orla Walsh sat quietly by herself, still shaken by recent events. She was an Irish lady in her fifties who had been a bookseller in Skibbereen. Years ago, she had come to Baltimore with a wagon full of books, hoping to start a new life for herself, but had been snubbed by the population from day one. She had not reckoned on the women of Baltimore. To them, she was nothing more than a papist blow-in from Skibbereen.

The women of Baltimore were ordinary working-class people, fishermen's wives and fish plant workers who were fiercely Calvinist. They did not like Orla's superior air and shunned all her attempts to befriend them. That was not true, of course, for their children. Her books opened up new worlds to them. Orla knew most of the youngsters who came in to look at her books and, especially eight-year-old Phoebe, with whom she often struck up long conversations.

"Wanna cup, Missus Walsh?"

"What is it you have there, child?" said Orla, taking the tin cup that Phoebe held out to her.

"Mum says it's got some flour in it, maybe some olive oil and vinegar, and dark stuff," replied young Phoebe.

"Well, let me have a taste, dear. I only want a taste."

Orla sipped the gruel and made a disdainful grimace before she smiled at Phoebe, who was watching her closely.

"Is it bad, Missus Walsh?"

"No, it is not. It is nourishing, my dear," said Orla. "It tastes of olives. Here, take the cup with you."

Young Phoebe returned to her mother at the food table where the women and children were distributing the fish and bread. She collected a cup for the Harris children and went off to serve them.

"It's some kind of gruel," said Mrs. Harris, tasting it. She passed the cup on to each of her three children in a circle.

"Drink some, Becky."

Becky grimaced at the taste and handed it on to her brother, who eyed the dark liquid with suspicion.

"We don't know when we will eat again," said Mrs. Harris. "So drink some of it."

The boy sipped the gruel and passed it along to his older brother.

"You won't like it, gran," said the older boy to his grandma. "It tastes something awful."

As the women lowered the hammocks and put their youngest to sleep, Felix sat with Ciara and the Osburne maid, Roisin, near Mrs. Evans and her ten-year-old son Amos.

"How is your ma?" asked Ciara.

"She is not her usual self," replied Felix. "I try to keep her spirits up, but she seems to have lost all hope."

"Well, my boy, she got her comeuppance today," said Mrs. Evans with a cynical laugh. "Emma right attacked her."

Felix nodded.

"S-o-r-r-y for your m-a-a-a," attempted Roisin in halting English. She was twenty-five years old and had curly blond hair and a mole at the corner of her mouth. She was terribly shy and spoke with a stutter. She looked very plain indeed sitting next to the uncommon beauty of Ciara.

"She'll be all right, I'm sure," said Ciara, putting her hand on Felix's shoulder to comfort him. The effect of her touch was to make him more nervous than before.

"What do you think is going to happen to us?" asked Ciara.

"We'll be fine, Ciara," said Felix. "I think this will be a great adventure for us all."

"Slavery ain't no adventure that I want to live," said Mrs. Evans mournfully.

"But ma, we'll see new places and people," said Amos with a look of wonderment.

"Heathens," said Mrs. Evans. "They are all heathens, Amos. Sinful people who are going to sell us body and soul."

The cover of the woman's hold was removed and the women and children looked up to see a crew member attach a safety rope to a scuffed and bruised Ellen Hawkins. The man climbed down, helping Ellen descend, using the rope to prevent her from falling. All eyes were on the Harris maid as she descended slowly into the dark hold. Several women rushed to her aid as she reached the bottom and the janissary removed the rope from around her waist. She had cuts on her face, but everyone's attention was on the bloody rag wrapped around her left hand. The three Harris children ran to embrace their maid as Mrs. Harris observed her with disdain.

"What did they do to your hand, Ellen?" demanded Mrs. Harris. "Let me have a look."

The women crowded around as Ellen removed the filthy bandage. There was a collective gasp as she pulled the last of it away. There were two stumps covered in dried pine tar where Ellen's fourth and fifth fingers had once been. The wedding band was gone.

"Oh, my God. You poor thing!" said Mrs. Harris as the women and children gathered around to comfort her.

The male captives on Captain Khalil's ship had spent a horrible night in the company of the dead man. The body rolled obscenely with the motion of the ship, and in the cramped space, it was impossible for those closest to get away from it. It was not until dawn that the hatch cover came off and several janissaries descended the ladder. They kicked the men out of the way as they went over to have a look at the dead man. They stood over him for a while, using their bandannas to cover their noses. After a brief conversation in Sabir, they left the man and returned to the ladder.

With the improved light coming from the hatch, Thomas Payne stood up and went to have a look at the body. He stepped back in shock.

"It's typhus," said Payne in a gruff voice. "I saw it in Kinsale last winter."

John Amble looked alarmed and joined Payne near the body. The dead man showed red spots on his abdomen, chest, and the back of his hands. Amble turned to his new friend.

"I think your man here has typhus," said Amble, stepping away from the body.

"*Mais non, ce n'est pas possible,*" said Jacques, who quickly stood up and joined them. "The red spots, it's not typhus."

"You think it's a rash?" asked Amble.

"If it's typhus, we are all dead," said Jacques.

A panic took hold of the French and Portuguese captives as they heard talk of the hated disease. The fear on their faces was palpable as they tried to move as far away as possible from the body.

With the dawn came a grey day and a sky spotted with rain clouds. The westerly winds were driving them towards the French coast. They could see the bay of Lambaol as they passed Ushant Island on their way south. They were on the lookout for French men of war. The most dangerous part of their voyage was crossing the Brest roadstead near the French naval base, with ships coming and going, second only to the risks for mariners navigating around the Finistere islands.

Murad stood at the tiller and scanned the horizon with a telescope. He had to avoid all contact with enemy vessels, French or British. He planned to go into a bay on the east side of Molene Island and wait for darkness before venturing out again and crossing the bay to Sein Island to the south. The corsair xebecs carried the Dutch flag, so there was a good chance no one would notice them in the islands. They passed Molene without seeing any French ships and then sailed back around to the northeast to enter the bay on the east side of the island. As they came into the shallow waters of the bay, a sailor stood on the prow with a sounding line and a lead weight. They were coming in fast on the tide and they had to be very careful not to run aground.

Murad dropped anchor in the bay and noticed Arturo Khalil approaching in a small dinghy. He smiled with satisfaction at his colleague, happy about their excellent start on their return voyage. Of course, he had hoped for better things, an Indiaman full of exquisite spices or Spanish gold, but they had met their quota of slaves for the voyage south. He was tired of this work and the dangers lurking along the coast.

Khalil climbed quickly over the rail and requested, *sotto voce*, a meeting in Murad's cabin. Neither man spoke again until they were sitting down for a coffee in the captain's cabin.

"How many?" Murad asked grimly.

"One dead," said Khalil. "We threw the body overboard this morning. I had Marcellus look at the others. Six of the men are sick with something, but none have the rash."

"If it is typhus, Arturo, all your captives will be dead in a week."

"What do you want me to do? The crew is afraid."

"What does Marcellus think?"

Marcellus was Khalil's first mate. The man was no expert, but he had some basic notions of medicine from his father, who had once been a physician in France. In the absence of anyone else, his opinion would have to do.

"He's not sure," admitted Khalil. "He says it could be something else, some kind of fever."

Both men knew that captives died below decks all the time. Conditions in steerage were abysmal, rife with vermin and disease, and even the most heartless of corsairs knew there was no money in dead captives.

"The dead man?" asked Murad. "Who was he?"

"He was French."

"Put the French and Portuguese on deck for a few days and increase their rations," said Murad.

"What about the English and Irish?"

"Leave them below. They'll be all right. Put Marcellus in charge of looking after the French and Portuguese. It may just be a fever."

"How are your women and children?"

"No one is sick, but we must be careful. Keep your janissaries away from the sick men. If they catch the malady, we could lose half our complement of soldiers before we get home."

With a soft, westerly breeze, Khalil's ship followed his sister ship out of the bay in the moonlight. They headed south around the small island and then sailed in a southwesterly direction across the Brest roadstead and down the French coast. The French and Portuguese captives sat shackled together on the deck near the forecastle, under the surveillance of three heavily armed janissaries. They had eaten well for the first time in a month, and they looked hopeful as they watched Captain Khalil give orders to his crew. They knew they were back in France and their chances of being freed had increased substantially with the large number of French naval vessels in the area.

Captain Murad urged his ship to its maximum speed and soon they were sailing close to the wind at ten knots. He planned to sail some twenty-five miles south and then turn east heading for Sein Island and the coast near Audierne on the Goyen River. They were in desperate need of food and fresh water, which they could only obtain in the rivers and farmlands along the coast. They had not visited either town on their way up, so Murad felt that their chances of being attacked by local French militias were low.

It had been a long night in the hold, with frequent outbursts of tears from the women and children. They woke up to the sound of two janissaries, a fat jovial Italian by the name of Marco and Diego, a skinny Spanish *renegado*, descending the ladder with the food trays. They brought boiled fish and a bucket of dark gruel, which they installed on a makeshift table lit by two tallow candles in the dim light. The women and children were hungry going into their third day of captivity. Emma and the children helped with the food distribution. Ciara divvied up the fish and the children carried around the tin cups of gruel.

Young Phoebe set out with two cups and sought her old friend, Orla Walsh, but the woman had disappeared from her usual corner. She now sat three families down behind a hammock in the darkest corner of the hold, reciting in Latin from her prayer book.

Phoebe went over to say hello.

"Mornin', Missus Walsh. You wanna cup?"

"Yes, thank you, my dear," said Orla. "I'm hungry today. I don't know why."

Phoebe gave her the cup, and she quickly drank down the dark liquid, making a grimace.

"Would you like some fish with that?" asked Phoebe.

"No, thank you."

"My ma says everyone must eat something."

"Maybe later, my dear."

In the dim light, Phoebe's eye caught the reflection of a page in

Orla's book of hours. She smiled at Phoebe and showed her an illustration of the arrest of Jesus.

"Jesus was arrested by the Temple guards, my dear. It happened shortly after the Last Supper."

The miniature prayer book was an immensely valuable family heirloom in the 17th century. Printed on fine vellum, the illuminated manuscript was often passed from a husband to his bride on their wedding day. It contained the hours of the Virgin Mary written in Latin with devotions to be made during the eight canonical hours of the day: matins, lauds, prime, terce, sext, none, vespers, and compline.

Phoebe was all eyes as Orla turned the pages and arrived at a section on the turbulent lives of the saints. She showed Phoebe a picture of Saint Christopher carrying the Christ child across a river.

"That's Saint Christopher saving the baby Jesus?" said Phoebe with pride.

"Yes, it is, my dear," said Orla, turning the page to a picture of Saint Leger.

"That's Saint Leger, who was blinded by a soldier."

Phoebe was shocked by the horrific image of a soldier gouging out the eyeball of the saint. Orla quickly moved on.

"Here you have Saint Brigid of Kildare. You must know her. She's the patron saint of Ireland."

"My pa says she could turn water into ale."

"Yes, I've heard that one. So you know the story of Saint Brigid's cloak?"

Phoebe shook her head.

"Saint Brigid was a nun who wanted to build a convent but had no land on which to build it. She asked the King of Leinster for land, but she was laughed at by his courtiers. Brigit prayed and prayed and asked God to soften the heart of the king. She returned to see the king, and this time asked only for the land that her cloak could cover."

"But a cloak covers nothing?"

Orla took off her own brown cloak and held it up before she spread it over the nearby hammock.

"You are right. A cloak doesn't cover much. But when Brigid placed it on the site she had chosen for the convent, the cloak started to get bigger and bigger until it was big enough to cover all the land she needed for the convent. The King of Leinster had a change of heart and gave her permission to build the convent."

Phoebe smiled and promised herself to tell her mother and her sisters about Saint Brigid's cloak.

"I've got to go," said Phoebe, still holding a cup full of gruel.

"Here, take the book with you."

Phoebe hesitated and looked around nervously.

"No, take it," Orla gently pressed the miniature prayer book into the child's hands. "Take good care of it now. You can bring it back tomorrow."

"Thank you, Missus Walsh," replied Phoebe, as she hid the book in the pocket of her coat. She collected the empty cup and left to make her rounds.

Back at the makeshift food table, fat Marco was talking to Ciara as the cook passed down another tray of fish from above.

"You want the blanket for yourself?"

"No, not for me. For my mistress, Missus Evans. She gets cold at night."

"I will ask permission."

"Thank you, Marco."

Marco found himself bewitched by the lovely Ciara, as did his friend Diego.

"It is nothing, miss," said Marco, grinning. "You know the proverb: *Far d'una mosca un elefante.*"

"No, I don't. What is this elephant?"

"I think you say make an elephant out of a fly?"

"You mean make a mountain out of a molehill, no?"

"Yes, that's it, miss. A blanket is a blanket, it is nothing."

The dawn came up wet and frigid for the month of June. On deck, Murad was watching a fog bank move in from the east. He called to a sailor and barked an order in Sabir. The crew eased the lateen sail, and the ship slowed perceptibly as they entered the fog.

According to his calculations, they were close to Sein Island off the coast of Finistere. He could just make out the rocky promontory and the furious waves on the western shore, which had wrecked dozens of ships over the years. The fog engulfed the corsair ships and soon they could barely make out the bow of the ship from the stern. They sailed on in a southeasterly direction to avoid the island and to bring them closer to their rendezvous at Audierne. The fog got thicker and thicker, and soon they had lost all contact with Khalil's xebec. They were leaving the eastern shore of Sein Island when a ship appeared out of the fog on their port side, coming straight at them. By sheer luck, Murad had been looking in that direction at the right time. He quickly ordered the man at the tiller to turn hard to starboard, bringing the ship around to port.

"*Attention, attention, bateau droit devant,*" yelled a French sailor. This was followed by a flurry of urgent orders in French as the crew of the frigate realized what was happening. Seconds later, the massive ship swept past them, so close that even in the fog Murad could make out the seemingly endless row of gun ports along her flank. Murad's xebec had narrowly missed being cut in two by the heavy oak prow of the frigate.

For now, the frigate has disappeared in the fog and Murad ordered the tiller back to port to resume their original course. He ordered his gunners to man the stern- and bow-chasers, although he had no illusions about the outcome if they encountered such an adversary again. In these waters, it could only have been a French man of war. Now they would be out looking for him.

Six

"Parliaments are all together in my power.
As I find the fruits of them good or evil,
they are to continue or not to be."
King Charles I

London

It had all started with Charles I's unshakeable belief in the divine right of kings to rule and therefore no man, politician or soldier, had the right to question his reign. But in 1628, the position of the king as absolute monarch was seriously challenged when Parliament demanded that he stop trying to raise money outside the institution of Parliament. The members had the impertinence to demand that he put an end to imprisonment without trial and the use of martial law against his citizens. Charles eventually grew tired of Parliament's insistence that money had to be accounted for and spending curbed. In 1629, he simply dismissed Parliament and decided to rule the kingdom alone, relying on the Privy Council to handle the administration of the government.

The king had been furious after learning of the attack on the English colony in Baltimore and a meeting of the Privy Council had been hastily convened. The grey-haired members were the survivors of bitter disagreements with Parliament. They sat at a long table in chambers as Richard Boyle, the Earl of Cork, stood up to address the council while William Gunter, dressed in his best brown suit, waited in the vestibule to be called.

"The attack on Baltimore was both outrageous and unprecedented, my Lords," said Boyle. "We all agree on that, but we need to consider what dangers lie ahead. I hear on good authority that the Turks intend to surprise the whole southern coast next year, distributing their fleet according to the strength of each port. Three evils will follow from this: the exode of people from the harbour towns; the end of the pilchard fishery; and the stopping of the flow of coin into the realm."

The Secretary of State, Sir Dudley Carleton, known as Lord Dorchester, had been listening attentively from his place at the table. He was a long-standing diplomat and often advised the king on foreign affairs. Now he put down his pipe and addressed his colleagues.

"The king and I are concerned by the lack of protection along our coasts. It appears that the two captains appointed to guard the coast are at each other's throats and blame each other. We must find where the negligence lies and stamp it out."

"Hear, hear," murmured the councillors.

"My Lords, Captain Francis Hooke of the *Fifth Whelp* maintains that our admiral, Sir Thomas Button, has pocketed the money for supplies, leaving Hooke stranded in port. He is making a lot of noise and has protested to the Admiralty. We cannot—"

Lord Dorchester stopped abruptly in mid-sentence and appeared to notice William Gunter for the first time. Gunter had been called by Boyle and had just come into the room.

"Who is this man?"

"He is with me, my Lord," said Richard Boyle. "His name is William Gunter. He ran the pilchard fishery in Baltimore and lost his wife and seven boys to the corsairs. He would like to have a word."

"Good morning, Mister Gunter," said Lord Dorchester.

Gunter stood against the far wall and coughed nervously before speaking.

"My Lords, thank you for your time."

"Please speak up, sir."

"I recently lost my wife and my sons when they were carried away by the Turks during the raid on Baltimore. In our village, 87 women and children and 20 men were seized by the Turks. They burned our homes and killed two local men."

Gunter stopped for a moment to gauge the sympathy of the room. The outrage among the lords was palpable.

"I've come here to ask the king to ransom our people from the Turks and bring them home. The pilchard fishery in Baltimore is finished without them. No one wants to live there anymore and everyone is in fear for their lives."

Sein Island, France

Murad stood nearly motionless near the tillerman, his eyes searching the swirling fog. The fog had lifted a bit and he could just make out the prow of the ship from his position at the stern. They were moving slowly southeast towards the mainland. He had put his crew on full alert and doubled the men at the oars in the event they had to move to the windward in double-quick time. It had been over an hour since he last heard a shout from Khalil's xebec.

With no sign of the French ship, Murad rang four bells to mark the breakfast call at six a.m. The sailors and janissaries silently went to the galley in the ship's stern to fetch their meal. The crew observed an unfamiliar routine working two ten-hour watches — a night watch from eight p.m. to six a.m. and a day watch from six a.m. to four p.m. with two dogwatches in between. The dogwatches were changed frequently to allow the crew to get the rest they needed.

The cook appeared on the poop deck, bringing the captain a mug of hot tea. *It was going to be a very long day*, thought Murad. *Where was Khalil's xebec in this fog? What was the French man of war doing in the vicinity? Was the ship actively looking for the marauding corsairs or was it a simple coincidence that they had run into her?* Murad felt they were safe for the time being, as long as the fog remained in place.

About a mile away, Captain Khalil was watching closely as a sailor put out a sounding line as they moved east away from the Island. The first mate appeared from the prow with a Frenchman in tow.

"This man knows the island, captain," said Marcellus. "He says you are too close to the shore."

Captain Khalil looked down at the slight Frenchman, who barely came up to his shoulder.

"My name is François Moulin, *capitaine*," said the man. "I was born on these islands. You are going to run aground on the *chaussée de Sein*."

"And what is this *chaussée*?" asked the captain, looking about nervously.

"A series of reefs," Marcellus answered in Sabir, "running east and west of the island."

"*Soyez sur vos gardes, capitaine,*" said the man excitedly.

Khalil didn't need a translation to understand. The tide was pulling them in the direction of the reef. He turned to the tillerman and ordered him to turn to port, bringing the ship to starboard and away from the reef.

"Thank the man, Marcellus. Give him some brandy and some for his mates."

Marcellus nodded and left with the Frenchman.

As Murad struggled to find his way out of the fog, the women and children slept through the day. For hours, the ship barely moved, so it was unnaturally quiet on board. Felix sat with the Evans family, chatting with Ciara as the others dozed.

"What do you think will happen when we get to Algiers?" whispered Felix.

Ciara smiled mischievously.

"A strapping young fella like you, you'll be sold as a slave to work in the fields," said Ciara with a laugh. "Me, I'll be the new concubine of the Sultan."

"You're not serious," said Felix.

"Serious, of course I'm serious, sweet boy. I've always wanted to be rich and powerful."

Felix did not look amused. He knew Ciara was laughing at him. She was beautiful enough to seduce the richest of men. Her stunning good looks would make her irresistible to the Turks in North Africa.

"I'm only joking," said Ciara, playfully jabbing Felix in the ribs. "I only said that to tease you."

"Maybe a rich man in Algiers will buy you," concluded Felix with a frown.

The Pierse girls, Eunice and Dinah, were playing quietly with a doll while their exhausted mother slept soundly beside them. Young Phoebe, the oldest of the girls, was glancing furtively at the remarkable illustrations in the miniature prayer book which she had hidden in her bedclothes. Each illustration was a story unto itself and she had hundreds of questions about the saints in the prayer book.

Children in Baltimore knew little or nothing about the saints. Sainthood was not discussed by the Calvinist radicals of Baltimore, whose aim was to purify the Anglican Church, by eradicating the perceived remnants of Catholicism. Calvinists believed that ordinary people could prove in their daily lives that they were worthy of receiving salvation, just like God's chosen. By doing good works and living a pious life, they too could aspire to sainthood.

Eunice called to Phoebe, who hid the book before standing up and going over to talk to her sisters. She suspected that her mother would not approve of the prayer book, nor would her neighbours. Orla would be subjected to constant harassment by the women if her secret got out.

On deck, the weather was clearing rapidly. The fog had lifted to reveal the French coast in the distance, bathed in sunshine. Murad was nervous as he kept watch for the French frigate and his sister ship. There was not a ship in sight, but that could change quickly. He decided to make a run for the coast and try to find shelter in a bay. He ordered the crew to raise the mainsail. The offshore breeze picked up, and they were soon racing eastwards towards Audierne.

Captain Khalil's xebec was still locked in dense fog. Despite Moulin's warning, they had still managed to run aground on a shallow part of the reef. The crew tried to winch the ship off the reef using the anchor, but the chain kept slipping. Several sailors and a few janissaries were busy removing oars from below decks and hauling them forward to the prow. They were going to use the oars to lever the ship off the reef. After a furious effort, the men succeeded in lifting the ship just enough to clear the reef. As they drifted away, the weather cleared and Khalil ordered the crew to raise the mainsail. They soon found themselves in an empty ocean with no sign of their sister ship.

The ship's bell rang eight times to signify the first dogwatch, and the crew dropped their things and went to the galley for their evening meal. Down in steerage, the English and Irish captives were stirring. They could hear the men working on the deck and wondered what was going on.

"We're movin' again," said Thomas Payne, listening to the waves hitting the hull. "They got us off the reef. Now we're movin' again."

"I told you we was in France," said William Mould to Corent Croffine.

"How do you know that?" asked Croffine.

"Course, we are," said Payne. "We've been sailin' east for two days."

"We gotta try somethin'," said Hugh Pierse. "We're not that far from home."

"We must be in Brittany," said Richard Watts. "We escape this ship and we're home in no time."

"Let's make a deal with the French," added Watts.

"What kinda deal?" asked Pierse.

"Goddamn it, Hugh!" Payne snapped. "It ain't difficult to understand. We jump 'em the first chance we get."

"We got nothing, we ain't armed," complained Croffine.

"We're sailing again, this boat is running fast," said Mould. "We could make a move when they stop for water."

"Righto, cully. They gotta take on water soon enough, and the fish ain't gonna last," said one of the Irish fishermen.

"The French are with us. They've suffered worse than us," added John Amble. "We should talk to them when we get a chance."

Suddenly, the men jumped at the sound of an explosion. The sound was like that of an eighteen-pounder being fired at close range. Clearly, a foreign ship was firing at them. They looked around, horrified. They were trapped in the steerage hold. If the xebec sank, they would all drown like rats.

Seven

Goyen River, France

Captain Murad was on deck as the xebec sailed up the silent river on the incoming tide. They passed rich farmlands and rolling hills as they moved upstream. Murad had posted a sailor on the prow with a sounding line, who called out the water depth at regular intervals. There was no one around. Not a farm animal nor a labourer could be seen in the fields. Murad suspected their friendly Dutch flag on the mast was convincing no one. A river like the Goyen would normally be full of small boats, fishing the rich waters at the mouth or hauling cargo up and down the river at all hours of the day. Today, it was unusually quiet.

Murad and his men would have to hurry to lay in their water supplies and then get away before they attracted too much attention. On the deck, Aga Santos had mustered fifty men for a scavenging expedition. The janissaries wore their military uniforms and Murad had no doubt that the very sight of them would be enough to discourage any opposition from locals.

The French man of war had lost Murad's ship in the fog, but had found a consolation prize in Khalil's smaller xebec, now a sitting duck as the frigate came out of the fog. *Le Cyne* had the advantage of the weather gauge as it bore down on Captain Khalil's ship. Khalil instinctively turned his ship due south to avoid the frontal attack by the French frigate. They were massively outgunned, but if they could get up to speed fast enough, they might still outrun the French ship. A xebec with a good wind could make nearly fifteen knots against the frigate's ten. What they could not do was outrun the cannon fire of the big eighteen-pounder mounted on the frigate's bow.

Khalil knew that surrendering to the French was an impossible choice. The French would hang every last member of the crew and the entire contingent of janissaries. There would be no mercy for his men. His only hope was to get away. As he thought about his options, another shot from the frigate whistled overhead. From the sound, he could tell that it had missed his lateen sail by only a few yards. If the next one was a direct hit, they would be at the mercy of the French ship. Khalil quickly turned the xebec to port to reduce his exposure to the French bow-chaser and to give his stern gunner a better angle on the Frenchman.

As another shot from the frigate landed wide, Khalil ordered his gunner to fire a twelve-pounder at the French ship, hoping to discourage the enemy. It was a lucky shot. The ball struck the frigate's upper topgallant and ripped a large hole in it. That effectively ended the chase as the xebec quickly gained sufficient distance from the frigate so that the French cannon fire fell short.

Murad's xebec was moored near the shore. The crew, helped by several janissaries, was busy filling empty barrels of water from a spring above the river. While some hauled the empty barrels to the source, others rolled the full barrels down one by one to be loaded into a dinghy and brought over to the ship. The Baltimore women and children were taking the air on the deck, watched by a handful of janissaries. The young children pranced around, playing tag or inventing games in their heads.

Murad watched the idyllic scene from the railing near his cabin. With the threat of typhus hanging over them, he needed to keep his captives healthy, and this meant giving them every opportunity to breathe fresh air and take in the sunshine. Sickbed captives would not fetch a good price at the slave market in Algiers.

There were two camps of women on deck: the friends of Sally Gunter on the port side and those who favoured the rebel Emma Pierse on the starboard side. Sally's youngest boys were running around the deck while their mother was chatting with Mrs. Croffine, Mrs. Roberts and Mrs. Harris. The Harris maid, Ellen, looked better and her left hand had been bandaged in a clean white cloth.

On the starboard side, Emma and her mother were chatting with the younger women, including Mrs. Evans and her maid Ciara, Bessie Flood, the Meregey maid, Deirdre, and the redhead Besse Peeters. Joane Broadbrook wandered about between the two rival camps with her two boys. She was going into her sixth month of pregnancy and was not feeling well.

A janissary was chatting with young Giles Gunter while plucking away on the strings of his lute. He was a Dutch janissary like the captain and spoke English with ease.

"Hey, little man, do you know 'Sing a song of sixpence'?"

Giles nodded shyly at the man and a group of children came over to hear what the man was saying.

"I know it, sir," piped up young Phoebe.

"Then sing it for me," added the man.

Phoebe and her sisters, Eunice and Dinah, recited the song from memory as the janissary improvised the music on his lute.

> *"Sing a song of sixpence,*
> *A pocket full of rye.*
> *Four and twenty blackbirds,*
> *Baked in a pie.*
>
> *When the pie was opened,*
> *The birds began to sing;*
> *Wasn't that a dainty dish,*
> *To set before the king.*
>
> *The king was in his counting-house,*
> *Counting out his money;*
> *The queen was in the parlour,*
> *Eating bread and honey.*
>
> *The maid was in the garden,*
> *Hanging out the clothes,*
> *When down came a blackbird,*
> *And pecked off her nose.*
>
> *There was such a commotion,*
> *that little Jenny wren*
> *Flew down into the garden,*
> *and put it back again."*

The mothers were watching the children sing when they saw Orla

Walsh come up from the hold and search for a quiet spot on the deck. They separated to give Orla room and to keep their distance from the papist woman. The mothers clapped their hands at the end of the song as the children listened to a Turkish theme on the lute.

Two janissaries appeared on the ladder, carrying several stinking buckets of human waste. As they emerged from the hold, Felix and Caleb moved away from the railing to give the men room to dump their buckets over the side. In the crowd of children, young Malcolm spotted a miniature prayer book lying on the deck and picked it up. He went looking for his mother and gave her Phoebe's prayer book. Joane took it and put it in her pocket for safekeeping. She would find the owner later when she was feeling better.

The contingent of janissaries under the command of Aga Santos marched along the east side of the river towards the town of Audierne. They stopped from time to time to run into a house or a barn looking for valuables and food supplies. The janissaries in their bright colours, flashing their yatagan sabres and muskets, looked irresistible. They would strike fear in the hearts of any locals who happened to see them. Along the way, they seized a wagon and a horse to carry the loot. They already had quite a bit of plunder, including silver and pewter plates, knives, sacks of grain, bags of flour and salt, and iron tools. When they reached the town, they found the houses abandoned. They went from house to house, loading up the wagon with additional items. They raided a barn and found a cow, which they quickly hooked up to their wagon.

A mounted rider appeared suddenly from behind a building. He fired a shot with his musket and galloped away before the janissaries could fire back. There was no use in pursuing the man and no one had been injured. They finished searching the houses and headed back to the boats. They had accomplished what they set out to do. They had added to their food supplies and struck fear in the hearts of the local population. No one would dare come after them without a large force of trained soldiers.

Back at the ship, the loading of fresh water continued as the sun went down. Just before dark, three Frenchmen appeared on horseback on the other side of the river and stopped to observe the corsair ships. They must have been surprised by the number of women and children on the deck. They quickly retreated upstream with news of their discovery. *Who were all these women and children? Were they French? Where did they come from?* The news would spread like wildfire in the French heartland.

The evening meal was a festive occasion for the women and children on board the ship. Captain Murad had invited them to share the sides of beef cooking over an open fire on the shore. The cook had butchered the cow and the horse to provide for the evening meal and to put away a supply of cured beef and horse meat for the voyage. The salting of the meat would go on all night.

The janissaries lit a torch to illuminate the women and children on the deck and put additional guards around the boat. The captives were starving for a decent meal after having eaten nothing in the last twenty-four hours. The stewards, Marco and Diego, served the women succulent beefsteaks, lightly burned on the outside and raw on the inside. It was a magnificent meal for all concerned and everyone ate to their hearts' content. Soon the children were nodding off, and it was time to go to bed.

The janissaries lit tallow candles in the hold and helped the mothers carry the sleeping children down the ladder for the night. Many of the janissaries had fond memories of their own children, abandoned when they left their homelands. They found themselves becoming attached to these children, who were now their prisoners. The women found these men quite endearing and their humanity attracted them. It would not be long before romantic attachments would form between the men and the female captives on board the ship.

Orla Walsh had eaten well and sat in her usual place in the dark hold, but was unable to sleep. She found it difficult to believe that she was so far away from Ireland and felt confident that no one would dare come after her in the hold of a corsair ship. She was free for the first time after years of oppression, but she felt restless and uneasy as she closed her eyes.

The day was dawning cold and wet when Khalil's xebec appeared in the bay and sailed upriver to join them. It had been a long night of loading water barrels and salting meat for the crew. The cooking staff were still at it when the first bell sounded at four o'clock in the morning. As the new shift took over the loading, they stopped what they were doing and cheered the arrival of their friends.

A sailor went to the cabin on the poop deck to tell the captain the news. As Murad appeared on deck, he could see Khalil's exuberant crew waving from their ship as they smelled the cooking on the shore. The French captives shackled together near the railing stood up to get a better look at the French countryside. The companion xebec swung to starboard and dropped its anchor in the shallow water near the freshwater spring. Khalil looked exhausted as he climbed down into the dinghy and came across to give Murad his news. He was led to the captain's cabin where he was served Turkish coffee in a tiny cup along with a glass of jenever, a gin made in Holland.

"I wondered what happened to you," said Murad, "after we lost you in the fog."

"We were attacked by a French man of war, captain. We had to run a long way south to get away," said Khalil. He stopped as he saw the smile on Murad's face.

"You saw her?"

"Yes, she almost cut us in two in the fog. We were lucky."

"A frigate *Le Cyne*?"

"Yes, I believe so."

They lifted their glasses.

"*Proost*," said Murad. "I'm happy to have you back."

They drank their coffee in silence.

"What about the typhus, any new cases?" asked Murad.

"No, sir. The prisoners are looking much better after a few days on the deck."

"I'm sure they are. The foul air in steerage is the death of any man."

"How is the loading going?"

"We'll finish by the end of the day," said Murad. "Why don't you get some food, Arturo? We'll talk later."

Khalil stood up and left.

At four bells, the breakfast call went out and the janissaries on Murad's xebec appeared from below decks and greeted their newly arrived comrades who were already finishing up their meal. Captain Khalil had brought the English and Irish captives on deck to join the French and Portuguese and had shackled every second captive. They were ravenously hungry and ate the burned beef, licking their fingers, and washing it down with water from goatskins. It was a joyous moment for the men, their hunger sated, to smell the fresh air of the river and the surrounding farmland, but the peace was broken by cries from the women's hold. The men stood up, the husbands and fathers worried about their wives and children.

Fat Marco was the first man to pull off the hold cover and look down at the frightened women below. He quickly descended the ladder, followed by several janissaries. There was complete pandemonium among the women and children.

"Calm down, calm down, please," said Marco in his Italian-accented English to the distraught women. "What is the matter?"

Sally Gunter appeared next to him and took his arm. She was accompanied by Felix and his brother Caleb.

"Something terrible has happened, sir. Please come this way."

Eight

An hour later, the women and children had all been removed from the hold and were taking the air on the deck. They were elated to see their husbands and fathers on the companion vessel. Food was served to the women and children while Felix Gunter was questioned by Captain Murad on the poop deck.

"So Felix, you and your brother found the body?"

"Yes, sir."

"Did you know the lady?"

"No, sir."

"What were you doing up so early in the morning?"

"We were on our way to the head when we saw her."

"What did you see?"

"Well, we saw the blood, sir. The way she was lying."

Felix looked distracted, and Murad pounced.

"What did you do to her?"

"I didn't do anything to her, sir," said Felix, shocked to be a suspect in the death of the woman. "I hardly know her."

Murad knew the Gunter boys were the only young men in the hold, and he figured that one of them must have had something to do with the death of the woman.

"I think it is time you told me the whole story. What were you really doing?"

"There is nothing to tell, sir," pleaded Felix. "Missus Walsh is an Irish lady from Skibbereen, a Roman Catholic. We're Anglicans. We ain't allowed to talk to Catholics, the reverend says so."

"Yes, but why would someone want to kill the woman? To steal her money, perhaps?"

Felix looked around nervously.

"I wouldn't know, sir."

Murad descended the ladder into the empty hold, followed by his colleague, Captain Khalil. They followed Marco to the back wall, where they found the body of Orla Walsh, who had been stabbed multiple times.

"Have you found the knife?" asked Murad.

"No, sir," said Marco.

"We can't have this kind of thing going on," insisted Murad. "Have you searched the women?"

"No, sir."

"You know that woman will cost us?"

"Yes, sir."

"Ransoms are higher for women like her. I hear she was an educated woman."

Khalil turned to Murad and waved Marco away.

"I'll handle it, sir. We'll find the knife."

An hour later, Khalil and the janissaries had searched the entire hold, going through the belongings of each family and shaking down what clothes they had. They found nothing, and Khalil was convinced that he was being played by the women. He ordered Marcellus to have the body wrapped in white muslin and removed.

Fear gripped the women and children as the body was hauled gently up the ladder to the main deck. They moved as far away as possible from the body of the woman, silently muttering prayers for her. Hugh Pierse called across to his wife, Emma.

"Emma, dearest heart. What's happening?"

"The Irish woman, Missus Walsh. Somebody kilt her."

"My God, how'd she die?" asked Richard Meade.

"She was murdered, the poor woman was murdered," yelled back Mrs. Harris.

"That makes no sense," added Thomas Payne.

"How you doin', Emma darling?" asked Hugh.

"Doin' fine," replied Emma. "The girls miss you."

"How are the children?" asked Payne, calling to his wife and children, who waved at their dad.

"The woman was stabbed to death," Mrs. Croffine called to her husband Corent. "We ain't safe here, dear."

Corent shrugged at this comment while his wife looked nervously at Roisin and Deirdre, two Irish maids standing nearby. The Croffines hated the poor 'shanty' Irish of Roaring Water Bay more than most people in Baltimore and didn't hide their dislike.

In death, Orla Walsh was just another poor dead woman, neither Roman Catholic nor Anglican, but a woman who deserved respect. The whole ship appeared to mourn her death after the janissaries had carefully deposited her body wrapped in white muslin at the mast. Marcellus noted that the women had again separated into two groups: one gathered around Sally Gunter and the other around Emma Pierse. Accompanied by Marco, he went over to talk to Sally.

"Have you found out who killed her?" demanded Sally.

"Not yet, milady," said Marco. "This is the second mate, Mister Marcellus. He wants to talk to you."

"I know nothing about the Walsh woman, sir," said Sally. "She was not one of us, she being Catholic and all."

Marcellus was looking down at young Caleb standing by his mother. The boy was only twelve years old, but looked older.

"What about you, son? You ever talk to the lady?"

"No, sir. I never met her," said Caleb.

Sally interrupted Marcellus and whispered something in his ear. Marcellus looked over at the group of women around Emma Pierse, who were watching him interrogate the Gunters. There was obviously some hostility between the two groups of women.

An hour later, the women and children had returned to the hold and Felix was upside down with his feet strapped to a wooden plank near the mast. It was uncomfortably hot on the deck in the scorching sun, and Felix was sweating profusely as he awaited his punishment. The male captives on Khalil's ship had been returned to steerage and there were only a few janissaries on the deck of the larger xebec to observe the *bastinado*. A heavily muscled man took off his shirt and picked up a cane, striking the empty air around himself several times to get the feel of it. Captain Khalil nodded to the man to start the punishment. The first blow to the arches of Felix's feet knocked the air out of the lad and he screamed.

"I've told you everything I know," he protested.

Khalil ignored the boy, and the second blow was doubly painful. The aim of the *bastinado* was not to cause permanent injury to the toes and heel of the foot, but to maximize the pain and to render the torture victim pliable. The third blow elicited a muted squeal from the boy as he tried to control his fear of the cane and the pain from his bruised arches. He knew he had a high tolerance for pain. All the Gunters were like that. He had seen his father William suffer from a terrible injury in a boating accident when he was still a young boy, but the man had scarcely felt the pain. His father had told him that pain was connected to emotions. If he withdrew into himself, the pain would go away.

Marcellus leaned down to question the boy.

"So what will it be, Felix? You ready to tell us what happened?"

Felix said nothing, ignoring the second mate.

Another blow of the cane fell on Felix's sore feet and then another, and still, the boy ignored the questions.

Two stout janissaries hauled young Felix into Captain Murad's cabin and set him down at a low table. His face was flushed red, and he looked exhausted. His swollen feet were killing him. He could barely walk on them. The captain watched as a servant brought in a tin plate of beef and set it down in front of Felix.

"Eat. It will do you good. Have a glass of wine."

Felix was surprised as the captain poured him a glass of red wine. After the foot lashing, he hadn't expected to be treated so well by the captain. He was starving and didn't need any encouragement to eat. He picked up the red meat with his fingers and ate quickly. The meat was delicious, and he washed it down with the wine under the captain's watchful eye.

"Feeling better, young man?" asked Murad.

"You didn't need to beat me, sir. I would have told you."

The captain nodded, watching the boy patiently.

"I only have one thing to say."

"Yes."

"It's about the knife wounds, sir."

"What about the wounds?"

"I got a look at the wounds when Marco came below. They were very small puncture wounds."

"What are you saying?"

"The width of the blade, sir. It must have been a filleting knife."

"So?"

"I'm a fisherman, sir. I work on the boats. I never worked in the fish palace. Those are jobs for women."

Murad watched Felix as he drank more wine. He realized that the boy was very observant and not some ignorant fisherman's son. He had a good head on his shoulders.

"You think it was a woman?"

"It has to be, sir. It wasn't me or my brothers and all the women work with filleting knives."

"We searched the hold and didn't find any knives."

Felix said nothing to this as he finished off the plate of beef.

"It's easy to get rid of a knife, sir."

Murad stood up and made to go out on deck.

"What is going to happen to us, sir?" asked Felix.

"You'll be sold in the slave market, my boy. Women are much in demand, not so much men."

Murad left, and when he returned, Felix hadn't moved. He sat there silently, thinking about the coming ordeal of the slave market. *Would his family survive being sold off to the highest bidder?*

Murad looked at the boy and sat down again.

"We've all been slaves once or twice in our lives, Felix. A lot of janissaries were slaves, even *renegadoes* like me. I'll see to it that your new life is not so bad."

"Thank you, sir."

"What do you know about Orla Walsh?"

"Not much. My pa said she arrived at night in a wagon with a load of books."

"You think she was fleeing someone or something?"

"I don't know, sir, but her arrival in Baltimore got a lot of local tongues wagging. There were rumours about the Irish evicting us Anglicans from Baltimore."

"Yes, but who would want to hurt a book lover? You never borrowed any books from her?"

"No, sir, but many people in Baltimore enjoy a good book from time to time."

The servant returned with two cups of Turkish coffee for Murad and his guest. Felix put a teaspoon of dark molasses in the small cup.

"There was a lot of blood, sir."

"Yes, there was."

"Blood stains a lot, sir," said Felix with a questioning air.

The captain shrugged and then jumped up as a janissary came in with urgent news. He rushed out on deck, leaving Felix alone. Moments later, two janissaries came in and lifted Felix clean off the ground as they hustled him out of the cabin.

On the deck, there was a great flurry of activity going on. A contingent of janissaries had just arrived on foot from the mouth of the river with bad news. They had spotted a French ship in the bay. Captain Murad was giving orders to his first mate, and the crew was preparing for a quick departure. Janissaries were hauling the last water caskets in a dinghy to Khalil's xebec while the cooks were bringing in their barrels of salted beef. The crews were scrambling to get their ships ready to sail.

It was getting dark as Felix was helped down into the hold by the janissaries. They put him in a sling and dropped him down to his mother and six brothers.

"What's going on, Felix?" asked his brothers, clamouring for information.

"We're leaving. There's a French ship in the bay."

"What happened to you, son?" asked Sally.

"Why can't you walk?" asked Caleb.

"It's the soles of my feet," said Felix. "They hurt too much."

"Let's get him over to the hammock," said Sally. "Let him breathe."

She grabbed Felix around the waist and, with Caleb's help, they stumbled over to the hammock where Felix could lie down.

"They beat the soles of my feet with a stick, ma," said Felix. "I'm all right now."

"They beat you?" asked Caleb. "Why?"

"They thought I knew something about the murder."

"Let me see," said Sally, picking up one foot and then the other. There were red welts all over his arches.

Mrs. Croffine and Mrs. Harris came over to hear the news.

"What happened to him?" asked Mrs. Croffine.

"They call it a *bastinado*," said Caleb with great pride. "They beat the soles of his feet."

"What did you do, Felix?" asked Mrs. Croffine.

"Nothing, Missus Croffine, nothing," replied Felix. "They wanted me to talk, but I don't know anything about that woman."

"He's telling the truth," said Sally.

"There's a French ship in the bay," said Felix to the women.

The news cheered the women and children. A French ship in the bay could be their salvation.

The corsairs were soon ready for departure, but they had to wait for the ebb tide to get them down the river. At six bells, the janissaries went in groups to the galley for their evening meal. Meanwhile, Captain Murad climbed into a dinghy with two of his best rowers and went down to the mouth of the river to get a look at the French ship. It was slow going, moving against the flood tide in the moonlight. After an hour of paddling, they arrived at the mouth of the river and put in to shore. The French frigate *Le Cyne* was standing offshore half a mile away.

Murad observed the ship for a long time. *Le Cyne* was not a good sailor and swung this way and that in the swell. She was a square-rigged ship, and he bet she wouldn't be able to maintain a course close-hauled to the wind. It would be easy to outrun her. The prevailing wind in the bay was favourable, as it was coming from the southwest.

Murad had a plan. Under the cover of darkness, the corsairs would float down the river with the tide and work their way east, depth sounding in the shallow water. They needed to be in the deep water of the bay before they were spotted by the frigate at sunrise.

At the request of the women, Marco had placed a candle near the ladder to illuminate the hold at night. The children and most of the women were fast asleep when Ciara got up and came over to talk to Felix. She stepped carefully around the Gunter boys, who were asleep on the floor. She kneeled close to Felix and whispered in his ear.

"Felix, wake up."

Felix woke with a start and was pleasantly surprised to see Ciara's lovely mouth and long eyelashes inches from his face. It was almost too much for him.

"What did you tell Captain Khalil?" asked Ciara.

"Nothing," said Felix. "I know nothing about the murder."

"Then why did they punish you?"

"I got the *bastinado* because they thought I might know something."

"You do know something?" asked Ciara.

"No, Ciara, I don't know anything. You're not funny. That poor woman was stabbed to death."

Ciara kissed Felix on the cheek.

"What was that for?" asked Felix, blushing.

"You handsome devil. Who do they think kilt the woman?"

"They don't know. I told them it had to be a woman."

"Why?"

"The knife, Ciara. The filleting knife."

Ciara looked surprised. She had taken Felix for a dumb adolescent boy with a crush on her, the kind that was easily manipulated and blinded by their sexual drive, but Felix was different. He was an intelligent, even devious young man, behind that nascent moustache of his.

"I have never owned a filleting knife, Ciara, and neither have my brothers. It must be a woman who worked at the palace."

"Who does the captain suspect?"

"He doesn't have a suspect."

Nine

Two hours before dawn, the corsair ships floated silently down the river with the ebb tide. At the mouth, a thick fog was coming in and obscuring the visibility. They hugged the eastern shore, depth sounding in the shallow water as they went. With the fog it took them more than an hour to get into the deep water of the bay. The subterfuge had worked. The corsairs slipped out of the bay unbeknownst to the French. They sailed in a southeasterly direction towards the Penmarch peninsula and, from there, the plan was to sail due east and tuck in behind Tudy Island.

Of course, the fastest way home would have been to avoid France altogether and sail due south and west, but they needed food and a constant supply of fresh water, which could only accessed in the rivers along the coast. They feared the horrendous storms in the Bay of Biscay, which were comparable to those encountered in the Drake Passage on the southern tip of South America and in the South China Sea. No xebec could withstand the fierce storms in the bay, so they sailed close to land where they could quickly find a safe harbour in bad weather.

Tudy Island, France

They arrived in the early afternoon. Tudy island was a finger of land on the eastern shore, protecting the entrance to the village of Pont-l'Abbé, a few miles to the northwest. The village had been founded by a monk in the 14th century. Captain Murad knew it well and had stopped here before on his way up the coast, as had other corsair raiders, so he doubted there was going to be much benefit to a raid in the area. The locals feared corsair attacks and would have run for the hills, abandoning their homes and farms.

Nevertheless, Murad ordered Aga Santos to send two contingents of fifty janissaries to scavenge the area for food and valuables. One contingent was to follow the western shore towards Pont-l'Abbé with the help of Captain Khalil's xebec and the other was to march inland along the eastern shore of Tudy Island. Murad told the aga to fire a musket if he needed help.

Khalil loaded the men for the western shore and took them deep into the bay, landing on Queffen Island, a short march away from the village. The tide was out, and Aga Santos ordered his men into the muddy water and up the riverbank. They soon disappeared from view as Khalil waited on the island for their return.

The janissaries expected to find empty farmland and nary a soul, but as they neared the village, they noticed that there were people everywhere who quickly picked up their things and fled before them. The people of the *Pays Bigouden* were descended from a pre-Celtic race of inhabitants and were fiercely independent. Their women wore tall lace bonnets typical of the region and they didn't take kindly to foreigners.

Santos watched as his men ran off to pursue the fleeing women and children through the backyards of farmhouses and barns. He was left with a dozen men and none with muskets. What had started as an ordinary scavenging mission now became a race to capture as many men, women, and children as possible. When they found a woman they fancied, they would force her to the ground and rape her, often in front of her children or parents. These horrific scenes played out in house after house as the janissaries rampaged through the village. A janissary kicked a barn door open and seized a young girl cowering in a corner. He was about to throw himself on top of her when her grandfather appeared behind a bale of hay with a loaded musket.

"*Monsieur, vous avez pris mes deux fils, mais vous n'aurez pas ma petite fille,*" said the old man as he shot the janissary point blank in the chest.

The family had suffered enough from corsair attacks. Two boys had been taken in other encounters, but the grandfather refused to give up his granddaughter. A second janissary heard the gunshot and ran into the barn to help his colleague. He approached the proud old man standing over the body of the dead janissary with his sabre and was about to hack him to pieces when a pitchfork was thrown from above, piercing his neck and knocking him to the ground. The grandmother in her white lace bonnet stood up in the loft, brushed herself off, and looked down at the dying man.

The old and young put up a fierce fight against the unsuspecting janissaries. They were attacked by desperate people with muskets, farm tools, and knives. The town had been warned about the raiders in an urgent message from Audierne and Quimper that arrived the same morning. A contingent of local French militia was quickly assembled near the Hôtel de Ville and marched down the road to engage with the enemy. There were a dozen young men under the orders of a captain, an old geezer with grey hair and a large moustache. Most of the men had muskets while some wielded pikes. They wore their mismatched blue and red uniforms with pride. Santo's men laughed at this rabble of toy soldiers and raised their sabres to prepare for an attack.

The old geezer in command didn't look like much, but he seemed to know what he was doing. He barked an order to his men, who halted twenty yards from Santos' janissaries and raised their muskets. Santos suddenly realized that none of his men had their muskets with them and ordered them to charge, but it was too late. Their only hope was that the militia would panic and run. The young French militiamen were frightened but held their ground as the janissaries came at them.

"*Feu*," growled the French captain to his men. The volley instantly killed six janissaries before they had closed half the distance. Aga Santos looked on, aghast, at the slaughter of his men. He had never had to fight a disciplined infantry force before. In the brief moment of silence that followed the musket shots, Santos and his men turned and ran. They had no desire to face a second volley or to impale themselves on the militia's pikes. The janissaries sacking the village heard the shots and emerged in the streets with their captives, mainly old women and children. The men were loaded down with plunder, some with silver plates and candlesticks, bottles of wine, and other common household valuables. They immediately released their captives and ran with their loot to join up with their colleagues on the road. Some of them were cut down by the second volley of musket fire, while others were pursued by a motley collection of villagers, firing old muskets and wielding farm tools and blades of every description.

It was a rout. The enraged villagers fell upon the janissaries while the militiamen attacked with their pikes. Santos had never witnessed anything like it before, armed resistance against invincible Turkish janissaries. It just didn't happen. His contingent of soldiers was in tatters as they made their escape. Men and women, young and old, came out of their houses and stood with the militia. It was a Pyrrhic victory for the villagers that had come at a great cost. They cheered their victory. They had killed twenty janissaries but had lost an equal number of their own citizens.

It was the most ignominious return from a raid that he had ever witnessed. Captain Khalil stood on the shore at Queffen Island and watched as Santos and the remaining men stumbled in disarray back to the ship. They had no captives with them and carried little, if anything, in plunder. The wounded men hobbled along behind the others, but what was more astonishing was the number of men missing.

Khalil had heard the volley of muskets from the village and had wondered what was happening. It was obvious they had been attacked. He was furious at Santos for having made such a cock-up of what was just a routine scavenging operation. The important thing in a raid was to get in and get out with as much loot as possible, and to strike fear into the hearts of the local people, but the aga had somehow lost control of his men and never imagined a counter-attack. Khalil turned his back on Santos and his men as they climbed on board, and ordered his crew to get ready to push off. He could only hope that Captain Murad would not blame him for Santos' failure.

Back on Tudy Island, the eastern contingent had arrived with two goats, a roe deer and a dozen pheasants. They had encountered no resistance on their march along the eastern shore. The cooks were at work butchering the goats and cooking the evening meal on an open fire on the beach. It was going to be another lovely evening with fresh meat and water for everyone. In the distance, Murad's men could see Captain Khalil's xebec steer towards them on the shore.

In the hold, it was hot and airless, and most of the women and children were sleeping. Joane Broadbrook was feeling better. She sat up with young Malcolm as Liam was having a nap. She was reading the Latin text in the miniature prayer book and examining the beautifully illuminated pictures with her son. Joane was deeply religious, as were most of the English colony in Baltimore. She wondered where this extraordinary book of hours had come from. In the margins, there were pencil markings with what she surmised to be the dates of birth and death of members of the family who had originally owned the book.

"What is this one, ma?" asked Malcolm.

"It's the life of Christ, Malcolm," said Joane. "See Jesus holding the cross."

Joane carefully turned the pages.

"This is the prayer at vespers, Malcolm: *'Deus, in adjutorium meum intende. Domine, ad adjuvandum me festina.'*"

"What does it mean, Ma?"

"It means: 'O God, come to my assistance, O Lord, make haste to help me. Glory be to the Father, the Son, and the Holy Spirit—"

"As it was in the beginning—," added Malcolm, grinning.

"—is now and ever shall be, world without end. Amen," completed Joane. "You remember the words, Malcolm."

"Yes, ma."

They could hear angry voices coming from the deck above them. Joane kissed Malcolm and put the prayer book away.

Murad was absolutely furious and stormed around his cabin as Aga Santos sat in penitence at the low table. He had dismissed Captain Khalil when he realized that the man was in no way responsible for the disaster. He had to figure out what to do with the good-for-nothing commandant of his janissaries.

"Now tell me again what happened," he said. "And do not lie."

Santos was petrified. He knew Murad well enough to know that when he went quiet like this; he was at his most dangerous. He told the whole story again, leaving nothing out. By the time he had finished, he thought Murad was going to explode.

"What were you thinking?" Murad asked. "You allowed yourself to be ambushed."

"I'm sorry, Captain," Santos stammered. "We never expected to be attacked."

"That," Murad said, "is the point of an ambush."

"I mean, we never expected to be shot at, sir."

"Of course you didn't."

Murad sat down and drank some water, ruminating on this embarrassing episode.

"You were routed by a bunch of ragtag militiamen and a few armed civilians. You've got to maintain discipline among your troops, Santos. You can't let your men run off to rape and plunder and leave you with a mere handful of soldiers. That is quite inexcusable."

"I'll do better next time, sir."

"The pasha may want your head on a pike, Santos, when he hears about it."

After the breakfast meal in the hold, the women rested while the children played. Emma's girls were boisterous in the early morning. They had found a piece of twine and were jumping rope in the tight quarters of the hold. Emma put up with it because it kept their minds off the murder of Orla Walsh. Phoebe and Eunice held the rope for young Dinah who sang the first line of the song, followed by Phoebe on the second and Eunice on the third.

> *"When shall I marry?*
> *This year, next year, sometime, never.*
> *What will my husband be?*
> *Tinker, tailor, soldier, sailor, rich-man,*
> *poor-man, beggar-man, thief.*
> *What will I be?*
> *Lady, baby, gypsy, queen.*
> *What shall I wear?*
> *Silk, satin, cotton, rags.*
> *How shall I get it?*
> *Given, borrowed, bought, stolen.*
> *How shall I get to church?*
> *Coach, carriage, wheelbarrow, cart.*
> *Where shall I live?*
> *Big house, little house, pigsty, barn."*

Mrs. Harris stopped in the passageway to watch the girls singing the nursery rhyme. When they had finished, she continued on, going past them and stopped to look down at an object underfoot. She picked up a brown cloak, thinking it might have some value, and noticed five bloody holes in the coarse hemp fabric. The cloak was stiff with dried blood. She dropped it immediately.

"The blood," she cried to the women nearby.

"What is it?" asked Emma.

"The cloak. It's covered in blood."

"Well, don't look at me, you old harpy," said Emma. "It wasn't me who put it there."

Ten

Quiet reigned in the hold until the moment Mrs. Harris held up the bloody cloak. Then all the women started talking at once and their voices woke the sleeping children. They were all thinking the same thing and regarded each other with growing suspicion. *The murderer is among us and we are all in danger of being murdered in our sleep.* Sally Gunter was conferring with her friends and throwing angry looks at Emma Pierse and Bessie Flood.

"I'm not guilty, Sally," said Emma. "I'm not guilty of killing that woman."

"We need to turn the cloak over to the captain," said Mrs. Harris. "He'll decide if you are guilty or not."

"He's a bloody pirate, a murderer, and a slave trader," said Bessie Flood. "What does he know about justice and truth?"

"Bessie's right," said Mrs. Evans. "He's an outlaw. They'll hang him if they ever catch him."

The Irish maids Roisin, Ellen and Deirdre sat with the children listening to the back and forth of the women's arguments, until young Phoebe stood up to defend her mother.

"My ma ain't guilty," Phoebe cried, on the verge of tears. "You're innocent, ain't you, ma?"

Phoebe ran to her mother and threw her arms around her.

"Thank you, my dear," said Emma, turning away from the child to confront her nemesis. "You may have noticed, Sally, that your friend found the cloak all by herself. Maybe she put it there."

"She's right," said Emma's mother. "She put it there."

Emma and her mother's comments were followed by open threats from Mrs. Harris and the Gunter quarter.

"Why don't we just leave it for the janissaries to find," suggested Besse Peeters, sitting near Emma.

"Give it to Marco," said Mrs. Croffine.

Captain Murad and his men were getting ready to leave Tudy Island. Khalil had cleared the decks and sent the French and Portuguese prisoners back to steerage. Murad stood on the forecastle, watching his men pull in the mooring lines. He was concerned by the freshening wind and had noticed the change in direction when he had first come on deck an hour ago. The wind was blowing from the south and he spotted a rain squall coming in from the west. He felt he had to get his men away as soon as possible since Tudy Island was not a good place to weather a bad storm, but more importantly, Santos' bungled raid had revealed a sobering fact. An overconfident local militia could be a genuine threat to his men, and he would be derelict in his duties if he remained in the vicinity, vulnerable to attack.

Murad knew the coast well. He had been here back in 1627 when he led a raid on Iceland for the pirate Republic of Salé. The sheer audacity of the raid was remarkable — a three-thousand-mile sail from North Africa to Iceland and back. It had made his reputation as a daring corsair raider when he returned with two ships and a few dozen Icelandic and Danish captives. He had not been responsible for the horrific Algerine attack on the east coast of the island that occurred two weeks later. The Algerine raid was infamous in the history of piracy after the corsairs killed some thirty islanders and captured four hundred.

From Tudy Island, the way south followed the curve of the Atlantic coast. There was always the risk of running into naval vessels, so they would give a wide berth to towns such as Concarneau and Port-Louis. Murad had seen enough French men of war for one trip. He planned to sail due east and work his way along the coast to the mouth of the Aven and Bélon rivers, where he could find refuge by sailing up either river depending on the prevailing winds.

In the hold, the women were arguing again. Felix sat with his brothers, holding baby Walter in his arms. He was getting bored watching them. He found it hard to believe that any of these women were capable of stabbing Orla to death. The cloak was a woman's garment that could have belonged to Orla or any of the women. Maybe Orla had covered herself in the cloak when she slept. He had examined it earlier and noticed that the holes corresponded to her stab wounds. Then again, the murderer might have used the cloak to protect her own clothes. By pressing the garment against the victim's chest and stabbing through the coarse fabric, the assailant reduced the blood spurts and avoided getting blood all over her clothes.

He glanced over at Ellen, who looked pale and withdrawn. She had not said a word after her wedding ring ordeal and wasn't interested in the murder. Joane Broadbrook was not well, and appeared to be bored by the arguments. The Ryder, Pumery and Croffine ladies remained outraged by Emma's accusations while others like Roberts, Meade and the Irish maid Deirdre showed no interest at all in the debate. The women were clearly frightened by the thought that there was a murderer among them. Many tried to look unconcerned by the arguments put forward by the women, but their faces revealed their unease and fear of another attack.

They were crossing the bay opposite the town of Concarneau when the weather made a turn for the worse. The ships were sailing close to the wind and making good time. The wind was blowing hard, and it wouldn't take much for the waves to swamp the boats. The xebecs were not suited for heavy weather. Murad looked to the northwest and saw that Khalil's smaller vessel was already struggling. The continental shelf along the French coast extended far out into the sea, resulting in relatively shallow waters and rough seas.

Murad turned in time to see a flock of white birds approaching from starboard. They were gannets, always on the lookout for herring and mackerel. They were large white birds with streamlined bodies made for diving and wings edged with dark brown feathers. Murad watched as they plunged headlong into the sea, spouts of white water marking their impacts. Moments later, they resurfaced, some still swallowing their prey, and then took off again to continue the hunt. It was a stunning display, and when Murad looked up at the lateen sail, he saw one of them perched on the mast, looking down at him.

Murad took this as a favourable omen. Like many sailors, he was a superstitious man. At sea, he often had to make life-or-death decisions, and those decisions were often ruled by circumstances over which he had no control. Omens were important to him, and this one told him to find refuge as soon as possible in a safe harbour.

Captain Khalil's xebec was in trouble. The male captives in steerage were standing in water that was almost up to their knees and the situation was getting worse as each massive wave broke over the bow of the ship. The crew had descended to the bilge pump and the prisoners could hear them pumping hard to reduce the weight of water in the ship. The pump room was just next door to steerage and near the mainmast.

A Frenchman climbed to the top of the steerage ladder and observed the land off to the north through a pinhole in the cover. He could see Concarneau disappearing in the northeast as they rounded the cape at Trévignon. He called down to his friends.

"*La houle est forte. Nous allons vers l'est.*"

"He says the swell is bad," said John Amble to his English friends. "We're going east."

When the Frenchman came down, an agitated Hugh Pierse quickly climbed to have a look. He hurried back down, looking perplexed.

"The bastards are praying," said Pierse. "There are a dozen of them janissaries on deck and they're praying something fierce."

"They're Mahometans," said Amble. "Of course, they're praying. They fear for their lives, just like we do."

The prisoners were getting restless. The water was above their knees. They were starting to wonder whether they would survive the crossing. Jacques waded through the rising water to have a word with his friends, John Amble and Thomas Payne.

"*Messieurs, nous avons un plan.*"

While the English and Irish had slept through the night on Tudy Island, the French and Portuguese had talked for hours on end. They had reached some kind of agreement among themselves.

"I hope you do," said Payne. "I don't like the look of this water."

"Don't worry, *messieurs*," said Jacques. "The captain will soon find calmer waters. Then we will execute our plan."

"What plan?" asked Amble.

"*Nous allons saborder le bateau,*" whispered Jacques.

"I don't like it," said Amble.

"Wait, John. Let's hear it," insisted Payne.

"*Le plan est de saborder le bateau près de la rive.*"

"You want to scuttle the boat near the shore," said Amble. "You've got to be mad."

"Bloody hell, mate, what kind of plan is that?" asked Payne. "Scuttle the ship and we all go to the bottom with it."

"It's decided, John," said Jacques with a look of grim resignation.

"It's a desperate plan but we don't have a choice."

Jacques returned to join his compatriots.

"They're going to scuttle the damn ship," complained Payne.

"He did say it was a last resort," added Amble.

Payne relayed the plan to Hugh Pierse and the other men, who shook their heads and thought it a mad scheme.

Murad's xebec headed straight for the mouth of the Aven River and calmer waters beyond as the winds blasted out of the south. They had started their day with twenty-five-knot winds and ten-to-twelve-foot seas, but now the winds had reached gale force, blowing at forty knots as they raced into the mouth of the river. The wind dropped suddenly, and the crew breathed a sigh of relief as the flood tide moved them up the river. It had been a close-run thing.

Khalil's xebec had fallen behind. It was riding dangerously low in the water and just made it into the mouth of the river. Once in the calmer waters, the xebec moved sluggishly up the river on the tide away from the storm. The men who had been working non-stop for hours on the bilge pump were knackered. The ship was out of danger, so Khalil ordered them out of the pump room and told them to rest up as the ship moved up the river.

As soon as the crew were gone, a Portuguese man used a gaff to hack away at the heavy wooden door into the pump room. The prisoners had spent hours in mortal terror of drowning and were desperate to break out of the hold. Thomas Payne got up and grabbed an iron bar, ripping it from the wall with great force. He joined the Portuguese man and started attacking the bottom of the door. Soon, there were four or five men with rudimentary tools doing the same.

A Frenchman climbed to the top of the steerage ladder and observed the river through the holes in the cover.

"*C'est bon, on est rendu*," he confirmed to the others.

John Amble looked at Jacques.

"*On est dans la rivière*," said Jacques with a complicit air. "The water is not very deep here."

Amble turned to his English friends.

"We're into the river. We're going to make a run for it."

Suddenly, everyone seemed to be on the same page, but no one knew for sure whether there was an escape route through the pump room.

Captain Murad looked back with concern at his companion vessel, which appeared to be very low in the water. He could try to turn his ship around and head back, but the tide was against him. He observed Captain Khalil on deck, yelling at his crew as his xebec sank slowly into the river. The janissaries on board were busy removing their bedding and personal objects from their sleeping quarters and dumping them on the main deck. Others had put down their prayer mats and were busy praying. The crew ran hither and thither trying to find a reason for the sinking of the ship. It was total chaos on deck as the ship sank slowly into the mud.

In steerage, the water level was now above the head of the tallest man and the men were clinging to the wooden beams and ladder. The door to the pump room was open, and the men had to hold their breath and duck underwater to get through the door before climbing the ladder to the deck. A cry went up as a dozen men on the ladder made a dash for the deck. Soon everyone was clawing their way out of the hold and making for the pump room ladder.

Eleven

Aven River, France

The first prisoners raced across the deck to the port side and jumped into the river as the janissaries watched in astonishment. Most of the French and Portuguese were already in the water and struggling to get to the shore when the English and Irish emerged on deck. A handful of janissaries surrounded them with their sabres and drove them back. The French and Portuguese scrambled up the riverbank and headed for the trees. The janissaries were in no position to stop them.

The fugitives glanced back at the xebec in the river and swore never to allow anyone to take them prisoner again. Several English captives had jumped overboard, but the janissaries followed them into the water and held them back with their sabres. Captain Khalil took charge and shouted at his men not to lose any more captives. On the deck, John Amble and Thomas Payne were surrounded by janissaries with sabres. Amble smiled as he saw his friend Jacques scrambling up the hill opposite. When the fugitives got to the top of the rise, they looked back momentarily at the ship to confirm that they weren't being followed and waved to the English and Irish prisoners on deck before heading off in a westerly direction. Hugh Pierse stood on the deck and had tears in his eyes as he realized there would be little hope of escape from now on.

Captain Murad appeared on the shore and descended the river on foot to find out what was going on with Khalil's sinking xebec. The ship sat on the bottom of the river, but the crew was working the pump again and slowly raising the ship.

"What happened?" Murad asked Khalil when he arrived.

"They pulled the stop cock and flooded the hold. They came up through the pump room, sir."

"Damn, how many did we lose?"

"At least a dozen, sir. Most of them were French and Portuguese. Our men were busy saving their own things when it happened. No one saw it coming."

"How long will it take to refloat the ship?"

"We should be clear by tomorrow, sir. Then I will get the carpenter to replace the door so they can't get in there again."

"You are a very unlucky man, Arturo."

"Yes, sir."

"The pasha will make you pay for the loss of those men. Nothing I can say will change his mind."

Murad watched Aga Santos order his men to give each prisoner ten lashes as punishment for trying to escape. The first in line was Thomas Payne who was tied to the mast by two janissaries and then a third man laid into him with the lash. He grimaced at the pain but said nothing, putting a stoic face on his suffering. The other men stood in a line, waiting for the same.

The storm in the bay went on all night unabated. Khalil's crew worked non-stop pumping the water out of the hold. They were relieved every hour. By daylight, with the tide coming in, the ship was floating higher in the water. Captain Murad returned in the morning to consult with Khalil.

"We are going to be stuck here for a few days until the weather improves," said Murad. "I'm going to send out a hunting party. We need fresh meat and this area is teeming with game."

A servant brought in Turkish coffee and served it at a low table in Captain Khalil's cabin.

"I want you to get Santos to put together a contingent of janissaries," said Murad, "and go after the prisoners who got away."

"But, sir, you don't think that those men are long gone," said Khalil. "They've had a full day to get away and Santos' men have been busy at the pump all night."

"They are janissaries, Arturo. They are made of sterner stuff. Get that idiot Spaniard to roust them and send them out."

"Yes, sir."

"You've cost us a dozen prisoners, Arturo. Find some more Frenchmen to replace them and we are quits."

Captain Khalil nodded as Murad stood up.

On the riverbank, Aga Santos had lined up his janissaries. Each man carried a musket, and ball and powder in a pouch at the waist. Several of the men had crossbows slung over their shoulders as they headed out, climbing to the top of the hill and disappearing from view. Meanwhile, Murad put together his own hunting party from the remaining janissaries and they set off along the riverbank to the north. Captain Khalil set to work with his carpenter, repairing the wooden door into the pump room. The water level was now only knee-deep in steerage.

The morning meal was served to the women and children in the hold by Marco and Diego. The food was salt beef and the usual dark gruel. Emma Pierse and the girls served the food, as was their habit. As Marco was lowering a second tray of food from the main deck, he noticed a piece of paper with a message on it stuck to the ladder. He wasn't sure he understood what it meant, so he collected the scrap of paper and slipped it into his pocket. After the meal was over, Marco went to see the captain and gave him the scrap of paper with the blocky letters written in charcoal. It read: WE FOUND A BLOODY CLOAK.

It was later that morning that they came for Emma. She was indignant and struggled with the janissaries. She cursed Sally Gunter and Mrs. Harris. Emma's girls screamed as she was taken away and their grandma had to console them. As she climbed the ladder to the deck, Mrs. Harris thrust the blood-stained garment into the hands of a janissary. She looked satisfied that her game plan had worked. There was no doubt in her mind that Emma was culpable.

Emma Pierse was brought into the captain's cabin and her legs were kicked out from under her. She collapsed at the low table as Captain Murad entered the room and looked down at her. Emma was a firebrand, red-faced and angry, but she was very attractive, with her dark hair and white skin. *She will bring a good price in the Algiers slave market*, thought the captain as he sat down opposite her.

"What can you tell me about the murder, Missus Pierse?"

"Nothing."

"Your friends think you are the murderer."

"Sally Gunter and her friends, they are lying, sir. I have three little girls. Why would I commit such an awful crime?"

"What is going on down there, milady?" asked the captain. "Why are your people at each other's throats?"

"Let me tell you something, captain. We live in a small community. We all work at the fish palace, so sometimes there are tensions between us."

"Tensions!" exclaimed the captain, holding up the blood-stained cloak. "See this cloak. A woman was stabbed to death right under your nose and you talk about tensions."

Emma quickly became very calm and reflective. She found the captain to be well spoken for a pirate and was surprised by his intelligent manner.

"Orla Walsh had this old house with lots of books in Baltimore, sir. My girls went there often. She was always very nice to my daughter Phoebe, loaning her books to read. The day before she died, she lent her a prayer book."

"A prayer book?"

"A book of hours, sir. A beautiful book with the order of prayers, readings from the scripture, and such like. It was a prayer book for Catholics."

"Where is this prayer book now?"

"We don't know. Phoebe lost it. She thinks someone took it from her when she was on the deck."

"Why would someone want to kill Orla Walsh?"

"I don't know, sir. She was a nice lady, but many people in Baltimore wanted her gone because she was a papist."

The French and Portuguese fugitives were making their way slowly to the northwest. They were tired and hungry after walking for hours on a meagre meal of berries and crab apples. As they trudged along in the rain and wind, they heard a hunter's call to his dogs. Moments later, they threw themselves off the trail as a stag bounded along, followed by barking hounds. As they watched, several noblemen on horseback galloped past them in hot pursuit.

Jacques and his friends exchanged fearful glances when they realized that they were trespassing on land belonging to the local nobility. This was a very serious criminal offence in France, punishable by hanging. Only the local nobility had the right to hunt. They quickly got to their feet and moved under the cover of trees to the north.

The Duke of Quimperlé and his master of the hunt were riding splendid white horses and carrying crossbows in their mad dash after the hounds. They were followed by the duke's son, his groom, and two stable boys whose job would be to butcher any large game and bring it home. As they raced south, the riders didn't notice how distracted their hounds had become. The dogs were picking up the scent of unwashed humans on the trail and going off in different directions. The riders ignored the dogs and raced after the stag.

Santos heard the shouts and the thunder of hoofbeats and motioned to his men to close ranks. A moment later, the stag appeared at the top of a rise and hurtled down towards them, only to be felled by a crossbow bolt from one of the janissaries. The dogs followed, coming over the rise and barking madly as they surrounded the dying stag. The horsemen made no attempt to slow as they came over the rise at a full gallop.

Where they had expected to see a fleeing stag, they found themselves facing fifty armed soldiers scattering before them. The horsemen tried to pull on their reins, but they couldn't stop their mounts from colliding with the soldiers. The Duke of Quimperlé instantly recognized the danger and fired his crossbow into a janissary as he found a path through the compact men. The duke's son followed the master of the hunt but was on a nervous mare that took another path through the soldiers and somehow got turned around. The horse pitched backwards and the young man was thrown from his horse. The janissaries still in a state of shock, surrounded the young man with their sabres as they awaited the attack by what appeared to them to be a superior force of cavalry.

As they galloped away to the east, the French noblemen could hardly believe their eyes, running into a contingent of Turkish janissaries invading their private hunting domain. They pulled up to collect themselves and the duke dismounted. It quickly became apparent that his son was missing. The duke looked at his hunt master and then the groom, for an explication.

"*Où est mon fils?*" screamed the duke. "Where's my son?"

"I didn't see him, *monsieur*," replied the hunt master.

"What about you boys?" asked the duke of the groom and the stable boys.

"We followed your horse through the soldiers, *monsieur*," said a stable boy. "We didn't see him."

The duke turned to his hunt master and ordered the wizened grey beard to return to the woodland, where they had encountered the soldiers, to have a look. Grim-faced, the hunt master turned his horse around and galloped away.

"Go with him," said the duke to the groom and the stable boys. "He probably fell off his horse. I'll wait for you here."

Murad was prostrated on his prayer mat in his cabin, praying to Mecca, when two muscular janissaries shoved Felix inside and closed the door. The captain ignored Felix and finished his prayers before he stood up and greeted the young man.

"Can I offer you a coffee, Felix?"

"Thank you, sir."

The captain snapped his fingers, and a servant came into the cabin. He muttered something to the man, who left to fetch the coffee.

"Tell me, Felix. Have you ever considered becoming a Muslim?"

"No, sir."

"How old are you now?"

"Fourteen years old, sir. Fifteen in September."

"It's your choice. No one can force you, but I can tell you from experience that things will go much better for you in Algiers if you are learning to become a Muslim. The same goes for your brothers."

Felix nodded.

"If you desire it, just tell me and I will arrange for lessons for you and your brothers on board the ship."

"Thank you, sir."

The servant arrived with two cups of Turkish coffee. Felix added a teaspoon of molasses before sipping the hot drink.

"I had a talk with Emma Pierse," Murad said. "Orla Walsh had a prayer book. Have you seen it?"

"No, sir."

"She gave it to one of the Pierse girls the day before she died. Do you find that strange?"

"I don't know, sir. Maybe she was tired of it."

"A prayer book is very personal, Felix, like a copy of the Quran. You keep it close."

"You think she wouldn't do that?"

Murad nodded.

"You know what a book of hours is, Felix?"

"No, sir."

"It's a liturgical book. Roman Catholics use it to pray seven times a day. They pray on rising in the morning, at the lighting of the evening lamp, at bedtime, at midnight and so on. She would not have given it away without a reason."

"Why would she give it away?"

"That's the question, my boy."

"I saw the cloak, sir."

"Yes, so did I."

"She was killed by someone who hated her, sir. She was a frail woman. One stab would have been enough."

"She was killed for a personal reason? Someone hated her?"

"Yes, sir. I would think so."

Ten miles away in a French game reserve, Aga Santos had the miracle he so desired. The fallen horseman — hardly more than a boy, really — had survived with nothing worse than a severe headache. When he had finally regained consciousness, he had haughtily informed his captors that he was Jean-Marie de Bancalis de Maurel, son of the Duke of Quimperlé, no less. He demanded a safe return to his family.

Santos smiled at the boy. He knew that Captain Murad would be only too pleased to do exactly that for a price. Ransoming captives and slaves was standard practice among the Barbary corsairs, and if the family acted quickly enough, they could even negotiate his release before the ship left the coast.

At dusk, Santos and his men returned, leading four new captives and their horses, one of which was loaded with the disembowelled stag. The groom and the two stable boys had been captured when they had come looking for young Jean-Marie, but the duke's hunt master had escaped. As they descended to the riverbank, a welcome cry went up from their comrades, some of whom were having a wash in the river while others were relaxing on the grass. One of the janissaries had been wounded by a French crossbow and another had been injured by a collision with a horse.

Captain Murad exited his cabin to watch the men arriving. He was not terribly concerned about losing a few janissaries during the voyage. It was expected. They were the Pasha's men and were easily replaced. What was a constant concern for Murad was the loss of his captives to violence or sickness, which cut into the profit from the voyage.

The second contingent of janissaries had arrived earlier with a load of game animals, including a roe deer, a wild boar, and several pheasants. Already the cooks were busy preparing the evening meal and there was a pleasant smell of cooked meat hanging over the camp.

Murad joined Khalil and Santos on the deck of the smaller xebec now returned to its usual height in the water.

"Aga Santos was just telling me," said Khalil, "that they couldn't find the French captives, but they ran into a hunting party. That young man over there is the son of the Duke of Quimperlé."

Captain Murad glanced at the captives. The capture of the young nobleman changed everything.

"We shall ransom him," said Murad. "His father must be very rich."

He smiled and clapped Santos on the back.

"Keep up the good work, Santos. Let me have a talk with the young man."

The duke's son was taken to Murad's ship and offered a glass of Dutch jenever in the captain's cabin. The lad seemed to appreciate the gesture.

"*Votre nom, s'il vous plaît*," asked Murad in French.

"*Je m'appele Jean-Marie de Bancalis de Maurel, Duc de Quimperlé.*

"You are the son, *le fils du Duc de Quimperlé*?"

"*Oui, monsieur*. I'm very proud of my family."

"I'm sure you are," Murad said wryly. "Here is what we can do to help you. Do you understand?"

"*Oui, monsieur.*"

"I am going to send one of your men to find the duke. If he can pay a ransom for your life, you will be set free. If not, you will come with us to Algiers, where you will be sold into slavery."

Jean-Marie's eyes widened in shock.

"*Bien sûr, il va payer*," said Jean-Marie, recovering his wits. "He will pay."

"I am going to send for your men. You choose which of them will deliver the message. He must return with the money by eight o'clock tomorrow morning or we will be gone."

"*Oui, monsieur.* I will send Alphonse, the youngest. He will need a horse."

"Good, we agree. He must leave now."

Twelve

Ransom demands were not always well received. On at least one occasion, Murad's demand for ransom had been returned with a scribbled note informing him that there was no need for the captive to be returned at all. More often than not, the ransom offered was too little and too late. In these cases, the negotiation was better left to others and handled by Algiers. Ransom amounts then doubled or tripled depending on the capacity of the families to pay.

Murad had no idea how the Duke of Quimperlé would react to the kidnapping of his son, but he knew better than to assume that he would just meekly pay the ransom. That was the most likely outcome, but Murad knew from past experience that members of the aristocracy could be unpredictable. There was always the possibility that the duke would call out the local militia and attempt a surprise attack. That would be a very foolish thing to do, but Murad was taking no chances. As soon as the stable boy Alphonse had ridden away, Murad had ordered Aga Santos to post pickets along the ridge on both sides of the valley.

In the early morning hours, the stable boy returned to the encampment. Both the boy and his mount looked exhausted as they approached the ships moored along the riverbank. Murad looked up at the heights, squinting against the sun, and observed the watch party signalling that all was well. There were no uninvited guests trailing the boy. All was well as he awaited the ransom payment.

Down in steerage in Khalil's refloated ship, the French nobleman's son, his groom, and a stable boy waited for news of the ransom exchange. It had been a horrible night in the humid air of the hold, still wet through and full of mosquitoes and fleas. They could hear the mooring lines being slackened and the grinding noise of the anchor chain being lifted.

"*Je crois que nous sommes sur notre départ,*" said John Amble in a kindly tone to the young nobleman, indicating they were about to leave.

"*Non, ce n'est pas possible, monsieur,*" said Jean-Marie, alarmed. "They must first let me go!"

John Amble looked surprised by Jean-Marie's reaction. Why would the captain let this Frenchman go while the English and Irish remained prisoners in the hold?

"Maybe they have forgotten you, sir," suggested Amble.

"No, that is not possible," replied Jean-Marie.

The young Frenchman stood up and stumbled over to the ladder to the main deck. He looked up, hoping to see the hatch open and his wish for freedom granted, but nothing happened.

In the hold of Murad's ship, the women and children waited for their morning meal. Felix sat with Ciara and Mrs. Evans as the Pierse children played in the hammock nearby.

"You're very quiet, Felix," said Mrs. Evans. "Cat got your tongue?"

Felix blushed as the women observed him. He had been withdrawn and anxious after his meeting with the captain. He hadn't told Sally or the boys about the captain's offer.

"The captain is taking a liking to young Felix," said Ciara.

"No, he ain't, Ciara," said Felix. "He asks a lot of questions about the murder."

"The murder?" asked Mrs. Evans.

"Yes."

"But you know nothing about the murder," said Ciara.

"Of course, I don't. The captain likes to talk. He talks about the murder and Islam."

"Islam?" asked Mrs. Evans. "That evil man."

"He told me that things would go easier for me and my brothers if we convert to Islam," blurted Felix.

"Well, of course, it would," added Ciara.

"He offered to give us lessons, Ciara, to teach us the ways of Islam."

"You're not thinkin' of 'turning Turk'?" asked Mrs. Evans, clearly troubled by the thought.

"I am and I ain't."

Murad was drinking his coffee as Khalil arrived with a leather satchel containing the ransom for the duke's son.

"Here it is, sir," said Khalil.

Murad hardly looked at the satchel.

"Now the storm is over, we need to make up for the wasted time," said Murad. "The plan today is to make it to Groix or Noirmoutier."

The captain explained how he planned to descend the river on the ebb tide and, keeping as far offshore as possible, sail past Port-Louis and St. Nazaire, two major ports with French naval vessels protecting the coast. There were natural harbours on the south side of Groix Island and the east side of the Noirmoutier peninsula that could be used in the event of bad weather.

The captain picked up the satchel and dumped a leather pouch on the table. He emptied a pile of gold ecus into his hand and examined them closely.

"The duke," said Murad with a cynical air, "must be a very rich man. We'll talk to him again once we reach Algiers."

Murad waved to his servant to bring out the bottle of jenever.

"Would you like a glass before we start our day, captain?"

"Yes, sir," replied Khalil.

The captain poured the jenever into two tiny shot glasses, and they drank to their success.

The corsairs descended the Aven and set sail for Groix with a westerly wind. After the storm, the sea was relatively calm with its long Atlantic swells. They made good time sailing due south and then made a turn to the west for Groix.

In steerage, young Jean-Marie sat with his head in his hands. He had refused to talk anymore. He could hardly believe that his father had not paid a ransom for his liberty, but here he was on a slave ship heading to some godforsaken country under the worst conditions imaginable.

A janissary removed the hatch and a young man descended the ladder to join the men below. It was Jean-Marie's stable boy, Alphonse. Jean-Marie jumped up, furious at the young man.

"*Vous avez volé la rançon!*" screamed Jean-Marie, hurling insults at the boy and slapping him across the face.

"*Non, monsieur,*" said Alphonse. "*Je l'ai apporté selon la volonté de votre père.*"

Alphonse tried to tell Jean-Marie that he had brought the ransom money. He had not stolen it, but Jean-Marie continued to pummel him with his fists.

Thomas Payne stood up to separate the Frenchmen.

"*Calmez vous, messieurs*. Calm down, please."

Jean-Marie was enraged by his circumstances. *How could this happen?* he asked himself. *He had sent the boy to collect the ransom money and here he was.*

"*Mais, je suis encore prisonier dans ce bateau déguelasse.*"

"*Ils vous ont déjoué, monsieur,*" said Amble with a laugh. "They played you and your father."

"They're feckin' pirates," added Payne. "That's what the bastards do. They steal from people."

Hugh Pierse and the rest of the captives chuckled to see Jean-Marie's desolate air.

The hatch came off again and a tray of venison descended to the men below. The men stood up to eat and some of them drank from a ladle in the water barrel. John Amble collected an extra plate of meat for Jean-Marie and brought it over.

"*Vous devez manger,*" said Amble. "It's good, you'll see."

Jean-Marie ignored Amble and went off to sulk alone in a corner.

Yeu Island, France

The corsair ships arrived at Groix early in the afternoon and continued their run as far as Yeu Island. Yeu had an excellent natural harbour on its south side, which put them in a good position to make the long passage past La Rochelle and the Gironde estuary near Bordeaux. These were treacherous waters for corsairs with many French naval vessels patrolling the coast.

They sailed into *Port de la Meule*, a little cove protected by a breakwater as the light was fading. They immediately spotted a fishing skiff in the bay that seemed to be down on its luck. The tide was out, and it lay on its side in the mud. Captain Murad sent a dinghy with five janissaries to check the area for any French people living on the island. The men quickly disembarked in the shallow water and ran up the sand to take position around the fishing skiff. They climbed on board and woke two men who were sleeping in the empty vessel. The janissaries shackled the men together and led them back to the dinghy. They send three janissaries off to do a recce of the island and seize any locals they could find.

An hour later, the two fishermen were hauled into the captain's cabin. After the coffee was served, the captain arrived with a French-speaking janissary. He smiled at the men and turned to his colleague.

"Ask them what they were doing on their boat."

The janissary questioned the men, who murmured a reply in heavily accented French.

"He says they ran aground and ripped a hole in the bottom of their boat," said the janissary. "They were going to repair the damage and sail home."

The conversation continued in French.

"They are brothers, Pierre and Jean-Marc. They are from Croix-de-Vie in the Vendée."

"Ask them about French naval ships in the area."

The men grinned, nodding affirmatively at the question.

"They say they saw the *Grand St. Louis* last week off Croix-de-Vie with the *Neptune* and the *Licorne*."

The corsairs left Yeu Island at dawn with their two new captives. Captain Khalil swore that he would find more Frenchmen to replace the captives lost on the Aven River. As they headed south, they could just make out a ship off in the distance, heading in their direction. Captain Murad used his telescope to determine the origin of the foreign vessel. He quickly turned to Khalil on the sister xebec and yelled across.

"He's bearing a Spanish flag, Arturo. I know the captain. He's from Salé."

The xebec was almost identical to Murad's ship except for the ensign, since Murad was still showing his Dutch flag. The foreign ship approached until it was within shouting distance. It was in terrible shape. It looked like a heavy ball had ripped through the crew's quarters and destroyed part of the forecastle.

"What happened, Peter?" yelled Murad across the water.

Peter was an English pirate, a *renegado* like Murad, who sold his slaves and plunder in Salé and other ports on the Atlantic Coast of Morocco.

"It's not too bad," Peter shouted back. "We ran into the French fleet last night on our way up. We were lucky."

"How many ships?"

"Three ships of the line, Jan. Be careful, amigo. Adios."

The English pirate waved as his lateen sail caught the wind and drove him north.

Murad knew many of the English corsairs. He had been harassing Spanish shipping as a Dutch privateer when he had been captured in the Canary Islands by Salé corsairs. He had turned Turk' in 1618 and gone to work as a corsair himself.

"I did her hair once," said Bessie Flood, watching Emma brush Phoebe's hair in the dim light of the hold.

"You did?" exclaimed Emma.

"She came to me one day and asked me to cut her hair."

"You didn't refuse?" asked Mrs. Roberts.

"She seemed so desperate," said Bessie. "It was the only Christian thing to do. I've cut all your hair. I couldn't refuse Orla. I went to her house one morning, and she showed me all those fine books of hers. She was proud of her books."

Mrs. Roberts and Mrs. Meade sat in a circle near the Pierse children.

"Well, after I cut her hair, she invited me to have a sherry with her in the garden."

"I thought you didn't drink, Bessie," said Mrs. Roberts.

"Well, I like a sherry from time to time. We got to talking."

"I can't believe you talked to that woman," said Mrs. Meade.

"Orla was easy to talk to. She told me about her family and how she had been married to Gilly MacCarthy, the illegitimate son of Florence MacCarthy. The Irish prince they have locked up in the tower in London."

"She married a MacCarthy?" exclaimed Mrs. Meade.

"Orla said the marriage failed in the first year when she couldn't get pregnant. Gilly beat her and kicked her out of the house."

"She told you this?" asked Emma.

"Yes, dear. She was married to those damned MacCarthys, so I felt some sympathy for her. Orla managed to salvage her family's books, but she got nothing else. They treated her like dirt and chased her out of Castlehaven. She moved to Skibbereen and then on to Baltimore."

"How was that old house of hers? I remember the roof used to leak," said Emma, who had lived across the road as a child.

"It still leaked, but it didn't bother Orla none," said Bessie. "She complained about people trespassing at all hours of the night."

"People visited her at night?" asked Mrs. Meade, intrigued.

"She told me that she could hear people moving about downstairs in her house late at night. When she got up in the morning, she would find the mess they left behind."

"Did they take anything?" asked Emma.

"Orla said she didn't notice anything missing."

Arcachon Bay, France

By the end of the day, the corsairs had sailed a long way south, keeping a watch for French naval vessels and giving a wide berth to Ré Island, La Rochelle and Oléron Island. After passing the Gironde estuary, they hugged the coast before putting in at Arcachon Bay in Gascony. They anchored near Cape Ferret with its sand dunes. It had been a long, uneventful day. The women and children were allowed up on deck to eat their evening meal. The opposing groups of women maintained their distance on deck. They waved at their menfolk when they appeared in shackles on the deck of Khalil's ship. The men were surrounded by janissaries who weren't taking any chances.

A rumour was spreading among Sally's friends that Emma had made an arrangement with the captain. She was obviously a slut and had offered her body to the pirate who let her off the hook. In their minds, there could be no other plausible explanation that the woman was still walking freely around the hold.

The next day, Murad sent Captain Khalil in his xebec along Cape Ferret to the north to make a visual inspection of the bay. It was the usual scavenging expedition, looking for potential captives, game, and abandoned farm animals. They were not to dawdle because Murad wanted to catch the ebb tide out of the bay and set sail for the Spanish coast later in the morning.

Khalil's xebec ran aground when he tried to sail around Bird Island in the middle of the bay. They had to wait for the tide to free the ship. While they waited, Khalil sent five janissaries to the island in a dinghy to catch seabirds and waders in the marshy land around the island. They used nets to capture the marsh birds, including bitterns, moorhens, godwits and rails. On their return, the men discovered several adult turtles on a sandy beach on Cape Ferret. They collected them and returned to the xebec to unload.

When they returned to the mouth of the bay and joined their sister ship, the ebb tide was just starting and Captain Murad was eager to get moving. He ordered Khalil to follow his ship on its way out of the bay. They had to be very careful at the mouth of the river. There was a strong current pulling them south and driving them close to the Arguin sandbank. Murad had posted a sailor with a sounding line on the prow to call out the depth as they went through the passage.

Both ships had no sooner passed out into the ocean when they were surprised to see three ships less than a mile distant heading south. Murad had no way of knowing who they were, but the three ships — the *Grand St. Louis*, the *Neptune* and the *Licorne* — were unmistakably men of war, probably the same French naval vessels he had been warned about. They had the advantage of the weather gauge with the wind at their backs. The *Grand* closed for the attack, followed by the two others.

Captain Murad immediately sized up the situation. There was no way he could outrun the French ships while they were still in the shallow water of the bay. He ordered his crew to the oars while he told his gunners in the bow to get ready to fire. While his crew drew out the oars and brought down the mainsail, he waved to Captain Khalil to follow him. The corsair ships began moving away from the shore and heading directly into the wind towards the *Grand*, whose bow-chaser was already lobbing eighteen-pound balls into the sea short of the corsairs. The xebecs sat low in the water and, as they came within range, the gunner on the *Grand* adjusted his aim lower so that his bow-chaser was not shooting over the heads of the corsairs. Captain Khalil followed his friend Captain Murad as they risked everything rowing into a sea battle with a far superior foe.

Thirteen

Lekeitio, Spain

As Murad's xebec closed with the French ships, the gunner on the *Grand* was again shooting over the heads of the corsairs, the eighteen-pound balls passing just over the top of the masts. The gunner on Murad's ship now had a large target for his twelve-pound bow-chaser. He got lucky on his first shot and tore a hole in the mainsail of the *Grand* which reduced its speed. The *Grand* was still coming and would still be able to rake them with a 32-pound broadside. The frigates *Neptune* and *Licorne* were overtaking the *Grand* and firing their bow-chasers.

Captain Murad ordered his crew to draw up the oars and raise their lateen sails as they closed on the French ships. Captain Khalil followed suit, pulling up his oars and raising his mainsail. As their sails caught the wind, the corsairs pulled away to port at a ninety-degree angle, reducing their exposure to French cannon fire. The *Grand* fell behind as the *Neptune* and the *Licorne* turned to starboard to try to catch the corsairs who dashed away from their path. The corsairs were soon making twelve knots against the six knots of the French naval frigates.

It had been a desperate move. By attacking the French ships head-on, they had snatched victory from the jaws of defeat. A raking broadside by any of the French ships would have instantly destroyed the xebecs, smashing them into matchwood. It had been a battle of bow-chasers with the xebecs offering smaller targets. It was sheer luck that they had escaped the destruction of their ships and the slaughter of everyone on board. The French liked to make an example of Barbary raiders when they caught them. The corsairs soon lost sight of the French frigates and were well on their way towards the Spanish coast.

Captain Murad could just make out the mouth of the Lea River in the Basque country. As they approached the estuary, they could see an old Gothic basilica on the hill, the Church of Santa Maria, in the fishing village of Lekeitio. Murad and Khalil had been here before on their way north and had found the village abandoned by its citizens. As they came in, the ebb tide drove them back and they were forced to drop anchor in the bay. They would have to wait for the tide before they made their way up the river.

As the cooks went ashore on the eastern side of the bay and started to prepare the evening meal of deer and turtle meat, Murad sent Aga Santos with fifty janissaries in Khalil's xebec across the bay to the village on the western shore. It was a routine scavenging expedition to search for valuables and food left behind by the local population. As the janissaries moved through the streets, Santos knew they had been spotted hours ago by the locals. The janissaries broke down the door to the bakery and found the oven still warm. They grabbed several sacks of flour before they walked out. In a *taberna* on the main street, they discovered a large quantity of wine and hauled out as many barrels as they could. They put the wine and flour and other foodstuffs on a cart they had stolen to haul back to the ship.

As they approached the Church of Santa Maria, the front door opened and a child ran into the street. Santos sent several men into the church to investigate. After a few moments, his own curiosity got the better of him and he followed his men inside. He was dumbfounded by what he saw. A lone priest stood at the altar reading from Isaiah 41.10 in Latin:

> *"Ne timeas, quia tecum sum,*
> *ne declines, quia ego Deus tuus;*
> *confortavi te, et auxiliatus sum tibi,*
> *et suscepit te dextera justi mei."*

("Fear thou not, for I am with thee; be not dismayed; for I am thy God: I will strengthen thee; I will help thee; I will uphold thee with the right hand of my righteousness.")

The priest's words echoed around the nave, and even Santos was spellbound. An Italian janissary crossed himself. The soldiers stood there in awe of this man who risked being slaughtered or enslaved.

Santos realized that his men were waiting for him to give the order, so he went to the priest, raising his sabre. The priest stood fast, his gaze serene and unafraid. It was unsettling, and Santos hesitated as he got ready to strike down the man. He had never killed a priest before. He thought he might ask the man to leave or simply seize him and make a captive of the man.

A flurry of musket shots suddenly erupted outside the church and saved Santos from killing the man. The priest's gaze never wavered as Santos gave orders to his men to leave the church. He could feel the man's eyes on his back as he hurried out of the church. As they ran outside, several janissaries were struck down by musket shots coming from behind the gothic columns of the portico where a small group of Spanish soldiers was gathered and making a stand.

The janissaries panicked and ran off towards the ship, leaving Aga Santos and a handful of men struggling with the cart full of loot. The janissaries near the cart opened fire on the Spanish soldiers and then ran for cover while the Spanish reloaded their muskets. This gave Aga Santos and his men just enough time to get away with the cart and move it down to the dock. As Santos and his janissaries unloaded the cart onto the deck of the ship, the Spaniards celebrated their victory by parading around the square with their muskets raised and the little boy on the shoulders of his father. People began to emerge from their houses and fill the street as they joined in the celebration.

Captain Khalil's crew shoved off and the xebec rowed across the bay to join Captain Murad on the opposite shore. This was another defeat for Santos, who knew Captain Murad would not be happy with him.

"I heard the shots from the church. What happened?" asked Murad.

"There was a Spanish force, sir, hidden near the church. They caught us in a crossfire and killed five of my men."

"The Spanish were expecting us," replied Murad. "We will have to be more careful."

"What is the plan, sir?"

"We eat first and then we head west."

Mundakako River, Spain

Captain Murad knew the coast well and used the cover of darkness to sail west to the large Mundakako River estuary. They sailed upriver with the tide, passing the fishing village of Mundaka and a spit of sand into a secluded lagoon.

The stop was necessary. They were nearly out of fresh water, the one thing they couldn't do without. A ship's company could do without food for a week, but not water. Daybreak revealed a freshwater stream feeding into the lagoon, not a hundred yards from where the two xebecs were moored. Murad gave the order, and the crews of both ships wearily began loading the empty wooden casks into the dinghy. It would be another long day.

As the morning light penetrated the gloom of the hold, Marco and Diego delivered the morning meal to the slumbering women and children. Emma and her children got to work serving the salt beef and gruel when they heard Phoebe scream from the depths of the hold. She stood with a cup of gruel in one hand, looking up at the Osburne maid, Roisin, hanging from a beam in the deep shadow of the hold. Her eyes were glazed over and there was spit on her face. Phoebe dropped the cup and ran back to her mother.

Marco and Diego pushed their way through the terrified women and children to find the dead maid, swinging back and forth gently with the motions of the ship. Diego climbed onto the back of his friend Marco and unhooked the rope around her neck, lowering the woman to the floor. They could see the reddish marks of the rope on her neck. It was not hard to imagine how she had managed to climb up to the beam. There were wooden boards fixed at regular intervals along the wall.

After emptying the hold once again, Captain Murad came below to examine the dead woman. This was the second death of a captive on the voyage and would need some explaining when they got to Algiers.

"Who is this woman?" asked Murad.

"She was a maid, sir, a very nice girl," said Sally. "She worked for Mister Osburne in town."

"Do you have any idea why she would kill herself?"

"I don't know, sir," said Sally, standing next to Felix and his brothers. "I'm surprised that no one else has tried it, sir. On account of our situation."

Murad looked at Sally with a quizzical air as he turned to Marco and Diego and said: "Let's get her up on the deck."

The two janissaries threw a sheet over the dead woman and then hauled her body over to the ladder where she was winched up to the main deck using the sling.

Later, the women and children were on the shore eating their breakfast meal on the grassy riverbank surrounded by a janissary guard. The death of the woman had frightened the children. There was already gossip circulating about Roisin and how her death might be connected to the murder of Orla Walsh. The children sat quietly in a circle and ate silently until Marco and Diego arrived with a set of boules. They watched as Marco drew a circle for the jack, the small target ball, on a flat area above the creek. Then Diego pulled several wooden balls from a burlap sack and lay them on the ground. Marco then threw the jack into the circle to start the game. He picked up a ball and threw it as close as possible to the jack. It was then Diego's turn to throw a ball, and the game was on.

The Gunter boys came over to watch and Marco handed Caleb a ball to throw.

"Go on, lad," said Marco. "Let's see you play. Try to put your ball as close as possible to the jack."

It wasn't long before there was a circle of children watching the game as their mothers talked about Roisin's untimely death. Several women called out the news to their husbands, who were in shackles, taking the air on the deck of Captain Khalil's xebec. The men were closely watched by armed janissaries as they walked around the deck.

It was stifling hot in the depths of the empty hold. A woman covered from head to toe in a white shawl searched the belongings of the Pierse family in the dim light, rummaging through the children's toys. She then moved on to the belongings of the Gunters, the Croffines, the Ryders, and so on. Two janissaries descended the ladder to fetch the stinking buckets of waste from the head. They hauled them over to the ladder where a rope and hook were installed to help remove them. As they were hoisting the last bucket, they noticed the woman approach and follow them up the ladder.

The relaxing day on the shore helped calm the children's fears. The crew had worked hard all night to reload the water casks, and the ships were ready to sail in the early morning. Before they left, the janissaries dug a grave for Roisin in the field near the shore. Deirdre said a few words for the dead maid, followed by a prayer by Sally, Ciara, Ellen, and Jenny. Most of the women shunned the ceremony because suicide was a sin for Catholics as it was for Anglicans.

An hour later, the corsairs exited the lagoon and floated down the river past the village. Murad brought his ship in close to shore so he could have a look at the village. It was a tempting target, with the church so close and not a sign of resistance in the village. He was about to order a quick sweep of the village when he changed his mind. There had been far too many unpleasant surprises recently. If they were attacked again, they risked being delayed and missing the ebb tide. The potential cost was not worth the candle. They veered away and descended the river estuary to the sea.

Murad sailed west, giving the town of Bilbao a wide berth. It was a major port in the crown of Castile. Murad hoped to reach the bay at the mouth of the Agüera River after a few hours of sailing. Out in the Atlantic, the xebecs were buffeted by heavy seas, but once Murad had satisfied himself that they were not unmanageable, he ordered that young Felix be brought to his cabin for a word. He turned over the ship to his first mate and went inside to have a look at his charts.

It didn't take long for Felix to appear. Two large janissaries came in and sat him down at the low table.

"What can I get you, Felix? Would you like a coffee?"

"Thank you, sir."

The captain bellowed something in Sabir, then sat down. Moments later, a servant hurried in with a pot of coffee and poured two cups for the men. Felix put in a teaspoon of molasses and stirred the cup, waiting nervously for the captain to speak. Murad waved the servant away and only spoke once the door was closed.

"So Felix, what do you make of the hanged woman?"

"I'm not sure, sir."

"You must have an opinion."

"Roisin killed herself. She worked as a maid for Mister Osburne. She must have lost all hope, sir."

"Suicide is a sinful act, Felix. For Muslims, but it is also true for

Catholics and Protestants like yourself."

"Roisin was not sinful!" retorted Felix angrily. "She was a good person, always very nice to everyone."

Murad gave him an amused look.

"Anything else?"

"I wonder how she did it, sir, how she got up there to hang herself?"

"Marco thinks she climbed the wall and slipped the rope over the beam."

"She must have been very strong, sir, to do that."

"She was a maid, Felix. Women can be very strong. They work hard."

"I don't believe Roisin killed Orla Walsh, sir. She was a gentle person, incapable of violence."

"So who killed Orla Walsh?"

"I don't know, sir. It has to be someone else, someone with a motive. Roisin wouldn't hurt a fly."

"Well, I intend to find out the truth, Felix. We will find Orla's murderer."

"Yes, sir."

The servant brought in the bottle of jenever for the captain and poured him a glass.

"This maid, she was Irish like Orla Walsh and both were Catholics?"

"Why yes, sir?"

"How many Irish women do we have?"

"Deirdre, Ellen, Ciara?"

The captain nodded and drank from his glass.

In steerage, the French nobleman's son, Jean-Marie, had been seasick on and off for several days and was not eating. He sat alone in a corner and talked to no one. The stench in steerage was suffocating. The walls had dried out, but the bilge water sloshed about, making life below deck very uncomfortable. The young man had a delicate disposition and the rejection of the ransom money had taken its toll. He was utterly dispirited and had given up hope of returning to his homeland.

John Amble had tried several times to talk to the young man, but he had brushed him off. The groom, Antoine, had brought him food, but he refused to eat, only taking a bit of water. After several days, Antoine got up and crossed over to sit with Amble and Payne.

"I'm worried about the boy, *monsieur*," Antoine said in halting English. "He is often sick."

"He must eat or he won't survive the voyage," said Amble. "What can we do?"

"I don't know, but this cannot continue," said Antoine.

"I'll have a talk with the first mate," said Payne, looking at the emaciated boy.

"*Oui, s'il vous plaît*," said Antoine. "Maybe the captain can do something."

Fourteen

Agüera River, Spain

They sailed west and arrived in a wide bay. The flood tide brought them up the river near a tall mountain with a flat-topped rocky promontory shrouded in clouds. They were sheltered from storms and the country around the bay offered the prospect of good hunting for wild game. As soon as the ships had put out their mooring lines, Captain Khalil came over to have a talk with Murad. They stood on the deck and watched the cooks getting the evening meal ready.

"The French lad looks sick, sir."

"You need to take very good care of that young man, Arturo. He's a valuable asset. The ransom for the boy will be high."

"I'm thinking of putting him in with the crew, sir. The men can watch him."

"No, Arturo," said Murad, shaking his head. "That will not do. You will share your cabin with the boy. When you are not there, leave two janissaries to watch him."

"But sir, he's a prisoner!"

"It doesn't matter. I want his father to think we are taking very good care of him. For heaven's sake, he is the son of a duke."

Captain Khalil glared at Murad, but knew better than to argue further.

It was a hot summer day. There was a large field beyond the sandy beach and Murad decided to let out all the captives at the same time. The conditions below decks were intolerable. Murad knew he risked losing many of them to sickness and fever if he kept them locked up in the stifling air of the hold. They needed fresh air, and the children needed to play. It was as much a business decision as an act of kindness. They would bring better prices at the slave market if they remained healthy.

Murad watched as the guards deployed and the men, women, and children invaded the shore. The men were on one side and the women and children were on the other. Within minutes, many of them had discarded their clothes and plunged into the cool water of the river. After a refreshing dip, the mothers got to work washing clothes and spreading them out to dry on the rocks near the shore. Some of the men sat naked in the sun a hundred yards away on the sandy beach, while others played a game of three shells and a pea to pass the time. It wasn't long before several janissaries had joined the captives for a swim in the river.

The evening meal was served in the nearby field. The janissaries allowed the men to join their wives and children for a few hours. There was a lot of weeping and tears as the men ran to embrace their wives and children. It was a very moving moment for all concerned. For a short moment, the families held out hope that their lives might return to some kind of normalcy, but it was all an illusion. They were going to be sold in the Algerine slave market where no life ever remained the same.

Beef, deer and turtle meat were served to the captives and several bottles of Spanish wine circulated among the captives. The celebration continued late into the evening and a game of boules was played with the children. It was by far the happiest moment for the mothers and their children in many weeks.

After the meal, Felix went over to see Deirdre, who was sitting with Ciara, Mrs. Evans and her son.

"Felix, you spend more time with the captain than you do with us," commented Ciara.

"I have little choice, Ciara," said Felix as he turned to speak to Deirdre.

"The captain wants to talk to you."

"Why?" asked Deirdre, looking alarmed.

"I don't know," replied Felix. "Don't worry, Deirdre. He only wants to ask you a few questions."

Deirdre stood up. She was an attractive dark-haired woman about thirty years old with a snub nose and a rosebud mouth. Felix felt vaguely guilty as he led her back to the ship. It was through Felix that

Murad knew how close she had been to Roisin.

Deirdre and Roisin had known each other all their lives. Both came from poor families in Roaring Water Bay and had been sent to work as maids in the prosperous community of Baltimore as soon as they were old enough. Deirdre had worked as a maid for the Meregey family and was in charge of two young children.

Murad was having a drink with Marcellus on the main deck. They were in good spirits, laughing and making jokes. As Deirdre arrived, Marcellus stood up to give her his chair and nodded to the captain as he left. Murad smiled at Deirdre as she sat down.

"I'm sorry for the loss of your friend," said the captain.

Deirdre had not expected to receive condolences from the captain. She lowered her eyes to her lap. Murad glanced at Felix and gave her a moment to compose herself. When Deirdre looked up, she was teary-eyed and sad.

"I've known Roisin my whole life, sir. We are from the same village."

"Do you know why she would kill herself?"

"No, sir," Deirdre replied. "She was always very shy. She had a bad stutter — people made fun of her, so she was never much of a talker."

"A stutter?" asked the captain.

"She had difficulty talking, sir," said Felix, standing nearby.

"You mean *stotteren*," said the captain.

"Yes, sir," said Deirdre. "When it was bad, she could hardly put two words together."

"Did you know Orla Walsh?"

"I knew who she was, but I never talked to her."

Murad glanced at Felix. It was an unspoken question.

"Missus Walsh was from Castlehaven, sir," said Felix. "Deirdre and Roisin are from Roaring Water."

Murad nodded vaguely, his eyes on Deirdre.

"Do you think Roisin killed Orla Walsh, Deirdre?" asked the captain suddenly.

"No, sir!" blurted Deirdre at the question. "That is not possible. Roisin was a sweet person — she would never hurt anyone."

As the light started to fade, the janissaries separated the men from the women and children and led them back to their ship, leaving the women and children in the field. The men were sent below while Marcellus installed Jean-Marie in Captain Khalil's cabin. He gave him a straw mattress and put him in a corner of the room while a janissary fixed shackles on his legs to confine his movements.

"*Vous avez de la chance, monsieur,*" said Marcellus. "This is the captain's cabin."

Jean-Marie looked around at his new environment with suspicion as Marcellus left the room.

The mothers and children tramped back to the ship and were locked up for the night in the hold. The children settled in quickly, falling asleep as their mothers folded their clothes, reflecting on a lovely evening. In less than an hour, virtually everyone in the hold was sound asleep.

Felix fell asleep dreaming of Ciara. The dream seemed so real that he could feel her hand touching his cheek, her lips on his own. He jolted awake to find Ciara kissing him on the mouth.

"Ciara," cried Felix in a loud voice.

It was no dream — it was real. Ciara pulled back enough to clamp a hand over his mouth.

"Keep it down, Felix," whispered Ciara. "You handsome devil."

She gave him another very long, lingering kiss. Felix didn't want it to end, but finally Ciara pulled away and looked down at him with those lovely green eyes of hers.

"What are you doing here?" said Felix in a whisper. "What did the captain want to know?"

"Nothing. He had a few questions for Deirdre."

"He thinks Deirdre killed Orla Walsh?"

"No. I don't think so. He wanted her to talk about Roisin."

"The captain suspects Roisin?"

"He suspects everyone, Ciara."

Ciara nodded and then nuzzled his cheek.

"We'll talk in the morning," she whispered. "Go back to sleep."

She tiptoed away in the dark. His imagination was running wild and his heart was pounding so hard he thought it might burst out of his chest. He thought of Ciara's body so close to his own and he was sure of only one thing. There was no chance of sleep at all.

"Captain Murad, wake up!" Marcellus yelled as he threw open the cabin door. "There's a Spaniard in the bay."

Dawn was coming up on a wet, foggy morning as Captain Murad ran out on deck. He could just make out the flag and mainsail of a large ship anchored a mile away in the bay near the tall mountain.

"Muster the crew," he whispered to Marcellus. "Get the dinghy ready and put the oars out, but do it quietly."

When the dinghy was ready, Murad climbed aboard and with the help of a sailor was shuttled across to Khalil's xebec. Murad disappeared in the fog and voices could be heard over the water before the captain returned several minutes later. The sailors on Khalil's xebec were already putting out their oars and raising their mooring lines. It would not be easy rowing against the ebb tide, but they might have no choice.

Twenty minutes later, the corsairs had put some distance between themselves and the Spaniard by rowing up the river. They hugged the shore, where they were no longer visible to the enemy ship hidden by the tall mountain. Murad realized they were locked in, and their only hope was that the Spaniard would sail away sooner or later. There was, of course, the third option, but it would be dangerous.

After consulting with Khalil and Santos in his cabin over coffee and shots of jenever, Murad ordered Santos to put together a contingent of twenty janissaries and take them upstream to hunt for wild game, while Murad and Khalil took ten of his men downstream to have a look at the Spanish vessel.

It all started with a complaint by Emma Pierse about Felix's meetings with the captain and soon became a fierce argument in the hold.

"All I'm sayin', Sally," said Emma in a loud voice, "is that lad of yours should stop talkin' to the captain. He's a damned pirate."

"Felix can talk to whoever he wants to," said Sally.

This was followed by vocal support from Mmes Harris and Croffine while Felix sat quietly with his brothers and Ciara. The boys were busy playing a game of three shells and a pea.

"He's gonna get us all killed, that Mahometan bastard," said Bessie Flood. "You cannot trust the man."

"He wants to convert the boys to Islam," said Mrs. Evans. "He wants to turn our children into heathens."

Sally looked at her son in disbelief.

"Ma, he only said that things would be easier for us if we converted. That's all," insisted Felix.

"My son ain't gonna convert," insisted Sally. "He ain't no heathen."

"Why is he helping the captain, then?" asked Bessie. "He told the captain about Deirdre. What's he tellin' him about Emma and me?"

The argument had been festering since the night before when Deirdre had told everyone about her conversation with the captain. It had started again the following morning when Ciara had wasted no time claiming that the captain was looking for the murderer and would soon be coming for one of them.

"He ain't helpin' the man," protested Sally, frustrated by the complaints. "He's just talkin', that's all."

"Sure he is," Bessie snorted derisively, "but that kind of talk could get us killed."

Murad and Khalil climbed the flanks of the mountain to get a better look at the Spanish ship. It turned out to be a merchant vessel, not a warship, even though several twelve-pound guns were visible. It was sitting on the sand at low tide close to the shore. From what they could see of the main deck, a carpenter was trying to fix a broken rudder, sawing away at a large piece of wood while another man was shaping some kind of fitting with an adze.

Khalil and Murad looked at each other and grinned. This ship wasn't a threat. It was an opportunity. They could seize it and make off with its cargo.

Late in the afternoon, Santos's men returned with a wild boar and numerous waterfowl. It had been a good hunt and although the pork was forbidden for Muslims, it would make an excellent meal for the Christian captives and janissaries. The others would have to satisfy themselves with salt beef and waterfowl.. As he came on deck, Santos was surprised by the agitation among the ship's crew and janissaries. They appeared to be preparing the ship for an attack, bringing up munitions for the stern chaser, loading muskets and sharpening blades. He quickly sought out Captain Murad to find out what was going on.

"We'll wait for the ebb tide tonight and then make our move," said Murad.

"Won't they see us coming with a full moon?" asked Santos as Khalil joined them.

"They won't be expecting an attack from the land side," Murad told him. "How many men do you think they have, Arturo?"

"Maybe twenty or thirty at the most," shrugged Khalil dismissively.

Murad rubbed his hands together.

"I have planned a little distraction that should help hide our intentions," said Murad, smiling at his colleagues.

The moon reflected off the water as the xebecs glided down the river with the tide. They had stowed the sails and were moving fast with the help of their oarsmen. It was just after two o'clock in the morning, and they hoped to catch the Spaniards asleep in their bunks.

Captain Khalil's ship led the way with several women and children on deck. Deirdre, Besse, Sally and her boys, Felix and Caleb, had been chosen to stand on the deck and make the ship look less threatening from a distance. There was not a single janissary to be seen on the deck as they came around the flank of the mountain and entered the bay. Captain Murad held back as a precaution and let Khalil mount the attack. The women and boys were easily recognizable in the moonlight. Felix and Caleb were fascinated by Khalil's two gunners, who were loading their twelve-pound bow-chasers. They had never seen a sea battle before and were looking forward to the entertainment.

Fifteen

Captain Khalil ordered his rowers to accelerate the pace. "*Avanti, avanti,*" he called to his men. His oarsmen responded, and the ship shot forward. They were fast approaching the cargo vessel and still could see no activity on board the ship. Captain Murad's xebec followed Khalil's ship and planned to come around from the other side when suddenly the Spaniard fired its stern-chaser. The women and children dropped to the deck as the ball whizzed harmlessly over their heads.

The Spanish ship immediately sprang into action with its crew smartly raising the anchor and unfurling the sails. It was going to be a closely contested battle as Khalil's janissaries swarmed onto the deck with their muskets and sabres ready to board the enemy vessel. Felix and Caleb were in the thick of it, huddled with their mother and the other women near the gunwale. They watched in awe as the janissaries climbed onto the long prow of the ship to be the first to board the Spanish vessel. With its square-rigged mainsail open and gathering the wind from the southwest, the Spanish ship started to move out of the bay towards the east with the xebecs in hot pursuit.

Khalil's gunners fired their twelve-pound bow-chasers at the Spaniard, hoping to put a hole in the mainsail, but were having trouble adjusting the range of their guns. The Spaniards fired a second stern-chaser, and the ball crashed through the captain's cabin several feet from where Jean-Marie sat in shackles. Seeing the destruction, Khalil had enough and quickly veered away, avoiding further damage to his ship. He ordered the crew to pull in the oars and to raise the lateen sail which fluttered in the wind. Captain Murad had seen the damage to Khalil's ship and decided not to pursue the Spanish vessel.

It had been a good plan, but obviously, the Spaniard had seen them coming. You never knew until the last moment what the enemy was planning. Murad, who had been both attacker and defender in many sea battles, knew all the tricks and the most important was to be ready to change your plans at the last moment.

Sally sat with her two boys in a corner of the captain's cabin next to Besse and Deirdre. Jean-Marie sat across from them while a carpenter worked on repairing the damaged wall. The boy had perked up on seeing the women and even attempted to engage Besse in conversation.

"*Qui est cette jolie femme?*" asked Jean-Marie, looking squarely at Besse.

"*Je suis Besse, monsieur.*"

"*Vos cheveux sont magnifiques. Vous êtes anglaise?*" asked Jean-Marie, admiring the young woman's red hair.

Felix spoke before Besse could reply. He did not like the young Frenchman with his aristocratic airs.

"We are English, but we come from Ireland, *monsieur*," said Felix. "This is Sally, my mother, and these ladies are Deirdre and Besse."

"Good day, *mesdames*."

The women smiled at Jean-Marie and Besse blushed.

"When we get to Algiers, I will be ransomed," said Jean-Marie with pride. "My father gave money for me, but the captain is a pirate."

Jean-Marie gave the women a wistful glance.

"The captain is a thief."

Felix was about to make an ironic comment to this rich Frenchman when he stopped himself just in time. He realized that he would again be taking Captain Murad's side.

Murad was at the helm as they passed the rocky headland guarding the bay. He had been frustrated by his recent engagements with the Spanish and French and wanted to put some distance between himself and any enemy pursuers. They sailed west on a heading that would take them past the towns of Laredo and Santander and eventually Gijon.

That afternoon they arrived at the wide mouth of the Eo River. Both Murad and Khalil had been there before. It was the perfect jumping-off place for corsairs rounding the Galician peninsula with its heavy naval presence at Ferrol and Corunna. They would need to top up their water casks again and find food for the large number of captives and janissaries.

Ribadeo, Spain

The corsairs sailed a long way up the river estuary, past the tiny village of Ribadeo on the western shore, until they came to a brook emptying into the bay. They dropped anchor and the crew started hauling the empty water casks over to the riverbank with the help of the dinghy. The janissaries under the command of Aga Santos formed up on the shore.

It was another hot, windless day in July and the sun beat down mercilessly. Santos sent a squad of fifty sweating janissaries south to look for game on the east side of the river. The river ran along the western flank of the Cantabrian mountain range which teemed with wild boar, roe deer, rabbits and bears. Aga Santos then boarded the smaller xebec with the remaining janissaries and Captain Khalil took them across the water to the village of Ribadeo to scavenge for food and valuables.

As Sally Gunter and her sons descended the ladder into the hold, the younger boys Lionel, Geoffrey, Giles and Cecil ran to them. Young Walter in Jenny's arms called for his mother. Sally kissed the toddler while Felix and Caleb hugged their brothers. Deirdre and Besse soon appeared, and the other women crowded around them for news of the attack on the Spanish ship. When they learned the Spaniards had fired a cannonball that had crashed through the wall of the captain's cabin, they were in shock. *What were they doing in a war with Spain?* thought the women. *That only happened in places like Kinsale or off the coast of Plymouth with the Spanish Armada. They were lucky to have survived the Spanish attack.*

After the evening meal, the conversation turned to ransoms
"What's a ransom?" asked Caleb.
"A ransom is a payment for your liberty," replied Felix.
"Why is the Frenchman going to be ransomed?" asked Geoffrey.
"Because his father is the Duke of Quimperlé," said Deirdre. "He's a very rich man in France."
"Well, that's just fine for nobs like him," said Emma. "I doubt we fish palace workers are gonna be ransomed by a duke."

"Of course, we'll be ransomed!" exclaimed Ciara. "I'm sure they're talking about it right now in Castlehaven, maybe even in London."

Felix and his mother exchanged a look, but neither had the heart to say anything.

Ribadeo looked like a ghost town. Santos, mindful of his previous misadventures, ordered his men to stay alert as they disembarked on the dock and climbed the hill to the magnificent Franciscan monastery founded by Benicasa de Tudesco, a disciple of St. Francis d'Assisi, after St. Francis' pilgrimage to Santiago de Compostela in 1214. They saw no one and reached the monastery without incident. They knocked on the door, but no one came to open it. The door was solid oak braced with iron crosspieces and far too strong to be breached with the blades carried by the janissaries, so Santos took four men across the street to the blacksmith's shop, the most likely place to find the tools they would need to pry open the door. He told the rest of his men to fan out through the narrow streets and grab whatever food or valuables they could find.

The door to the smithy was unlocked, so Santos's men went inside to have a look around. They needed iron bars and sledgehammers to break into the monastery. They found what they were looking for and stopped dead in their tracks near the forge. The body of a man lay on the floor in an advanced stage of decomposition. From above, they thought they could hear the voices of children. They exchanged a look, and two men cautiously went upstairs to investigate. The stairs led directly into a small, windowless room, stiflingly hot, with a ceiling so low that the two men could hardly stand upright. They sheathed their weapons when they saw a woman lying on a straw bed with two small boys sitting close beside her. The woman looked sick, close to death, and one of the janissaries approached the boys and was pulling them away when he noticed the angry red pustules on the woman's face and hands. He quickly jumped back, fearful of catching the disease.

Outside the shop, Santos looked down to see an emaciated young girl, perhaps five years old, standing in the dusty street and imploring him for food.

"*Comida, por favor.*"

He took a step towards the little girl, just as the four janissaries ran out of the shop, their faces white with fear.

"What is it?" Santos demanded.

"There's a dead man inside and a sick woman upstairs," said one man.

As Santos looked up, he noticed a small sign in Spanish in the window: "*Tienda cerrada, viruela*" (shop closed, smallpox).

"Stay back," Santos ordered the men. "Stay back and don't move."

Santos was scared to death of smallpox and with good reason. Many years ago, half his village in Spain had been struck down with the disease and he had never forgotten the blighted lives and hardship it had caused. Now he knew why this village had appeared so quiet and empty.

The janissaries did as they were told. They stood where they were, not moving. They could have pretended to have seen nothing, but the Janissary code of honour was very strict. Each man must protect his brethren from infection and disease. They had to accept temporary isolation from their comrades.

The little girl understood none of this. The whole agitated conversation had been in Sabir. Santos spoke soothingly to her in Spanish, but she was too hungry to be denied. She approached him again, and if anyone had been watching from a distance, they would have been puzzled by the sight of five strapping soldiers running away from a little girl.

Meanwhile, the other men had managed to pry open the door to the monastery and had gone inside looking for plunder. They went from room to room collecting silverware and gold religious ornaments only to discover that a mysterious disease had struck down the residents. There were victims in the chapel, in the library, and in the cells throughout the building. The janissaries panicked and dropped their loot before they ran out into the street.

Santos quickly called his men to attention. He borrowed a musket and fired a warning shot. Suddenly, janissaries began to appear from shops up and down the street and ran to join them.

"The pox is in this town!" yelled Santos. "If you touched any dead or sick people, stand over there."

He waved a hand to where the four men from the smithy stood apart from their comrades. No one moved to join them.

"We didn't touch anyone, sir," said one man who had just come out of the monastery.

"But you were inside with the dead?" asked Santos.

"Yes, sir."

Santos could not take a chance. It would only take one infected man to spread the disease.

"You heard me," yelled Santos. "Get over there. That's an order."

The man and his mates shuffled glumly over to the contaminated group as the adjutant arrived with a pot of red hematite and a rag taken from a house across the street. He approached the group huddled together and daubed their clothes with red ochre. The men were furious, but their code did not permit them to protest further. They dutifully fell into line, trailing the other janissaries as Santos marched them back to the ship. The men carried bags of grain and silverware and led a donkey on a chain.

Across the street, the young girl stood in the doorway of a shop and watched sadly as the soldiers started to leave. A young janissary ran across the road and tossed her a bread crust that he had taken from the kitchen of the house down the road. It landed in the dusty street, only a few feet away. She gave him a shy smile as she snatched it up and ran away.

As the janissaries loaded the donkey and loot into the xebec, the red-ochre men were ordered to embark last and remain together on deck. The main squad of janissaries wanted nothing to do with these men. No one wanted to risk infection.

"Are you sure there are no others?" asked Murad when Santos and Khalil had reported the smallpox on their arrival. Like everyone else, Murad had been puzzled at first when Khalil's xebec disembarked the contaminated group of men on the beach a good distance away from the others, but then understood when he saw the splash of red on their clothes. He knew what it meant, and it worried him. Smallpox was a terrible disease and highly infectious.

"Yes, sir," said Santos. "These are the men who went into the smithy and the monastery. They found bodies and sick people inside both places."

"Did they touch anyone with the pox?"

"I don't know, sir. They were in contact with the victims."

"They brought nothing back."

"No, sir. Just some silverware, a few sacks of grain and a donkey. We did not dare bring anything else."

Greed was one thing, foolhardiness quite another. Every sailor had heard tales of ghost ships, sailed by men dead from the pox. In the cramped quarters of a ship, the pox would spread like wildfire.

"Very well," Murad sighed.

He leaned against the rail and looked across the water at the red-ochre men. They sat idly on the beach, guarded by a watchful cordon of janissaries keeping their distance. The captives, both men and women, were awaiting their evening meal on the shore and speculation was rife about the little group of red-ochre men. *Why was the captain singling out these men?* they thought. *What had happened to them? Were they to receive some kind of punishment?*

Murad glanced down at the near shore. The evening meal was cooking over an open fire.

"Get everyone fed, Arturo. Tomorrow, we'll decide what to do. Keep those men in isolation on the shore. I don't want them anywhere near the ship."

"Yes, sir."

"And don't forget to feed them."

Captain Murad could be a ruthless man and under no circumstances would he risk his human assets during a voyage. He had to think of the pasha's profit. He would have to quarantine these men for a few days and keep an eye on the others who had gone into the town. It would only take one infected man to spread the disease.

After the meal, Marco and Diego played a game of boules with the children. Felix played against Caleb and Ciara soon joined them. She had the uncanny ability to place her ball right next to the jack whenever she so desired. Her throws were almost magical, and the boys were hopelessly outplayed.

"Ciara, you are too good at this game," complained Felix. "Your turn, Caleb."

Emma Pierse and the women watched from the sidelines as Caleb launched his boule with wild abandon.

"Your turn, Ciara," said Felix.

Ciara stood at the end of the pitch and launched the ball with just enough backspin so that it rolled to a position inches away from the jack.

The janissary guards came over to watch the game. One of them seemed more interested in the women gathered there than the game of boules. He was a handsome fellow and rather tall. He seemed to have eyes only for dark-haired Emma Pierse and the redhead Besse Peeters.

"Ain't he the handsome one," said Emma to her friends, smiling at the attention she was getting from the man.

"What are our husbands going to say?" said Mrs. Evans with a laugh.

"We ain't got no husbands, no more," said Mrs. Croffine. "Soon as we're sold in that market in Arabie, our men will be gone forever. We'll be lucky to keep our kids."

"Don't say that," said Mrs. Roberts, mother of three young children. "They can't take our kids from us."

"They can do any damn thing they want," Bessie Flood frowned. "Ain't that the truth, Emma?"

Emma ignored her. She was busy flirting with the tall janissary who seemed to fancy her.

The men sat on the grass and watched their womenfolk and children at play. John Amble and Thomas Payne were talking together while Jean-Marie sat nearby.

"We're in Spain now, maybe Galicia," said Payne.

"A lot of Irish came to Galicia," said Amble, "after the battle at Kinsale."

"I think I've been here before. It looked a lot like this."

"When was this?"

"Years ago, we sailed here one winter to buy a butt of wine," said Payne. "We sold it in Roaring Water for a nice profit, as I remember."

"If I could get away, how long would it take me to walk home?" asked Jean-Marie wistfully.

"We must be almost a thousand miles from your home, Jean-Marie," said Amble.

"On foot, it would take a month or more," said Payne. "With a horse, you'd get home sooner."

Jean-Marie glanced at the small group of men off by themselves in the field.

"Why do those men have red marks on their clothing?" he asked.

Payne and Amble exchanged a look. The boy was clearly unaware of all the gossip circulating about the red-ochre men.

"They're marked men. They've got the pox," said Amble. "That's why they're keeping them apart."

"*La variole, monsieur?*"

"Oui," confirmed Amble, "they've got the pox."

"*Non, ce n'est pas possible,*" exclaimed Jean-Marie. "We had *la variole* in our town and a lot of people died."

"The captain won't be taking any chances, Jean-Marie," said Payne. "My bet is he's gonna leave those fellas behind when we sail away."

Ciara returned to the ship, smiling at the young janissary, guarding access to the hold. She climbed down and was on her way to the head when she saw a flash of pale bodies in the shadows. The noises she heard were unmistakable — a couple was having sex in the dark perimeter of the hold. They were so intent on what they were doing that they didn't know or care about her presence. Ciara kept going until she reached the head and pulled the crude divider closed. She listened, a faint smile on her lips, as she did her business. When the noises stopped, she ventured a glance at the couple. They were getting dressed.

Ciara stood up and, as she left the head, she had a brief glimpse of the couple in the shaft of light near the open hatch. They paused a moment, long enough for the janissary to pull the woman close for a final kiss. Ciara stifled a giggle as she realized who they were. Emma Pierse had wasted no time getting it on with the tall janissary. As Ciara arrived on the main deck, she noticed the tall janissary looking her way as he walked along the beach with Emma Pierse.

Ciara was walking away to join the others when she was stopped by the guard. He was a strong, dark-skinned man with a muscular build. He grabbed her arm and pushed her in the direction of the crew accommodation.

"I don't feel well," complained Ciara to the man.

The guard ignored her protests and pushed her harder, knocking her down. He grabbed her by the neck and dragged her backwards. Ciara bit down hard on his arm, but the man just twisted around and flung her down the steps into the below decks. She looked around for help, but there was no one there in the tight passage between the pairs of oars suspended in the air. The oar holes were plugged, and it was dark in the room. The guard smiled at Ciara, anticipating the pleasure he was going to have beating her into submission and then raping her. He tried to seize her arm, but Ciara was faster and pulled away from the man, heading ever deeper in among the oars. He was enjoying himself as he stood between her and the exit to the main deck. He picked up a whip used on galley slaves and went after Ciara.

Sixteen

In the hold, the women and children were just drifting off to sleep when they were awoken by a lot of shouting and noise coming from the main deck. The women were tired from their long day in the fresh air and sunshine, and had been looking forward to a quiet night. They listened to the angry voices and wondered what was going on. It was spoiling the end of a very pleasant evening.

In the captain's cabin, Khalil and Santos were having a heated argument.

"You have a murderer among your crew," yelled Santos. "It's as simple as that."

He was standing nose to nose with Khalil and was as furious as Murad had ever seen him.

"What was one of your men doing down in the crew quarters?" asked Khalil angrily. "He shouldn't have been there."

"I have no idea," replied Santos. "Maybe he had a friend there."

"Enough," whispered Murad, trying to calm his officers.

"When someone attacks one of my men, they attack us all," charged Santos.

"I doubt the crew had anything to do with it," said Khalil.

Murad handed his officers a glass of red wine.

"Let's have a drink, *proost*," said Murad, raising his glass and pointedly waiting until his officers, still glaring at each other, touched their glasses to his.

"Good," growled Murad. "We'll sort it out tomorrow."

In the morning, Murad gave Captain Khalil the use of his cabin so he could question the members of his crew who had been on board the xebec after the evening meal. The first man was Mustafa, who had discovered the body.

"I was having a nap, sir. It was just after eight bells. I was going out on my watch when I noticed the dead man. He was lying on an oar. There was a lot of blood."

"When you were sleeping, were you awakened by any sounds?"

"No, sir. There are always noises coming from the main deck, but I heard nothing unusual."

"The dead man had been guarding the hold?"

"I wouldn't know, sir. We have our work to do and have little contact with the janissaries."

"Did you know the dead man?"

"No, sir."

"His name was Jamal. Maybe you played cards with him and his friends?"

"No, sir."

"Come on, Mustafa. We know that there are games going on every evening."

"I don't have time for cards."

"Maybe you don't play cards yourself, but you must have placed some bets?"

Mustafa nodded.

"I do sometimes, captain, but the amounts are small. I don't know this fellow, Jamal."

Khalil nodded and let Mustafa go. He didn't look like he was capable of murdering anybody. A second man came in and Khalil learned nothing new. After an hour, he knew there was a lot more interaction between the crew and the janissaries than met the eye. He was about to leave and get out in the fresh air when there was a knock on the door. He looked up and was surprised to see Santos standing there with a tall janissary.

"Captain Khalil," Santos said, "my man Agron was on the ship. He can tell you what he saw."

The night before, Murad had made it very clear to his officers that they were to be unfailingly civil to each other, especially in front of the men.

"Good," replied Khalil, gesturing for Agron to sit. The janissary appeared ill at ease as Santos left the room.

"What did you see?" asked Khalil.

"Not much, sir. I was accompanying Emma — Missus Pierse back to the hold."

Khalil looked at Santos's man with suspicion. He thought, *that was very kind of you, but what was a lecherous janissary like yourself getting for your services.* He had serious doubts that Agron could help him find the killer.

"You saw Jamal on the deck?"

"Yes, sir."

"Did you know him?"

"Not at all, sir."

"Who else was on deck?"

"I don't remember, sir."

"Did you talk to Jamal?"

"No, sir."

"What was he doing when you saw him?"

"He was standing near the ladder that goes down into the hold."

"He was guarding the hold?"

"I think he was, sir. It was very hot that day. There was nobody else around. Everybody was on the shore."

"Not everybody," said Khalil with an ironic air. "Not everybody."

In a corner of the field, Aga Santos accompanied a young janissary named Juan to talk to the quarantine men. They had just received their morning meal and were resting on the grass. Santos stood twenty feet away and called to the men.

"How are you feeling this morning?"

"We're fine, sir," said Carlos, a Spanish janissary standing to attention.

"No one has a fever?"

"No, sir."

"Good. We're going to be here for another day to see how you are progressing."

"Don't worry, Carlos," said Juan. "We're not going to abandon you."

Carlos was Juan's older brother. They had been captured together by Algerine corsairs five years earlier and had served as janissaries for the pasha ever since.

"Don't go any closer," Santos advised Juan. "I'm going back to the ship."

"Yes, sir."

The aga returned to the ship, leaving Juan in conversation with his older brother.

It was going to be another blistering day, and the heat in the hold would be intolerable. Captain Murad allowed the captives to go on shore. The women sat in the shade of the trees and watched their children playing a game of boules. Their menfolk sat further up the beach under a rocky outcropping, guarded by a dozen janissaries. From time to time, they ran naked into the river to cool off.

Felix and his brother Caleb were dozing sprawled on the grass under a tree as Ciara arrived.

"Felix, we need to talk," said Ciara, sitting down beside the two boys.

Felix gave Caleb a look and his younger brother went off to watch the game of boules. Ciara looked around to make sure no one was within earshot.

"There's been another murder," she whispered.

"What?" exclaimed Felix.

"I heard the crew talking. A janissary was killed last night. I think I saw the killer."

"But we were all on the shore yesterday, Ciara."

"I know. The murderer isn't one of us, Felix."

"Then who?"

She leaned in close to him.

"During the evening, I went back to the hold," confided Ciara, who now had the lad's full attention.

"I saw Emma with a tall man in the hold. They were going at it, having sex."

Felix stared at her.

She held his gaze and nodded.

"You're blushing, Felix. He's a janissary. Emma was making eyes at him yesterday?"

"Missus Pierse? But she's married to Hugh—"

"She's an attractive woman, Felix," said Ciara, smiling impishly. "I'm sure you've noticed, and she's not the only one carrying on with the men."

"You mean?"

"The women are talking among themselves, Felix. They know they're never going to be with their husbands again."

"But she's married and has three little girls."

"She'll be lucky to keep her girls, Felix. It's going to be that bad from what I've heard."

Felix looked annoyed as he learned about life's darker secrets.

"Emma didn't see me, but the tall janissary did."

"Are you sure?"

"Yes, he might come after me."

"What can I do?"

"Talk to the captain, Felix. He likes you. You have his ear. Find out what is going on."

After Ciara left, Felix spent the better part of an hour trying to think of a plausible reason to request an audience with the captain. He was already aware that some of the captives already looked at him with suspicion — few prisoners had any contact with the man, and certainly, none were on such good terms with him. He was soon tired of thinking about it and decided he didn't need a reason to see the captain. He got up from under the tree and walked down to the ship. A janissary took him to the captain's cabin where he found him alone looking at charts of the coastal waters.

"How are you, Felix?"

"I'm fine, sir."

"Would you like a glass of kümmel?"

"Kümmel, sir?"

"Yes, Santos's men found a bottle in the monastery. It's made with caraway seeds that come from Riga in Latvia."

The captain signalled for his servant to bring the bottle. The man returned a moment later with two glasses and a small squat bottle. The captain took the bottle and poured the colourless liquor into the glasses.

"It's very popular in Holland, Felix. In Spain, they call it 'Ribadeo kümmel' because Ribadeo is the only point of entry for kümmel."

The captain drank from his glass as young Felix sipped the strong liquor.

"What are the rules of war, Felix?"

"I don't know, sir."

"Come on Felix. Show a bit of imagination. I'll tell you what the first rule is. Know thyself. Know what you are capable of and not capable of doing."

Felix nodded at the wisdom of this comment.

"I think you already knew that one," said Murad, smiling. "When

Khalil gave you a *bastinado*, did you resist? Did you fight back?"

"No."

"You knew Khalil and his men could snap you in half like a twig, did you not?"

Felix felt vaguely insulted, but that was exactly what he thought.

"Yes, sir," admitted Felix.

"You see, Felix? You know more than you think you do."

Murad picked up his glass.

"Rule number two is to know thy enemy. Know his strengths and weaknesses. What is rule number three, Felix?"

Felix wasn't sure why Murad was asking him these questions, but for some reason, he wanted the captain's approval. He remembered something that his father had told him years ago. His father had talked about the famous battle of Crécy and how the English King Edward III had beaten the French commanded by King Philip VI at the start of the Hundred Years' War. Edward had chosen a defensive position on a hillside and with the advantage of their English and Welsh longbows, they had won a splendid victory over a much superior enemy force.

"That's easy, sir. Choose the battlefield."

"Very good. Yes, that's always a good rule — but not always possible. There is another rule that may be more important, and it has always served me well."

"What is that, sir?" asked Felix, with real interest.

"Always do the unexpected," said Murad. "War is chaos, Felix. No matter how well you think you've planned things, those same plans are often useless within the first hour of battle. Take advantage of that chaos. Try to create it in the mind of your enemy. If he expects you to go north, go south. If he expects you to attack, then save yourself by running away. You can always fight him another day. This rule has saved my life many a time."

Felix nodded his agreement as the captain finished his glass of kümmel.

"Always do the unexpected, Felix. By the way, how are our womenfolk?"

"Fine, sir. It's a lovely day. They are enjoying the fresh air with their children."

"Good for them."

Felix wondered how much he should say. Finally, he made the

leap.

"I heard that one of your men was killed yesterday."

"Yes, a very unfortunate case, Felix. A janissary was killed. It may be a revenge killing."

Murad poured himself another glass of kümmel.

"How did it happen?"

"He was stabbed to death below decks, near the crew quarters. One stab wound to the heart is all it took. He still had his *kilij* sword on his belt."

Felix sipped his kümmel.

"Who are those men marked in red, sir?"

"You're very curious, Felix, always asking questions."

"Are they sick, sir?"

"The town has the smallpox plague. Those men went into a house and may have become infected."

"What are you going to do with them, sir?"

"We will do what we have to do. We cannot risk them infecting our people."

Seventeen

Dungarvan, Waterford

No one knew why the Englishmen had come to Dungarvan. It was a tiny fishing village east of Cork with no claim to fame. The four horsemen wore mail, and three of the men carried pikes and falchions hidden in their scabbards in case of trouble. The fourth man, who was obviously the senior officer in charge, had a small pinched face and rode his horse with difficulty. He was clearly not used to charging around the countryside looking for fugitives. Irish villages were notorious for their hatred of English soldiers, and this one was no different from any other.

The officer did not want his target to give them the slip, so they made an early start. The men had spent most of the night drinking at an inn and were still drunk in the early morning hours when the officer had rousted them from the barn. The men grumbled as they mounted their horses and rode off in an easterly direction. They went past Dungarvan Castle, built in the 12th century, and crossed the bridge over the Colligan River, riding into the Abbeyside parish. They woke up the occupants of several cottages along the shore and demanded to know where John Hackett lived. No one appeared to know, or they refused to say. As they got to the last cottage in the row, a man clad only in his long underwear shot out the back of the house and ran for the hills.

Two of the horsemen took off after the man and ran him down. One man jumped down from his horse and tackled the fugitive to the ground. They walked him back to the officer, who was waiting at the house.

"Your name, please?" asked the officer.

"John Hackett, sir," replied the man.

"Hackett, you are under arrest and required to come with us to the Court of Assizes in Cork."

Hackett's frightened wife and child watched from the doorway. Neither spoke a word of English and indeed had rarely heard it spoken. No one in Dungarvan had ever been arrested by Englishmen from Cork.

"On what charge, sir?" asked Hackett, looking unperturbed.

The officer was annoyed by such insolence, but took the time to search through his papers but found no explanation.

"I'm afraid I don't know, Mr. Hackett," said the officer. "Please get dressed and provide for your missus and the child. We leave in ten minutes."

Ribadeo, Spain

It was after dark and the women had put their children to bed. Ciara and Felix sat with Mrs. Evans and her son Amos, who was already fast asleep.

"Ciara, my dear. Where did you learn to play boules?" asked Mrs. Evans in a whisper.

"Castlehaven, milady."

"I ain't never seen no fish plant worker play boules like that."

"I learnt it playing with the rich folk, milady. I was a maid for the MacCarthys for a while."

"You never mentioned it, Ciara."

"No, I suppose I didn't."

"What were they like?"

"I was lady-in-waiting to Ellen MacCarthy, milady."

"The wife of Florence MacCarthy?"

"The same."

"I don't believe you, you're lying again, Ciara."

"I am not."

"Ellen MacCarthy, you made it up."

"No, milady."

"Did she throw you out?"

"No, of course not."

"For lying or stealing, perhaps?"

Ciara glared at her and stood up. She walked away only to return later when Mrs Evans was asleep as were most of the exhausted women and children. It was becoming a nightly rendezvous, and Felix was alive with anticipation. After what seemed like a very long time, he heard a rustle of movement as Ciara pressed up against him, giving him a kiss on the cheek.

"Were you lying, Ciara?" asked Felix.

"No, I was tellin' the truth. I know Ellen MacCarthy. That's a fact. That woman knows nothing."

"Why did you come to work in Baltimore?"

"That's a long story. What did the captain tell you?"

"Not much."

"What do you mean?"

"We talked about the rules of war."

"The rules of war?"

"The captain likes to talk, Ciara. I asked him about the dead janissary. He says the man was stabbed to death, says it's a revenge killing."

"A revenge killing?"

"Yes, then he told me about those men with red marks. They have the smallpox plague, Ciara."

"Smallpox? Oh, God, no."

"Don't worry. The captain won't allow them to infect us. We are too precious for him to put our lives at risk."

At first light, Captain Murad and Aga Santos went to meet the red-ochre men under the trees after Santos learned that some of them were not feeling well. Standing at a safe distance, they called to the men who were just waking up after a long, uncomfortable night.

"How are you feeling this morning?" asked Santos.

"We're fine, sir," said one man.

"How many of you have symptoms?" asked Murad.

"Just Carlos, sir," said another man. "He says he has a headache, but I think he has a fever. He's very hot."

"You men stay away from Carlos," warned Murad.

"What do we do, captain?" asked Santos.

"Nothing. We do nothing."

Murad turned to Juan, who stood nearby.

"Juan, I think your brother has the pox. Stay away from him."

"What about the others?" asked Santos.

"We'll give them food and water for the first week. After that, they are on their own. They can take their crossbows with them."

The captain turned away and walked back to the ship, leaving the aga to deal with the problem.

"But sir, my brother will die if you leave him here," cried Juan to Murad, who waved him off.

"He'll die anyway," said Santos. "You better stay with him and take him home to Valencia if he gets better."

Juan glanced around, totally demoralized.

"Look at it this way, Juan," said Santos. "You might be able to save him. I've seen it before, but you will need to be very careful. Keep your distance at all times or you'll catch the pox yourself."

Santos called to the other janissaries who stood up to hear his words while the sick man remained on the ground.

"Listen to me. I'm releasing all of you from the service. As of today, you are freemen. You are no longer janissaries in the pasha's service. You can go home to your family. Get rid of your Turkish clothes. If the *soldatos* catch you, they'll burn you alive as heathens."

"We'll do it, sir," said Juan, speaking for the others.

"Of course you will," said Santos. "Remember, you were once proud janissaries and janissaries can do anything."

The corsairs raised their mooring lines and prepared to leave. The ships pushed off and a contingent of janissaries on deck waved at Juan and their sick comrades on the shore. An ebb tide whisked the xebecs out into the river close by the shore of Ribadeo, the ghost town where the victims of the smallpox scourge lay dead and dying. They were soon out into the bay and a brisk wind took them around the headland of Isla Pancha and into the Atlantic swell.

The next stage in their voyage would take them along one of the most dangerous parts of the Spanish coast. Captain Murad gave the area a wide berth sailing northwest and then west and south under cover of nightfall to avoid the naval shipping in the area around Ferrol and Corunna. Ferrol was a major shipbuilding centre and its port was the home of the Spanish navy in the north. It was from Corunna in 1588 that the Spanish Armada set sail for England on their disastrous voyage and the following year, Sir Francis Drake launched a massive attack on the city.

Costa da Morte, Spain

Murad sailed south as far as the Lires River. They arrived in the bay on a moonlit night and laid anchor in the shallow water near the beach. At first light, they entered the river estuary with the flood tide and took the right fork until they arrived at a freshwater spring on the shore. They had been here before and knew the area well. The crew immediately brought out the empty water casks and loaded them into the dinghy.

It was going to be another hot day, so the captain gave permission for the men and women to go ashore. A meal was served and the children soon entertained themselves by running about in the long grass. The men were kept at a distance from their womenfolk. It wasn't long before everyone was talking about the red-ochre men who had been abandoned at Ribadeo. No one felt any sympathy for the sick men and all believed the captain had done the right thing to abandon them.

As the day wore on, several male captives were having a nap under the trees away from the shore. They were under surveillance by a dozen janissary guards. From time to time, they would disrobe and descend to the river naked to cool off. Young Jean-Marie got up and joined John Amble, having a dip in the river. Thomas Payne sat on the beach drying himself next to Corent Croffine and Hugh Pierse.

"Be careful, Jean-Marie," said Amble. "*L'eau est profonde.*"

"Don't worry, John," said Jean-Marie as he swam further out into the river. The men watched as Jean-Marie disappeared below the surface and then popped up again.

"He swims like a fish," said Payne.

The other men laughed as they saw Jean-Marie plunge again, but this time, the young man seemed to be gone a long time.

"Where'd he go?" asked Amble.

"Over there," said Payne, pointing to where Jean-Marie's head had just broken the surface. He was already halfway across the river. He stayed just long enough for a deep breath of air and disappeared again.

"Good for him," added Croffine.

The next time they saw Jean-Marie, he was emerging naked from the river on the opposite bank and running for the trees. One of the guards spotted him and raised the alarm.

Several hours later, the janissaries had still not returned with their fugitive and Captain Murad was not happy. He summoned Khalil and Santos to a meeting.

"Still no news about the young Frenchman?"

"No, sir," replied Khalil.

Murad was furious. The young French aristocrat was a huge prize, perhaps worth more than the rest of the captives put together. Santos knew better than to make excuses. The guards he had assigned to watch the prisoners had not been paying attention. They had probably been straining their eyes to watch the women bathing and hadn't been watching the men.

"I have men out looking for him," Santos said, trying to sound confident. "We'll find him."

Murad stared at him for a long moment, then shook his head in a tiny movement that spoke volumes. He waved Khalil and Santos away and returned to his charts. He was interrupted moments later by a timid knock on the door.

"Come in," he said to Mustafa standing at the door, holding a dirty rag in his hands.

"Sorry to disturb you, sir," said Mustafa. "We found the knife."

The captain looked puzzled.

"The one that killed Jamal, sir."

Mustafa removed the dirty rag from the knife and handed it to the captain.

"Where was it?"

"It was under the oars, sir. We couldn't see it because it was too dark."

"Good work, Mustafa."

Murad looked at the knife. It had a narrow wooden handle and a thin seven-inch blade. It showed a lot of wear and tear.

"It's still got his blood on it," said the captain.

"Yes, sir. It's an ordinary fisherman's knife."

"Yes, it is."

It was getting late as a dispirited Santos took the dinghy to the far shoreline to await the return of his search party. He ordered the oarsmen to remain with him. If the lad was found, he did not want to waste any time getting him back to the ship. The men returned in groups and had seen neither hide nor hair of the lad in the swampy ground.

Santos was beginning to despair when two janissaries dragged a sun-burned and bloody Jean-Marie out of the trees and down to the dinghy. They had found him in an open field miles away, and the lad had been foolish enough to resist the men. Santos got up, reminding himself not to show the lad how relieved he was, and motioned him into the boat.

They rowed over to Captain Khalil's xebec. Santos boarded the vessel only long enough to order the boy to be tied to the mast and to administer a well-deserved *bastinado* as punishment. Santos and his oarsmen then returned to the far shore to wait for the rest of the search party. Conscious of his tenuous standing with Captain Murad, he had been careful to take a head count of his men before he dispatched them into the countryside. Now that he had recovered the French lad, it would not do to leave any of them behind.

After the *bastinado*, the janissaries carried the weeping lad to see the captain.

"Where did you think you were going?" asked Khalil. "There is nothing out there. We're in Spain, a long way from France. We cannot ransom you if you die of exposure."

Jean-Marie could only manage a whimper in response.

"You will remain in steerage for the rest of the voyage," said Khalil, glad to be rid of the young man. "Take him away."

Two janissaries lifted Jean-Marie off his feet and hauled him out of the cabin.

Captain Murad was happy to have the French aristocrat back. He called for a bottle of wine to celebrate his capture with Santos, Khalil and Marcellus. A servant brought in a bottle of red wine and poured glasses for each of the men. As soon as he left, Murad pulled out a chart of the coastal waters and laid it out on the table.

"We are leaving this evening," said Murad. "We will sail on the ebb tide and head south as far as Cape Finisterre. You remember the town of Fisterra?"

"Yes, sir," said Santos.

Khalil remembered their futile attack on the town on their way up the coast, which had ended abruptly when a Spanish ship appeared on the horizon. The captain still believed the rumours that there were hidden treasures in the Church of Santa Maria das Areas.

The cape was a slim finger of land pointing due south, with the town of Fisterra on the east side. It was the most westerly point of Spain extending way out into the Atlantic Ocean, and was the final destination for many pilgrims on the Camino de Santiago, being only a short distance from Santiago de Compostela.

"We will land our janissaries on the western shore after dark, " said Murad. "They will cross the headland to the town in the early morning hours."

"How many janissaries will we need, sir?" asked Santos.

"A full contingent," said Murad, still looking at the chart.

"You mean two hundred men, sir?"

Khalil's face wore a quizzical, almost impertinent air as he watched Santos trying to ingratiate himself with the captain.

"Not that many," Murad said, looking up. "A hundred men should do."

"What time will the ships collect us?" asked Santos.

"If there are no problems, we will arrive at the port with the high tide at around eight o'clock. That will give you several hours to search the church and the town."

Eighteen

Fisterra, Spain

During the night, the corsair ships hugged the west coast of Cape Finisterre as they approached the shallow water of their landing site in the dark. They came in from the north of the town of Fisterra so they wouldn't be spotted by local farmers or fishermen. The janissaries sat quietly on deck with their muskets, crossbows and sabres waiting for the order to go ashore.

As the boats closed on the beach, the men jumped into the waves and waded ashore. The landing was accomplished in less than a minute with the men running up the beach to find cover in the sand dunes while the two xebecs rowed back out to sea. Aga Santos ordered his men to stay hidden in the dunes and get some rest while he went off to do a reconnaissance of the town. He took only one man with him, a janissary by the name of Luis, who, like him, was a native of Spain. They wore nondescript clothing, not unlike that of Spanish peasants, and left behind their curved yatagan sabres. Both men were armed with straight swords and if the excursion went according to plan, they wouldn't have to use them.

If there were too many Spanish soldiers in town, they were to call off the engagement by lighting a fire on the beach an hour before sunrise. The ships would then return to collect the men. If it was a go, they were to collect the men on the other side of the cape.

Fisterra was quiet. The only sound was the occasional bark of a dog. Santos and Luis marched along the Paseo Ribeira near the port before they saw anyone at all. Two soldiers were lying in the street opposite the garrison building. Luis ran forward, intending to silence them with his sword before they could sound the alarm. He stopped in his tracks when he noticed that both men were fast asleep and stank of *oroju*, the Spanish grappa, with its sour, sweet taste. There was an empty bottle lying on the cobblestones beside the men.

Santos signalled for Luis to leave the drunks alone and to go check on the garrison building. There were no sentries guarding the gates as Luis crept silently into the building. Once his eyes adjusted to the darkness, he could see a large open room with a dozen men asleep in their beds and snoring loudly. Luis closed the door silently and left the building to join Santos, hidden in the shadows across the street. They went down to the harbour where there were several fishing sloops lying on their side at low tide. The sleepy town looked ripe for the picking.

An hour before daylight, Aga Santos and Luis returned to the dunes to fetch the men and set off for the town. They planned to start by ransacking the houses on the perimeter and work their way into the centre. The first houses they entered in the moonlight looked abandoned. They broke down doors and went inside, looking for valuables, but it was obvious that the occupants had moved out long ago from the layers of dust accumulating everywhere.

As they arrived on the Paseo Ribeira, Santos expected his men to have a fight on their hands as they encountered the Spanish soldiers, but the garrison was deserted and even the two drunks were long gone. They moved on past the harbour and warehouses until they reached the church. The church was their main prize, the purpose of the raid, and Murad believed it to be the repository of untold treasure. The breaching tools they had brought were unnecessary, since the door was unlocked and swung open easily. Santos and twenty of his men went inside, hoping to find objects of value in the nave. There was nothing on the altar, so they went into the vestry in search of vestments and sacred objects, but again, there was nothing of value.

Santos could hardly believe it. The church has been emptied of all its precious religious objects. Everything of value had been packed up and moved. He ordered his men to redouble their efforts and look for hiding places and secret rooms, but their efforts were in vain. The ransacking of the town and the church had been for nought. They had no captives and nothing to show for their efforts, except perhaps a few barrels of *oroju* they had found in the port. Captain Murad would certainly be frustrated after such a long night of preparation for the attack.

It was shortly after eight o'clock when Captain Murad and Captain Khalil sailed into the port with the tide. They found Aga Santos and his janissaries hauling the barrels of spirits along the dock. There were no captives and no treasure as far as Murad could see from the deck of his ship.

Murad called an urgent meeting with Santos and Khalil in his cabin. After the men had been served a glass of jenever, Santos told them about finding the two drunks asleep in the road on his reconnaissance sweep of the port and how they had failed to locate the church treasure.

"You say the town has been abandoned," said Murad, "but it still had several soldiers here only a few hours ago."

"Sir, we don't know where they went," said Santos.

"Philip may be a rich man and the King of Spain and Portugal, Aga Santos, but he isn't so stupid as to pay soldiers to guard an empty town."

"They could have left on a boat, sir," said Khalil.

"No, I don't think so. We'd have seen them leaving."

Marcellus appeared in the doorway.

"Captain Murad, there's a man here for Aga Santos."

Agron stepped into the room and was acknowledged by his boss.

"Aga Santos, can I have a word, please?" asked the janissary.

"Yes," replied Santos, hoping for some good news.

"We found some carriage tracks going north, sir. Maybe the soldiers left by the road."

Santos turned to Murad, whose eyes lit up.

"That's it, Santos," said Murad. "We must have just missed them. They can't be more than an hour or two ahead of us."

"But sir, they will certainly have a coach and horses and my men are on foot," protested Santos.

"The road north follows the bay. Let's load up and get after them."

Unknown to the raiders, the priest in charge of the Church of Santa Maria das Areas had loaded up the most precious possessions in wooden crates the previous day for the trip overland. The bishop of Santiago de Compostela had ordered their removal to a safe location, but had no faith in sea travel. It would have taken half the time to sail the crates south to the Tambre River and then on by coach to Santiago.

The priest was a man by the name of Pedro de Escalante, who had served with Ambrogio Spinola in the Low Countries during the Eighty Years War. His last battle had been the Siege of Breda in 1624 where he had been wounded and, after a long rehabilitation, he had returned to his home in Galicia. The bishop had rewarded the wayward priest with a new post in Fisterra, protecting the Church of Santa Maria das Areas.

No one was eager to look after a church in the exposed coastal area, especially a church that had long been the subject of so many rumours of untold treasure. The bishop doubtless felt that a warrior priest was the perfect solution. The church had been attacked many times over the last year by marauding foreign ships, and with Fisterra's under-manned garrison, the raiders kept on coming. Father Pedro had even buried the church's treasure for a time in different tombs in the cemetery to protect it from the raiders. There were gold-plated cups and chalices, silver crucifixes, statues and plates, priceless gold and jewel-encrusted monstrances with holy objects, gold pyxes and candlesticks, religious pictures and other liturgical items of great value.

They could not defend the church forever, and no one knew that better than Father Pedro, a man who had seen more combat than all the soldiers in the garrison combined. Replacements were slow in coming, reinforcements not at all, and his entreaties to the bishop and the Spanish military had been ignored. He knew the men had reached their limit, and several weeks ago he had made one last, desperate appeal to the bishop. It had actually been more of a threat than an appeal, but in the end, it had achieved a satisfactory result. The bishop had sent him a letter ordering him to remove the Church's precious objects to Santiago by the land route.

The plan had been to leave in the morning at daybreak, but during the night, he had been awakened from a recurring dream and by a strong sense of foreboding that he should not wait. He had learned to act on such feelings, so he had sent the cook to wake up the soldiers and get them ready to travel. He had collected his things and then followed her over to the garrison building. He had witnessed her attempt to raise the dead, the two drunken sentries asleep in the street. In that instant, he knew that any defence of the church in

Fisterra was a hopeless enterprise. They would never survive another corsair attack.

The garrison had an officer, but Father Pedro had long ago been accepted as their de facto commander. He stood in the middle of the square and barked orders, not caring if he woke the few remaining inhabitants of the village. An hour later, the horses had been saddled, and the coach had been loaded with its precious cargo. They set off in the dark on the road north, with Father Pedro accompanied by his housekeeper and cook inside the coach and two soldiers sitting up top, driving the horses. They were trailed by a dozen mounted soldiers, some of them undoubtedly asleep in the saddle. By seven in the morning, they were already at the top of the bay and heading inland towards Corcubion on the bay of the same name.

Father Pedro chatted with his housekeeper, Camila, and her younger sister Mariana, who cooked for him. Both women came from Fisterra, but their families had long ago left for safer towns in the interior. They planned to return to their families when they arrived in Santiago. As the women fell asleep one after the other, Father Pedro had time to reflect on the tone of the ultimatum he had sent to the bishop. It occurred to him that with the transfer of the treasure to Santiago and the virtual abandonment of the Church of Santa Maria das Areas, his service to the bishop might soon be coming to an end.

Corcubion, Spain

The corsairs sailed east and north, hoping to catch the heavily guarded coach. Captain Murad knew that the coast road went through Corcubion on the bay before heading inland to the east. He figured all it would take was a contingent of janissaries near the road and the surprise would be total.

As they arrived in the bay, there was no sign of a coach on the coast road, nor any activity in the town. They sailed further north and moored the two ships near the rocky shore. Aga Santos immediately called up his janissaries who lined up on the beach with their weapons. The plan was to climb up the cliff to the road and cut off the coach as it came along.

The coach rolled slowly north, with Father Pedro and the two women asleep inside. The two soldiers on top who were driving the team of four horses watched the road and struggled to remain awake in the heat. The twelve soldiers on horseback plodded along behind them. As they approached the top of the bay, Father Pedro woke up and looked out the window. He couldn't believe his eyes. A contingent of janissaries was running alongside the coach and firing their crossbows at the soldiers on top. The coach came to a sudden stop and Father Pedro jumped out the door, crashing into a man, who had been reaching for it from the other side. The impact knocked the sabre out of the man's hand, and in one movement, Father Pedro snatched it up and pivoted, beheading the man in a geyser of blood. Father Pedro knew a battle when he saw one, and he attacked in a flurry of action.

Aga Santos had been congratulating himself on a successful ambush. It had worked perfectly. The crossbows had taken out the two men atop the coach and at least six of the soldiers had gone down in two separate musket volleys, one from the front and the other from the inland side of the road. He watched the surviving soldiers turn their horses and gallop away, heading back to the town. Santos ran towards the coach when he heard a shout and looked up.

He froze, momentarily transfixed by what he saw. A man in the unlikely garb of a priest was a blur of deadly motion near the coach. Even as Santos watched, the man dropped to one knee and disembowelled a lunging janissary, somehow twisting the blade free in time to parry the assault of another.

Santos shook off his disbelief and ran towards the men.

"*No mates al cura, por favor*. Please don't kill the priest!"

No one was listening to him. The priest spun like a dervish, and his sabre slashed across the neck of a janissary. This was training and skill, not madness, the cut just deep enough to kill him, but not enough to slow the blade, a glittering snake that kept on going to ring against the blade of another sabre.

"Stop!" Santos bellowed.

A mob of vengeful janissaries had cornered the priest against the coach. The men heard their commandant's order and reluctantly backed away. They were sworn to obey Santos, but the priest was not. Later Santos would never understand what had compelled him to put away his sabre and step between his men and the priest. He had seen what the man could do and Santos knew he would have no chance against him if the situation deteriorated.

"You cannot kill them all. *Padre, por favor*."

"You will not harm the women?" asked Father Pedro.

Santos had seen no women, but he dared not take his eyes away from the priest.

"Of course not. We do not harm women," said Santos.

The priest nodded once, then dropped the bloodstained sabre on the road. He stood back, ready for his punishment.

"Tie his hands," said Santos to a janissary. "Let's have the women out and start unloading the coach."

The janissaries climbed up on the roof of the coach and delivered the wooden crates down to the men below. The two frightened sisters descended from the coach and stood next to the priest. The janissaries opened one crate after another, showing their colleagues various gold and silver cups and plates. The treasure was worth a fortune and would probably be sold back to the Catholic church one item at a time for a huge profit.

Shortly after the attack, the priest and the two sisters were sitting in the captain's cabin drinking coffee with Captain Murad. The pretty housekeeper, Camila, was scared to death and still shaking like a leaf, while her younger sister Marina showed no emotion at all. Father Pedro held her hand to help calm her down.

"You have been in a war, I think?" asked Murad as he noticed the long scar on the priest's wrist and arm.

"You are Dutch, not French?" asked Father Pedro, who had seen the French flag at the top of the mast as he came aboard.

"Yes, I am. Where did you fight, father?"

"Breda in Holland in '24, and other places."

"You are a priest now?"

"Yes, sir. I work for the bishop in Santiago."

"What were you doing with the church's treasures, father?"

"I was told to repatriate the church property, sir. The church in Fisterra is constantly under threat of attack."

"You killed four janissaries, father. My man Santos is not pleased."

"I'm sorry, captain," said Father Pedro, crossing himself. "I reacted without thinking. I will pray for them."

Murad nodded his approval.

"How long will you hold us, captain?"

"It is hard to say, but I would think you and your women will be ransomed within the year. The church looks after its own."

The two women looked at Father Pedro.

"*Rescatada por la iglesia*?" asked Camila.

"*Si,*" replied Father Pedro.

The sister's eyes lit up with hope for an early return to their former lives.

Nineteen

London

There was a nervous tension in the room as the Secretary of State, Lord Dorchester, cleared his throat and put down his pipe. The Privy Council was meeting again to discuss the Baltimore affair after Charles I had taken an interest in the case. Lord Dorchester had summoned Richard Boyle, the Earl of Cork, and Arthur Loftus to come to London to explain the facts of the Baltimore case once again.

"Gentlemen, the king has received no report from you with regard to the Turkish corsair raid on Baltimore," he told them sternly. "This will not do."

"My Lord, we have inquired into the question of the captain's negligence at the time of the raid," said Richard Boyle.

"Well, that's wonderful, but if that's the case, then where is your report?" asked Lord Dorchester, looking peeved. "We still haven't received it."

"Sorry for the delay, my Lord," said Boyle. "Captain Hooke has complained that he could not act against the corsairs for want of provisions. You will remember that on May 28 of this year, we provided Sir Thomas Button with a warrant of 200 pounds towards victualling both ships. On June 4, he claimed to have taken orders for victualling both ships so that on June 20, when the raid took place, the *Fifth Whelp* moored at Kinsale should have been able to act."

"That is exactly how the king sees it, gentlemen," said Lord Dorchester. "But why did he not act?"

"Captain Hooke complains that he has been badly and dishonestly victualled by Sir Thomas Button," said Boyle. "He claims that the want of victuals prevents him from dealing with the pirates, of whose depredations we hear daily complaints. I have met with the captain and he has shown me his sea log, which had been signed by the officers on the *Fifth Whelp*. It showed that after he arrived at Kinsale in April, he has been victualled from hand to mouth and hasn't been able to leave port."

"It must be remembered, my Lord, that the attack was delivered suddenly," said Arthur Loftus. "The invaders stayed only a few hours and the harbours in those parts are many and so far apart that it is impossible to tell where an attack may be delivered or how it may be forestalled. We have urged vigilance on the captains. On victualling ships, we have spent the sum of 3,649 pounds. Although we feel that Captain Hooke is at fault, we think Sir Thomas Button should be ordered to come before you and explain his position."

"Yes, I would like to hear what Sir Thomas Button has to say," said Lord Dorchester. "We have had many complaints from his superiors at the Admiralty about under-manned vessels and supplies."

Richard Boyle nodded his agreement.

"Captain Hooke has been ordered to put out to sea and has been victualled for one month. He is to patrol the coast," said Loftus. "But in the future, without sufficient supplies, he cannot be expected to continue to patrol these waters and have a dissuasive effect on the corsairs."

Corcubion, Spain

The corsairs left the bay heading south with a strong westerly wind hoping to make a long swing past Pontevedra, Vigo and Porto. The plan was to overnight in the Mondego River estuary on the Portuguese coast where there was a supply of fresh water and wild game. The captain opened another bottle of jenever and offered a glass to Father Pedro.

"Breda," said Murad with disgust. When he finally spoke, it was as if he was talking to himself. "We Dutch thought Breda was impregnable, a fortress."

"You were there?" asked Father Pedro.

"No, by then I was based out of Salé," said Murad. "Our fleet kept me informed. We thought Spinola would give up and go home after a siege of a month or two."

"Ambrogio Spinola never gave up on anything in his life, captain. He was a great military leader, but a very stubborn man. I'm sure you know he was an Italian *condottiere* from Genoa before he fought for Spain."

"His victory at Breda certainly restored faith in the Spanish army."

"We won the battle, yes — but it cost us too much. Too much gold and too many lives. It was the beginning of the end for Spain."

"I remember one thing, father. This is why Spinola will always be a hero to the Dutch people. When we surrendered, he could have had all the Dutch killed. Instead, he allowed Justin de Nassau to lead his men out of Breda with full honours. It was a remarkable gesture."

"I remember that day."

"No Dutchman will ever forget what he did."

"We have a saying in Spanish," said Father Pedro quietly. "*El valor del vencido es la gloria del vencedor.* The valour of the defeated is the glory of the victor."

"Another glass, father?"

"No, thank you."

"What happened when you returned home?"

"In Holland, we were fighting for the glory of Spain, while at home people were fighting to put food on the table. It was a terrible time for my family."

"So you joined the church, the priesthood?"

"Yes, sir."

The two men lapsed into silence, each lost in his own thoughts.

The two sisters were taken to the hold where the women and children were lodged. Camila followed her sister Mariana down the ladder into the hold where they were shocked to find some eighty women and children stuffed into every nook and cranny of space. A Spanish janissary helped the sisters find a free hammock while the English and Irish women stood by to watch.

"You can't have that one, dear," said Mrs. Meade, surrounded by her three children. "That one's mine."

The janissary led the sisters deeper into the hold where they found room. Deirdre approached the two women and offered her assistance.

"You are sisters?" asked Deirdre.

"Yes, my name is Camila. This is my sister Mariana."

"My name is Deirdre. If you need anything, come to me."

Next to the sisters, Joane Broadbrook sat with Malcolm and Liam, who were playing a game of three shells and a pea. The sisters watched the boys play and struck up a conversation with Joane.

"How old are the boys?" asked Camila.

"Six and four," replied Joane.

The sisters smiled timidly at Joane who was repairing a shirt with a needle and thread.

Mondego River, Portugal

The corsairs arrived after midnight in the river estuary on the ebb tide. They would have to wait for daylight and a flood tide before proceeding up the river. It was a quiet night as the crew lowered the mainsail. Father Pedro stood on the deck with Captain Murad watching the crew drop the anchor before he was led below to the crew quarters by the first mate. The captain had offered to lodge the priest among his crew so that he wouldn't have to put up with the abysmal conditions in steerage. The crew was not happy with this decision. They already knew all about the Spaniard's exploits and appeared evenly divided between those who wanted to kill him outright and those who were fearful for their own lives and would not dare close their eyes to sleep.

In the morning, two janissaries roused Felix from a deep sleep. They created quite a commotion among the women and children as they dragged him away. Felix climbed the ladder into the blinding sunlight on the deck. It took him a moment to get his bearings. The two corsair ships were entering a river and moving slowly upstream with the current. It was a cool morning, and the deck was slick with morning dew.

Felix heard a shout and looked towards the bow. A sailor was standing at the rail with a sounding line. He had just called out the depth and Felix could see Captain Murad and the first mate standing nearby, watching the water. He hurried forward to the bow and waited while Murad consulted with the man at the sounding line. Murad finally noticed him and turned away from the sailor.

"How are you, Felix?"

"I'm fine, sir."

"I have something to show you."

Murad pulled a knife from his cloak and stuck it in the soft wooden taffrail, leaving it there.

"Tell me what you know about this knife."

"You found the knife, sir," said Felix.

"Yes, we did, but not where you would expect it."

"This is an ordinary filleting knife, sir, like the kind we use at the fish palace back home."

"Is it the murder weapon?"

"I don't know, sir. Where did you find it?"

"We found it under the oars near the crew quarters, Felix. It was used to kill the janissary."

Felix was surprised by the discovery and suspected that the two murders must somehow be linked.

"But how did it get there, sir?"

"I don't know, Felix. That's why I'm asking you."

"It must be the same knife that killed Orla Walsh, sir," said Felix. "None of your crew carry filleting knives."

"No, they don't. The janissary was armed but didn't put up a fight, Felix. What does that suggest to you?"

"I don't know, sir."

"Come on, Felix. If he had been attacked by another man, he would have put up a fight. There would have been evidence of a battle, but there was no evidence."

"He was with a woman?"

"Good lad," said the captain. "That's it. It has to be a woman. The knife is very sharp, and the blade is thin. It would not take a lot of strength to stab a man to death with it. A woman could do it. Especially if the man had other things on his mind."

"A woman? You suspect a woman?"

"You are still quite young, Felix. A lot of your women have been carrying on with the crew and janissaries. The women flirt with the men, so there is a lot of coming and going in the evenings."

Felix felt his legs give out from under him just as the captain grabbed his arm. It had come to him suddenly. He didn't believe it at first. Now the evidence was right there in front of him.

"Are you all right, Felix?" asked the captain, holding his arm.

"Just a bit weak, sir."

"Come with me. We'll have our breakfast together."

The captain led young Felix away.

Twenty

The corsairs were moored near a freshwater creek about a mile up the river. The crew was busy loading the empty water casks into the dinghy and taking them to the shore as Aga Santos was putting together a contingent of fifty janissaries for the usual scavenging expedition. Murad gave the order to let the women and children out into the fresh air. The children ran ashore ahead of their mothers and soon there were cries of joy as they played tag behind the trees and bushes in the nearby field.

An hour later, the male captives arrived and were led further up the river, all except Jean-Marie, who was shackled to the railing of Khalil's ship. Father Pedro watched the men and women on the shore from the deck. He could just make out Camila and Mariana talking to Joane Broadbrook under a tree while her children played nearby.

Joane had her book of hours open in her lap with a picture of the nativity scene. It was Terce (the third hour) and she was reading the text in Latin about the angel visiting the shepherds. The two sisters appeared happy to have found such a pious friend among the women. Since Joane had acquired the prayer book, she seemed to have rediscovered her own spirituality.

At the end of the day, the captain had Deirdre delivered to his cabin. He sat her down and offered her a glass of red wine. After the wine was served, she sat there quietly smiling at the captain, confident of her position. She had done something to her hair, which set off her blue eyes and her alabaster complexion.

"Deirdre, my dear, I called you here for a reason," said Murad. "I want to know what you were doing on the ship the night the janissary was killed."

"But sir, I was not on the ship that evening," she replied, surprised by the question.

"You were seen in the hold by a janissary. What do you say?"

"That's a lie, sir!" protested Deirdre, her face flushed red with anger and her mouth contorted into a sulky pout. "I didn't return to the hold until after dark with the other women."

The captain leaned closer and took her hand in his.

"Why should I believe you, my dear?"

"I would not lie about such a thing."

"If it wasn't you, whom might it have been, pray tell?"

"I don't know, sir. It must have been someone else. Another maid, maybe Ciara. She worked for Orla's family once, and I don't think they treated her well. Perhaps she held a grudge."

Deirdre watched the captain anxiously for a reaction. He drank his wine and said nothing for a long moment.

"You say that my janissary was mistaken?"

"Ciara and I both have dark hair, sir. There is not a lot of light in the hold. Your man made a mistake."

"Would you like some more wine?" asked Murad.

"Yes, please."

"Deirdre or Ciara? Which one will it be?"

"Sir, it wasn't me. I'm innocent."

"I'm sure you are."

Murad smiled at Deirdre and she smiled back at him, confident she had deflected blame onto a woman she had never liked.

It was well after midnight when Captain Murad pulled a blanket over Deirdre's naked shoulders and went out on deck. It was quiet save for the hooting sound of a long-eared owl and the footsteps of the janissaries on guard duty. He waved at the guards onshore as he stood near the gunwale, looking down at the receding water. He liked the silence of the night and often did his best thinking during those hours.

He smiled to himself. Deirdre had certainly done her best to convince him of her innocence, but he could hardly blame her for that. Nor could he just accept her attempt to cast suspicion on Ciara. Baltimore was a small place, like his hometown of Haarlem in Holland. The same families spawned injustices and vendettas that festered for years, even decades. His own family had suffered terribly from the hate-filled gossip of the Calvinists and this had been his primary motivation for leaving Haarlem and becoming a Dutch privateer.

He would need a confession from one of the women before their arrival in Algiers. The pasha required accountability in all things and those who did not respect his wishes paid a heavy price. At the moment, all he had were two bodies, a bloody knife and cloak, and no explanation for the murders. *What motivated the assassin to kill?* he asked himself. *Ciara and Deirdre were young women with long lives ahead of them. It made little sense. There must be a reason for the deaths.*

In the normal course of a voyage, two deaths and a suicide were not so exceptional. People died for all kinds of reasons on board a ship. It was the cost of doing business. The pasha would look at Murad's manifest, duly make the appropriate entries in his ledger, and subtract the losses from Murad's share of the spoils. The captain sailed at the pasha's pleasure, and the pasha loved money above all else.

The captain returned Deirdre to the hold. He wanted to be alone to reflect on his plans for the next few days. He had enjoyed her company — her childish attempts to seduce him, the sex they had together and her stories about Roaring Water Bay over a splendid meal at midday. It was almost like being at home with his wives. It was a wonderful break from the stressful life of a corsair. A janissary took Deirdre back to the hold and helped her descend the ladder. Ellen approached her as she stepped off the ladder.

"Jimmy and Sophia were looking for you, Deirdre."

"I'm sure they were, Ellen, but I could do nothing for them."

"Don't worry. I looked after them."

"Thanks, Ellen."

The Meregey children were excited to see Deirdre and happy to have her back. The only person who was overly curious was Mrs. Harris, who wanted to know why she had been singled out by the captain. Deirdre shrugged her shoulders and remained silent.

Across the way, Ciara sat with Felix and Mrs. Evans. They had been chatting together and stopped when they saw Deirdre descend the ladder. She looked relaxed and confident, and Ciara had no doubt she was having sex with the captain. Ciara knew it would not be long before it was her turn.

The next day, they sailed out of the estuary and made their way south. They gave Lisbon a wide berth and reached Cape St. Vincent, the extreme southwest corner of Europe on the following day. They then turned east, hugging the coast as a massive storm was brewing in the Atlantic. There were huge waves running thousands of miles through the Gibraltar straits into the Mediterranean. They sailed past Sagres on the south coast and lingered off Lagos, trying to get a look at the Spanish ships in for repairs.

Murad had always dreamed of capturing a Spanish treasure ship loaded with gold and silver bullion, but these ships travelled in convoys from the New World to Seville and were almost impossible to attack on the open sea. Spanish galleons were general-purpose cargo vessels carrying all manner of cargo, including gold and silver from the New World, gems, pearls, tobacco, sugar and spices. They were well protected and had large guns below their decks. As they arrived in Spanish waters, these ships would sometimes require urgent refitting to replace jury-rigged masts, improvised rudders and tillers before sailing on to Cadiz in Andalusia, where their cargo would be offloaded for transport up the Guadalquivir River to Seville.

Murad knew of several safe harbours along the coast in the Algarve from Lagos to Faro where this kind of work would be carried out. He meant to have a closer look on his way home. He saw nothing of interest in the usual ports as they sailed east towards Faro. They stopped and turned about several times to get a better look inside the harbours, but found nothing of interest.

Arade River, Spain

After passing a large estuary, they glimpsed what appeared to be a large Spanish galleon in a narrow cove surrounded by high cliffs several miles east of the river. The ship was tied to a dock where workers were busy installing what looked like a new rudder. This was the routine kind of work required by ships damaged in storms after a long sea passage. The entrance to the cove was protected by a casemate on the seaward cliff with two eighteen-pound guns. One gun covered the outer cove and the other, the inner cove. Captain Murad signalled to Captain Khalil to turn his ship around, and they made a second, slower pass to get a better look at the ship and the soldiers manning the guns.

As they sailed away, Murad was excited by the prospect and they landed a few miles away on a sandbank in a saltwater lagoon. He immediately called a meeting with Khalil and Santos to work out a plan of attack.

"You saw the two guns, captain," said Khalil. "There's no way we can get through there."

"There is one way, gentlemen," said Murad with a smile.

"How is that?" asked Santos, intrigued by the captain's statement.

"We attack the casemate before we go in."

"You want to cut out a galleon?" asked Khalil, showing no enthusiasm for such a risky adventure.

"Not at all, Arturo. That ship will be nothing but trouble and far too slow to keep up with us," said Murad.

Khalil heaved a sigh of relief. He wanted to get home and didn't need any more excitement.

"We seize their gold and silver," said Murad with a glint in his eye. "Then we disappear."

Khalil's discouragement was only amplified by Santos' enthusiasm and eagerness to please.

After the evening meal, Captain Murad and Aga Santos left with a contingent of twenty janissaries for a reconnaissance visit to the area. The window for the attack was short. The ship might sail away as early as dawn tomorrow. They planned to climb to the casemate and have a look at the Spanish soldiers guarding it. If an attack was feasible, then Santos would leave an officer in charge of the men and return to the ship with the captain.

It was a difficult climb up a very steep cliff. The men attached themselves to a rope to avoid falling as they climbed higher and higher. They were exhausted when they arrived at the top. After a rest, they moved into position within a hundred yards of the casemate. From their point of observation, they could simultaneously maintain surveillance on the gunners and keep watch over the dockyard. The workers had already left for the day, but a small unit of about a dozen soldiers marched up and down the dock.

Murad had a low opinion of the capability of Spanish soldiers to protect such an important asset as a ship. Lack of discipline and drunkenness were common among the Spanish military classes. He expected half the men would be asleep or too drunk to defend the ship or themselves within the hour. He saw no movement on the galleon's deck, so he figured that the captain and the crew were probably having a night out in town, but that could all change at a moment's notice.

Murad conferred with Santos to fix a time for the attack and an abort procedure in case there was a reason to delay. The corsair ships would arrive from the east at the required time and signal the janissaries at the casemate with a lantern so they could start the attack. If there was fog, they would have a man whistle a tune from the main deck. Santos gave his orders to a reliable junior officer, who would command the attack before he and Murad started down the cliff to the beach below.

This was the kind of operation that corsairs dreamed of — to launch an attack on a Spanish galleon in the middle of the night without warning. The gold and silver bullion on board the ship would benefit every man on board. After expenses, half the profits would go to the investors and another half to the ship's company. The sailors would divide up some three percent of all profits while the janissaries would get only half as much since they were on fixed salaries paid by the pasha. The captain would receive a massive forty percent. It would be a very profitable venture for all involved.

Everyone knew they could earn more in one night than in an entire career at sea, and some might even be able to retire from the business and return home to their families from the profits. Most of the crew came from very modest backgrounds and had become corsairs in order to feed themselves and their families. They had only turned to piracy for the freedom it offered and the possibility of huge financial rewards.

It was already dark when Captain Murad and Aga Santos returned to the ships. Khalil was waiting for them on deck, and he summoned Marcellus to the meeting. The four men met in the captain's cabin and quickly reviewed the plan of attack.

"We enter the cove at three o'clock," said Murad. "Santos' men will take out the gunners as soon as they see us arrive. The flood tide begins at around two o'clock, so we should have enough water to get in and the galleon will be low in the water. This should be helpful when we offload the cargo to the dock and then onto our ships."

"It's going to be a moonlit night, sir," said Marcellus.

"We can't do anything about that. If there is a problem, Santos' man will signal us. Arturo, you will go in first and head straight for the dock. You will need to maintain total silence, not a sound, or we'll have the garrison down on our heads in minutes."

"What will you be doing, sir?" asked Marcellus.

"We'll follow at a distance in case of an ambush and we need to fire our bow chasers."

"How many men do we need?" asked Khalil.

"A full contingent, all of them. We'll need to unload that ship as fast as possible."

Twenty-one

At just before three in the morning, Santos's men attacked the casemate. The gunners and soldiers were half asleep in their bunks and gave little or no resistance. The janissaries raced inside the stone bunker and dealt lethal blows to the men inside with their yatagan blades. It was over in less than five minutes and a dozen men were dead. There had been no time to sound the alarm or fire off a gun to warn the townspeople.

Moments later, Khalil's xebec ghosted silently into the cove, carried by the incoming tide and with only the barest of effort by her oarsmen. She moved silently towards the dock and the Spanish galleon. The gunners stood quietly at their bow chasers ready to fire them in case of an attack. Murad's ship followed, but remained at a distance off the port side of the galleon.

There was no movement from the galleon until Khalil's xebec knocked up against the dock. A Spaniard smoking a clay pipe stood on the dock in the moonlight and raised his musket to challenge the newcomers. A janissary shot the man with a crossbow from the deck before he could fire his weapon. The janissaries jumped over the gunwale and ran along the dock, firing crossbows and hacking the Spanish soldiers to death with their sabres. A soldier asleep on the deck of the galleon woke up to the sound of dying men. He picked up his pistol, cocked it, and fired at the first janissary to climb onto the deck of the galleon. The pistol shot reverberated around the cove and dogs started barking. The silence was broken and the advantage of surprise was over.

Janissaries poured into the galleon and were about to enter the crew's quarters when they ran into several well-armed Spaniards surging up onto the deck. The Spaniards fired their pistols, killing several men before they were overcome by the janissaries' sabres. Nothing could rival the yatagan sabre in a close fight. Out in the cove,

Captain Murad ordered his men to make for the dock. The oarsmen bent to their task and the xebec glided slowly towards the port side of the galleon. Father Pedro watched it all from his position on deck. There was nothing he could do to help his countrymen who were being slaughtered by the janissaries. He had given his word to do nothing to displease the captain. He was a priest, so perhaps he could do something for the victims of the attack. No one stopped him as he joined Murad near the bow and scrambled over onto the deck of the galleon. There were a lot of dead or dying Spaniards on the dock, so Father Pedro went from one to another to give them their last rites and provide them with some comfort in their final moments.

Aga Santos and his men struggled to open a heavy wooden door leading to the below decks. Someone had locked it after hearing the rush of footsteps on the deck. The janissaries tried unsuccessfully to break through the door panels set in the heavy oak frame.

A voice was heard from within.

"*Quién eres*?" asked the voice.

"*Aga Santos*," replied Santos. "*Quién eres*?"

"*Yo soy el sobrecargo*," said the voice, indicating that the man was the ship's purser.

"*Abra la puerta*," demanded Santos.

There was silence as the men waited for a reply.

"*No es posible*," said the faint voice from inside the ship.

"*Abra la puerta ahora mismo*," ordered Santos, calling for the purser to open the door immediately.

The janissaries stood there waiting for an order as Captain Murad arrived and consulted briefly with his colleague.

"He won't open the door, captain."

"*Abra la puerta ahora mismo*," demanded Murad.

"*Es contra las reglas*," said the voice louder than before.

Murad was furious to see his plan falter at the very last minute due to one rule-bound Spanish purser who had locked himself inside the ship. He looked around, trying to find a solution, when Father Pedro approached and had a quiet word with him.

"He's just a poor man who wants to do right, captain," said the priest. "He'll talk to me."

"You think you can get him to open it?" asked Murad.

"Yes, captain, I do. We have an agreement?"

Murad was desperate and nodded his assent at the priest. He

waved his men away from the door and the priest approached.

"*Soy el padre Pedro de Escalante*," said the priest, announcing his presence in a grim voice. "*El barco se esta quemando.*"

He told the purser that the ship was burning and then recited a prayer in Latin to the dead:

"*Requiem æternam dona eis, Domine,*
Et lux perpetua luceat eis,
Fidelium animae, per misericordiam,
Dei, requiescant in pace. Amen."

There was a long silence among the men on deck and then suddenly, the door sprang open and a little man stood on the threshold. He was barely five feet tall and thin as a rake, with heavy glass spectacles sitting on a thin nose. He stepped into the arms of Father Pedro and thanked him for saving his life.

"*Gracias hijo mio,*" said the priest, putting his arm around the tiny man as the janissaries raced inside.

Up the road, Captain Murad and his men could hear the shouts of the Spanish garrison preparing to launch a counterattack. It would not be long before they arrived and a full-scale armed engagement would begin. Murad's men had lost a lot of precious time with the delay in getting into the cargo hold. The janissaries were already carrying crates and sacks of every description out of the Spanish ship and dumping them on the dock for the captain to sort through them. The cargo capacity of the galleon was enormous, so it was important to be selective about what they took and what they left behind. Murad's priority was the gold and silver bullion that Spanish galleons transported from the New World. They would have to leave the rest of the cargo, including valuable agricultural goods, lumber, spices, tobacco, and more exotic goods.

Murad was consulting with Aga Santos on the dock when he saw Father Pedro fast approaching.

"What is it, father?"

"Have you found your treasure yet?" asked Father Pedro.

"We're still searching."

"Look for a locked chamber in a wall near the captain's cabin," said Father Pedro, turning to watch the Spanish soldiers descending the road towards the dock. "My brother was a sailor on ships in the treasure fleet. He told me that only the captain and second mate were given access to the secret chamber on long voyages."

"Thank you, father," said Murad, smiling at his good fortune to have brought Father Pedro along.

Murad jumped over the gunwale and descended into the dark interior of the galleon. He stopped the janissaries carrying cargo up from the hold and had them examine the walls of the captain's cabin. It wasn't long before they had ripped away the wooden partition leading to the secret chamber and started hauling the heavy chests of bullion up the stairs to the deck. It took four men working together to lift each chest up the stairs in the dark. The chests contained gold doubloon coins, gold ingots, silver coins and emeralds. As the men were offloading the bullion into the two xebecs, the Spanish garrison attacked with muskets, pistols, and swords.

The women and children inside the hold of Captain Murad's xebec had heard the sounds of gunshots and the clash of weapons from afar. Now there was only silence and the rumble of running feet along the dock. No one had the slightest clue as to the nature of the belligerents. There was a tremor of optimism among the women that perhaps the corsairs had met their match with an English man of war and soon they would all be released. They had put up with so much over the last month that they felt sure that God would release them from their miserable fate. Then, suddenly all hell broke loose. There was absolute panic on the faces of the women and children as musket and pistol shots rang out and they heard the clang of steel from the sabres.

The Spanish soldiers poured onto the dock and attacked the corsairs with a volley of musket and pistol shots. Many janissaries were killed in the first volley and it looked like the Spanish had the upper hand until Murad gave the order to his gunner on the bow chaser. He had positioned his xebec on the other side of the galleon and his bow chaser was pointed over the gunwale directly at the surging Spaniards. Twelve-pounders at such a short range were terrible killing machines. Murad waited until the very last moment and then ordered the gunner to fire. A tremendous fireball of grapeshot hit the Spaniards, ripping its victims apart and scattering body parts all over the dock. The Spanish soldiers immediately withdrew, leaving dozens of dead men behind them.

At the other end of the dock, Thomas Payne in steerage had climbed the ladder to get a glimpse of what was happening. He could just make out the dock, the smoke in the air, and the Spanish galleon looming overhead. He called down to John Amble and the men below.

"Bloody hell, you won't believe this, John. We're in a battle with a Spanish galleon."

"Are they going to sink us?" asked Jean-Marie.

"It doesn't look like it," said Payne. "I think the Turkish chaps are winning."

"I hope they aren't taking any more captives," said Amble. "We don't have any space for them."

"They're unloading the treasure ship," said Payne. "They're going to be rich as Croesus."

The Spanish soldiers had moved back to the road and were waiting for reinforcements as Murad and Khalil distributed the remaining valuables in wooden boxes between the two xebecs. The dock was a scene of frenzied activity as the crates were torn open and rifled through for their contents. It was impossible to take it all. They had already stored the heavy chests of gold and silver bullion in their ships and, now with the dawn light, they were discovering other treasures, including gemstones, pearls, silks and porcelains in the boxes on the dock.

"Are you fully loaded?" Murad asked Khalil.

"Yes, sir," said Khalil, looking at his senior officer as if he were mad.

"Can you can take any more?" asked Murad.

"Not if I want to stay afloat."

Murad nodded and gestured towards the harbour.

"Lay offshore within musket range, if you can. Tell your gunners to be ready and leave half your janissaries with me so I can finish the loading."

"The tide, captain," warned Khalil.

Khalil shot a dubious glance at the harbour. The ebb tide had begun, and the xebecs were already below the level of the dock. It wouldn't be long before it was impossible to load them efficiently.

"I know. Hold on as long as you can."

There was a shout from the landward end of the dock. Both men turned to see one of Santos' scouts running towards them.

"They are coming, captain," the man cried.

"How many?"

"They are mustering in the village. A company, at least."

"Very well," said Murad, holding up a hand to silence the man while he turned back to Khalil. "Off you go, Arturo."

The janissaries, who had attacked the casemate, were arriving in small groups along the shore and Murad quickly put them to work, sorting through the contents of the remaining crates and helping to load the ship.

On the road, the Spanish garrison had filled out its ranks and was starting to move. They were fine-looking soldiers, well turned out in their impeccable uniforms, and marching twelve abreast and three deep with their muskets over their shoulders. The men in the back were volunteers and looked like farm workers with their pitchforks, pikes and sickles. The commanding officer was a fancy-looking martinet who had taken his time regrouping his forces and now he ordered them to march down to the dock and attack the heathen devils. They set off at a rapid pace in perfect order and descended the road to the harbour.

When they finally arrived at the dock, they saw a mess of boxes strewn here and there near the bodies of their comrades, but no sign of the enemy. Off in the distance, they could just make out the silhouette of the enemy ships in the morning mist sailing out of the cove on the ebb tide. The soldiers took up position and fired a volley of gunfire at the ships, but they were already out of range. Other soldiers ran along the shoreline hoping to get closer for a shot, but the corsairs were gone.

There was a strong southwesterly wind blowing as the corsairs emerged from the cove and sailed east. Murad figured it would be rough sailing with the big Atlantic swell for most of the day. After an hour, the corsairs sailed close in to land and entered a secluded bay. As Captain Khalil watched from the deep water, Captain Murad ordered his oarsmen to bring his ship close to the shore. Father Pedro jumped down into the shallow water and carried the sisters one at a time to the beach to avoid them getting wet. Camila and Mariana couldn't believe their good luck as they set foot on the sandy beach. They were free and going home to their families.

Murad stood at the prow of the ship and called to the priest.

"Father, come here."

Father Pedro returned to the ship and Murad gave him a leather pouch. The priest took the pouch and looked up at the captain.

"*Vaya usted con Dios*," said Murad. "You have a long journey ahead of you."

Father Pedro looked at the gold coins in the pouch. The funds would allow him and the sisters to travel north in comfort. He nodded his thanks to the captain.

"Thank you, father. We Dutch are grateful people."

With a wave from the captain, the priest headed off to join the sisters who were already climbing the beach towards a rocky promontory. After a few minutes, the priest and the two sisters had disappeared from view as Murad's xebec pulled away from the shore, her lateen sail catching the wind.

Twenty-two

" 'Tis two long years since sunk the town beneath that bloody band,
And all around its trampled hearths a larger concourse stand,
Where high upon a gallows tree, a yelling wretch is seen—
'Tis Hackett of Dungarvan — he who steered the Algerine!
He fell amid a sullen shout, with scarce a passing prayer,
For he had slain the kith and kin of many a hundred there —
Some muttered of MacMurchadh, who brought the Norman o'er—
Some cursed him with Iscariot, that day in Baltimore."
The Sack of Baltimore, Thomas Osborne Davis

Cork, Ireland

The Cork County Assize was held in the old brewery building, where the English circuit judge sat in judgment on a regular basis. After the Battle of Kinsale and the end of the Nine Years' War, the English conquest of Ireland was almost complete, and the authorities were able to implement their aim of anglicizing the Irish polity. One of the first steps was the rapid establishment of a national network of assize circuits. The Lord Deputy of Ireland, Sir Arthur Chichester, was convinced that ordinary Irish people would soon "warm to the benefit and blessings of English law."

The English judge sat alone, his files spread out before him on a long table, and listened to John Hackett's solicitor describing the actions of his client. A dishevelled Hackett sat next to his solicitor in a gloomy silence and glared occasionally at his erstwhile partner, Edward Fawlett. The English captain had been arrested in Castlehaven and sat at another table with his own solicitor. Each man had spent most of the day proclaiming his innocence and the other man's guilt.

"The Turks seized my client," declared Hackett's lawyer, "and

158

forced him to go with them to Baltimore, my lord. He made no mention of Kinsale to the corsair captain, my Lord."

The crown counsellor stood up.

"The testimony of Edward Fawlett confirms that it was Mister Hackett, who strongly advised the corsair not to go to Kinsale," said the counsellor. "He told the corsair everything he needed to know about the fort and the defences of the city and even mentioned the Spanish attack on the town had failed in 1601."

"Do you have anything else to say in defence of your client, sir?" the judge asked Hackett's solicitor.

"Yes, my lord. I have one more thing. My client is a good, honest man, a citizen of Ireland, and a fisherman with a wife and a child to support. He lives in Dungarvan and swears on his life that he has never set foot in Kinsale and has no knowledge of the city's defences. It is our opinion that it was Mister Fawlett who advised the corsair against an attack on Kinsale."

The crown counsellor exhaled loudly and scornfully.

"Yes, counsellor?" asked the judge, raising an eyebrow.

"Mister Hackett may never have set foot in the town, but you can be sure he fished along the coast there and would have known about the fort and its defences."

"Thank you, gentlemen, for your testimony," said the judge as he stood up. "I will take all comments into consideration and make my decision regarding this case within the hour."

Barbate, Spain

The wind picked up, and it was going to be a rough passage across the Gulf of Cadiz. The treasure fleet from the New World arrived in convoys at the ports of Cadiz and Rota. There had been two famous raids on the town of Cadiz, the first in 1587 by Sir Francis Drake, who captured six ships in the port and destroyed thirty-one others, and the second one in 1596 when an Anglo-Dutch fleet led by Robert Devereux and Charles Howard took captives, sacked and burned the town. These were dangerous waters for corsairs. If a Spanish ship saw a corsair in the vicinity, they would instantly give chase. Murad gave the towns a wide berth and sailed for Barbate in the south, near the Strait of Gibraltar.

They arrived in the Barbate River estuary in the late afternoon. A lot of the women and children had been seasick during the crossing. The swaying motion of the ship, the stink of the latrines and the excessive heat were intolerable. Murad ordered his men to let the women and children out on the deck while the oarsmen rowed the ship up the river during the slack tide, but he gave no order to Khalil to release the men. They passed the empty fishing village of Barbate, which had long ago been abandoned by the Spanish due to the incessant corsair raids. The captain was in a hurry to get in the water casks and make the passage east through the Gibraltar Strait.

Felix and Ciara stood on the deck, watching the shore as the ships moved slowly upstream. Deirdre, with the two Meregey charges, James and Sophia, came over to talk to them.

"Hello, Jimmy," said Ciara to the youngest.

"Hello," replied the youngster.

"And how are you, Sophia?"

"I'm fine."

"The captain is looking for you, Ciara," declared Deirdre with a self-satisfied look on her face. "The janissary saw you."

"Shut up, you stupid cow!" exclaimed Ciara angrily.

"You're the one they're looking for," hissed Deirdre. "You killed Orla Walsh."

"I did not!"

Felix could see the women were starting to attract attention, so he pulled Ciara away from Deirdre.

Captain Murad noted in his journal that the date was July 24, some thirty-four days since the attack on Baltimore. With a good wind, he estimated he could be home in four days. It had been a long and tiring trip, but he was once again a very rich man. On his arrival in Algiers, he knew he would be celebrated for his daring attack on the Spanish galleon.

After the ships were moored near the freshwater creek about a mile up the river, the captain allowed the women and children to go on shore for a few hours. Before Ciara could descend to the riverbank, two janissaries detained her. They grabbed her arms and led her away. Felix watched from the shore and then followed the men.

The captain was in his cabin on his prayer mat. He stood up as a janissary came in to announce the arrival of the young woman.

"Come in, my dear," said Murad to Ciara.

Ciara was brought in and sat down at the low table.

"You have been a thorn in my side for several weeks, young lady," said Murad. "You killed Orla Walsh and the janissary, Jamal, for no reason."

"I swear I did not, captain. That is a lie."

A servant came in and whispered in the captain's ear. The captain nodded and waved in young Felix.

"Well, Felix, it looks like we have finally found our killer. Ciara killed Orla Walsh and our janissary with the filleting knife."

"Sir, Ciara is not the killer. I killed Orla Walsh."

Felix's confession was a complete surprise for Ciara. She looked at him as if he were mad.

"You said it had to be a woman not a week ago."

"I lied, sir."

"Why would you do that?"

"Orla was a papist in our village. She was trying to convert our people and spying on us."

"That's very interesting, Felix, but what about my janissary?"

"I got rid of the knife by throwing it under the oars when I went to the crew quarters, sir," said Felix. "I have no idea who killed the janissary."

"You say that the knife was yours?"

"Yes, sir. Ciara had nothing to do with it."

Felix held Ciara's gaze. He was still hopelessly infatuated with the girl.

"Thank you, Ciara. You can go now; it looks like we have our guilty party."

Ciara was astonished by her good fortune. Just like that, she was off the hook for two murders. She stood up, smiled at Felix and went out the door. Murad took out a bottle of jenever and poured himself a glass. He was grim faced as he knocked back the gin.

"Felix, I suppose you know you are going to be punished for your actions and also for lying to me."

"Yes, sir."

"I have a son about your age back in Holland. I haven't seen him since I last set foot in my hometown. His mother wanted me to take him with me, but I felt the life of a corsair was too dangerous for such a young boy."

Felix was red-faced and nervous. He realized the game was up. He had lost and would have to pay the piper. The captain had not believed a word of his confession.

"You will be punished not for your actions, but for your stupidity. Only a very stupid boy would lie to save a woman."

In his mind's eye, his confession had sounded so reasonable, even logical, that Felix had almost convinced himself it was true. He realized that it had been a foolish thing to do.

At eight bells, the corsairs left the freshwater creek and the ebb tide took them downstream to the sea. The light was fading by the time they got down to the bay opposite the abandoned fishing village. Murad planned to sail due south to Tangier and then hug the coast of Morocco with the southwest wind taking him through the Strait. The north side of the strait was far too risky with the maritime traffic in and out of Gibraltar.

From the straits, he would sail due east, avoiding the traffic around the Spanish colony at Oran and Mers-el-Kébir. The Castilians under Cardinal Cisneros had captured the city in 1509 and had held it for over a century. The Spanish navy in Cartagena had several ships in and around Oran to protect their shipping from pirate attacks. There would be no more stopovers for food or water. He intended to make the 600-mile run to Algiers in two to three days with a good wind.

The men were always nervous when passing through the strait. Under starry skies, Captain Murad quietly gathered his crew and janissaries on deck for a traditional corsair ceremony. A sailor made a bundle of small wax candles and wrapped them together with a pot of oil. He lit the candles and then threw the package overboard as a present to the long-dead holy man who was believed to lie in a tomb on the south coast. The candles floated for a moment and then vanished into the depths as the men held up their hands, imploring the holy man's blessing and a safe passage through the strait.

After the ceremony, they sailed east at a reduced speed in order to avoid a collision with local shipping. The waters along the south coast were crowded with ships of every description — carvels, polacres, tartanes, settees, barks and galleys — travelling in one direction or another. By morning they were well out of the strait and heading due east with a good wind.

After the morning meal was served, two janissaries went to fetch Felix for his punishment. He was taken to the mainmast and turned upside down, with his feet strapped to a wooden board. A muscular janissary took off his coat and picked up the cane. Captain Murad came on deck and nodded for the *bastinado* to begin. The first blow knocked the air out of Felix and he screamed from the pain. He was determined to control his fear as he waited for the second blow. He knew he could endure a lot of pain, but even so, the sharp bite of the first few blows was hard to bear. He squeezed his eyes shut and determined not to open them again until the ordeal was over.

After ten blows, the captain told the janissary to stop. He descended to the main deck and kneeled close to Felix.

"You were stupid to fall in love with that girl, Felix," whispered Murad in his ear.

"Sir," acknowledged Felix, opening his eyes.

"You were doubly stupid," said Murad, "to try to save her by telling me that ridiculous story. Women are not to be trusted, ever. The Quran says that women are from hell. Never trust a woman, Felix."

"I'm sorry, sir."

"You are a good boy, Felix. I know you couldn't kill Orla Walsh anymore than that poor girl Roisin could have."

"What will happen to Ciara?" asked Felix.

"What did I just tell you?" asked Murad, shaking his head in exasperation. "Stop thinking about that evil bitch. She'll be sold to the pasha and will fetch a very good price when they learn that she murdered two people."

Castlehaven, West Cork

Justice was swift in Ireland in the 17th century. Someone had to be punished for the corsair attack on Baltimore and John Hackett of Dungarvan was the ideal candidate. He was a devout Irish Catholic who hated the English colonists in Baltimore for their Calvinist faith. He had accompanied the corsair captain during the attack and had been freed in return for his services. He was convicted on charges of treason — not for the obvious reason of piloting the corsairs to Baltimore, but for convincing the corsair captain not to attack Kinsale where a navy ship might have stopped him. Like the Scot William Wallace in the year 1305, his punishment was to be dragged by a running horse to the gallows.

It was a particularly cruel punishment. It began in Castlehaven, where a large crowd had gathered in the town square to see the English soldiers attach ropes to the prisoner. As the soldiers set off on horseback with Hackett in tow, the townspeople pelted the prisoner with stones and rotten fruit. In every little hamlet along the route to Baltimore, people waited on the roadside to throw stones at Hackett, who ducked and ran to keep up with the horses.

Dazed and bleeding, he somehow survived that gauntlet, only to be met by a vengeful crowd in Baltimore itself. Virtually everyone in the village had lost family members or loved ones in the corsair raid, and they maintained a merciless rain of stones on Hackett as the soldiers dragged him along the beach near the Cove and finally to a hill overlooking the bay. He was bleeding from a head wound and his clothes were in tatters when the English soldiers cut away his bonds, placed a noose around his neck, and roughly sat him on a horse.

There were ragged, profane cheers as they led the wretched prisoner to a large oak tree overlooking the bay where Captain Murad had anchored his ships on that fateful night. Beaten and barely comprehending, Hackett slumped miserably in the saddle as the soldiers heaved the other end of the rope over a branch and lashed it to the trunk of the tree. There was no ceremony beyond a brief reading of his condemnation and then a soldier simply kicked the horse in the rump, leaving Hackett dangling high above the hill visible to all in the bay below.

Among the crowd watching Hackett swing from the tree was Stephen Broadbrook, husband to Joane and father of Malcolm and Liam, now lost forever. He turned away from the grim spectacle and felt no satisfaction at Hackett's death. It would change nothing for him. His own guilt remained, and it festered in his heart like an evil tumour he could never remove. He had abandoned his wife and children in their moment of need.

Stephen had spent weeks alone in the emptiness of his broken-down cottage. Now, with autumn fast approaching, he was still undecided about what to do with his life. There were only a few souls still living in the village. The fishery was gone. A pilchard industry required a lot of hands on deck and there were simply not enough people to revive it. He had covered the blackened rafters of his cottage with the remaining thatch and wattle from other cottages and this helped keep out most of the rain, but the winds would surely blow off the thatch in November. He survived by fishing in the bay and scavenging flour, tea and other foodstuffs from the empty houses in the village. Stephen was not worried about another corsair raid because he had nothing more to lose. At night, he dreamed that the corsairs would return to Baltimore and take him away with them so that he could again be with his family, but no one ever came.

The day after the hanging, a two-wheeled dogcart pulled by a horse descended the steep road from the village to the cove and advanced along the row of cottages before it stopped in front of Stephen's old place. The passenger was a well-dressed, older gentleman who descended from the cart and looked up at the cottage. Stephen saw him through the window, and for a moment, he dared to hope. He took a deep breath and went outside to meet the man. The hope died the instant he saw the expression on Gunter's face.

"Broadbrook, you remember me?"

"Of course, Mister Gunter."

"I've just returned from London, where I presented our case to the Lords."

Stephen nodded but remained silent.

"I'm sorry, Broadbrook."

"What did they say?"

"Nothing much," said Gunter, who wouldn't look at Stephen. "It was all a waste of time, my friend. I'm sorry."

"But they must realize the threat to the community?"

"They don't care, Broadbrook. Nothing will come of it."

For a moment, Stephen felt a flush of anger. When there remained a faint hope that the government might ransom the Baltimore captives, Stephen could at least dream of his family's return. *Now Gunter had erased any hope he might still have?* thought Stephen.

Gunter looked sadly at the patchwork of new thatch on the cottage roof.

"I've moved on, Broadbrook. Sally and the boys won't ever be coming home. You must do the same."

Stephen said nothing. He was in no mood for advice.

"I've started a new business in Skibbereen," he said gruffly. "I'd like you to come and work for me. I can offer you a job and a place to live."

It was a very generous offer, something Stephen had never expected, but he found himself speechless. If he left the home he and Joane had built together, it would be the final betrayal.

Stephen turned his back on Gunter and returned to the cottage.

"You can't stay here, Broadbrook," shouted Gunter. "Come and stay with me for a few days and have a look around."

Stephen slammed the door, and all was silent as the driver turned the horse and dogcart around. Gunter climbed aboard and looked profoundly unhappy as he ordered the driver to leave.

Twenty-three

Algiers

A rab legend likens the ancient city of Algiers to a diamond set in an emerald frame. From the deck of Captain Murad's ship, the dazzling triangle of the city with its walls, its minarets and mosques, and its flat-roofed buildings appeared to glitter in the brilliant sunshine set against the greenery of the Sahel hills. The city's narrow streets descended to the harbour, where a large mole led to a rocky island with the formidable Bordj El Fenar tower and fifty-five cannons commanding the bay. As always, the town looked impregnable to Murad's eye. He knew that was due not only to the fortifications but also to its aqueducts, which would provide fresh drinking water in the event of a siege.

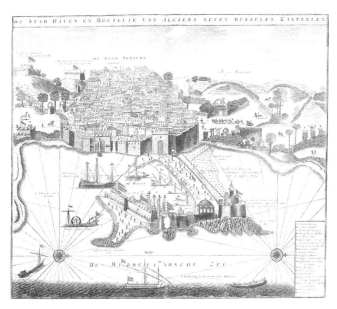

Their arrival in Algiers was heralded by cannon fire. The gunners at the Bordj El Fenar tower fired off a salvo, and Murad's gunners replied with their bow chasers. The thundering salvoes reverberated around the horseshoe bay and the atmosphere in the old city was electric as the curious hurried down to the harbour to get a look at the corsair ships and their slaves.

In the ship's hold, the terrified women and children took stock of their situation. All the gunfire and celebration could only mean one thing — they had arrived at their final destination. They needed to prepare themselves for whatever horrors were to come. The women cleaned the faces of their children and themselves as best they could and then looked to their own ragged clothes. After thirty-eight days at sea, they were left with the appalling prospect of more misery to come.

James Frizell had been in Algiers for longer than he cared to remember. He was employed by the powerful Levant Company, which had a royal charter for trade with the Ottoman Empire. Frizell negotiated with English merchant ships and was allowed to charge a fee for each transaction. Unfortunately, Algiers did not receive many English ships, so the pickings were slim for the English Consul. He lived from hand to mouth, often on credit, and it was a constant struggle to attract the attention of Parliament to his impoverished condition.

He lived in a flat on a narrow street at the top of a rooming house. He had chosen it for one reason. From the window, he could watch the arrival of ships in the harbour. It was not an easy life for a diplomat in a rough and tumble place like Algiers, where you could be jailed or beaten with sticks, and your house ransacked for no apparent reason. He felt like a slave himself and was so neglected by the English crown that his only desire was to go home.

His morning routine was to go down to the harbour for a coffee and watch for ships arriving in the port. He would take note of the date, the ship, and the number of people arriving. The year 1631 had been a busy year for arrivals. On the 8th of April, Frizell noted that thirty-eight English captives arrived on the *Falcon* from London. Then, in July, twelve more arrived on a ship from Weymouth. Most of the captives were English sailors who had been easy prey for the corsairs.

Frizell had started recording the number of English captives arriving in the port back in 1629. Since then, he had noted a fourfold increase in their numbers. Of course, they were just a small fraction of the total number of captives arriving in Algiers every year. Thousands of Europeans were being snatched up along the Mediterranean coast. It was estimated that thirty-five thousand European Christian slaves were being held in towns along the Barbary coast, including Algiers, Tunis and Tripoli. The captives were mainly fishermen and farmers living near the coast. The great majority came from Valence and Andalusia in Spain and Calabria and Sicily in Italy, where the slavers were particularly active.

Frizell had written to the English ambassador in Constantinople, Sir Thomas Roe, and warned him of the increasing number of English slaves arriving in Algiers. Roe sounded the alarm with his superiors in London by suggesting that the number of English slaves could rise to over a thousand a year and added the following note in his gloomy report: "*The corsairs say that, unless you send ransom money speedily, they will go to England and fetch men out of their beds as commonly as they used to do in Spain.*"

On the morning of the 28th of July, 1631, Frizell dressed carefully in a wool tunic and breeches and headed down to the harbour to fulfill his official role. He would faithfully record the names of the new arrivals and then try to get them released under some technicality. His options were limited outside of a general protest against the Algerine authorities. He walked the length of the mole to where Murad's ships were docked. A large crowd of slave traders, con men, *renegadoes*, and gawkers of different nationalities were already forming along the mole to watch the parade of slaves that would follow.

As the crowd grew in number, Frizell elbowed his way up to the gunwale of the first xebec. There he saw the first English women and children emerge from the hold, blinking in the bright sunlight. On the other vessel, the men started to appear from steerage, one at a time, as the janissaries installed heavy chains around their necks and ankles, linking one man to the next.

As the women and children surged onto the deck and the men lined up to be chained, Frizell was astonished by their number. He wrote later in his reports to the crown that something quite unique had happened. Captain Murad had carried away an entire village of men, women, and children. The men were shackled together in bunches and then lined up on the dock in the sweltering heat. The women and children were brought over and lined up behind the men.

Captain Murad, resplendent in a dark doublet and turban, took his place in front of the cortege alongside Captain Khalil and Aga Santos in their best clothes. A contingent of officers and janissaries guarded the flanks and brought up the rear. This was the captain's moment of glory for all of Algiers to see. The triumphant procession set off along the mole to the city walls, the sound of the clanking chains not quite drowned out by the excited shouts of the crowd. The *renegadoes* were already talking up the captives with offers to help guard their valuables and to work for their release. They knew better than anyone how to exploit their own countrymen and make a profit for themselves by haggling with the slave traders.

Frizell joined the procession, walking alongside the captives and making introductions to the disoriented and frightened men and women. He approached the pregnant Joane Broadbrook, who was struggling to keep up with her sons Liam and Malcolm.

"What is going to happen to us, sir?" asked Joane.

"You are going first to the palace, milady. I will notify London of your plight and we will try to ransom you and your sons later."

"I will pray for a miracle, sir. I don't believe in ransoms. I've heard only the rich get ransomed."

Frizell started to say something, but then thought better of it. He knew the poor woman was right. He bowed to Joane and moved on to provide support for a new group of captives.

As the cortege advanced along the mole, the captives noticed the gangs of slaves hauling rocks to shore up the breakwater from the ever-encroaching sea. They walked past the enormous cannon known as the *Baba Merzoug* (Blessed Father) that had protected the city from foreign invasion for decades. It weighed twelve tonnes and was twenty-two feet long. It could fire huge projectiles at ships within range. It was later renamed *La Consulaire* after the French Consul Jean Le Vacher was supposedly fired out of the mouth of the cannon. He was accused of being a traitor after the French bombarded the city in 1682.

As they passed through the city gate into the narrow streets, they witnessed the chaos of life in Algiers. Two slaves had been driving a wagon loaded with wine in the narrow street and had damaged the side of a building as they tried to make a sharp turn with their wagon. Now they appeared to be stuck, incapable of either advancing or going back. People swore at the men and threw rotten fruit at them, while their owner rushed forward with a lash to beat them into submission. In an alley, beggars shouted at the captives to throw them a few coins. The cortege marched on and curious eyes examined them from the *souk*'s dark interior. They caught the glimpse of a boy naked to the waist in the dark interior of a tannery being beaten by an old man, a woman crying behind her display of new cotton fabrics, and a woman bargaining with a local merchant about the price of a chair.

After weeks of fear and privation, the onslaught of sights, sounds and smells was overwhelming. The kaleidoscope of vibrant colours in Algiers startled Felix. He stole looks at his fellow captives and saw that they were just as stunned as he was. The brilliant sunlight that reflected off everything made the colour of the purple irises, the red oleander and the white jasmine in their window boxes even more intense. He heard the shouts and jeers of onlookers, the calls to prayer from the minarets, the cacophony of unidentifiable languages in the *souk*, the gurgling of water in the fountains, and the clanking chains of his fellow prisoners. And he saw more races of people than he had ever known existed. There were fierce-looking Arabs everywhere, but also ebony giants from Sub-Saharan Africa next to tall, blond Scandinavians and short, stocky Asians. It was almost too much for a boy from Baltimore who had never ventured far beyond his own parish.

Behind Captain Murad and the janissaries walked the French and Portuguese captives followed by the Baltimore men, the Devon sailors and the Irish fishermen. Young Jean-Marie de Bancalis de Maurel, who hoped to be ransomed by his father, was chained to his groom and his two stable boys. Hugh Pierse was chained to John Amble and Thomas Payne. They struggled to keep up as the chains around their necks chafed in the heat. Behind them came William Mould, Corent Croffine and Richard Meade, wearing clanking leg irons, which made walking difficult.

Sally Gunter led the Baltimore women and children, holding young Walter in her arms, followed by Jenny with young Giles and Cecil, and the older boys Felix, Caleb, Lionel and Geoffrey. The physical similarities of the Gunter boys attracted the attention of the crowd, who were greatly amused and pointed fingers at them.

Behind the Gunters came Mrs. Ryder with a son and daughter, followed by Mrs. Croffine with a daughter and Mrs. Evans with her son. Behind them came Ciara, looking stunningly beautiful in her ragged clothes. She was followed by Mrs. Harris with her mother and three children, and her maid Ellen of the missing fingers. Deirdre followed them with the two Meregey children. Emma Pierse with her rouged cheeks and dark beauty was accompanied by Phoebe and her aging mother, who held the hands of Eunice and Dinah.

Next came young Besse Peeters, who attracted appreciative stares from the crowd for her lovely red hair, followed by blonde Anna Lorye and her four children, Bessie Flood and her son, and a long suite of mothers with children.

There were over fifty children of all ages in the cortege and they were all eyes for the exotic birds and people in the *souk*. Felix, whose feet were killing him, slipped in behind Mrs. Evans and her son to have a word with Ciara.

"You want some kind of medal for saving me, Felix?" teased Ciara, happily noting the openly flirtatious glances of the men in the crowd.

"Certainly not," replied Felix.

"You got the *bastinado*. The captain was not happy with his favourite son."

"I'm not his son, Ciara."

"Yes, you are! He has adopted you, Felix."

Felix shook his head ruefully. He had sacrificed himself to save this girl from punishment, but she showed no sign of being grateful for it. The captain had been right.

"Tell me why you did it, Ciara. Why'd you kill Orla Walsh?"

"I suppose it won't hurt to tell you now that we've arrived," she shrugged. "Orla stole a prayer book from my mistress, Ellen MacCarthy. It was a family heirloom, worth a fortune, and Ellen wanted it back. I told her I'd get it for her."

"You came to Baltimore looking for a prayer book?"

"Yes, but not any book. A book of hours, Felix."

"So you found Orla Walsh and then were captured like the rest of us?"

"Yes, ain't I the lucky one," said Ciara bitterly. "When I arrived in Baltimore, I couldn't just walk up to Orla and demand the book. I had to find work as a maid to stay in the town long enough to search her house."

"But why did you kill her?"

"I confronted her one night, and she said she didn't have it anymore."

"You killed her," said Felix, who realized that he hadn't known Ciara at all. "You killed her because she didn't have a book."

"No, Felix. I killed the bitch because she lied to me. She knew where the prayer book was but wouldn't tell me. I could have sold that book to gain my freedom, and she wouldn't tell me where it was. She deserved to die."

"What about the janissary? Did he deserve to die too?"

"That tick-bellied oaf was going to rape me," snarled Ciara. "I let him come at me and then I ran my knife straight through his heart."

Felix was shocked into silence. Ciara's callous disregard for human life was astonishing. There was no trace of remorse in the girl at all. There was something very ugly in her character, hidden behind her lovely facade.

"Goodness gracious, Felix. I killed that impudent toad and I'm glad he's gone from this world," said Ciara, touching his arm.

"The captain says you'll be sold to the pasha, Ciara."

"Well, I do hope so."

PART TWO

ENSLAVED

Twenty-four

"Se ti sabir, ti respondir;
Se non sabir, tazir, tazir.
Mi star Mufti: ti qui star ti?
Non intendir: tazir, tazir."
The Mufti speaks in *lingua franca*
Molières's *Le Bourgeois Gentilhomme* (1670)

(If you know the lingua franca, you will reply.
If you do not know it, be silent, be silent.
I am the Mufti. Who are you?
If you do not understand, be silent, be silent.)

They made their way up the steep hill on Great Market Street to the palace of the Dey. The street was a long *souk* with tradespeople of all kinds selling a multitude of wares and services — butchers, bakers, tailors, cobblers, candle makers, barbers, clerks for letter writing, lawyers, farriers, smiths, textile traders, seamstresses, tannery workers, carpenters and craftsmen working glass and metal. As they looked back down the street, the Baltimore captives could see the flat roofs of the town, the city squares with their freshwater fountains and the flower gardens overlooking the harbour, where there was a fleet of over a hundred ships of all descriptions. Algiers was a clean and prosperous metropolis, but it had a dark and terrifying underbelly.

As they entered the palace through the huge wrought-iron gate, they admired the white, three-storey stone building with its fountains and lemon trees. The cortege came to a stop at the canopied entrance. An army of porters and horse-drawn wagons soon arrived from the port carrying the most prized valuables taken from the ships, in particular, the chests of bullion and the priceless gold and silver religious and liturgical articles.

Murad led the men and women captives through the door into the palace, leaving the children in the courtyard. The Gunter boys watched from the shade of the lemon trees as their mother disappeared into the building. Little Liam looked up at Felix, his eyes welling up with tears.

"Where's my ma?" he asked.

"Don't worry, Liam," Felix told him, trying to sound more confident than he felt. "She'll be back soon."

The truth was that he didn't have any idea what was going to happen. He gave Liam an encouraging smile, even though he suspected there was much worse to come. He was spared further questions from the children about their parents when they discovered the fountains. After the long walk from the harbour, the children were thirsty and eyed the cool water spilling into the fountains. Felix didn't have the heart to stop them. He was more exhausted than thirsty, so he was content just to lie down in the shade and doze.

Malcolm and Liam hurried over to the fountains and were soon joined by the Gunter boys and the Pierse girls. None of the children had ever seen a water fountain before, and the gargoyles around the central column frightened them. Water poured from the mouths of the gargoyles and filled the reservoir.

"It's good, Liam, it's fresh water," said Malcolm, dipping his cupped hand in the clear pool and drinking from it.

Liam, reassured by his brother, followed his example. The children who had been intimidated by the fierce gargoyles, no longer hung back. They rushed to splash water on their faces and satisfy their thirst. Within moments, over fifty children were laughing and splashing each other around the fountains.

Inside the palace, the men and women were cowed into a stunned silence. None of them, not even Jean-Marie, the haughty French aristocrat, had ever seen anything approaching the opulence of their surroundings. They were transfixed by the gleaming marble columns, the olive wood ceilings and the luxurious furnishings.

The pasha's officials were sitting on plush sofas on the raised dais beneath the *baldachin*, a cloth canopy of state that dominated the dais. They waited patiently as the janissaries herded the captives into two long lines of men and women. When there was a semblance of order in the room, Murad and his officers entered and approached the dais to greet the officials. The distinguished Algerine admiral Ali Bitchin, an expatriate Venetian and a *renegado* like Murad, rose from his place on the dais to greet the captain and congratulate him personally on his hugely successful run.

"Captain Murad, I heard the news and hurried over here to welcome you back," said Bitchin with the voice of a man accustomed to command.

"Thank you, Ali."

"I hear you seized the cargo of a Spanish galleon."

Murad nodded and smiled at his friend.

"You must come by and have a drink with me, Jan. I want to hear all the details of that attack."

"Of course, Ali."

While they waited in silence for the pasha to arrive, they heard the voices of children coming from the courtyard.

It had all started with Malcolm, more daring than the others, who had climbed into the shallow water of the fountain to collect the copper coins glinting at the bottom in the sunlight. Liam had joined him, as had the older girls and boys. Malcolm had taken it a step further when he decided it would be easier to get the coins if he plunged his head into the water to get closer to the bottom. It wasn't long before all the children were climbing into the fountain and doing the same. They were soon competing among themselves for the most coins, wildly splashing each other with water and for a few precious moments having the time of their lives when suddenly a loud cry was heard from the front entrance.

Aga Santos was apoplectic with rage, standing there on the portico bellowing at the mob of children to behave themselves when Captain Murad appeared at the palace door.

"Santos!" Murad yelled. "Can't you control the children?"

"I'm trying, Captain," Santos replied as the children jumped out of the fountains and, dripping wet, ran back to sit under the lemon trees.

"Don't worry, Santos. They are just children, and we both know what is ahead for them. Let them play."

Murad looked fondly at the children. He had become attached, as he always did. This was the last time he would see them before they were sold in the slave market, and he felt a responsibility towards them. Their mothers and fathers would soon be gone from their lives and he only hoped that they would move on to a better life.

Another hour passed before Pasha Hussein, the Dey, made his appearance. The men and women were exhausted from standing in line, waiting to be inspected. The men were on one side and the women on the other, and the smell of sweat, faeces, and outright fear was overpowering. A courtier had brought a chair for pregnant Joane Broadbrook, who was looking very pale and stressed. The pasha suddenly swept into the room past the marble columns, the filigree panels and the Sago palms, followed by a small group of courtiers. He was an impressive figure, wearing a turban with a glittering diamond crescent and topped with two large ostrich feathers. He wore a sash adorned with jewels and a broad scimitar in a fine velvet sheath. The captives watched the pasha claim his place on a carefully arranged pile of damask pillows on the dais and consult with his courtiers on the order of the day.

Outside in the courtyard, the children sat quietly in the shade of the lemon trees, watching the janissaries haul the heavy chests of bullion and the gold and silver religious articles from the wagon. Captain Murad stood near the wagon helping Aga Santos supervise the unloading. The pasha's courtiers would require a detailed list of all the precious loot before there was any distribution of riches.

Felix woke up suddenly, chiding himself for having lost track of time. He got up and his bruised feet protested with every step as he went looking for his brother Caleb. Then he heard the voice of the captain calling to him from the wagon.

"Felix, we do not have much time."

Murad's expression was grim as he took the two boys aside.

"You boys need to prepare for the slave market."

"Sir?" asked Felix, rubbing his eyes.

"The buyers will be asking questions," said Murad impatiently. "Tell them you and your brothers are learning to become good Muslim boys."

Felix and Caleb nodded.

"Tell them you had your first lesson with me on the ship and we talked about the Quran, the spoken word of Allah revealed to the Prophet Mohammed. What's a *surah*, boys?"

Felix and his brother exchanged blank looks.

"Try to remember this," sighed Murad. "A *surah* is a chapter of the Quran and the Quran is the 'spoken word' of Allah. It is meant to be read aloud."

The two boys heard a voice calling for the captain.

"Things will go easier for you and your brothers if you say you are learning about Islam. I am not joking about this. It will save you many beatings, so try to remember what I have just told you. A *surah* is a chapter of the Quran."

"Yes, sir," said Caleb. "A *surah* is a chapter of the Quran and the Quran is the spoken word of Allah."

"Very good, Caleb."

Murad heard the voice calling from the portico and for a moment, he looked like he was going to say something, but then he gave a curt nod and was gone.

Captain Murad hurried into the palace and sat down near Santos and Khalil as they waited for the pasha to start his inspection of the captives. A courtier invited the captain to accompany the pasha in his inspection. The captain joined him as he advanced slowly along the line of men.

"This one," said Murad, stopping in front of young Jean-Marie, "is the son of the Duke of Quimperlé, sir."

"Very good, captain."

"Monsieur," pleaded Jean-Marie, "my father is rich. He will pay the ransom."

The pasha looked at the young man for a moment, then whispered in the captain's ear.

"4,000 ducats for this one, captain," said the pasha with a smirk. "The boy flaunts his father's riches. He'll pay for his pride."

The pasha continued down the line of men with his courtier suggesting which slaves were best suited for the pasha's service, invariably the fittest men among them were chosen. The chains were removed from five men—John Ryder, William Arnold, Richard Meade and the two French brothers, Jean-Marc and Pierre of Croix-de-Vie. They were immediately marched out of the room. The law allowed the pasha to take one in eight male slaves who would be sold off to the militia at a profit. Another courtier removed the chains from Jean-Marie, who would be the guest of the pasha until the ransom from his father was paid. He would be lodged in the town at the pasha's expense until the day he was given his freedom.

The remaining men were led out of the room in their chains while the pasha began his inspection of the women. Murad and the courtier exchanged a knowing look. The pasha was always on the lookout for beautiful and exotic women, either for himself or for trade, and to his eye, the pale-skinned English and Irish sort were the best of the lot. The same one-in-eight rule applied to women as it did to men.

He stopped in front of Joane Broadbrook and looked down at her large belly.

"Hello, my dear. Are you carrying a boy or a girl?"

"I don't know, sir. Only God knows."

"Yes," nodded the pasha. "I imagine your God would know."

He moved on down the line, showing little or no interest until he came to blonde, blue-eyed Anna Lorye. She flinched, but said nothing as he touched her cheek.

"This one is very beautiful, captain."

Murad had been through this ritual many times before with the Dey. He could have predicted which of the women would appeal to the man. They moved on, stopping in front of Ciara.

"Another beauty, captain," smiled the pasha, delighted. "You've done well."

It was obvious to Murad that even the jaded pasha would find Ciara beautiful. She was the diamond in the rough of all the women in the room.

"You better take her, sir," said Murad in a conspiratorial whisper, "before the slave market doubles her price."

"And why is that?" asked the pasha, intrigued.

"She's a killer, sir."

"A killer?"

"Twice. A woman and a janissary."

The pasha raised an eyebrow and was impressed to have a woman assassin among his slaves. During the exchange, he had scarcely taken his eyes from Ciara, and unlike the other women, she had returned his gaze, unafraid.

True to form, the Pasha's inspection of the women took much longer than that of the men. The pasha paused to look at tiny Jenny, the black Jamaican woman with bird-like features, and then stopped to admire Besse Peeters' red hair and Joyce Watts' striking blue eyes and pale skin.

It did not matter to the pasha, if a woman had been married or was a mother of young children. Infidel marriages were all invalid under Islamic law. The women were no longer human beings with rights, but infidel prisoners of war — known as *tutsaklar* in the Ottoman states of North Africa.

If a woman struck his fancy, he could keep her. She might end up in his own harem or be sent to a harem in Tunis or Tripoli, or on to Constantinople as a tribute to the Sultan. The word 'harem' came from the Arabic word *harim*, which meant the private part of the house set aside for the women of the family. The chosen women were destined to become concubines, maidservants or simply companions to provide amusement.

Murad had seldom seen the pasha as awestruck as he had been by Ciara. He could decide to keep her, but based on her beauty alone, she would be sold at an exorbitant price. Her talent for murder would increase her value among the buyers. The pasha could even gift her to a political rival who he wanted eliminated.

There was a sudden stir as Aga Santos marched the children into the room, forming them into a line for inspection. The Gunter boys were at the front of the line from the youngest to the oldest and the pasha stopped to observe the similar family traits of the boys.

"Who are these boys?" asked the pasha.

"They are the Gunter boys, sir," replied Murad.

"Why are they all so wet?" asked the pasha, looking at their sodden clothes.

"They were splashing water from the fountain, sir."

The pasha nodded, smiling at the boys.

"Who is the tall one?"

"This is Felix, sir. I gave him some lessons about the Quran on the ship. He and his brothers want to become good Muslims."

"Very good, captain. We need more young men like them."

It did not take long for the pasha to finish inspecting the children. They would be sold for a good price to rich families as houseboys and kitchen maids. The men were good for work as galley slaves, field labourers and construction workers, but the real money was with the women. The pasha stopped to consult with his courtiers. After a moment of animated conversation, one of the courtiers pulled Anna, Joyce, Ciara and three pretty young women out of the line and led them to a small anteroom.

Anna and Joyce's children suddenly burst into tears as their mothers disappeared from view. They had been together on a horrendous voyage lasting some six weeks, and now their mothers were to be taken away from them. It was too much for the children. Nothing could comfort them.

Even for Murad, the heart-rending scene was painful to watch. He was about to turn away when one of the pasha's courtiers approached and whispered in his ear. Murad nodded, his eyes searching the room for Felix and the Gunter boys. There was a sudden flurry of activity at the door of the anteroom where Ciara and two other women had been sequestered. Anna and Joyce were struggling with two large female guards in a desperate effort to reach their children, while Ciara had taken advantage of the distraction to run over to Felix and grab him by the arm.

"Felix, do something!" she screamed at the lad.

The idea that Felix was in a position to do anything for Ciara was absurd. The janissaries were already moving the women and children out of the room, but if Felix was foolish enough to help her, it would go very badly indeed, especially if the pasha's guard got involved. Murad hurried over to intervene if necessary.

"Felix!" screamed Ciara again as she struggled with a minder.

Felix had always come running before, but not this time. He silently mouthed the words 'good luck' as he was shepherded out of the room. The lad had obviously taken the captain's advice to heart, but Murad had little time to be pleased with himself. Ciara saw him coming and immediately shifted her entreaties towards him. Her arms were seized by the two minders who were about to drag her back into the room when Murad held up a hand and they stopped.

"I want to be ransomed, captain."

"But you've been selected by the pasha, my dear," replied Murad. "It is the greatest of honours."

"That's not fair. I know people who will pay a ransom for me."

"It's too late for a ransom, Ciara."

She stared at him, disbelieving, then unleashed a wild series of threats and invective that Murad had no desire to hear. He waved his hand dismissively at her, and the two minders hauled her away. *If I were the pasha*, the captain thought wryly, *I would sleep with one eye open with this woman.*

Twenty-five

*"It was a pitiful sight to see the captives put up for sale:
wives were taken from their husbands and children from
their fathers. They sold the husbands on the one hand,
the wives on the other, ripping their daughters from their arms,
leaving them with no hope of ever seeing each other again."*
Father Pierre Dan, French Trinitarian priest

T he Baltimore captives were marched out of the luxuriously furnished palace down the street to the infamous Batistan slave market. The market itself was nothing more than an ordinary street, closed at both ends, to form a large shaded concourse crowded with excited slave dealers. As the captives entered the street, the men were immediately separated from the women and children. They were held in an enclosed area invisible to their wives, where they were made to wait. Meanwhile, the women and children were taken to a similar pen on the other side of the street.

It was exceedingly hot in the pens under the blazing sun. In the women's enclosure, the male auctioneers quickly got to work. Sally Gunter commanded their attention because she was dark-haired, porcelain-skinned and still attractive at thirty-six and was accompanied by her seven sons. An auctioneer asked her questions in heavily accented English.

"Milady, these are all your boys?"

Sally tried to speak, but she was terrified that she would be separated from her boys. All she could manage was a nod.

"Six boys and a baby?" said the auctioneer, looking at Jenny holding baby Walter.

Sally nodded again.

"What is your trade please?"

"At home, I managed a fish plant, sir," murmured Sally with

difficulty.

"Ah, you are a manager," said the man, holding up his hands in a pantomime of counting his fingers. "So you can do sums?"

"Yes, sir."

"And what about your boys? What can they do?"

"The oldest, Felix and Caleb, have worked on boats. They are good boys."

"Come with me, please."

The auctioneer led the way and Sally was led into a partitioned sales tent where several dealers sat on a bench, waiting to have a look at her. The dealers had paid to have exclusive access to the slaves before they were shown on the street to other buyers and the crowds of onlookers. Before Sally could utter a single word, the auctioneer ripped the dress off her shoulder, revealing her naked breasts. She cried out and covered herself with her arms.

One dealer after another came over to examine her. They walked around her silently as if she were a slab of beef, squeezing her sagging breasts, sticking fingers in her mouth, and making lewd jokes in Sabir. After the dealers were satisfied, the auctioneer dragged Sally half-naked out of the sales tent into the street so that the crowd could view her.

"Look at this fine woman," the auctioneer said in Sabir. "She has worked in a counting house. She can do sums. She has seven sons. Starting bids are at one hundred Spanish dollars."

Sally cringed, frightened and humiliated, as the bidding began. The price climbed quickly, and she was sold within minutes for one hundred and fifty dollars. The bids were in local *patacoons* or Spanish dollars.

The auctioneer roughly grabbed her arm and pulled her back into the sales tent so she could get dressed while his colleague led Felix and his younger brothers, all except the toddler Walter, into the street so the buyers could get a look at them.

"Six boys and a baby," announced the man to the noisy dealers. "Imagine the good luck these boys will bring you."

"They're infidels," growled an older dealer.

It was an obvious attempt to keep the price low.

"How old is the tall one?" asked another.

The auctioneer turned to Felix, who had picked up a few words of Sabir in his time on the ship. He looked up, forcing himself to face the crowd. His brothers were depending on him.

"Answer the question," ordered the auctioneer in Sabir.

"I am fifteen years old. My brothers and I are learning about the Quran, the spoken word of Allah."

There was a low murmur of approval from the crowd. The auctioneer let it die down before addressing Felix again.

"Who taught you, boy?"

"Captain Murad, sir."

"These boys were taught by Murad Reis," announced the man. "They will become good Muslim boys."

The auctioneer was taking a calculated risk. He hoped to score a higher bid for the boys. There were two schools of thought about the value of slaves and they largely depended on what the buyer planned to do with them. Many believed that conversion to Islam increased the value of a slave in the short term, while others bought slaves intending to ransom them later. They knew that no Christian nation would ransom boys who had "turned Turk" so they were often less interested in making an offer.

"Starting bids at fifty dollars each for the two oldest boys," said the auctioneer. "Twenty dollars each for the five youngest. That makes a total of two hundred dollars for the lot."

A man bid one hundred dollars for Felix and Caleb, followed by a second bid of one hundred and twenty dollars. No bid came in for the other boys, so the auctioneer offered the five youngsters to the merchant who had bought Sally for fifty dollars. He accepted, and the deal was done.

That ended the bidding, and Felix and Caleb were quickly led away by the buyer before Sally could say goodbye to them. When she came out of the sales tent, Felix and Caleb were gone and her sons were very upset.

"Ma, they took Felix and Caleb," cried Geoffrey.

The youngest boys burst into tears as Sally put her arms around them to try to comfort them.

"I'm here, my dears," said Sally.

The sale was over for the Gunter family and it would be years before Sally saw her older boys again.

In the men's pen, an auctioneer removed Thomas Payne's chains and led him into the sales tent.

"What is your name?"

"Thomas Payne."

"What is your trade, sir?"

"Fisherman."

"Take off your shirt."

The auctioneer helped Payne off with his shirt, exposing his white skin and muscled forearms, and led him out into the crowd on the street.

"A strong man, a fisherman. Starting bids at fifty dollars."

The auctioneer held up Payne's forearm like a boxer in a prizefight and walked him up and down the street in full view of the crowd as he waited for the dealers to place their bids.

"Please make your bids."

One dealer offered sixty dollars, and another brought it up to seventy dollars, closing the deal. The dealer led Payne away.

In the women's pen, Emma Pierse was next in line, along with her mother and three girls.

"Tell me about yourself," said one auctioneer.

"What is it you do?" asked another.

"I'm a fish plant worker, sir."

"Those girls are yours?"

"Yes, that's Phoebe. She's the oldest and the other two are Eunice and Dinah."

"And the older woman?"

"She's my ma."

An auctioneer held back the mother and the children, while another led Emma into the sales tent where she was roughly stripped to the waist. She was shocked by the brutal treatment, but made no sound as the men pinched her ample breasts and looked into her mouth. The auctioneer then dragged her into the street where the crowd jeered at her and others made rude signs before the auctioneer brought her back before the dealers.

"Look at this woman with her dark hair and lovely skin. She'll make a handsome wife for someone. Starting bids at seventy dollars," yelled the man.

The bids came in fast and furious in small increments, going from eighty dollars to a high of one hundred and twenty-five dollars. The sale was over, and Emma returned to the sales tent to collect her clothes. The children were then led into the street, along with their grandma. They were terrified as they were paraded up and down in front of the raucous crowd.

"Here's the grandma," yelled the auctioneer. "She can clean the house and sweep the floor. And here are three girls who can help her. Fifty dollars for the mother and twenty dollars for each girl. One hundred and ten dollars for the lot."

The dealers were not as enthusiastic about the mother and the girls. Several low bids came in. The mother and Phoebe were sold for sixty dollars to one dealer while the youngest girls, Eunice and Dinah, were sold to another for thirty dollars.

The grandma and Phoebe were led away by the dealer and the youngest girls became hysterical as they were ripped from the arms of their older sister. When Emma realized what was happening, she ran out of the sales tent to see a buyer struggling to remove Eunice and Dinah. Emma was quickly dragged away by two guards, but remained inconsolable, screaming at the auctioneers who laughed at her. Emma didn't know it then, but she would never see her own mother again.

It had been a very long and frustrating day for James Frizell. He climbed the stairs to his flat, perspiring in the heat after trying for hours to intervene in favour of the Baltimore slaves. He had argued with the pasha's courtiers that the Baltimore raid was illegal and contravened Sir Thomas Roe's peace agreement with the Turkish Sultan. Roe had been the English ambassador to Constantinople in the 1620s and had obtained certain privileges for English merchants trading with the Ottoman Empire. He had negotiated a treaty with Sultan Mourad IV in 1624 to release several hundred Englishmen held captive in Algiers, and Frizell had assisted the ambassador in the exchange.

Frizell's arguments now fell on deaf ears. The courtiers had made a show of listening politely and then ignored everything he had said, blandly pointing out that the relations between the Sultan and Algerine Turks were no longer what they had been, and that as a result the pasha now considered that all previous arrangements with the Sultan no longer concerned him or his corsairs. It had been a hopeless endeavour.

Frizell unlocked the door to his flat and wearily sat down at his desk. His only recourse was to prepare a report for the court of Charles I. He had hardly begun when he heard the landlord pounding on his door.

"*Monsieur Frizell*, you are late with the rent again, sir."

Frizell didn't move, hoping the landlord would leave him in peace.

"*Monsieur Frizell*, we give you one day, no more," said the voice on the landing.

Frizell could hear the man muttering to himself as he turned away and went back down the stairs. He heard the downstairs door slam shut and stood up. He went to the open window where there was a breeze coming from the harbour. He watched as the landlord in a turban and djellaba stalked off down the street and entered the corner café.

The knock on the door had driven home what a failure his day had been. As discouraging as it was, he reminded himself that the English captives were going through much worse. They had been forcibly taken from their homes to a frightening and alien land, treated like animals, and today their families were being torn apart at the slave market. Frizell knew that he was the only one who could do anything to help, even if it was just to write a report that would soon gather dust at His Majesty's court. He poured himself a large whisky and sat down to write:

Humble petition from James Frizell to the Lords.

Most humbly showeth onto your Lordships that since the receipt of Your Lordship's letter to me as of July 22, 1629, here hath been taken to this place of new English captives to this day the number of 340 persons remaining here, of which 89 of them are women and children taken lately from Baltimore, with 20 men only. The rest were taken out of several ships and barks that they have sunk at sea. And this is but a beginning of the mischief that they intend to do hereafter.

Frizell stopped writing and leaned back in his chair, thinking about his angry landlord. He was the representative of the English government in Algiers, yet despite his repeated appeals to Parliament, he was not compensated sufficiently to pay his own rent. He read what he had just written and smiled bitterly at his own hubris. *How could he presume to help the Baltimore captives when he could not even help himself?*

Twenty-six

In the women's pen, young Besse Peeters was next in line. She was sixteen years old and a pale redhead wisp of a girl. The auctioneers quickly saw in her an opportunity to get top dollar from the dealers.

"Hello, who are you?" asked an auctioneer.

"I'm Besse Peeters, sir. I worked at the fish palace."

"Ah, a fish plant worker?"

"Yes, sir."

"Are you here alone?"

"Yes. I have no family with me."

The auctioneer grabbed her arm and hustled her into the sales tent where he ripped at her clothes. Besse fought back after the man had pulled her blouse off, revealing her small, pert breasts and white skin with freckles.

"I ain't takin' off me clothes, you black-poxed bastard," screamed Besse as she clawed at the man with her fingernails. She drew blood, and the enraged man raised a fist to strike her when a second auctioneer intervened.

"My dear, this is a slave market," he said with great patience. "It would not do to have such a lovely face disfigured by a bruise or missing teeth. We can't sell you if the buyers can't see you. It is much better if we sell you today at a high price. The higher the price, the better the buyer and the better you will be treated."

Besse stared at the small, wizened man for a moment. He had a kindly face and spoke good English. She finally relented, reluctantly shedding her clothes and putting up no resistance as he took her arm and guided her before the dealers. She froze in terror as they began their inspection. One after another, they pawed her breasts and probed her mouth with their dirty fingers, but their real concern was elsewhere.

"Are you a virgin?" asked one dealer.

Besse was shocked by the question. She crossed her arms over her chest and fended off the grubby hands of the dealers.

"Course I am," she blurted.

"Have you been with a man?" inquired another dealer.

"Certainly not," said Besse. "I'm only sixteen."

"Bids start at one hundred and fifty dollars," said the auctioneer.

A dealer fired back in Sabir that nothing was settled until he could examine the girl.

"Place your bids, gentlemen."

Besse's youthful beauty meant she was destined to be sold to a wealthy older man, and the question of her virginity was the key to her value. The dealers waited patiently, and it was apparent that no bids would be forthcoming until they had the requisite guarantees. The auctioneer took a deep breath and then summoned an old woman, wielding a long stick, dressed in a black *m'laya* and face mask. She walked around the terrified girl, murmuring something under her breath as she pinched and prodded her, then beat her with the stick to drive her back behind a curtain for a more intimate examination.

The auctioneers and dealers fell into an awkward silence, broken only by Besse's whimpering, punctuated occasionally by the slap of the stick against her flesh. The dealers grinned at each other, aroused by what they imagined was going on with the lovely young infidel, and the long wait only heightened their anticipation. Besse suddenly emerged, driven out by the old crone.

"She is indeed a virgin," the woman murmured with a toothless grin as one of the men slipped her some coins and sent her on her way.

This was the confirmation the auctioneers needed to start the bidding. To whet the appetite of the dealers, Besse was hauled topless into the street in the blazing sunshine, where the crowd was practically salivating at the sight of the lovely redhead.

"This lovely girl is a virgin," announced the man, holding up Besse's arm triumphantly. "Bids start at one hundred and fifty dollars."

The Prophet Muhammad had written that "paradise is under the feet of the mother," so the atmosphere in the sales tent was dramatically different for Joane Broadbrook who was visibly pregnant. The auctioneers fawned over her. A pregnant woman, whether she was Muslim or infidel, commanded the respect of these men. The dealers didn't dare poke or manhandle a pregnant woman as they had done so roughly with the other women.

"How long before the child is born?" asked an auctioneer as he showed her to the dealers in the sales tent.

"Ten weeks, maybe more," replied Joane.

"And your boys, how old are they?"

"Six and four, sir."

"What is the work you do?"

"Seamstress, sir. I make clothes."

The auctioneer led Joane into the street in front of a crowd of dealers and gawkers to whip up interest. The Muslim crowd admired Joane's belly and waved their support. There were no lewd gestures as there had been for Besse, only silent reverence for a mother with child. The dealers realized the value of a mother with child and also the potential for ransom.

"This woman is a seamstress," said the man. "She makes clothes. Bidding starts at one hundred and twenty dollars."

The sales price rose incrementally to finish at one hundred and fifty dollars. Joane was returned to the sales tent while the auctioneers brought out her two boys, Malcolm and Liam, who were terrified by the noisy crowd.

"Here are two boys, six and four," said the auctioneer. "We'll start the bidding at ten dollars each."

There were no bids at all for the two boys. Then a bid came in from the dealer who had just bought Joane and the price went up to one hundred and sixty dollars.

The bidding was over and Joane nearly collapsed with relief when the auctioneer led her back into the street. The crowd cheered as the boys ran to their mother. Joane had spent the whole day dreading their separation. She cried softly and hugged them close. She thanked God for what she knew to be a miracle. She did not know what lay ahead, but at least they would be together.

The auctioneers spent less time selling the men than they did the women. Unskilled male captives were destined for hard manual labour and English slaves were among the least prized of all. They were traded at a fraction of Spanish, Italian and French workers because the English government refused to ransom their own citizens. The questioning of the English and Irish was cursory at best.

"What is your trade, sir?" an auctioneer asked Corent Croffine.

"I'm a fisherman," Croffine said with some pride.

"What about the others?"

"They're fishermen like me, sir."

"Good," said the auctioneer, visibly unimpressed.

He used a key to release Croffine's chains and those of Abram Roberts, Richard Lorye, Ould Hawkins and Hugh Pierse. The five men were led before the crowd in the street, arousing little or no enthusiasm among potential buyers. In a very brief, perfunctory bidding process, all five men were sold for forty dollars each.

The next man up in the men's enclosure was John Amble. The auctioneer released his chains and questioned him briefly.

"What is your name?"

"John Amble from Baltimore," replied Amble.

"What is your trade, sir?"

"I'm a smith, sir."

"A smith?"

"Yeah, you know, I make metal parts. A blacksmith."

"Ah, a *forgeron*," said the man, using the French word.

"Yes, sir."

"Take off your shirt."

The auctioneer pulled off Amble's shirt, exposing his white skin and several black-scarred burn marks on his arms. He then led him out into the street.

"This man is a smith. He makes metal parts. Starting bids at one hundred dollars."

A dealer shouted an offer of one hundred and twenty dollars. The auctioneer held up Amble's large, black-scarred hands and walked him up and down the street.

"Look at the burn marks on his hands. He is an experienced metal worker and hard to find. One hundred and fifty dollars and he is yours."

A dealer raised his hand, and the sale was done. The dealers were always on the lookout for skilled workers who invariably sold at a higher price.

At the end of the gruelling day, the male captives were marched to the *bagnio* near the main gate. It was a three-storey building with cell blocks on each side around a central courtyard with a chapel in the middle. The *bagnio* had originally been a bathhouse and was now used as an all-purpose prison for slaves. They were common enough in Algiers, the largest of them housing over two thousand prisoners.

As exhausted and disoriented as they were, the English and Irish captives were astonished by the relaxed atmosphere of the prison. In the yard, there were shops and *tavernas* where sailors and *renegadoes* from all over Europe sat in the shade drinking wine and smoking hashish in pipes. It was a cruel illusion. These men were freemen, so they could come and go, and do what they liked. They could order hot meals and drinks, and even consume pork in the cafés. The slaves, on the other hand, could do nothing of the sort. They had no money and survived on bread and water provided by their *patrons* and whatever else they could steal during their long hours of work on the outside. The gates were opened early in the morning and closed late at night so the locals could dine and drink in the stalls all day and into the night.

The slaves were treated like chattel. Their chains were removed, and the guards pushed them into a line at the barbershop where they were shaved of their hair and beards. They were then ordered to strip and go to the showers. Their ragged clothing from the voyage was thrown away, and they were provided with clean clothes — a shirt, a sleeveless waistcoat, a baggy, skirt-like garment, and thin-soled Turkish slippers. The feeling of relief, even pleasure, that these clean clothes afforded the new arrivals was shattered when the guards roughly affixed a heavy metal ring to each man's right ankle. The ring would remain in place permanently, although there was a chance that with good behaviour, it would be removed one day.

The new arrivals struggled to find an empty hammock in the sleeping quarters of the overcrowded jail. The hammocks were slung, one on top of another, with a communal ladder to climb up to them. The men were exhausted, and many were overcome with grief over the loss of their wives and children. They fell asleep to the cries of the weeping slaves and the shouts of the guards.

The sun was not yet up and the men were awakened by the guards banging on the metal bars of their cells. It was time to start their first day of work. They were hustled out of their cells into the prison yard where they waited for their new owners to collect them and take them to the job site.

While the men were lodged in the *bagnio*, the women and children were cared for by their new owners. They were often lodged near their *patron*'s home and taken directly to their places of work. The care was often worse than that provided by the *bagnios* and many were abused by their new owners. Like the men, the women and children were quickly put to work for the benefit of their new *patrons*.

The chance of survival was slim for many of the Baltimore slaves in the state *bagnio*. Men like Ryder, Arnold, Meade and the two French brothers were destined to the worst possible fate for a slave in Algiers. They were 'condemned to the oar', which was worse than working in the pasha's fields and the rock quarries. Galley slaves were literally chained to the oar and worked to death. They worked, ate and slept tied to their benches with no time off. When a galley slave died, his body was unceremoniously dumped overboard at sea and a new slave took his place.

Twenty-seven

Autumn 1631
Felix & Caleb

"A trabajo cornutos; can d'infidel a trabajo!" Pananti, 1841
(Get to work, cuckolds; infidel dogs, get to work!)

The Mitidja plain was a vast agricultural sweep of land that ran east to west in a narrow band along the coast. The fields changed little with the seasons. They were hot and dusty most of the year, with a heat mirage stretching to the horizon. The fields produced the wheat and barley used for making bread in the bakeries of Algiers. On an isolated farm, Felix and his younger brother Caleb worked from sunup to sundown milling the grain produced by the Saidi family while they dreamt of their home back in Baltimore surrounded by the sea.

Omar Saidi lived with his family in a stone cottage on a large plot of land. The boys were lodged in an open-air hangar at the end of a dusty track where a donkey went around and around, hour after hour, milling the grain. The millstone was made from strong volcanic rock and was in two parts: a lower stone called the meta, and an upper stone, the catullus. The catullus was concave and shaped like an hourglass, with a hole through its centre for a wooden beam and a hopper at the top through which the grain was poured. When the beam was turned by the donkey, the catullus rotated against the immobile meta, milling the grain. The animal-driven rotary mill increased the flour output and its quality as the donkey could drive the mill for hours at a time.

For the system to work, the hapless donkey had to go around the millstone at a slow, but constant speed, and the only way to ensure that was for one boy to walk behind the animal and use a stick to keep it moving. The other boy brought in the grain in a wheelbarrow and constantly replenished the supply of grain in the hopper. The only way to relieve the tedium was for the boys to periodically switch places. After the milling was complete, the boys emptied the meta base of flour by filling sacks with grain for transport to town.

Omar Saidi had lost his first wife to the plague and lived with his mother and three young children in the stone cottage. While the mother prepared meals for the infidel boys and taught them how to be good Muslims, Omar liked to show them who was the boss. From time to time, he would take them out behind the mill and give them both a good lashing with his whip.

Felix had grown strong working in the fields. His hair was closely cropped, with a long braid of blond hair at the back to show he was an infidel. He was growing a beard and a moustache. Like his brother, Caleb had a similar haircut and braid and looked older than his thirteen years. The boys no longer wore the heavy metal iron ring around their ankles that they had worn during their first month on the farm.

Every week, Omar went to town in a wagon with sacks of flour, dates and nuts, leaving his mother in charge of the boys and their lessons in Islam. Omar was a lapsed Muslim. He loved to drink and play cards with his *renegado* chums at the *bagnio* and buy himself one of the attractive ladies that hung around the bars. When he returned to his house after a day or two of drinking and whoring, he would go down to the mill and complain to the boys that he could barely live off the proceeds of their work. He would insist that grain production was down because they were not working hard enough.

Felix and Caleb missed their mother and brothers and wondered what had become of them. They liked mother Saidi, who read to them every week from the Quran and from time to time they enjoyed the occasional meal with the family. They liked to play with the Saidi children who came around every day bringing them their meals. The boys had their own prayer mats at the mill and prayed five times a day.

It was a good life for a slave. The work was not too hard, and the boys ate well. There was even a semblance of family life, and after a time, Felix and Caleb even came to think of Omar's mother as 'Grandma Saidi'. But Felix had not forgotten Ciara. He often dreamed about her and wondered what had become of her. *Was she married to a rich merchant? Had she been chosen by the Sultan himself and now lived the life of the idle rich?*

Ciara

Ciara stood on the top deck of the ship along with a dozen other concubines, staring raptly at the extraordinary vista of Seraglio Point from the Golden Horn. It had been a long, miserable sea voyage to Constantinople with stops in Tunis, Tripoli and Cairo to embark slaves and other merchandise on its way to the Turkish capital. It was the first time in her life that Ciara had felt intimidated by other women. There were women around her from parts of the world she could only imagine. There were black women from the sub-Sahara, blonde women from Scandinavia, olive-skinned Latin women, and exotic women from Egypt and Morocco. As different as they all were, they had one thing in common. They were all stunningly beautiful. After the ship had moored at the dock, several curtained two-horse carriages arrived to take the women to the Topkapi Serai, the Sultan's seaside palace. The palace was a vast estate three miles in circumference and home to the Sultan's janissaries, bureaucrats, eunuchs and concubines.

As lavish as the Dey's palace was in Algiers, it was nothing compared to that of the Sultan. The carriage drove through the Imperial Gate and entered the first courtyard, known as the 'parade courtyard', where court officials and janissaries would line the path dressed in their best clothes to hail the Sultan on parade days. From there, they passed through the Gate of Peace into a bucolic world of gardens and cypress trees, followed soon after by the Gate of Salutation, which took them into the second courtyard. This was the centre of the Sultan's power with the palace hospital, the bakery, the janissary quarters, the imperial harem and the Divan council chamber. At the end of the courtyard, the Gate of Felicity marked the entrance to the Sultan's private living quarters. No one was allowed to pass through this gate without his permission.

The carriage stopped at the door to the harem and the busy sounds of city life were replaced by the sound of the wind in the trees and the gurgling water in the fountains. The beautiful slave women in the carriage didn't know it yet, but this was a one-way trip. They would never be allowed to leave the harem and return to their old lives.

Ciara would be one among a thousand slave women in the harem, which existed solely for the pleasure of the Sultan. The private quarters of the Sultan and his sons were forbidden to other men, except for the black eunuchs guarding the palace. The building was a labyrinth of three hundred tiled rooms connected by courtyards and gardens. The new arrivals were forced to convert to Islam and receive training in palace etiquette. They were taught to read and write, play a musical instrument and sing for the pleasure of the Sultan. The head of the harem was the mother of the reigning Sultan or the *Sultan Valide* as she was called, who was responsible for selecting wives or concubines for her son.

The organization of the palace and its hierarchy had developed over the centuries to preserve the power of the Sultan. If a Sultan took a wife from a prominent family in the Turkish capital, then the family would be able to exert influence over the Sultan. To avoid this, the Sultan only procreated with his slave concubines so his offspring were completely independent of any exterior influence. This meant that every new emperor was the result of a union with a slave. Any slave who bore the firstborn male became immensely powerful if she and her son survived until his ascension.

The women in the harem were divided into various classes. There was the Queen Mother on top, below her the *kadin*, the four wives who were the first to bear male children, and below them were the *ikbals*, the four personal favourites of the Sultan who were his regular consorts. All the women were there for the pleasure of the Sultan, but the vast majority hardly ever saw him and never expected to sleep with the man.

Ciara's first day was a dispiriting whirlwind of sights and sounds. The new arrivals were led into a long and very narrow dormitory where they were issued a bed and then were subjected to a humiliating medical examination by a physician. Most daunting of all was their meeting with the Queen Mother, Kiosem, who had to approve of their presence. She was a Greek woman who wielded an enormous amount of power in the harem. One of her duties was to select the most seductive women for her son, Murad IV, but it was clear from her tone at the meeting that none of the slave women were ready for such an honour. They would have to be taught storytelling, poetry, music and the fine art of seduction, but before their training could even begin, they would have to start their servitude at the bottom of the hierarchical ladder as lady's maids or *odalisk*, preparing tea and reading from the Quran.

Ciara had always relied on her ability to beguile virtually any man she ever encountered, but looking into the shrewd, coal-black eyes of the Queen Mother, she realized she was powerless. She was in a different world now, a world controlled by a woman impervious to feminine subterfuge. Ciara and the other concubines had developed a kinship of sorts during their voyage, but after that horrible first day, she saw them in a very different light. They were no longer her friends, but competitors in her fight for promotion within the harem. They would use all their feminine wiles to prevent her from getting ahead. This was not a game she had ever had to play before.

She had been foolish and vain to think that it was an honour to be chosen to serve in the Sultan's harem while her friends were being sold like cattle at that horrible slave market in Algiers. Life in the harem was going to be a hundred times worse than a cloistered life in a monastery in Ireland, and she had never envisioned such a future for herself. She went to bed that first night, utterly discouraged.

Joane

In a narrow alley off Grand Market Street in Algiers, a stairway in the back of the building led to a third-floor shop with a dozen women sitting at tables, sewing *ghlilas*. The *ghlila* was a traditional Algerian waistcoat in satin, velvet or damask with a wide neckline, decorative buttons and enriched with gold threads. Falling mid-length with short sleeves, they were the height of fashion in Algiers and the demand for them was high among wealthy women across the city.

Maria Bouziane kept a close eye on the needlework of her workers. She was a Spanish *renegado* whose clients were difficult to please but were willing to pay a high price for the best quality work. Most of her seamstresses were Berber and their families had a long tradition of embroidery.

One woman stood out. Her pale complexion and blonde hair set her apart, as did her work. The other women had been sewing ghlilas for years and their fingers moved with lightning speed while the blonde worked at a much slower pace as she became familiar with the embroidery of each garment. Joane was a fast learner and Maria had no complaints. She had bought the English woman and her two sons on impulse at the slave market. A dealer had told her the English woman had experience making clothes, so she had jumped at the chance to buy a skilled worker for her shop. Joane had not cost her much and was already making money for her, while she had to pay the Berber women each day for their artistry.

The Bouziane family lived on the first floor of the house with their servants lodged in a shed in the alley. Maria had arranged for a midwife to assist in the birth of Joane's child. Joane had named the baby girl Evelyn, after her grandmother. Maria had hired a wet nurse to look after the baby while Joane returned to work in the shop.

Maria was impressed when she saw how quickly Joane had mastered the fine embroidery that went into the production of each ghlila. Joane got on well with the young Berber women and soon became an integral part of the workforce. Maria took a liking to Malcolm and Liam, who helped load boxes, sweep the floor, and make the tea. They were hard-working boys and always ready to help.

Maria hired a barber to cut the boys' hair, leaving the familiar long braid in the back common to all infidel children in Algiers. When Joane saw the boys' hair, she was enraged that she hadn't been consulted. She knew better than to confront Maria about it. She was a slave and not in a position to confront anyone. She knew Maria had only done it for the boys' own good. There was already talk among the neighbours against the two Christian boys at the workshop.

Maria's meddling, however, did not end there. Not long afterward, she had proudly informed Joane that she had been to the mosque and found an Islamic teacher for the boys. Joane tried to remain calm, but she seethed inside. She was proud of her Calvinist upbringing and 'turning Turk' was the worst kind of abomination in her view. Joane knew that Maria had been raised as a Catholic in Spain and only meant to help the boys. She had 'turned Turk' herself before she married her husband Medhi Bouziane and was now perfectly integrated into Algerian society. She obviously wanted the same for the boys, but Joane could not help but resent Maria's intrusion into her life. She was ashamed of herself for not standing up to the woman, but she knew it would not go down well for her or her children if she refused all her *patronne's* attempts to improve their lives. Still, it hurt her deeply that her own sons were being pressured to abandon their religion.

In other respects, Joane had to concede that she and her boys were well-treated and very fortunate to be together. The Baltimore raid and the misery it had provoked had severely tested her faith. During the voyage, Joane had found solace in her readings from Orla's prayer book, which had rekindled her own religious beliefs. She longed to pray in a real church. She had heard about the Anglican Church of the Holy Trinity in Algiers and the Reverend Devereux Spratt, who had been a slave himself for several years before an English captain ransomed him. Instead of returning to England, Spratt had remained in Algiers as a free man, ministering to the Anglican congregation in the city. Joane desperately wanted to attend the Sunday service and take the boys with her, but Maria had categorically refused. The boys were doing well in their Islamic studies and she didn't want Joane to compromise their relationship with the mosque.

Maria found it difficult to refuse Joane, who was becoming her best worker. She worked long hours and had a real talent for embroidery. The Berber women were certainly good at their work, but they were young and often made mistakes, which were costly to fix. Joane was always cheerful and kind and soon the young women began to count on her to look over their work. It was not long before Maria with Joane's help, reorganized the production chain into three groups of workers — those who cut the fabric, those who prepped and sewed the garments, and those who did the finest embroidery and finishing work. The result was a significant increase in production and the women were happier when they caught their mistakes earlier and didn't have to deal with rejects.

Joane had few complaints. Maria saw to it that her baby Evelyn was well cared for and her boys were happy. They got along well in most respects until religion entered into the equation. It was not the first time that religion had been a divisive issue in Algiers and would not be the last.

Twenty-eight

Payne

The *bagnio* was silent as a tomb when the guard struck Thomas Payne awake with his baton. He struggled to climb down from his hammock and was then led down a dark passage to the street, where a wagon drawn by a mule was parked. It was full of empty cages of the kind used to transport farm animals. The guard attached Payne's foot ring to a heavy chain and pushed him into a filthy cage, smelling of animal dung. Payne sat on the dirty straw and could barely sit up as he watched a ten-year-old boy arrive and stand next to the mule with a stick in his hand. The guard nodded to the boy, who tapped the mule on the rump with the stick, and off they went.

Ten minutes later, they pulled up at the State *bagnio* and the guards loaded two men in similar cages on the wagon. One was a large Slav with massive forearms and the other was an ebony Yoruba tribesman from West Africa. The boy checked that the men were locked in before trotting off to get them bread and water for the road. Ten minutes later, they left the town through the city gate and were on the road going west.

The slaves had no idea where they were going, and what work they would undertake. They were allowed out of their cages for toilet breaks and for meals, but remained chained to the wagon at all times. The boy spoke Arabic and very little Sabir, so the men could only communicate by signs. After their first meal on the road, there was no danger that they would try to escape. The boy brought them to an open-air kitchen off the road where each man was served a large plate of chicken and rice, and a glass of red wine. Their faces lit up at the food and they made jokes among themselves as they regarded the quiet boy. Back on the road, the men were soon dozing off under the white canvas awning on the wagon.

Payne awoke in the heat of the afternoon and watched the boy leading the mule on a long flat road through rich farmland. He began to wonder where they were going and why his new owner was feeding him so well. He couldn't complain after he had gone hungry for weeks on end. The other men were wide awake and watching him. The Yoruba tribesman rubbed his hand over his belly and shot Payne a questioning look. He seemed to be asking himself the very same question.

The second day on the road, they stopped again at a roadside kitchen and ate a large plate of lamb stew and couscous, and drank more wine. After three days of wonderful food, the men hoped their leisurely days of travel would go on forever. They were soon to realize that the owner was only preparing his slaves for the hardest physical work imaginable, that of a quarry worker.

They arrived in the village of Kleber near an imposing chain of mountains which ran inland along the coast from Cape Aiguille as far as Algiers, to the east. It was from these grey mountains that the Romans had procured their Numidian marbles. Pliny had written that Numidia produced nothing remarkable except marble and wild beasts. The first Numidian marble was brought to Rome in 78 BCE and used for the door sills in the house of Consul Marcus Lepidus. The consul was later criticized for his *faux pas* of using the most prized Numidian marbles for thresholds and floor coverings, instead of putting them on columns and wall coverings.

When Payne looked up at the mountain before him, he thought he saw snow on parts of the rock face, but it was only the quarried rock that gleamed in the sunlight. The mountain was honeycombed with quarried rock faces and narrow ledges cut into the mountain. It was serviced by a rough mountain trail that descended to a narrow, winding road at the bottom of the pit. The road exited the quarry near a wooden hut which served as a shelter for slaves working in the pit.

The quarrymen exploited the natural fissures in the rock to extract the massive blocks of marble. They inserted wooden wedges into the fissures and then soaked them with water to evenly expand and split the marble into large sheets. The Berber tribesmen doing this work were small, lean greybeards, who worked alongside the slave crews, moving the huge blocks of creamy white marble called *marmor bianco* down the mountain. Wagons drawn by oxen carried the heavy slabs of marble by road to the city.

The new slaves were quickly put to work. Their chains were removed, and before they went to work, they were given another very satisfying meal in the open-air shelter and kitchen at the top of the rock face. The Berber cutters sat apart from the slaves and slept in a wooden shack on the site. The slaves were provided with hammocks and slept in the open, watched by three armed guards.

The first week was the hardest for the new arrivals. They tore muscles and struggled in desperation with the twenty-ton slabs of marble, which had to be manhandled down from the rock face by a dozen men with ropes. They were so exhausted from their ten-hour work shift, they could barely eat the evening meal before falling asleep. With time, they adjusted to the workload and managed to better conserve their energy.

In their second week, two slaves were killed when the marble slab they were moving tumbled down on top of them. They were quickly buried in a cemetery at the bottom of the pit, and a week later, two new recruits arrived in the familiar wagon to replace them. Clearly, slaves were not expected to survive for long at the quarry doing this kind of dangerous work.

Besse

Besse did not know whether she was fortunate or not. She had been bought by Mustafa Touati and, although she did not know it at the time, he was a very wealthy man who had known the pasha's family since childhood. Of course, no one told Besse anything. She was just another slave woman to be delivered to her new owner.

She was put in a wagon with sacks of grain and agricultural produce and transported beyond the walls of Algiers into a new and exotic landscape. They travelled very slowly through vast tracts of farmland in the blistering heat, and Besse soon succumbed to sleep. She did not wake up until the wagon finally lurched to a stop in Baba Hassen and she got her first glimpse of the Touati estate. The manor house was the stunning centrepiece of a veritable oasis with beautiful gardens and gently gurgling fountains. It was so far removed from anything in her experience that it was like something out of a dream.

That had been months ago, and over time, the dream had been replaced by a new grinding reality. Touati, a distinguished-looking man in his sixties, had not even deigned to speak to her. Instead, he had relied on his three wives to welcome the new slave into the household. It was a strange welcome indeed. They had wasted no time giving her a long list of housework to do, including washing clothes and scrubbing floors. The wives believed that infidel slaves needed to be worked hard to gain their place in paradise.

Touati's first wife, Hamia, was the only one of the wives who actually spoke to Besse. She finally revealed the reason Besse had been brought to the estate. Besse was to become Mustafa Touati's fourth wife. In his sixties, he had three wives and seven children. His first wife had made him proud with one son and three girls. His third wife Fatima had given him another son and two girls, while his second wife Alicia had remained infertile and couldn't have children. Alicia and Fatima took little interest in Besse and it soon became apparent that it would be Hamia who would decide her suitability for marriage. There was little subtlety in her approach. Besse would have to renounce her Christian upbringing and convert to Islam after she became Mustafa's fourth wife. She did not elaborate on what that meant, but after weeks of servitude, Besse could only hope that her life would improve as a married woman.

Although Mustafa continued to ignore her, Besse did what she was told and was unfailingly respectful to Hamia and the other women. She feigned an interest in the teachings of Muhammad and tolerated the seven children who were often just as disrespectful as their mothers. It was another three months before Hamia announced that the Touati family had gotten permission from the mosque for the marriage. Although the Islamic faith frowned on interfaith marriages, it made an exception for Muslim men who were allowed to marry Christian and Jewish women, but not for Muslim women who wanted to marry non-Muslim men. The mullah would allow the marriage, but Besse would have to agree to convert to Islam after the marriage.

The wedding itself was overwhelming, unlike anything Besse could have imagined. It was a traditional marriage ceremony and celebration, a gruelling marathon that lasted three days and left Besse emotionally and physically exhausted. The first day, Hamia escorted her to the *hammam*, the Turkish bath, where she would be ritually cleansed of all impurities to ensure the prosperity of the new couple.

She was dressed in a traditional caftan dress and wore an ensemble of pearls and gold jewellery. The other wives helped to dress her, showing not a hint of jealousy or resentment at the marriage. Indeed, the preparation for the marriage was so reverent and uncharacteristic of the women that Besse almost felt as if they were treating her like a long lost sister. But deep down, she realized that there would never be any love lost between them. It was all in aid of pleasing Mustafa.

There was no question Mustafa Touati would be pleased. With her red hair gleaming in the sunshine, she looked magnificent as she strolled into the garden holding the hand of her new husband, dressed in a black *jabador* embroidered with gold thread. Their arrival for the ceremony elicited audible gasps of admiration from the wedding guests. It was a glittering assemblage of important people bearing gifts of all kinds.

In her time at the estate, Besse had barely exchanged a word with her new husband. Now, during the ceremony, they exchanged just enough words as were necessary to cement the marriage. The rest of the protracted celebrations were an exhausting and dispiriting blur. It was clear to everyone that the wedding guests were there to celebrate Mustafa and not his bride. They were business associates and local politicians who wanted to be seen among the pampered elite. Besse was an exotic prize, a symbol of an old man's presumed virility and nothing more.

Besse had never seen anything like it in her previous life in Baltimore. She had been in a dream and now it was over. After the last of the guests had departed, Besse waited for her husband to appear. She had never been with a man before and did not know what to expect. The leering slave traders had made much of the fact that she was a virgin, so Besse could only imagine what would come next.

Nothing. Nothing happened. She spent the entire night alone in her marriage bed, her heart pounding in anticipation and fear. She awoke in the early morning hours to discover that her new husband had never ventured into the room and was away on a business trip. Life quickly returned to normal as she slaved in the kitchen as a maidservant for the wives and the children. The women treated her well in front of the children but were harsh when alone with her. They would scream at her to hurry up and do this or that, and tell her she was just another stupid *renegado*.

From time to time, she would see Mustafa coming and going, but he remained aloof and showed no interest in her. He made no attempt to consummate their marriage and Besse regretted a little the fact that she was still a virgin. She came to believe that her marriage ceremony had been a dream and had never really happened. When she fell asleep at night, she hoped that the dream would end and she would wake up back in her bed in Baltimore.

She noticed that Mustafa's younger brother Farid would often spend several days in the house when his brother was away. Farid was a handsome man, polite and well-dressed, and Besse felt a frisson of interest whenever she saw him. The women of the house seemed to dress more elegantly in his presence, as if they were competing for his affection. The second wife, Alicia, would spend hours in front of a mirror primping for his visits. Besse found this quite unusual behaviour for the brother of their husband.

As the days and weeks passed, Besse found it difficult to sleep at night, no matter how tired she was. She would wander aimlessly through the house, often harbouring wild thoughts of escape that she knew were impossible. It was the only time when she was free of the constant demands and orders that dominated her life. It was a large house with three wings, one for each of the Touati wives and a large communal room for the children. Besse lived in a small room for servants at the back of the house.

Her routine was to first look in on the children. She wondered how they could look so adorable in their sleep and treat her so monstrously throughout the day. She shook her head and continued walking aimlessly through the dark hallways of the house leading to Hamia's wing. Besse froze when she heard Hamia suddenly cry out in distress. *Was it real or imagined?* she asked herself. Her first instinct was to knock on Hamia's door to see if she was all right, but there was a risk to that. If she had imagined the cry and woke Hamia up for no reason, there would be consequences. The private quarters of the wives were inviolate, and she had been warned not to enter those rooms. On the other hand, if Besse was right and Hamia was in genuine distress.

Besse ventured a few steps closer to the bedroom door, and again she heard the muffled cries from behind the wall. They were not cries of distress, but quite the opposite. They were cries of pleasure, and they came not only from Hamia, but also, unmistakably, from a man. Besse knew little of such things, but she was no fool. Alarmed, she backed away into the dark recesses of the house and returned to the safety of her room. She shuddered at what would have happened if she had mistakenly disturbed Hamia and Mustafa while they were making love. No matter how good her intentions were, she did not want to think about the punishment Mustafa would have imposed on her. Then she remembered something.

Mustafa was away in Constantine for a week.

Amble

In the dark pit of the forge, men were making steel blades by forging and tempering the iron. The heat from the charcoal-fired forge was oppressive. John Amble was sweating as he manufactured the knives, heating the blades until they turned yellow and became malleable, and then hammering them on an anvil to create a single-edged, six-inch blade tapered to a razor-sharp point. The finished blades then went to a master craftsman who made the traditional brass-inlaid decoration and wrapped the handle with metal wire. The decoration was believed to have magical power and to protect the user against the Evil Eye.

There was nothing fancy about *bousaadi* utility knives. They were common all over Algeria and were named after the town of Bou Saada in the Algerian Sahara. They were the weapon of choice of the Berber tribes along with the *flissa*, which was a longer knife or a short sword. The charcoal used in the forge was made from red oak in a cupola on the owner's farm. Amir Nasri was a successful landowner and had dozens of slaves working for him. It took four logs of red oak fed into the cupola to produce just one log of charcoal, and only burning charcoal could produce the high temperatures needed to melt iron.

The entry-level smiths were French, Italian and English slaves who had been bought at the slave market for their experience in working metal parts on an anvil. The master craftsman and his two sons were Berber tribesmen from the south. Amble and the other smiths were lodged in the *bagnio* and released every morning to Nasri's servant boy to start their day at the forge. The boy led the men in chains past the bakery where they collected two rolls of black bread before they went to work. It quickly became apparent to Amble and the others that the food rations were not sufficient to keep a man alive for long. They would starve to death if they didn't find a way to supplement their meagre food ration.

It was the Italian smith, Luca, who quickly recognized the value of the carbon steel used to make the blades at the forge. The steel alloy was better than anything he had worked with back home, so he stole a piece of the unfinished metal in his first week on the job. The steel came from Toledo in Spain and comprised an amalgam of hard and soft steels that were forged together. Weapons made from Toledo steel were the finest in Europe.

At the *bagnio*, there was a trader by the name of Hakim Kermali who knew all the metal dealers in town. He offered to buy all the metal that Luca could steal from the shop. Luca recruited his friends, including Amble and others, to pilfer the occasional metal blade from their workplaces. If everyone was in on it, Luca figured it would be hard for the boss to detect who was doing the thieving. It turned out to be a serious miscalculation. The sudden appearance of the hard-to-get Toledo steel in other shops around town made Nasri suspicious. The knife manufacturing business was a small community, and it did not take long for Amir to link Luca to the loss of Toledo blades. Fortunately for Amble and the others, that was as far as it went. Luca endured his punishment of fifty lashes and his exile to the hard life of a galley slave without ever revealing the names of his friends who had helped him.

Among his other duties, Amble was in charge of delivering the sweet tea that the men at the forge consumed in large quantities throughout the day. He soon became friends with the master craftsman and his sons, who showed him their brass-inlaid handiwork. Amble was appreciative of their work, even though he could only grunt his approval with a few words in Sabir. One day, the oldest son took him aside and showed him a beautifully finished *bousaadi* knife in its leather scabbard. Amble examined the brass inlay on the blade, which was different from the Nasri brand, but just as impressive.

"You sell this for me in the market, *vendir*," he said in Sabir.

Amble remained silent as he admired the knife. He was wary of the Berbers. They were great craftsmen and friendly enough, but there could always be an ulterior motive. After what had happened to Luca, he didn't want to lose his job at the forge, but he desperately needed money. He nodded at the boy and took the knife, hiding it in his waistcoat. He knew of only one man who could tell him what he needed to know.

Back in Baltimore, Amble had been known as an honest tradesman. He still was, but slavery had changed him. Algiers was a different world, and although he would never feel entirely comfortable in it, he had learned that some risks were worth taking. That evening after work, Amble sat down with Hakim in a *bagnio* stall and asked him a few questions.

"What do you know about *bousaadi* knives, Hakim?"

"I've got one myself," said Hakim, touching his shirt where he hid his knife. It was a tradition among Algerian men to carry knives on their persons for protection against thieves and assassins, and for domestic use.

"How much are they selling for?"

"I don't know, maybe five or more, depending on the quality."

Amble drank the wine offered by the trader and wiped his moustache. His black beard had filled out, and he looked like any other Muslim man in the city. He slipped a hand into his waistcoat and took out the *bousaadi* knife the Berber boy had given him. The trader removed the knife from the scabbard and closely examined the brass inlay.

"I've never seen a blade like this, John," exclaimed Hakim. "You made this yourself?"

"No, Hakim. How much would you pay for such a knife?"

"Maybe eight, not much more."

"Good, Hakim. I'll talk to my man."

Hakim returned the knife to Amble, who knew that the trader was sold on the knife. Hakim had seen all kinds of *bousaadi* knives and could easily identify the manufacturer by the decorative marks that appeared on the blade, but he had never seen such fine brass-inlay handiwork before.

It wasn't long before their business took off. Hakim succeeded in selling a batch of over a hundred knives to a man from Tripoli who asked no questions. There was little or no risk in selling knives outside Algiers, but it would be several weeks before Amble felt reassured and stopped fearing discovery. With money in his pocket, he could now dream of one day buying his freedom from Amir Nasri. All he had to do was to survive long enough to make it happen.

Twenty-nine

Ryder & Meade

If there was one man on board the pasha's galley who was valued more than anyone, it had to be old Nate, an English fisherman from Weymouth who was thin as a rake and had a long beard down to his belly button. He sat naked with skin like an old prune on a bench between two hulking German rowers who did most of the rowing for him. He wore a scrap of disgusting sail cloth around his privates and screamed when anyone tried to interfere with his two companion oarsmen. His prickly character and outrageous behaviour were enough to keep his fellow oarsmen at a distance.

The galley was a large xebec with a shallow draught, fifteen pairs of oars, and ninety oarsmen below decks. Most of the pasha's oarsmen lasted less than five years before the bad food and the enormous physical strain killed them. Just in the past month, five men had been found dead at their oar.

It had been four months since the slave market in Algiers. Richard Meade and his mates had been taken immediately for duty aboard the ship. They had been chained to the rowing bench ever since. They ate, slept, and even urinated on the same bench with absolutely no respite. Some days, they were forced to row non-stop for up to twenty hours without a break.

There was little comfort in the fact that they were still together. They were emaciated, with sunken cheeks and skeletal frames. Their clothes had long since worn out and disintegrated, leaving them naked and often freezing in the wet conditions below decks. Meade shared a bench with John Ryder and William Arnold of Baltimore, all of them straining on the same oar. The oar directly in front of them was manned by the French brothers Pierre and Jean-Marc from Croix-de-Vie and a Portuguese man.

Nate was the ship's mascot. He looked to be in his sixties, but it strained credulity to think that a man that age could survive so many years under conditions that routinely killed younger, stronger men. He had been with the ship for some twelve years and even the captain was amazed that he had survived all that time. Early on, before they knew better, Meade and his mates had the temerity to ask the guards about Nate, but they learned nothing and were beaten with a lash for asking.

Meade became obsessed with old Nate. If he could find out what was Nate's secret, he might have some remote hope of surviving on board the ship. One day, in spite of the hostile Germans, he had screwed up enough courage to ask Nate directly. In an eye blink, the wizened old man had transformed into a satanic dervish, screaming and unleashing a vicious torrent of spittle and obscenities at Meade and his friends. They had recoiled as one, horrified at the sight of the man, and in shock from the load of offal and profanity that rained indiscriminately down on them. Meade had made a grave mistake, but at last, he had an answer. The secret to Nate's survival was simple: he was mad. He lived in a fantasy world. It didn't matter whether he lived or died, he was already free.

Nate was a sorcerer, even if he did not know how he did it, he kept them all alive on the ship where staying alive one more day was a victory. There had been many times when the galley had come under heavy fire from enemy ships and, against all odds, they had escaped with little or no damage. It was the same with storms. The galley always managed to find a safe harbour in raging seas when Nate was with them. There had been other captains and officers, but no matter who was at the helm, the ship always came through.

Then one morning, everything changed. They were sailing off the north coast when Nate was found dead at his oar. The entire ship went into mourning. Even the captain came around to have a look at the old man and to supervise the removal of his body. It was unheard of for a captain of one of the pasha's galleys to show concern for an oarsman, but Meade believed the captain to be a superstitious man and saw the death of their mascot as a bad omen.

An hour after they found Nate, they had dumped his body unceremoniously overboard and a new man was already sitting in his place. This did not go down well with Nate's two German colleagues, who refused to work and were half-heartedly whipped by the guard who was as dispirited by Nate's death as everyone else on the ship.

They sailed on with heavy hearts, and that same afternoon, they were spotted by a squadron of Spanish warships who took up the chase. The pasha's galley was a fast ship, but it would not be fast enough to escape the lateen-rigged caravel attacking them. They were outgunned and the caravel had the wind gauge. The captain had no alternative but to make a run for the shallow waters of a nearby bay. They could make seven knots in short bursts, but the caravel was coming fast and had the wind at its back.

Meade and his fellow oarsmen had no idea what was happening, but they could see the growing desperation of the guard as he tried to whip the men to a greater effort. The oarsmen could only row for so long before they collapsed on their oars from sheer exhaustion. The sweat poured off their bodies as they struggled to pick up the pace. Meade knew there was little hope when he saw his friends slowing down. They were dead men. They knew it. If they weren't killed by the cannon fire, then they'd die by drowning.

The galley returned fire, but it was not a good sign. It meant that the caravel was drawing closer and coming within range of the xebec's smaller guns. The next Spanish salvo was thunderous and close, its eighteen-pounders raking the xebec's hull and smashing bodies, oars, and benches to pieces. The lower deck was awash in blood and severed limbs with water pouring in through gaping holes in the side of the ship. Moments later, the two ships came together and the oarsmen could hear the shouts of the Spanish boarding party as they swarmed the deck in a riot of clanging swords and gunshots. The pasha's janissaries put up a fierce resistance, but the battle was already lost.

Galley slaves feared above all drowning in a sinking ship, and ironically, it was the devastating cannon fire of the Spaniard that saved them. The oarsmen near the bow struggled to hold their heads above the rising water. Through the holes in the hull, they could see that they were in a bay in shallow water and the ship was slowly sinking to the bottom. They could do nothing but pray as the water rose around them. The impact of the shot shattered the wood around the bench supports. Meade didn't hesitate. He took a deep breath and plunged his head underwater in a desperate attempt to pull the chains free from the broken bench supports. The chains slipped free, and he surfaced, gasping for breath, arriving face to face with his friend Jean-Marc. They both had the same idea. Six men on two oars were now free, although encumbered by the weight of the chains themselves. They struggled through the rising waters to escape. When they reached the stairs, they found the body of the dead guard, felled by a musket shot. Meade grabbed the man's keys from his belt, then used them to unlock his ankle chain and those of the other five. They could do little more for the slaves on the bench nearest the stairs, so Meade tossed them the keys and followed his friends to the deck above.

It had been a slaughter. There were dozens of janissaries and Spanish soldiers lying in bloody heaps around the deck. The mast was gone, along with the poop deck and the captain's cabin. The xebec had run aground a hundred yards from a deserted beach.

The sudden arrival of the six naked slaves on deck had stunned the former combatants into silence. Finally, it was broken by a shout from a Spanish officer in a nearby pinnace.

"*Quién es usted?*"

"*Somos esclavos,*" replied Jean-Marc.

The officer watched as more slaves appeared on deck. He shook his head sadly at the sight of them. They had lost their clothes and were in even worse condition than Meade and his friends. The Spaniard stared at them for a long moment and then spread his arms wide with a triumphant smile.

"*Son hombres libres, señores,*" shouted the officer, loud enough for everyone to hear.

The slaves looked at each other. They could hardly believe the officer's words after the hell they had endured on the ship. Jean-Marc was the first to react.

"We are free," he said, grabbing his friend Richard and John by the shoulders and jumping up and down with joy.

"We're free," repeated Richard quietly smiling, beside himself with an emotion he had not felt for a very long time.

"We're naked," said William Arnold, smiling.

"Naked and free!" shouted John Ryder.

Besse

Besse was the only woman among the five men in her class. The students all came from Christian countries and were under pressure to become good Muslims and adapt to their new lives. They sat in a semicircle on prayer mats before their teacher, a young man by the name of Bashir with a flop of hair over one eye. Besse liked her teacher, who answered every question with such passion that it was no wonder that he was popular with his students. He spoke French and sometimes English to help his students understand the subtleties of the Quran.

Bashir had known from the first day that the beautiful young redhead would be a distraction in the class. She attracted furtive looks from every one of the smitten young men. He had put a stop to that early on, making it clear to all of them that the teachings of the *Quran* demanded their undivided attention and that anything less would result in their removal from the class. He had to remind himself every day that the same admonition also applied to the teacher, inwardly chastising himself every time his eyes lingered on the infidel woman for too long.

Besse was known to be the fourth wife of a very powerful man in town. The mullah had promised the Touati family that Besse would have access to Islamic teaching, but since she was the lone woman requiring it, he had taken the extraordinary step of admitting her to an all-male class. Bashir had no illusions about what would happen if any unfortunate incident took place in his class. He kept to a strict routine, and part of that routine was to ask his students at the end of each day if they had any questions.

This time, the first question came from Besse.

"Sir, what does *zinah* mean?" she asked.

Bashir was a modest man, and the question had surprised him. He felt his face flush red with embarrassment as if any association with such a horrid word would compromise his own health and security. He took a deep breath to compose himself before he spoke.

"*Zinah* is the worst crime that a man or a woman can commit. It is a *hudud* offence. The Quran prohibits unlawful sexual relations, and the punishment is one hundred lashes. Of course, there must be proof and four Muslim eyewitnesses are required."

The question had literally sucked the air out of the room. There was an eerie silence as the male students took this in.

"*Zinah* is a very serious offence," continued Bashir. "In cases of adultery, fornication, rape and incest, the eyewitnesses must witness the act of penetration."

"Thank you," said Besse, unabashed.

Besse was absurdly naïve about sexual matters and wondered whether this wasn't what they called adultery in her own church in Baltimore. She had simply been curious as to how adultery was treated in the Muslim religion.

It had all started after another nocturnal wandering in the darkened manor house when Besse had observed Farid stepping out of Alicia's bedroom half-naked and heading for Fatima's wing of the house. Farid was a very nice man, but he was showing quite a different picture of himself, a shameless carnality bedding his brother's wives.

"Any more questions?" asked Bashir.

The students looked at Besse as if they suspected her of having committed *zinah* herself. There were no more questions, so the students got up to leave.

"Good day, sir, *maa al salam*," said the students.

"Maa al salam," said Bashir, who had decided that Besse's question had been more than enough for one day. His usual practice after dismissing a class was to remain in the room for a few minutes, but this time he invented a pretext to go looking for an older colleague.

As Besse left the mosque, she noticed Bashir staring at her from the open door across the courtyard. A colleague arrived and Bashir joined him inside. Over their morning tea, Bashir asked his friend a question.

"Have you ever had to explain *zinah* to a class, Ahmed?"

"Never," Ahmed said, raising an eyebrow. "Who asked you that?"

"A young woman. She is English, a new student."

"Oh, yes, the Touati woman. I heard the mullah put her in your class."

"She wanted to know what it meant."

"As good a reason as any," Ahmed smiled. "I suppose she didn't know what she was asking about until you told her. That does not change the innocence of the question."

"Of course, Ahmed."

"Ah, be careful with her, Bashir," said Ahmed, giving his friend a knowing look. "What does she look like?"

"She's a redhead and very attractive."

"Mustafa Touati must be getting on in years," mused Ahmed. "Perhaps she is not so innocent after all."

It had been two days since Besse had asked her question. She was back in class and immediately felt a strange tension in the room. Gone were the smiles and the friendly air of the last few weeks. She noticed a difference in how she was treated by her male classmates and by Bashir himself. She knew enough of the Muslim faith to know that she must have transgressed an unwritten rule, and while occasionally she would still catch surreptitious looks from her classmates, the looks had changed. They had become threatening, even predatory, and she found herself hurrying out of the classroom at the end of the day.

Bashir hardly looked at her at all. She had the uncomfortable feeling that he was angry with her. Perhaps he had been offended by her question. That was a shame because the classes had been a welcome relief from the unrelenting drudgery of her life at the estate. Her last thought before falling asleep was that she did not want to give up on her classes, which were her only escape from the boredom of her new life.

Suddenly, she could not breathe. She jolted awake in her bed in the early morning hours as a firm hand was placed over her mouth. She struggled, but the assailant was too strong for her.

"Don't scream," Farid hissed. "If you scream, I will kill you."

He kept his hand over her mouth until she nodded, her eyes wide with shock. He removed his hand and picked up a candle beside the bed, lighting it from a tinderbox. Besse sat up in bed. She had no idea what was happening.

"Get up and follow me," he ordered.

After Besse had put on a cloak over her nightdress, Farid led her out into the garden, away from the house. It was a moonlit night, and he sat down in a wooden chair wet with dew near the fountain, motioning Besse to take the other one.

"I am hearing things about you, Besse," Farid said, his voice low and menacing. "You have been talking at the mosque."

Besse remembered her question to Bashir and felt trapped.

"But Farid, I am not talking at the mosque."

"Yes, you are, my dear," said Farid angrily. "I am hearing rumours."

"Rumours?"

"I think you are asking questions?"

He knew she thought. She did not know how, but he knew.

"Sometimes we ask questions of our teacher, Farid."

"You asked your teacher about *zinah*, didn't you?"

"Yes."

"Why did you ask that question?"

"Because I did not know what it meant," said Besse. She could see Farid was getting angry, but she had a temper of her own.

"And what were you told?"

"I was *told*," Besse said, her eyes glinting with mischief, "that *zinah* is the worst crime a man or woman can commit. It is fornication between men and women who are not married to each other."

The smug look on her face told Farid that the cat was out of the bag. He erupted from his chair and, in the same movement, seized Besse and dragged her towards the fountain. She fought hard, but she was no match for him. He plunged her head underwater and held it there. Finally, he relented, releasing his grip and letting her up. She sagged against the edge of the fountain, alternately gasping for breath and coughing up water.

"What are you trying to do, Besse?" Farid's voice was almost plaintive. "You have started these rumours. We offer you a good life here in our family and you want to destroy us? I should kill you."

Besse was enjoying herself. Farid was caught in a lie, so she thought her best defence was to go hard and attack. She was a tough, resilient girl from a hardscrabble background used to standing up for herself. She had fought against the bullies at school and her Calvinist parents.

"*Zinah* is a *hudud* offense, Farid," said Besse with a smirk as she got to her feet and stepped away from the fountain, fixing him with a knowing look. "It gets you the supreme punishment. One hundred lashes. One word from me, Farid, and the mosque will come looking for you."

Farid shoved Besse away and stepped back. He had never encountered a woman like this. He had expected her to be terrified of him, but he was the one who was feeling threatened. He knew there were rumours already circulating among his friends in Algiers about his regular visits to his brother's estate, but he had no way of knowing what he was up against. *Who had Besse talked to in town other than her teacher?*

Farid had wanted to kill her, but cold logic had overcome his desire for vengeance. He knew it would be difficult to explain her death to the family and the people at the mosque. It would create a terrible scandal in the town. Besse could stir up people at the mosque. Things were unravelling faster than he could control them.

"I can kill you, Besse," warned Farid. "It would be very easy for me to hurt you."

"I'm a married woman now, Farid. I'm your brother's wife, a Touati just like you. You can't touch me."

Besse stepped closer. She expected him to try to slap her or give her another dunking, but there was no way she wasn't going to win this.

"You can't touch me, Farid. Give me my freedom and I'll go away."

"I don't own you," he protested. "My brother does."

"Then give me money and a new life."

It was as if Besse had read his thoughts. He stared at her and realized then that this fierce slip of a girl had completely outwitted him. She would poison his life if he did not find a way to do what she wanted.

Thirty

Sally

Sally had been fortunate in her new job. She had most of her boys with her, and she had the comfort of familiar faces around her. There were six women from Baltimore in her group — Flood, Harris, Ryder, Croffine, Meade and Roberts. She had worked with most of them, salting pilchards at the fish palace back home.

The bakery was near the city wall, only a stone's throw away from the *bagnio* that housed the enslaved prisoners. It was a large, busy operation with several beehive ovens near a large open fireplace on the main floor. It provided bread to the entire slave population of the *bagnio* paid for by the slave owners, who were responsible for their upkeep. Each morning, the prisoners filed by a service window to collect their bread ration before going off to work, and all these transactions were duly noted in a register at the bakery.

It was hot, exhausting work in the sweltering heat of the bakery. The ovens had to be heated for around four hours with well-tended fires before they were hot enough to bake the bread. The work started around midnight with some fifty female slaves standing side by side at long tables, preparing dough made from local wheat and barley flour. After the kneading and proving, the dough would sit in a warm room and rise for an hour before being baked in the oven for a short time. Every twenty minutes, loaves of freshly baked bread were removed from the ovens before reloading. It was a model of efficiency compared to the chaos that had reigned before Sally had arrived.

On their first day of work, Sally and her friends had been shunned and belittled by their coworkers. The bakery was run by a bossy French woman who slept with the owner, an Arab named Rachid. She jealously guarded her position, both in bed and out of it, and it was clear she was not interested in entertaining any ideas or suggestions coming from her staff. In those early days, Sally had other things on her mind. She had to find a place to lodge her youngest children during the long nights, and once again, she was fortunate. The French woman had put ten-year-old Lionel, eight-year-old Geoffrey and six-year-old Giles to work sweeping the floor and distributing bread to the slaves in the early morning hours. The other boys, Cecil and the toddler Walter, were too young to work, so Sally had found a refuge for them in a back room where they could sleep through the night. She was not the only slave in the bakery with children. Mrs. Roberts had a young daughter with her, while her older girl had been sold at the slave market. The other women had lost their husbands and their children. Every night in her prayers, Sally thanked God for allowing her to keep her younger boys and not to have to endure the debilitating loneliness of her friends.

At the outset, Sally had known little about operating a bakery, but she was a fast learner and knew a lot about organizing workers. The Baltimore women were used to working with Sally, and she was soon able to introduce improvements to the production chain. Rachid was not a stupid man, and he could not help but notice the changes, despite his paramour's efforts to hide them. Not long after that, the French woman left his employ and Sally quietly took over the daily operation of the bakery.

Unlike her predecessor, she made new slaves welcome and brought in a cook and two assistants to prepare regular meals for her workers. She also allowed the women unlimited access to bread for themselves and their children, and she even turned a blind eye if they stole small quantities of bread to sell or barter in the market. While the women slept during the day, the cook and her assistants looked after the younger children. Their mothers were happier, free from worry about their offspring, and worked that much harder.

Gradually Sally transformed the bakery into a well-oiled machine, churning out a huge production of bread each morning. She was proud of her coworkers, and the owner was happy. She was always exhausted at the end of the night shift, but before sleep, she found time to think about her two oldest boys and wonder how they were doing.

The other Baltimore women did not have the weight of Sally's responsibilities. They had more time on their hands and their lives took on a new turn when they went to the *tavernas* at the *bagnio* during their afternoon breaks. There they met slaves like themselves and freemen from all over Europe and North Africa, who bought them drinks and flirted with them. The men were just as lonely as the women, having lost their own wives and children. The women rejoiced in their new liberty.

None of this would have been possible in Baltimore with its rigid puritanical attitudes towards women where a father or an uncle would always be around to give a woman a dressing-down in front of the family if she stepped out of line.

Besse

There was no way Besse could stay in the Touati house any longer. Farid had promised to talk to her later, but she could not trust what he said or what he might do to protect his family secret. She had to get away. She got dressed and collected her things as she waited for the sun to come up. She would need to leave as soon as possible. It was a long walk to town. She pulled a dark cloak over her haik and veil before exiting her room. The house was quiet and Farid must have returned to bed.

It took her a full hour to walk to town unobserved. There were farmers on the road heading for the fields just as the dawn light came up. It would not do to be seen alone on the road without a male companion, so Besse had to hide from time to time in the bushes on the side of the road to avoid being seen. Once in town, she walked quickly to the mosque, hoping to catch Bashir as he came in. She waited for two hours before she saw her teacher arrive. He saw her at almost the same moment. A look of alarm crossed his face and, for an instant, Besse was afraid she had made a mistake. He hesitated for a moment, then crossed the street.

"What are you doing here?" he demanded.

"I need your help," said Besse. "I need to talk."

"Not here, please. It is dangerous."

Bashir looked around, fearful of being seen alone with the wife of an important local man. It was early, but the street was already starting to fill with people.

"Follow me into the mosque," he said gruffly. "Then wait in the vestibule."

He turned away before she could say a word and crossed the street, disappearing into the mosque. She stood there for a moment and fought off her instinct to run away. She was already attracting curious looks in the street. She took a deep breath and crossed the road to the mosque, where she waited dutifully in the vestibule, assailed by self-doubt. She didn't know if she could trust Bashir to help her.

An hour later, she had her answer.

Bashir watched the street from his classroom window, then hurried downstairs when he saw the dogcart coming towards the mosque. He was waiting at the door when the horse pulled up and Farid and his brother's first wife, Hamia, stepped out.

"You've done the right thing," Farid told him as two servants dragged Besse out onto the street.

Bashir wasn't so sure. The beautiful infidel woman had put him in an impossible position. He was only a humble teacher, so she should have realized there was nothing he could do for her. She was the wife of a powerful local man. As soon as Besse had settled in the vestibule, Bashir had dispatched a messenger to the Touati estate and posted the two servants to watch over her.

"What's wrong?" asked Bashir. "She seems to be very agitated."

Besse's eyes were wild, like those of a frightened animal, and for a moment, she looked straight at Bashir with a gaze of pure hatred. He looked away, telling himself that he had done what he could for her.

"An anxiety attack," said Farid.

"She's very young," said Bashir. "Maybe she needs to talk to someone, to another woman."

"I'm sure she does," said Farid. "I'll let Hamia handle it. It is not a concern for men."

"Very well," said Bashir. "*Salam Alaikum.*"

They watched as the servants lifted Besse and put her in the cart next to Hamia, who made a show of comforting her. Her words seemed to calm and reassure the girl, who stopped struggling. She sank back into the cart with a look of utter desolation on her face.

Farid wasted no time leaving the mosque. He drove as fast as he could in the direction of the manor house. Hamia sat next to Besse, squeezing her arm until Besse pushed her away. Her heart sank when

Farid pulled the cart to an ominous stop on a deserted stretch of road near a grain silo.

No one spoke as Farid seized Besse by the arm and dragged her into a white stone building next to the silo, followed by Hamia.

"What is going on?" screamed Hamia. "Tell me, you little bitch."

"Nothing," whimpered Besse.

"You are telling lies about our family."

"I'm not telling lies."

"Yes, you are. You have been talking to that man at the mosque. What have you told him?"

"I told him nothing."

"Liar!" screamed Hamia.

Farid stood at the door as Hamia went after Besse, pulling her hair, slapping and kicking her, and calling her names.

"Come on, spit it out. You were telling lies about Farid and our family. Weren't you?"

"No, I said nothing to anyone."

Hamia wanted nothing less than a full confession from Besse. She wanted the English bitch to grovel at her feet, demanding forgiveness to save her life. What Hamia couldn't know was that Besse was a fighter. She was young and strong for her age, while Hamia was in her forties and had lived an easy life on the estate with servants to do the heavy work. Hamia pulled a small knife from her belt and lunged at Besse, who easily stepped aside, keeping her distance. She knew she was in a fight for her life and was vaguely aware of Farid standing at the door, watching them. Suddenly, all the rage pent up in Besse exploded.

As Hamia came at her again, Besse punched her hard in the face with her fist. She staggered backwards, blood streaming from her nose, and Besse seized the opportunity to wrest the knife from her hand. Now she, in turn, attacked Hamia with her own knife, and the older woman screamed in pain as the blade slashed her arm. Besse was raising the knife again when Farid grabbed her arm and pulled her away.

"That's enough, both of you," said Farid as he pulled a cotton handkerchief from a pocket and gave it to Hamia to wrap around her bleeding arm.

Hamia ignored the handkerchief and flew at Besse again, but this time Farid effortlessly pushed her away.

"We're going to return to the house and I don't want to see any more fighting," said Farid.

"I'm going to kill her," murmured Hamia.

"No, you're not," insisted Farid.

Farid took the knife away from Besse and led her out of the silo as Hamia wrapped her bleeding arm with the handkerchief.

"What does Bashir know?" asked Farid.

"I told you, Farid. He knows nothing," said Besse. "Give me my freedom and all your problems go away."

Emma

A new arrival in Algiers was turning heads. The city consumed vast quantities of wine for a predominately Muslim country. Janissaries, Christian slaves, European diplomats, sailors and others drank Mascara and Tlemcen wines grown in the vineyards near Oran. A pipe of wine (126 imperial gallons / 570 litres) could be purchased for as little as sixteen Spanish dollars. There was good money to be made in the sale of wine, but the new arrival from Virginia was offering tantalizing profits.

> *"Life is a smoke! —If this be true,*
> *Tobacco will thy Life renew;*
> *Then fear not Death, nor killing care*
> *Whilst we have best Virginia here."*
> Early 17th-century poem extolling
> the virtues of Virginia tobacco.

Tobacco was making its entry into European markets and was starting to arrive in Mediterranean ports. The English had imported half a million pounds of the stuff in the previous year and everyone sang its virtues. Tobacco was known to have cured the migraine headaches of Catherine de Medicis in the 1560s and the French called it "*l'herbe à tous les maux*" (the plant that treats all pains) because of its extraordinary healing properties. The tobacco arrived in hogsheads — barrels filled with dried, pressed tobacco — and had to be broken down and sorted for sale by the pound and the ounce. There were two kinds of tobacco. One was mild and sweet-scented and the other, Orinoco, was the stronger of the two.

In Algiers, there was a rush to get it to market and wine merchants were going all out with the sale of tobacco. They put together teams of female slaves to cut up and sort the tobacco leaves on large tables in warehouses behind their shops.

Emma Pierse worked on an assembly line of ten slave women, including the Baltimore maids Ellen and Deirdre and the tiny Jamaican nanny Jenny. They spent each day chopping and sorting tobacco leaves for ribbon cut, coarse cut and rope tobacco. It was hard, dirty work sifting through the dried tobacco leaves, and they were covered with tobacco dust from morning to night. They were lodged above the shop in a stuffy dormitory and took their meals in the kitchen, so the smell of tobacco clung to their hair and their clothes and followed them everywhere.

It had taken several weeks before the *patron* trusted Emma enough to run the occasional errand for him, and another few weeks before she felt comfortable walking around what to her, was a huge, teeming metropolis. One day, she delivered a pound of tobacco to the owner of the café opposite the wine shop. She was on her way back when she saw a familiar figure sitting at a table in the café. Her heart leapt. It was Agron, the janissary she had made love to on the ship during their long voyage from Ireland. She wanted to say how happy she was to see him, but she was too ashamed of her appearance. She brushed the strands of tobacco from her apron and hurried back across the street. Halfway to the wine shop, she heard his voice calling to her.

"Emma? Is that you?"

She stopped and turned to look at him. His skin was very dark from the sun and he looked tired as he got to his feet. His *bork* lay on a chair and he had a cotton bandage on his leg.

"What happened to you, Agron?" she asked.

"It's not serious, Emma. Just a scratch. We got in a fight with the Spanish."

"You were attacked?"

"Yes, it was quite a battle."

"Can you walk?"

"Of course, but with a limp. Where are you working?"

"At the wine shop."

"So you are one of the tobacco girls?"

"Yes."

"What about your girls, Emma? I remember Phoebe, the oldest."

"I've lost them, Agron. They were taken from me."

"I'm sorry, Emma. The slave market is a heartless place."

The memory was all too much for her. She burst into tears and fled across the street.

Over the next few days, Emma found herself stealing glances at the café opposite the shop. *Will Agron come back?* she asked herself. *Why would he? I looked so awful,* she thought.

A week later, Agron suddenly reappeared sitting at the same table. She spotted him as she came into the shop from the storage room with several boxes of cut tobacco. When the *patron* left the shop to see a supplier, she picked up a box of cut tobacco and hurried across the street. Agron looked up and smiled as she dropped the box on his table.

"They are watching me," she warned him, looking back at the shop. "Pretend you are a customer. Pick up the box and look inside."

Agron did as he was told, feigning great interest in the tobacco in the box.

"I've found a good job for you, Emma," said Agron, making a show of smelling the freshly cut tobacco. "You would be working for a friend of mine, a goldsmith."

Emma stifled a sudden impulse to hug him. She was speechless. Agron kept up the pretence, shaking his head dismissively.

"Lovely tobacco, Emma," said Agron, looking pleased as Emma picked up the box and closed the lid. "Can you slip out after work?"

Emma's hands were trembling, and she leaned in close to whisper in his ear.

"Nine o'clock in the alley," she stammered. 'Don't be late."

Agron nodded, and she started back across the street. She reminded herself that she had just been turned down by a customer and that a happy smile on her face would look out of place. When she entered the shop, the assistant challenged her.

"Who was that man?" he demanded.

"Just a customer, sir," she shrugged. "Wanted to see what we're selling."

It was a long, tense wait until nine o'clock. The wine shop had closed for the day and the women had returned to their quarters above the shop to have a wash and get ready for the evening meal. Emma cleaned herself up as best she could, but didn't try to improve her appearance in any way or rouge her cheeks. It would only arouse suspicion, not just from the *patron* and his assistant, but also from her co-workers, whom she knew better than to trust.

The hubbub of the evening meal offered her the chance she needed to slip out unnoticed. It was the best part of the day for the women who enjoyed the chatter around the dinner table. After a long wait, she was finally able to detach herself from the others and go out through the back door to the alley. She didn't want to miss Agron, so she arrived early and had to wait for twenty minutes before he finally appeared at nine o'clock. He was strolling nonchalantly down the alley when she stepped out of her hiding place. He gave her a big smile and leaned in to kiss her on the lips, but she turned away and offered only her cheek.

"Are you all right?" he asked.

"I want out of here, Agron," she said. "I want to be free."

"I said I'd help you if I could."

"Thank you, but what kind of work is it?"

"My friend is a goldsmith, Emma. He needs someone to help in his shop."

"I need money, Agron."

"I told him that, too," he said, proud of himself. "He'll pay you a small monthly bonus in cash for your expenses. He's a Jew, but an honest Jew."

Emma smiled at Agron. She was elated and couldn't wait to leave the tobacco sorting job. She grabbed him and gave him a real kiss.

"You will have to be patient. My friend will make an offer for you, Emma, but it can take time. Don't make yourself too indispensable, you know, cutting tobacco."

"Yes, Agron. I will not be a good worker."

"My friend will send a man to negotiate the price."

"I have to go before they notice me missing," she said. "When can I meet your friend?"

"Tomorrow," Agron promised. "I will bring him to the café. He'll buy a box of tobacco from you."

"Thank you, Agron," she said, embracing him again.

He tried to pull her in close, but she danced away, a look of pure delight on her face. Agron watched as she dashed off down the alley.

Thirty-one

Three Years Later

September, 1634
To the King's most excellent Majesty.
The humble petition of James Frizell on behalf of himself and eight
hundred of Your Majesty's subjects who are now slaves in Algiers.
Most humbly showing:
That the unfortunate and miserable prisoners and slaves having been
taken and are still detained in a most lamentable condition by reason of
breaking of the peace formerly made and confirmed by Sir Thomas Roe,
then ambassador at Constantinople, betwixt Your Majesty's subjects and
the corsairs of Algiers, have at divers times requested and long hoped for
their redemption of their miserable bondage. But same as not redeemed, no
fruits of Your Majesty's intended clemency towards them.

Please read my humble petition to appoint commissioners to find
ways and means for the preservation and deliverance of Your Majesty's
miserably suffering subjects and note that the number of unfortunate
English prisoners has doubled in Algiers.

James Frizell, British Consul, Algiers

Felix & Caleb

It had been three long years since the boys had come to the farm. It was a lonely place for the two young men. Felix was nineteen and his brother Caleb was sixteen. They were strong, healthy lads working the land and had grown close to the Saidi family. They were up every morning before sunrise to pump water and carry the buckets to the main house, then empty the pisspots and carry the night soil out to the fields before they started their day at the mill. Grandma Saidi still read to them from the Quran every week and had grown attached to her English boys. They had learned to speak Arabic and had become practising Muslims, stopping work to pray five times a day. They had lost their infidel braids and wore their hair and beards long. Even Omar had stopped complaining about the boys and whipping them for no reason when he returned drunk from town.

Felix had become disillusioned with his life on the farm. He felt he was missing out on what a real life had to offer. He could be struck down by lightning tomorrow and he would have seen little or nothing of the world. He liked the Saidis and his brother Caleb seemed happy enough, but Felix wanted more, much more. Was he destined to follow a donkey around a millstone for the rest of his life? The question tormented him every morning when he got up with the dawn.

It happened in the last week of September. Omar had gone to town in the wagon with the sacks of flour, dates and nuts. He was usually gone for two to three days before he returned, but this time he didn't return. It had been over five days since he left the farm. The family was worried about him and Grandma Saidi came to talk to the boys to see what they knew. Of course, the boys knew nothing about the comings and goings of their *patron*. It was not normal for him to go away for so long.

At first, Felix thought he was seeing things. He glanced up from behind the plodding donkey and noticed an odd silhouette on the dirt road. It was over a mile away and all he could make out was a wagon and some horses behind it. Alarmed, Felix called to Caleb, and the boys ran out to the edge of the road to get a better look. The wagon was moving slowly, but as it got closer, they could see nothing threatening about it. The horses were riderless, tethered behind the wagon, and after a few moments, they could see that the man driving the wagon did not look anything like Omar.

The Saidi farm never received visitors, and now there was someone coming to visit them. Felix and Caleb exchanged a worried look as they waited by the side of the road. Finally, the wagon pulled up in front of them and the man grinned at them through his large beard. There was something familiar about the man.

"Captain Murad?" Felix blurted, astonished.

"The very same," Murad said, his eyes twinkling, "but just a little older."

The captain descended from the wagon and engulfed the boys in a bear hug. Felix thought the captain looked much older and diminished with his stooped shoulders, grey beard and thinning hair. Of course, the man was in his sixties and had survived a long time in a tough world when many of his contemporaries had died violent deaths, fallen into poverty or simply disappeared at sea.

Murad stood back, looking them up and down.

"Look at you both," he beamed. "You have grown into strong young men."

He went to the back of the wagon, motioning the boys to follow. They gaped in surprise when Murad opened the tailgate. Omar Saidi was sound asleep in the back of the wagon. Felix was about to wave at the Saidi children, but somehow, they already knew. They spilled out of the house and ran towards the wagon. Murad pulled Felix and Caleb aside as the children swarmed their father, shrieking and laughing. They were soon joined by their grandmother.

"*As salamu alaikum,*" said Murad to the grandmother and then turned to the boys and spoke in English.

"Mister Saidi likes to drink and play cards," he told them. "Unfortunately, he is not very good at either. Fortunately, I am very good at both. He lost at primero, so he gave me his slaves to pay off his gambling debt."

Felix and Caleb stared at him, dumbstruck.

"You mean us?" Caleb asked.

"That's right. *Ti star franco,* lads. You are freemen."

"We're free," exclaimed Felix.

"Yes, you are. I am setting you both free," said Murad, patting his pocket. "It says so on a signed certificate I have with me."

"We're free," said Felix again. "Can we return to Algiers with you, sir?"

"Of course you can."

Freedom in a place like Algiers was a daunting prospect, thought Felix, glancing at his smiling brother.

Felix and Caleb were both surprised at how hard it was to leave. Omar Saidi had been a mean and often unpredictable *patron,* but over time, he and the boys had forged an uneasy truce. The children were attached to the boys whom they thought of as big brothers, and Grandma Saidi — well, she was very special. As far as she was concerned, the boys had become her own. When Murad and the boys said their goodbyes and mounted their horses, the children started to cry.

They were not the only ones. Grandma Saidi stoically turned her back on the boys, hiding her tears, and followed Omar back to the house. The boys tried not to show it, but their eyes were moist when they stopped waving to the children. No one spoke for a long time, and then Felix broke the silence.

"Captain Murad?"

"Yes?"

"What do we do when we get to Algiers?"

Murad made a show of thinking about it.

"Well, you're free," he mused. "You can do whatever you like, but as it happens, I've been looking for some bright young lads to sail with me on my next voyage. Do you think you two might be interested?"

They stared at him, speechless, hardly believing their good fortune. Murad chuckled and returned his attention to the road. It was still a long way to Algiers, and when they got there, he had another surprise waiting for the lads.

After their long ride from the Saidi farm, the captain and the boys were tired and hungry. They dropped off the horses at a livery stable on Great Market Street and Murad took them to a café in the *bagnio*. After the isolation of the farm, Algiers was a new and exciting revelation. The boys had seen very little of the town during their brief and frightening time at the slave market. They drank their first glass of ale after three years of seclusion, marvelling at the swirling human tapestry at the *bagnio* — and all in the presence of the great Captain Murad, a man they thought they would never see again. The boys were stunned by their abrupt change of fortune and were more than a little drunk. It was hard to tell whether the intoxication they felt came from the ale or from the miracle of their freedom.

"Who was the greatest general the world has ever seen?" asked Captain Murad.

"I wouldn't know, sir," said Felix, looking amused by a street barker with a clown's hat, making a fool of himself in the market.

"Every heard of Hannibal Barka, Felix?"

"That's the man who crossed the Alps with thirty elephants," said Caleb. "Omar Saidi talked about him."

"He was a Carthaginian general, boys, a very great military leader. He took a huge army with horses and elephants across the Alps and attacked the Romans. Carthage was a very great power in Roman times and their Numidian cavalry was the best in the world. You'll see the ruins of Carthage when you get to Tunis."

Felix vaguely remembered his schoolteacher talking about the Romans and their battles with Carthage.

"Hannibal fought many battles against the Romans, but his greatest battle was the battle of Cannae in the south of Italy. The Romans lost 50,000 men in just one day, Felix. Hannibal fought with his Spanish mercenaries and Gauls in the centre of his line and put his hardened African forces on the flanks along with his superior Numidian horsemen. After the Romans attacked his weak centre, Hannibal pulled his men back in a controlled retreat, drawing in the Roman infantry. He has soon encircled the enemy by using his hardened troops to attack from the flanks and his cavalry to attack the rear. The slaughter was terrible. Livy described it as the worst disaster in battle ever suffered by Rome."

"What happened to Hannibal's elephants in the battle, captain?" asked Caleb.

"I think they had all died by the time Hannibal got to Cannae, lad."

"Didn't the Romans attack Carthage and burn it?" asked Felix.

"Yes, they did, but much later, after Scipio Africanus defeated Hannibal at the battle of Zama. The Romans dominated the seas and attacked the Phoenician warships in the bay, burning them before they entered the city. They slaughtered the people and razed the city. You remember the rules of war, Felix?" asked Murad.

"Yes, sir," said Felix, distracted by the people on the street. "Know thyself and know thy enemy."

"Very good. What's the third rule, Caleb?"

"I'm not sure, sir."

"Didn't Felix tell you the rule?"

"No, sir."

"Choose the battlefield, sir," said Felix.

"And what if you cannot choose the battlefield, Caleb?"

Caleb looked at his brother.

"Do the unexpected," said Caleb with a smile. "That's the part Felix told me to remember."

"Very good, son. War is chaos. Nothing ever happens as it should. You must always be ready to do what no one expects."

The boys remained silent, happy just to watch the people coming and going in the street. It was amazing how pleasant it was to just to sit on a street corner and watch life go by.

Murad had been about to say something when he looked up and his face creased into a wide grin.

"Ah, there you are," Murad said. "Sit down. We've been waiting for you."

Felix and Caleb hadn't been aware they'd been waiting for somebody. They watched as the bearded man pulled out an empty chair and sat down.

"You found them," the man said to Murad.

"I said I would, didn't I?" said Murad. "Lads, you remember this man?"

'You remember me?" asked the bearded man, looking directly at Felix. "I was there when Captain Khalil gave you the *bastinado*."

"Marcellus!" Felix exclaimed.

"That's *Captain* Marcellus to you," said Murad. "He was recently promoted. That's probably why you didn't recognize him. He's cleaned up and doesn't look so scruffy anymore."

The *bastinado* was not a happy memory for Felix, but there were some good moments with the captain that he remembered. He reached across and shook Marcellus' hand.

"So Marcellus, are we ready to go?" asked Murad.

"I think so, captain," said Marcellus, who looked at the boys for a long moment.

Felix and Caleb stared at each other, suddenly alarmed at being left to themselves in this strange, chaotic city.

"What about us?" Caleb asked, his voice almost comically plaintive. Felix shot him a reproving glance.

"I'll see you both tomorrow morning," said Murad with a warm smile. "Go to the harbour where you will find my ship."

"What do we do tonight?" Caleb asked his brother.

"Did I ever tell you I have four sons of my own?" Murad asked the boys.

Caleb glanced quizzically at Felix, who shrugged. He couldn't recall Murad ever mentioning his family before, and it seemed odd that he would now. He and Caleb had other things to worry about, like finding a safe place to sleep for the night, and Murad's sudden digression was not helping.

"My youngest son, Anthony," Murad continued, "is a little older than you are, Felix. He lives with a German woman on the Hudson River in New Netherlands. I haven't seen him or his brothers for a very long time. I've been thinking about them a lot lately and it reminded me how important family is."

This coming from a man who tore my family apart, Felix thought bitterly, but he kept silent. He knew he would never be able to pardon the captain for enslaving his family.

"You lads were hard to find," said Murad, "much harder than your mother and your brothers."

Murad pointed at the bakery across the street.

"Your mother and brothers work over there. They're waiting for you."

Felix and Caleb stared across the street, hardly daring to believe it. They stood up nervously.

"Go on, lads," said Murad cheerfully. "I'll see you in the morning."

Felix and Caleb nodded their thanks and ran off to find their family.

Thirty-two

Joane

On Sunday morning, Joane was up with young Evelyn at the crack of dawn and looking forward to her day. The baby in the family was now four years old. She was a beautiful blonde child with blue eyes and a lovely personality. Maria and the Bouziane family adored little Evelyn, particularly Maria's two daughters, who never tired of playing with her. Malcolm had turned ten and his brother Liam was going on eight years old. They were both in school and spoke Arabic fluently with the extended Bouziane family.

Joane had few complaints. She had her work and her children were happy. She missed her husband Stephen and her church in Baltimore. She had no friends and no one to confide in. She couldn't share her thoughts with Maria, who had thrown away her Catholic upbringing to marry a Muslim man. Joane didn't want to start over. She wanted to go back to her old life, but it was quite impossible.

Joane had fought tooth and nail with Maria over her right to go to church. Maria had finally relented and allowed Joane to go alone, but she was adamant that the boys should not accompany her. It would only create gossip among her Muslim neighbours, and that would not be good for either of them.

The Anglican Church of the Holy Trinity was in an unlikely spot, tucked away in a long, narrow street where the traditional *mashrabiya* balconies of one house almost touched the balconies on the other side. It was a modest wooden structure, its only distinguishing features a single stained-glass window and a red door. From the outside, it hardly looked like a church at all. That was probably the reason it had survived for so long.

Joane pushed the door open and stood in the entrance for a moment. It was her first visit, so she took her time entering the chapel and looking around. The chapel was already filling up with people. The congregation was a mixed crowd of freemen and slaves from across Europe, some of whom she recognized having seen them around the *bagnio* in the old quarter. There were English, Irish and French Protestants, Dutch reformists, German and Danish Lutherans, and others. She found a pew in the back next to a small rumpled Englishman.

"This your first time?" asked the little man with a smile. "Where are you from, love?"

"Ireland is my home, sir," replied Joane with a nervous smile. It felt strange and wonderful to be conversing in English again with an adult. She hadn't done that in months.

"Lovely place it is, love. Pray tell you're one of those English slaves from Baltimore?"

"Yes, I am. And yourself?"

"We were taken from the *Mary* by a heathen mob of pirates. We were on our way to Providence Island in Central America to start a colony of good Christian people when we were attacked."

"I'm so sorry, sir."

"Don't matter none. Do you know the reverend?"

"No, sir. This is my first time here."

"Well, we all love Reverend Spratt. You might not know it, but he was a slave here for a time before he was ransomed by an English captain in Leghorn (Livorno). He's a good Christian man and decided to stay on after they freed him."

They looked up as Reverend Spratt entered and nodded to the faithful before leading the crowd in a prayer from the altar. The prayer itself was reassuringly familiar, and Joane was just so happy to be in a church again. After she had kneeled down for the prayer, she noticed that the little man next to her had disappeared, as had several other parishioners. She found that very odd, but Reverend Spratt and the rest of the congregation appeared not to have taken any notice.

The reverend bid the congregation to join him in singing the first hymn. Joane loved to sing, and she had never heard a congregation sing so enthusiastically and so — well, loud. It was so loud that it took her a moment to become aware of the background noise. It sounded like sawing and hammering. Some kind of repair work was going on in the basement. The church was very old and obviously in need of repair, but it was quite unacceptable to make such a racket while people were trying to worship. Still, she seemed to be the only person bothered by the noise. The service continued with sermons, bible readings and Holy Communion along with the noise of sawing and hammering.

After that first service, Joane had even considered not returning, but she couldn't stay away for long. Her faith was too important to her, and the service was a weekly respite from living as a stranger in an alien land. She only wished that Maria would allow her boys to come with her. In the weeks that followed, she came every Sunday. She was still looked upon as a newcomer, so she knew better than to complain about the noise. She got to know the wee little man in the rumpled suit. His name was William Okeley. He was a slave too, but years ago, his *patron* had told him to earn his keep or he'd be thrown out. Algiers was no place for a homeless white man, so Okeley had gone to work in a succession of exhausting, menial jobs so he could pay his *patron's* rent. The first months were hard, but he managed to scrape together two dollars a month to stay under his *patron's* roof. It took a long time, and although he didn't make enough to buy his freedom outright, he did save enough to open a wine and tobacco shop and then branch out into a partnership manufacturing waterproof canvas clothes.

It was a lucrative business in a seafaring city like Algiers, and in spite of his eccentric appearance, William Okeley was an enterprising, intelligent man. Okeley and Joane would sit side by side in church, and every week he would disappear as soon as the service got started. It soon became clear to Joane that something was going on down there in the basement and it was better that she didn't ask what it was.

Felix & Caleb

The white spaniel ran out of the city gates, closely avoiding a kick from one of the guards. It had a white nose and body with brown spots on its flanks and head. It belonged to Murad Reis and was a Dutch hunting dog, a breed that was popular in the coastal communities of Holland. It ran quickly along the mole, avoiding the slave workers and the fishermen returning from a night at sea with their buckets and nets. A boy tried to stop the dog, but it snarled aggressively at him and he let it go.

There was a cortege of some fifteen foreign captives and numerous janissaries coming along the mole, led by a flamboyant corsair captain with a large red beard and plumed *bork*. They were returning from a raid with a rich prize and on their way to the palace of the Dey. In the middle of the cortege, there was a distinguished and very handsome woman holding the hands of her two children, accompanied by a nanny two steps behind carrying a baby and followed by numerous servants with suitcases and hat boxes. She was the wife of the Duke of Lucca, a tiny Italian duchy in Tuscany, and had been captured off the Italian coast as she sailed from Marseille. The Leghorn shipping agent in Algiers would be alerted within the hour, and the negotiations would begin for a huge ransom.

The white spaniel dodged the foot traffic and sniffed the air. There was a smell of fear on the captives as they trudged along the mole. The spaniel spotted the friendly face of the six-year-old boy, who patted it on the head and dropped to a knee to stroke its fur. The boy called to his mother.

"*Mamma, guard il cane*. Can we keep it? It is like Uncle Flavio's dog."

"*No, Marco, e impossible*. We cannot keep a dog. Let it go."

The cortege had slowed and was provoking jeers from the gawkers. A janissary pushed the dog away and tried to give it a solid kick to its flank but missed. The dog barked and ran off as the cortege moved forward again.

Even in the crowded harbour of Algiers, Murad's ship stood out. Felix and Caleb instantly recognized it and walked down towards the ship. They could see Marcellus at work with a carpenter on deck, but there was no sign of the captain. They were about to go on board when they heard a dog barking and a white spaniel bolted past them. Marcellus looked annoyed, then stepped over the gunwale and kneeled close to the dog, who licked his hand.

"Is that your dog?" asked Caleb as the boys approached.

"No," Marcellus replied brusquely, kneeling to calm the animal. "It belongs to the captain."

The boys watched curiously as Marcellus probed the dog's collar and came up with a tightly rolled sheet of parchment. He unrolled it and squinted to read the minuscule handwriting. His face darkened as he read the contents, then folded the parchment up and put it in his pocket. Felix could contain himself no longer.

"What is it?" he asked.

"The captain won't be coming today," said Marcellus, looking around anxiously. "He's in hiding."

"Hiding?" asked Felix.

"His villa was attacked last night and burned to the ground."

Felix looked shaken and Caleb confused. They couldn't imagine Captain Murad hiding from anybody.

"You boys better come aboard," said Marcellus, scooping up the panting spaniel. He led them to the captain's cabin, a place Felix remembered well. Marcellus ordered coffee from a servant and then motioned for the boys to sit down.

"What do you boys know about sailing?"

"Well, sir," Felix said, "we've been on boats all our lives—"

"—fishin' for pilchard," added Caleb with a wide grin.

"We're not looking for fishermen," said Marcellus, "but you know that already."

Felix and Caleb nodded. They had seen enough during the long voyage from Baltimore to understand what they were getting into. Felix was about to say as much when they were jolted by the impact of a ship hitting against their ship's hull. Marcellus was up in an instant, heading for the main deck. The boys followed, the spaniel right behind them.

A boat had smacked into Murad's xebec and five men had boarded the ship wielding sabres. Marcellus recognized the men as janissaries for hire. They had seized the carpenter and his assistant and quickly taken control of the ship. They ran into the captain's cabin and then started a search of crew quarters.

"Don't worry, boys," said Marcellus. "I know these men. They are Ali Bitchin's men."

"Where's the captain hiding?" asked a burly janissary as he thrust his sabre into Marcellus' face. "Where's Murad Reis?"

"I don't know," said Marcellus, pushing the blade away from his face. "He didn't come by this morning."

The white spaniel was barking at a janissary who disliked dogs and had taken a swing at it with his sabre. The dog jumped up and ran into the arms of Marcellus.

"Hey, be careful with the dog," said Marcellus.

Marcellus gave the spaniel to Felix for safekeeping. The dog licked Felix's face before he handed him off to Caleb, who loved dogs. The burly janissary had finished his search of the boat and called off his men. They quickly clambered back into their boat and rowed back to their berth in the inner harbour.

"Come on, lads," said Marcellus. "We've got work to do. The captain wants you to learn all there is to know about sailing a ship."

They returned to the captain's cabin with the dog and sat down at the low table. The servant had laid out the coffee and a bottle of Murad's private stock of jenever for Marcellus.

After dark, Marcellus called a dogcart for the two boys and sent them off on a mission. The dogcart drove them along the mole into the old city. As they were approaching *La Consulaire*, Felix noticed a second dogcart following them. They drove slowly along the dark streets into the *souk*, giving every opportunity for the men following them to move ahead, but the dogcart slowed when they slowed and remained behind them at all times. Many shops were closing up, but there were still a lot of people in the cafés and bars around the *bagnio*. As their driver turned suddenly into a narrow street, the two boys jumped down and ran into the *souk*. Their dogcart continued on, followed by Ali's surveillance team.

The boys were afraid they might have been spotted as they walked through the *souk* to the café that Marcellus had mentioned. They entered the café and sat down, and a waiter brought them two glasses of ale. After an hour, a bearded man arrived, paid for the ale and led the boys through the streets to a mosque. Their guide knocked on the door and a moment later, a mullah opened it. He dismissed the guide, lit a tallow candle with a taper, and led them upstairs to the residence.

Captain Murad stood in the darkened room, waiting for them.

"Hello, lads," said Murad, gesturing towards the mullah. "This is my good friend, Mullah Akeem. He has taken pity on me in my moment of need."

"*Assalamu alaikum*," said the boys to the mullah.

Mullah Akeem nodded.

"These are my Muslim boys, Akeem. I told you about them. This is Felix and his brother Caleb."

The mullah smiled at the boys and left the room.

"So what news have you?"

"Ali's men searched the ship this morning," said Felix, handing Murad a scrap of parchment. "Marcellus says he will sail for Tunis tonight."

Murad picked up the candle left by the mullah and read the note in the candlelight. He sank into a chair and motioned for the boys to sit with him. Felix and Caleb exchanged glances. This was not the Captain Murad they knew.

"What is going on, sir?" asked Felix. "Marcellus said you are in hiding."

"I have no choice," said Murad. "At least not for now. Algiers is run by the Dey, Felix. But he has no power, the power is in the hands of Admiral Ali Bitchin and the Diwan. Ali used to be a corsair raider like me, but now makes his money by extortion."

The boys were at a loss to understand the political life of Algiers. They had grown fond of the captain and felt sympathy for him after his fall from grace. He was no longer the proud corsair captain parading through the streets with chests of Spanish gold and silver. Times had changed and now he was a pariah in his own town. He had liberated them from the Saidi millstone and given them a better future, but what was to become of them now?

"These last few years," said Murad in a whisper, "I've tried to live quietly away from the Diwan and the petty jealousies of my colleagues, but nothing seems to work. I've put aside ambition and eschewed all vanities, but to no avail. Sometimes one just has to submit to the will of others, however outrageous, and continue on. There are battles in life that cannot be won."

Felix could never have imagined Captain Murad like this. The captain was sounding downright depressive when a twinkle suddenly appeared in his eyes. An attractive woman and a young boy stood in the shadows of an adjoining room and approached the circle of light from the candle. The boy scampered forward to give the captain a kiss. He smiled shyly at Felix and Caleb before the woman, obviously the boy's mother, chided him gently and led him out of the room. Murad watched them leave, the brief animation in his features disappearing as the woman softly closed the door behind them.

"I have something for you," Murad told the boys as he stood up and went to a nearby table, rummaging through the papers until he found what he wanted. He turned back to the boys and put two official documents written in Arabic on the table.

"These are your 'free cards'. They are invaluable. Do not lose them."

Felix picked one up and gave the other to Caleb.

"Sew them into your clothes and keep them on you at all times. They prove you are freed slaves."

Felix looked at his card, in stunned silence. He had picked up a good deal of Arabic from Grandma Saidi and could just about read the text. The free card bore the official seal and across the top, his name was written in Latin script along with his country, his height and his hair colour. Below that, there was a terse, official message declaring the bearer was not a slave and could not be put to work as one. The bearer was not allowed to leave the city, but with the payment of an additional tax, he could even do that.

Felix stole a glance at Caleb's card. Other than the name and personal details, they were identical. They were both freemen, and they had the documentation to prove it.

"Thank you, sir," he stammered, momentarily overcome. He heard Caleb echo the same words, and from the sound of his voice, his brother was fighting back tears. It was incredible that the captain, even in the midst of fighting for his life, had found a way to keep his word and do the impossible.

"I expect things will be back to normal soon," said Murad. "In the meantime, you'll be staying here with the mullah."

"Are we in hiding too?" asked Caleb, his eyes wide.

"Yes," Murad told him. "It is too dangerous otherwise. I will be gone for a few days, and *Insha'Allah,* I will be successful in turning the tide. While I'm gone, you must not go out or be seen. Ali has spies everywhere."

Thirty-three

Emma

The workshop was always busy, with young men filing, sawing, forging, casting and polishing all kinds of metals. They made silverware such as plates, cups, goblets, and utensils. They made gold rings, brooches, earrings, bracelets and necklaces. There was a huge demand for gold and silver jewellery in Algiers. The work required a great deal of skill, and it took years for the average apprentice to master.

Emma had a good eye and a talent for putting the finishing touches on various pieces of jewellery. She would often finish the work of an apprentice, in addition to keeping the register of sales. She soon became a valuable asset to the shop. In her second year, her friend Agron disappeared. He did not return from a voyage to Funchal in the Madeira Islands. Emma went down to the port to enquire and learned from his shipmates that he had been killed during a skirmish with the Spanish. It was a common fact of life among janissary families. The breadwinner would often end up in a shallow grave in a foreign land or his body dumped at sea.

It was during this sad time that Emma started her search in earnest for her mother and children. Phoebe would now be twelve years old while Eunice would be going on ten and Dinah nine. Slave girls worked long hours doing housework, making beds, washing clothes and cleaning kitchens. When the girls were twelve or older, they would be sold as wives to older men or ransomed off if they were still Christians. Emma discovered that the rich would often rotate a slave girl through their various family households, depending on the workload. This made them very hard to find.

Emma had paid a bribe to a contact in the palace and obtained a list of well-to-do slave owners. On her days off, she visited the homes of these people, looking for her daughters. *Where had they gone?* She asked herself the same question every night before she went to sleep. *They couldn't be too far away,* she thought. *She just had to find them.*

On her excursions, Emma always avoided official visits at front doors and preferred gathering information discreetly at back doors from the kitchen and servant staff. She would ask the names and ages of any Christian girls working in the house and when they had started work. This was usually enough to eliminate most of them. One day, as she was leaving a large manor house, she spotted several young girls being led by a servant to a mosque nearby. One of the girls looked foreign with her blonde hair and light complexion. At the mosque, she learned the girls were attending classes in Islam and how to become good Muslim women. There were some twenty girls in each class, taught by an older woman. Emma waited until the end of the class to see the faces of the girls as they came out of the mosque.

The mosque was fairly large, and Emma knew there might be other groups of girls attending these classes. She returned several times a week in the hope of identifying her daughters, but they never appeared. After a while, she realized she was spending too much of her time searching for families living within the city walls and not enough in the surrounding towns.

It wasn't long before her boss noted her constant comings and goings and had a word with her. They sat in his office drinking tea at the end of the workday. Ariel wore thick glass spectacles and had short, curly hair under his yarmulke.

"What's wrong, Emma?" he asked, genuinely concerned.

Emma remained silent, drinking her tea.

"I'm sorry to ask you this, but you seem distracted and your work is suffering. I am not complaining, I am just stating the obvious, my dear."

"I miss my girls, Ariel — and my mother," said Emma. "I miss them terribly."

"How old would your girls be now?"

"Phoebe is the oldest. She would be twelve."

"You realize, Emma, that they could be anywhere. In Constantine, Tlemcen, even Tunis."

"Yes, I know, but I have to try to find them."

"It's been what, four years since you arrived here."

"I have a list of houses with Christian girls, Ariel. I've gone to most of them."

Ariel looked alarmed.

"You must be careful, Emma," he warned. "The families might complain to the authorities — you could be arrested."

"I do it very discreetly," she assured him. "They don't know who I am. I never go to the front door."

"Still, it could be dangerous for you," said Ariel, shaking his head. He knew exactly the kind of complaint these people could be expected to make.

Ariel's wife had died in childbirth with her third child. He had two older boys to look after and they were well integrated into Muslim society. He worried about his reputation in the community and took on the responsibility of squiring Emma around the outlying towns as she searched for her girls and mother. They travelled in a dogcart and Emma always went to the back doors of the well-to-do to inquire of their kitchen staff. They also waited outside mosques for the Christian girls to emerge from their classes. After a month of visits, often accompanied by Ariel's two boys and festive meals in the small towns, Ariel was convinced that Emma's search was a waste of time.

"You cannot continue, Emma," he told her. "The longer you keep this up, the more distressed you'll become."

"I'm not distressed, Ariel. I'm persistent. I just don't give up easily."

"Look at you," said Ariel, throwing up his arms in exasperation. "You have this fire in your eye. It is eating you up, devouring you from the inside. You have to give it up."

"Enough," she said defiantly. "I will go alone as I did before."

Ariel sighed, not trusting himself to speak. After what seemed to them both like a very long time, Ariel raised his eyes to look at her.

"I will go with you," he said, "one last time. Sometimes, Emma, I have to wonder if you are my slave or I am yours. We will go and we will look and it will be the last time."

This did not go down well with Emma, who categorically refused to go on any more trips with Ariel. She would go alone for however long it took.

Ariel renewed his offer the following week, and Emma reluctantly accepted it. They left in the early morning and did a sweep of the towns east of Algiers. The first town was small, and as always, Ariel waited patiently in the cart while Emma canvassed the back doors of the few houses that looked like they could afford slave girls. The second town was larger, and they arrived just in time for the end of classes at the mosque. Ariel stayed with the dogcart while Emma stationed herself near the door.

Emma's heart thudded with excitement when she saw several Christian girls coming out, heading off to join their Muslim chaperones. She hadn't expected to see so many in one place. She looked closely at them as they passed, but none of them looked even remotely like Phoebe. Then they were gone, and her spirits plummeted. She was turning away when a lovely dark-haired girl, tall and slim, appeared in the doorway. She walked past Emma without even a glancing look. She was obviously hurrying to catch up with the others, but in that instant, Emma knew. She was astounded and could hardly move to get the girl's attention.

"Phoebe!" she cried out. "Phoebe, is that you?"

The girl whirled around to face her, and Emma's heart literally skipped a beat.

"Phoebe, it's me. I'm your mother!"

Phoebe wore a white haik and a veil. She looked annoyed by the presence before her.

"Go away," Phoebe cried. "I don't want to see you."

She looked like she was going to run away before Emma had time to talk to her, so she grabbed her arm.

"I'm your mother, Phoebe — I love you!" said Emma, pleading for a moment with her daughter. She was devastated after having dreamt of this meeting for so long.

"Let go of me," said Phoebe, trying to pull away. "You are no one anymore. I have a mother and a family. I don't need you."

"Where are they?" Emma held fast. "Where are your sisters and my mother?"

Phoebe stopped trying to pull away, and her voice softened, becoming a whisper.

"Grandma died in the first year, ma. I'm sorry. The work was too much for her."

They stared at each other through tear-filled eyes. Just for a brief moment, they were mother and daughter again. Then the moment was gone.

"And your sisters?" Emma asked finally.

"I have no idea," said Phoebe. She gently pulled her arm free from Emma's grasp. "I have to go."

Phoebe turned away and headed across the street.

Emma looked devastated as she watched Phoebe cross to her Muslim chaperone, an old woman dressed in black, who had been watching them from a distance. Emma ran into the street.

"Phoebe," she cried. "Where is grandma buried?"

Phoebe stopped walking and turned slowly to look at her mother.

"Where is she buried, dearest heart?"

Phoebe glanced at her minder standing near the dogcart, and then looked back at Emma.

"She was buried a Muslim, ma. They took good care of her. She's buried over there in the cemetery, far left corner."

"Thank you," said Emma, as she looked at her daughter's minder and her tone stiffened. She shouted: "I'm your mother, Phoebe. Don't you ever forget it!"

Phoebe glanced back at her mother, then she climbed into the cart and was gone. Emma crossed the road and waved to Ariel before entering the cemetery. She understood that her mother could not receive a Christian burial in a Muslim cemetery, so Phoebe's new family had buried her as a Muslim woman, which was the best they could do.

Joane

Joane's estrangement from her own family had started as the Bouzianes were preparing for the Eid al-Adha holiday, the 'Feast of Sacrifice' day that marked the end of *Hajj*, the five-day pilgrimage that all Muslims must undertake once in their lifetime. The Bouziane family went to the mosque for the celebration, but this year the school had organized the distribution of sacrificial goat meat in their neighbourhood. The Bouziane children had been recruited to go house to house with packages of meat and a collection box for donations. Maria had invited Malcolm and Liam to go with her own children.

"Eid al-Adha. Can you tell us what it means, Malcolm?" asked Maria while they were having dinner.

"It's the story of Abraham and his son Isaac, Maria," replied Malcolm in perfect Arabic. "Abraham was going to sacrifice Isaac on the mount, but Allah stopped him and he sacrificed a ram instead."

"Good, Malcolm," said Maria, nodding.

Joane looked at her son with pride. The story was the same in both religions.

"That's wonderful, Malcolm," said Joane.

"We learned it at the mosque, ma," said Malcolm.

"I'm sure you did, but I remember reading the same story to you on the ship. You don't remember?"

Malcolm shook his head and Joane felt a pang of regret. She had often read to her boys during that horrible voyage, but the child had no memory of it.

"We're going to celebrate the festival with Maria and her children," said Liam.

It was the first Joane had heard of it.

"Can I go with you boys?" asked Joane.

It was a simple question, and she expected her boys to welcome her participation. Her heart sank as she saw the boys glance at Maria for approval.

"You can't, ma," said Liam. "You're not a Muslim."

"It's only for Muslims," added Malcolm.

"He's right, Joane," Maria told her, smiling at the boys. "It's only for Muslims."

Joane glanced around the table and felt immensely tired as if the lifeblood had been squeezed out of her. *Don't they have any respect for me?* Joane asked herself. *I'm their mother. I brought them into this world.* She wanted to scream at Maria and the boys.

From that day on, Joane felt like she had ceased to exist in the Bouziane household. She was just another seamstress on Maria's staff, living in the shadow of her previous life. She continued to go every Sunday to Reverend Spratt's service at the Anglican Church of the Holy Trinity, but now she found herself pushing the red door of the church open on a Wednesday morning. She didn't know why she had come. She was supposed to go to the *souk* to buy some much-needed fabric for the shop but had come to the church instead. She felt very much alone and lost.

The church was empty and silent. She walked down the aisle to the altar and sat in the nearest pew. She felt better already as she peered at her book of hours. It was terce, so she started to recite her prayers when she heard a sudden clatter of footsteps behind her and turned to see a man burst into the church from the cellar, followed by a cloud of black smoke. He stopped and bent over, his hands on his knees and his shoulders heaving in a paroxysm of coughing.

Joane got up from the pew, tucking her precious prayer book in her pocket, and she went to the man's aid. His coughing subsided, and he stood up. The top of his head barely came past her shoulder and even though his face was covered in soot, she realized immediately who he was.

"Mister Okeley?"

The wee little man in the rumpled suit took a step back, his eyes widening in surprise.

"Missus Broadbrook," said Okeley. "I'm sorry, you startled me."

There were more footsteps on the stairs and a moment later, another man stumbled into the room, coughing and fighting for breath. The smoke was thicker than before, and it took him a moment to recover before he joined them in the aisle. He shot a quizzical look at Okeley.

"This is my good friend, John Randall," said Okeley, his tone more formal. "John and I have a shop in the *souk* where we sell clothes."

Joane smiled nervously, her eyes on the growing cloud of smoke flooding the interior of the church. It seemed an odd time for introductions.

Okeley followed her gaze.

"Oh, that," said Okeley, as he turned back and gave her a reassuring smile. "No reason for alarm, my dear. We're burning pitch in the cellar."

"To stop water from leaking in," Randall added.

Joane could stand it no longer. She brushed past the two men and fled the church for the fresh air outside.

Thirty-four

Felix & Caleb

After Captain Murad returned a week later, Felix and Caleb were able to step out into the open and resume their training with Marcellus. The captain never mentioned the cause of his quarrel with Admiral Ali Bitchin, who was by far the richest man in Algiers, and was building a huge mosque in the Zoudj-Aïoun district. Whatever it was, the captain had been successful in negotiating a truce and could now move openly about Algiers and resume his activities at the port. The boys understood none of it. They were burning with questions, but it was clear to them that the captain had no desire to talk about this dark moment in his life.

Marcellus related the local gossip about how Bitchin had wooed Princess Lalla Lallahoum, the daughter of Ben Ali, Sultan of the Kabyle people, with beautiful Persian carpets, silks and brocades of the Levant, diamonds from India and even gold from Peru, but still the princess had refused his offer of marriage. She had instead demanded that her suitor build a mosque to prove his faith, which surprisingly Bitchin had agreed to do.

The boys returned to Murad's xebec for their training. They were sensible enough to realize that fishing for pilchard was one thing and sailing into battle with corsairs was quite another. Wisely, they did what they were told and said little. Finally, it was time for a real test of their abilities. Their training on shore could only go so far, and Marcellus told them there were things that could only be learned at sea.

In the last week of September, Captain Murad's xebec weighed anchor and left the port, followed by a smaller xebec under the command of Captain Marcellus. Felix and Caleb were ordinary jacktars on Marcellus' ship. They were there to do all the tough physical jobs on a ship, from helping with the rigging, scrubbing the decks, repairing sails, manning the bilge pumps, hauling powder and ammunition to the gunners, and other jobs. They got on well with Marcellus and his first mate Allaire, a tough-looking French *renegado* with a scarred face. They were both intelligent, practical mariners, and encouraged the boys to do their best. The xebec carried the usual complement of janissaries and galley slaves, so the boys lived in the very cramped crew quarters in the bowels of the ship. They were reminded of their first voyage as captives on Murad's ship, but now they were freemen, spending their days in the open air and embarking on a great adventure.

Captain Murad was on another slaving mission along the coast of Sicily, which was an area under the protection of the Knights Hospitaller, also known as the Order of Knights of the Hospital of Saint John of Jerusalem. Their base was in Malta and they patrolled the Eastern Mediterranean to protect Christian merchant shipping from corsairs going to and coming from the Levant. Over the years, their moral decline had become self-evident. With dwindling revenues from their European sponsors, the Knights had turned to piracy. They plundered all manner of ships and sold the cargo for profit, just like their adversaries, the Barbary corsairs.

The corsairs sailed east along the coast, hoping to find some local maritime traffic to prey upon on their way. It was an uneventful voyage until they arrived at Cap Blanc, the northernmost point in Tunisia, where they planned to sail to the northeast around the western point of Sicily looking for slaves and plunder. Sicily and Naples were under the control of the King of Spain and the Knights were often seen in the area.

As they approached the cape, a storm was visible on the horizon and the wind had picked up, blowing from the northeast. Captain Murad decided to put into the Bay of Bizerte and its lagoon to wait out the storm when they sighted three ships flying the Knights Hospitaller flag heading their way and seeking refuge in the same bay. Murad was tacking to the southeast with Marcellus following in his wake when the enemy ships, with the advantage of the weather gauge, came at them out of the storm.

To avoid the enemy, Murad's xebec heeled away to the leeward going northwest, followed by Marcellus' ship. They could not retreat downwind much without risking running aground in the shallow water. At the very worst moment, the eighteen-pound bow chaser on the leading enemy caravel dismasted Murad's ship with a single shot. The ball smashed through the mainmast and tore a hole in the poop deck. The loss of sail slowed the xebec considerably. Murad had no choice but to go to the oars and try to make for the shallow waters of the lagoon. The enemy ships were coming on fast while the oarsmen struggled to pick up the pace. Murad's only hope was that the shallow draught of his ship would allow him to go where the Knight's caravels could not follow.

Marcellus still had the wind and quickly overtook Murad's vessel, heading northwest. As the Knights' ships turned their attention to Murad's xebec, Marcellus heeled his ship to the southeast and came at the caravels as they went after Murad heading for the lagoon. They were on a collision course with the caravels as the gunner on their twelve-pound bow chaser scored a hit with the second of two shots, destroying the mizzen sail on the closest caravel.

They were closing fast. Felix and his brother were hauling ammunition to the bow chaser when they were jostled astern by the janissaries scrambling forward to the prow. There was a shattering noise as the two ships collided and the knights swarmed aboard the xebec. They had the weight of numbers, and the janissaries were thrown back in a wild melee. It was an unforgettable scene. The knights surged forward in their chain mail with a white cross on their black cloaks brandishing heavy broadswords in a battle to the death with their avowed enemies in their red tunics wielding deadly yatagan sabres.

From the stern of the ship, Felix and Caleb could see the two enemy caravels in the distance pursuing Captain Murad into the lagoon. There was going to be a huge battle inside the lagoon, but Marcellus could do nothing for the captain with the hand-to-hand combat raging on his own deck. The knights were battle-hardened combatants fighting for God and their own purses. Their chain mail was proof against the most telling blow from a janissary sabre, and they relentlessly pushed the outnumbered janissaries back. It was turning into a slaughter.

"Turn that gun around!" bellowed Marcellus, fighting his way through the crowd and shoving Felix, Caleb, and the other crew members back towards the stern chaser.

"Grapeshot," he yelled.

Felix looked around and found the bags of grapeshot nestled underneath the bags of gunpowder near the gunwale. He grabbed a bag of each and ran to the gunner. The gun normally pointed aft, but Marcellus, Caleb and the others had wrestled the heavy gun around, reversing it on its pedestal so that its muzzle pointed directly down the centre of the ship. Marcellus knew they were losing the battle. Momentum was everything, and the knights had seized it with their initial rush across the deck, now slick with blood and littered with the dead and dying. The janissaries had been pushed back amidships and could not hold on for long.

Felix had practised loading the gun several times, but never in the heat of battle. There were several steps in the process, and this was no time to make a mistake. He helped the gunner load the gun, forcing himself to shut everything out. He rammed the grapeshot down the barrel and the gun was ready to fire. He was pulling back on the ramrod, thinking to tamp down the bag once more to be sure, when he glanced up and saw Marcellus fire a pistol straight at him.

Instead of dying where he stood, Felix was knocked to the deck by the massive weight of a knight collapsing on him from behind. The knight had broken through the crowd of fighting men, intent on killing Felix before he finished loading the cannon. Marcellus had seen the man rear up behind Felix, his bloody broadsword poised to split the boy from his shoulder down to his waist.

For a moment, the smoke obscured his view, and he did not know whom he had killed, the towering knight or the boy. Finally, the smoke dissipated enough to reveal the ramrod still jammed in the gun barrel and Felix staggering to his feet. He yanked the ramrod free and then sidestepped clear of the muzzle and raised his arms high. That was signal enough for the gunner.

Marcellus had done this only once before under Murad's order. He remembered what it had cost, but there was no other way to save his ship. There was sudden movement at the aft hatch, just forward of where he stood, and he was relieved to see his first mate Allaire signal his readiness. Marcellus gave the order, and the cannon roared. Grapeshot tore through the bodies of the knights and the janissaries on deck, killing friend and foe in one decisive blast. The shock value was enormous and Marcellus did not hesitate.

"Swords!" he screamed, dropping the pistol and charging through the smoke into the carnage on deck. Allaire and five crewmen wielding sabres erupted from the hatch and joined Marcellus in a headlong rush to clear the deck. It was a terrible butchery as Marcellus and Allaire hacked at the stunned survivors strewn across the deck, methodically killing any knight still breathing and exhorting the surviving janissaries to join in the slaughter.

Minutes later, it was over. The captain of the caravel had seen enough and poled his ship clear of the xebec, following his colleagues into the lagoon. Marcellus gave the order to turn the ship to the northwest and head for Cap Blanc, knowing he was in no shape to do anything but limp back to Algiers.

"It had to be done," said Allaire. "We would all be dead if you had not done it."

Marcellus remembered saying much the same thing to a distraught Captain Murad, all those years ago, as he observed the slaughter on deck and the shattered stern. The stern chaser was long gone, catapulted back into the sea by the recoil of the cannon blast.

"May God forgive me," murmured Marcellus as he looked at Felix and Caleb sitting side by side on the scorched deck in a state of shock. Marcellus had seen that look many times before, after violent confrontations with the enemy.

"You did well," he told the boys.

They seemed not to have heard. Like everyone else, they were covered in blood splatter and the only way to tell one from the other was the powder burns blackening Felix's left side. The blast from the cannon had nearly hurled him over the rail, and he was lucky to be alive.

Marcellus had no time for tears. The foredeck was covered in dead men. He ordered the crew to throw the bodies of the dead knights into the sea and scrub down the deck. The dead janissaries and crew would be returned to Algiers for burial. It would be a grim voyage with so many casualties among his own men. Marcellus wanted nothing more than to retreat to his cabin and close the door, but one of the many things Murad had taught him was that he needed to look to his crew and his ship first, regardless of what he wanted for himself. He turned when he heard the boys talking.

"The captain didn't choose the battlefield," said Caleb to his brother.

"No, he didn't," said Felix. "He barely knew his enemy."

"But he moved fast and did the unexpected, Felix."

"Yeah, you could say that."

"He headed for the lagoon," said Caleb with tears in his eyes.

At that moment, Marcellus realized something about the boys. The captain had been a father figure for them. He had looked out for them when no one else had and the boys loved and admired him.

"Why the long faces, lads?" asked Marcellus. "The captain has been at this for a long time. In a fight, his janissaries will serve him well. They may very well get away."

"You think so, sir?" asked Felix.

"Sure, the captain is a fighter. He won't give up easily."

Marcellus told them that the captain still had a fighting chance to defend himself and his men in the lagoon if they could only get ashore before the knights boarded his ship.

When the news of the sea battle against the Knights arrived at the port of Algiers, there was a general lamentation around town. Captain Murad was a legend and had helped make Algiers immensely rich over the years. Ordinary people were convinced that a turn of bad luck had struck the town and they might never recover.

Not a week had passed before Captain Marcellus was sent off on another mission by the pasha and he took the Gunter brothers with him. When they returned two weeks later, Felix and Caleb heard the bad news. Murad and his crew had been captured by the knights. There were alive and languishing in a prison in Malta.

Thirty-five

Besse

The café in Algiers was full of rumours about Captain Murad's fate. It was located in the *souk* not far from the *bagnio* and it served coffee, tea, wine, ale, hard liquor and traditional Algerian food dishes to local merchants, sailors and construction workers. Besse Touati, with her fiery red hair and youthful looks, stood at the bar and attracted lots of men to her stall. They sat there quietly drinking wine and *aguardiente* and admiring the pretty foreign woman who worked long hours serving customers and watching the cash box.

Besse was free of the household drudgery at the Touati estate, even though she remained the fourth wife of Mustafa. She enjoyed her independence and had made friends with many *renegadoes* in town. She lived in a flat near the bar and never returned to the estate near Baba Hassen. The café had belonged to Mustafa's family for years and was losing money when Farid offered it to her. She had put the deed in the name of her dead father, Robert Peeters, and gave it an English name. She called it the Good Luck Café (or the Café *Hazun Saeid)* named after a pub in Baltimore.

The café was soon a huge success. Every week, Farid arrived to collect his share of the cash receipts and was amazed at how Besse had turned the business around. Farid was making good money and was no longer under threat for his philandering at the estate. He got on well with Besse now that she was free and independent. One evening he even revealed the family secret when he told Besse that Mustapha had been rendered impotent as a young man due to a childhood injury and his condition had not improved over the years. He told her that it was important for a man in Mustafa's position to have a large family, and so Farid had offered to help his brother found a family. He was proud to be the father of all of his brother's children. He went on to tell Besse that not a single one of Mustafa's wives had never complained about the arrangement. Farid was the man behind the scenes and the de facto father of his brother's children.

Mustafa, on the other hand, had always been ashamed of his condition and, to show off the virility of the Touati clan, he had chosen Besse as his fourth wife. Besse was curious and asked Farid what his plans had been for her. Farid laughed as he told her that he had planned to seduce her and impregnate her, just like he had done with the other wives.

In Baba Hassen, the storm clouds were gathering and threatening the very fabric of the Touati family. The women were not happy with Farid's arrangement with Besse. Hamia expressed her unrelenting hatred of the 'little whore' who was enjoying her life in the city while she and the other wives slaved away at the estate. Hamia had convinced them that Farid no longer loved them and favoured Besse, giving her expensive presents. Jealousy festered among the women and they would often refuse to have sex with Farid as a form of protest. He shrugged it off, but the wives had much to be jealous about. Besse had a degree of independence beyond their imagining, and Farid, ever the philanderer, was strongly attracted to the young English woman. He had hoped over time his business relationship with her would somehow lead to her bed, but Besse was having none of it. She kept away from him and made her own life in town. She was constantly courted by the denizens of her café, many of whom were handsome janissaries and sailors.

It had started badly. In her first month at the café, she had been attacked by two young men with knives. She had been closing up one night when they came at her out of the alley. She bolted before they could get their hands on her and ran into the darkened *souk*, looking for a hiding place. She darted into a shop near the café and hid behind the counter. One man entered the shop and stood at the counter listening for sounds and then moved away. Besse managed to slip out of the shop and run into the street, where she stumbled into a party of drunk janissaries who recognized her from the café. They were only too happy to help a damsel in distress. They were just fanning out to find her assailants when her two pursuers ran out of the alley and straight into the men.

It was a colossal mismatch, and the only reason the assailants survived the beating was that Besse had her suspicions. She invited the janissaries back to her café for a drink to thank them for their gallantry on the condition that they take her assailants captive rather than just killing them outright. She was well known in Algiers, and estranged or not, she remained a married woman, the fourth wife of Mustafa Touati. That made her as untouchable as a woman could get in the old city.

She sent a servant to get word to Farid while she waited for him with the men at the bar. It was a calculated risk. By Besse's reckoning, the only person who could kill a Touati in Algiers and expect to get away with it was another Touati. There was a chance that it was Farid, who was behind the plot, but with her bodyguard of six burly janissaries, she knew she was safe, at least for the night. When Farid arrived in the early hours of the morning, he took one look at the terrified young men and recognized them immediately. They were gardeners at the Touati estate — Besse had thought there was something familiar about them. There was no doubt in Farid's mind. They had been hired by Hamia.

Killing the young men would serve no purpose, other than to alert Mustafa that something was dangerously amiss with his domestic situation. Much to the disappointment of the janissaries, Farid let the men go, along with a stern warning not to listen to his crazy sister-in-law ever again. Besides, thought Farid, good gardeners were hard to find.

That was the last Besse heard of Hamia. She died in a plague outbreak along with her husband Mustafa and most of the Touati children the following winter. Some 30,000 people perished that year as the disease took a terrible toll on Algiers, Tunis and other towns across North Africa. After the death of Mustafa, Besse inherited a sizeable sum of money from the estate and bought out Farid's share of the café.

As a free woman and recent widow, she thought about getting married to someone her own age. She fell in love with a French *renegado* who worked in the cloth trade and was often seen in her café. They were married six months later in the Muslim faith.

Emma

Emma felt the hot flush of amniotic fluid as her water broke. She was eight months pregnant and standing at the counter talking to a customer. Ariel rushed over to provide support and urgently called an apprentice to go across the road and get the midwife. Ariel led her upstairs to their private quarters.

Ariel had married Emma not long after her search for the girls came to an end. The marriage had been a small Jewish ceremony in the tightly knit Jewish community of Algiers. She had converted to Judaism at the request of the family. Ariel's people were Sephardic Jews who had been expelled from Spain in 1492 and had settled in the Maghreb under Muslim and Ottoman patronage. They felt at home in Algiers, but they knew how things could change very quickly for people of their faith.

Emma gave birth to a son. She was thirty-five years old and Daniel was her fourth child. She took a week off work and rested in the spacious apartment above the shop. Ariel was rapturous about the arrival of his son, as was his family. She had only just returned to work when she had a visitor. That in itself was unusual. She spent more and more time working on the accounts and ordering supplies, so she had less direct contact with the public.

"Hello, Emma," said Sally Gunter, standing at the counter talking to a young apprentice. She was fashionably dressed and looked relaxed and confident.

Emma was astonished to see Sally in the shop. Sally had never forgiven her for her behaviour on board the ship, and they had not parted as friends. She was the last person Emma expected to see. She looked at her nemesis for a long moment. Beneath her air of confidence, Sally had clearly dreaded this meeting and was distracted by the noise of the workshop with so many young men sanding, polishing, filing, and sawing metals.

"What do you want, Sally?" Emma asked coldly.

"This is my first time here. What lovely rings and brooches you have," said Sally, admiring the collection under the glass counter.

"What can I do for you, Sally?"

"You know I work at the bakery?"

"Yes, I've heard."

"Look, Emma. I've come here because I have some information

that you will want to hear. I also think it is time we were friends after all the bad blood."

"What is it, Sally?"

"I heard you got married again and have a new baby."

"Yes, it's true. We have a lovely boy. We call him Daniel."

"That's wonderful," Sally murmured absently, her eyes on the counter again. "I've come about Eunice."

"Eunice?" blurted Emma in disbelief.

"You know I'm the manager over at the bakery, so I see a lot of things. We get orders from all over town. Sometimes it's just a name on paper with an address."

"Yes," said Emma, eager to hear more.

"Well, we got an order last week from a regular client. It was just a scrap of paper. The writing was not very clear, and it looked like it was signed by a child. I could just make the name. It was signed Eunice."

"My Eunice?" Emma gasped. "You think it's her?"

"I don't know, Emma — but I knew I had to tell you. The name is uncommon. She has to be English with a name like that."

"Thank you, Sally. Thank you so much."

"Here," said Sally, pressing a scrap of paper into Emma's hand. "Here's the address of the house. I figure she works in the kitchen."

Emma looked at the address and then suddenly embraced Sally, who was speechless.

"Thank you, Sally," she said, wiping a tear away.

"Well, let me know if it's her. Bye, now."

Sally smiled at her as she left the shop.

Emma couldn't wait to visit the house. The next day, she dressed in a cloak and veil and set off with Ariel to the address Sally had given her. Ariel parked the dogcart down the street at a distance from the imposing house to avoid being observed by the owners. Emma took a deep breath before knocking on the kitchen door. She waited impatiently and when no one came to open it, she knocked again, harder this time. After a moment, a servant opened the door and ushered her inside.

"I'm looking for Eunice," she said in Arabic.

The boy put down the tray he was holding and went away to look for the girl while Emma waited on the threshold, her heart pounding, not sure what to expect. Then she saw her. The girl was ten years old, slim, with dark hair.

"Hello," she said in Arabic. "Can I help you?"

Eunice obviously did not recognize her own mother.

"Eunice," said Emma, her hands shaking as she removed her veil. She spoke in English. "I'm your mother."

Emma held her breath.

"Ma, is that you?" cried Eunice.

"Yes, my dear."

Emma lost her footing and collapsed, sobbing with joy as Eunice ran to her.

"It's me. I've been looking for you forever," said Emma.

She had looked everywhere for her daughters. She had found Phoebe, who at first had refused any contact with her, but had finally accepted to accompany her on a visit to her grandma's grave.

It had been a rainy day in the summer and the two women had huddled together under an umbrella near Ariel and the boys. Emma had put her arm around Phoebe, and her daughter had melted into her embrace. The frosty tone of their first meeting was gone.

Okeley

In the cellar of the Anglican Church, several men attempted to fashion a boat out of waterproofed canvas. William Okeley had designed the boat to take a small group of slaves north across the sea to Spain or Majorca. Today was the day of final preparations, and he had called a meeting to decide on their state of readiness. There were two carpenters, a sailor, a bricklayer, and two washermen employed washing and drying clothes down by the seashore outside the city walls. Reverend Spratt had been recruited as a marine consultant and was curious to see how the construction was going. *It's madness,* thought Okeley, *and I'm the maddest of them all.*

In truth, Okeley had a good life in Algiers, even if he was a slave. He had reached an uneasy truce with his master, helped by the fact that he had made the man a lot of money. In return, he had become more independent than most, but he was getting on in years and he desperately wanted to go home. During the planning stage, Okeley and his collaborators realized that they would have to smuggle the boat down to the shore in sections. The men had found a twelve-foot piece of wood for the keel, which they had sawed into two equal lengths because they couldn't reasonably hide it in their clothes as they left the city. The keel would have to be assembled in two six-foot lengths and joined together. The same principle applied to the ribs of the boat. Each rib would be in three sections, joined with nails inserted through holes. For the hull of the boat, they had stretched stout canvas twice over the frame and waterproofed it with hot pitch, tar and tallow.

Spratt examined the boat to see whether any of the seams in the canvas would leak water. He had a pitcher of water in one hand and a crucifix in the other. He said a prayer before he began testing. The pitch had been applied to the canvas to prevent leaks, but the men soon discovered that portions of the canvas needed more waterproofing.

"Well, what do you think, reverend?" asked Okeley.

"It should float all right, but you will need to do a final test before setting forth."

"Of course, reverend," said the little man. "Let's take it apart again."

The following Sunday, Joane arrived at the church and spotted Okeley in a pew. He waved her over.

"Missus Broadbrook, how are you?" asked Okeley cheerfully.

"Well, I was thinking of asking you the same, Mister Okeley. The last time I saw you, you were coughing something fierce from the smoke in the cellar."

"A horrible job it was, milady. We won't be layin' pitch no more for the reverend. No more hammerin'. It's all done."

"Good," said Joane as the reverend arrived.

There were a lot of happy, smiling faces in the congregation that day. Reverend Spratt started the service with a special prayer for all the sailors on the high seas who risked their lives in the hope of seeing their loved ones again. Joane glanced at Okeley, who was listening to the words with an enraptured smile on his face. He looked quite mad. She thought of the old phrase from Corinthians 11:19: "For ye suffer fools gladly, seeing ye yourselves are wise."

By the end of June, everything was ready. Two men hid the sections of the boat in their dirty laundry and carried them to a hiding place near a small hill half a mile from the sea. It took a full week just to get all the parts out of the city unobserved. On the night of the 30th of June, they were ready to go. The small group assembled in the dark near the hiding place and retrieved the sections of the boat. They carefully assembled the parts and put notches in the ribs and timbers for the oarlocks.

Once the boat was assembled, they hoisted it on their shoulders and carried it down to the shore. They had brought a supply of bread and goatskins filled with water for the voyage. They carefully laid the frail craft in the water and checked the seams for leakage. There were no leaks, and the boat seemed to hold up well in the waves. Okeley, the smallest man in the group, climbed into the boat. He was followed by a second man, and the boat appeared to float beautifully. The men were ecstatic. Then all seven men clambered into the boat and it sank. The small dinghy couldn't support the weight of the seven men.

"What are we going to do?" asked Okeley.

"Bloody hell, William," growled one man. "We've put a lot of work into this boat. What do we do now?"

"There's nothing for it," said Okeley. "We're too many. Two of us will have to stay behind."

He braced himself for a fierce argument, but for a few moments, there was nothing but a stunned silence. Then he heard a muffled grunt from the washerman, who was most nervous about going to sea in such a small craft. He waved his hand at the men and started for the shore. He was followed moments later by the second washerman. Okeley breathed a sigh of relief as the remaining men climbed into the boat. There were a few gruff farewells to their friends on shore, and off they went. They pulled away from the beach, rowing as fast as they could. Soon they were a mile or two out beyond the mole. Their biggest fear was to be spotted by a ship coming into the port.

They felt they were already making good headway north, but as the sun came up, they saw that they had barely cleared the bay. The wind had been pushing them back towards the shore, and it took several frantic hours of rowing before the city walls finally disappeared from view. The sun was merciless in spite of the breeze. It was then that they started to discover numerous small leaks along the canvas bottom. The boat leaked enough that they had to bail constantly just to stay afloat. Another disappointment was the store of bread which had gotten soaked in seawater during the night and the goatskins of water had become contaminated with salt. They would have no choice but to eat the bread and drink the water.

They headed north, using a marine compass that one of the men had brought with him. They took bearings each day and navigated by the stars at night, but by the fifth day, they were ready to give up. They were so dehydrated and burned by the sun that they had stopped rowing and were too exhausted to do anything but bail. Then one morning, a sea turtle broke the surface near the boat. The men scrambled to catch it, nearly capsizing the boat in their clumsy effort to haul it aboard. They chopped off its head and drank its blood. They ate the liver and flesh, which they divided up between them.

The turtle was a godsend. Without the turtle, they would not have lasted another day. It restored their strength and spirits, and they started rowing again. Later that day, they spied land on the horizon. They rowed all night and into the next day, finally coming ashore on the island of Majorca. It had taken them six days to row two hundred nautical miles to safety.

The English slaves, barefoot and in rags, were brought before the Spanish Viceroy at the Almudaina Palace in Palma. He was so impressed by the story of their escape that he paid for their food and lodging until they could arrange their passage back to England. The people of Palma held a public collection to buy clothes for the men and even rescued the boat from the beach and hung it in Palma's great gothic cathedral.

Thirty-six

Six Years Later

Payne

It was a hot summer day at the quarry in Kleber, and most of the men were off at the local mosque for the Friday prayer service. Only a few Christian slaves remained, including Thomas Payne, who had been promoted to the role of supervisor at the quarry. He looked a good deal older with his darkly tanned face, burned by the merciless sun after years of work at the rock face. The men were dozing in their hammocks after the midday meal, and they paid little attention when the owner's four-wheel buggy arrived at the quarry.

It was not an unusual visit, even on a day of rest. Ayoub Rahmani was getting on in years, but he never missed a chance to show off the quarry to prospective clients. He pulled the buggy to a stop and stepped down, followed by a rich merchant and his wife. The creamy white marble on the quarry walls gleamed in the sunlight and looked astonishingly pure. Rahmani confidently led the way over to the wall so the client could see the cutting techniques. The woman quickly lost interest in the visit and remained behind as her husband followed the old man for a closer look. There were wooden wedges stuck into the fissures in the rock near the cliff face. Rahmani was pointing to them and explaining to the man how the marble slab was removed when suddenly the ground under them gave way, taking the two men with it.

The thunderous crash awakened Payne and the other men, who jumped out of their hammocks and ran towards the cliff face. They found the woman looking down into the quarry where a huge cloud of dust billowed up from the pit.

"What happened?" Payne yelled at the woman.

"My husband," screamed the woman, grasping desperately at Payne. "My husband and Mister Rahmani — they fell."

Standing in a safe area near the cliff face, they peered down into the pit, where the cloud of dust obscured the bodies of the two men who had fallen a good one hundred and fifty feet onto hard, unforgiving rock. Their chances of surviving such a fall were minimal. There were only two ways to get down to the bottom of the pit. One was a winding and treacherous rabbit trail going from ledge to ledge until one arrived at the road at the bottom, and the other was to take the long circuitous route overland that led to the same road at the bottom of the pit half a mile away.

There was no time to waste. The men scrambled down the rabbit trail at the edge of the quarry. Even then, it took some ten minutes descending from one ledge to another before they found the fallen men. Ayoub Rahmani lay still, his head and neck twisted grotesquely on his shoulders. The woman's husband was unconscious and barely alive. Both his legs were broken, his skull fractured, and he would require immediate medical attention to survive. The four men lifted the unconscious man gently and carried him down towards the slave shelter at the bottom of the pit. There was nothing they could do for their boss.

The Roman villa sat within a walled compound perched on a rocky promontory overlooking the sea. It was the day after the accident and Payne had received a message from the family that morning requesting that the patriarch's body be transported to the family home as soon as possible. They had been watching for his arrival and a turbaned manservant opened the gate for Payne. As he drove into the courtyard, the servant respectfully inclined his head as the body of his master passed through. Payne drove the wagon into the courtyard and pulled up near an elaborate fountain and pillared walkway leading to the main entrance.

"*Sabah El Kheir*," said the old man, wishing Payne a good morning.

"I have the body in the wagon," said Payne, stepping down. "Can you tell the lady of the house that I've arrived?"

"Yes, of course."

The servant left Payne standing near the wagon, marvelling at his surroundings. He had been here many times before, but he was always impressed by the size of the villa. The house had been rebuilt over the centuries and had added Moorish columns and facades. It was ancient in design, but not in appearance. There was something eerily familiar about the place. Then he realized what it was — the same creamy white marble. The quarry dated back to Roman times, and the house shared its origins with the quarry.

The servant returned after several minutes.

"This way, sir," said the man, gesturing towards the ornate walkway leading to the front door.

Payne had often made deliveries to the villa but had never been invited inside. He removed his red, sweat-stained *fez* and brushed the dust from his hair and clothes before following the servant into the house. The room they entered was quite extraordinary. It was a Roman atrium with an opening in the roof. Sunlight streamed in and reflected off the rainwater in the pool. Payne was drawn by the play of dappled sunlight on the surface and the intricate design at the bottom of the pool. It was an image of a leaping fish pulling a chariot, and it was formed by hundreds of tiny, brilliantly coloured stones.

The air was cool in the atrium. He looked up to see the servant standing patiently at the side of a low table surrounded by cushions and inviting him to sit down. Payne was tired and hot from the journey and elected to remain standing as the servant withdrew. He stepped closer to the pool to get a better look at the picture of the leaping fish. Never in his life had he seen such an exquisite room with its high ceiling and marble floor.

A moment later, a young woman in her twenties appeared in the doorway. She was dark-haired and olive-skinned, and Payne surmised she must be the Rahmani daughter.

"Hello, Mister Payne. Please sit down."

Payne was surprised. He had never been invited to meet the Rahmani family, and the fact that the woman knew his name and spoke English was quite remarkable.

"You speak English very well, milady," said Payne.

"I'm from Oran, Mister Payne. My father was a wine merchant in the city and I was educated by Catholic missionaries."

"I haven't spoken English for over six years."

"I was always good with languages — Spanish, French and English. Do you like the atrium?"

"It's a magnificent room, milady."

"You know the Romans took a lot of marble from our quarry in their time, and this house always belonged to the owner. It has been rebuilt several times over the centuries."

For a moment she looked lost in thought, but then she remembered her guest.

"Would you like some tea?"

Payne nodded, and she clapped her hands, summoning an unseen servant.

"You have my husband's body?"

"Yes," Payne stammered, suddenly feeling very foolish. This woman was the wife of Ayoub Rahmani, not the daughter. He thought she was far too young and beautiful to be married to such an old man. The effect of her gaze was electric.

"My condolences. I'm sorry for your loss."

"My husband was very imprudent in going to the quarry. It is a dangerous place, is it not, Mister Payne?"

"Yes, it is, milady."

He was saved from saying anything else when a servant appeared with the tea service. Neither of them spoke again until the servant had poured the tea and left the room.

"Let me introduce myself, Mister Payne. I'm Zara Rahmani. My husband Ayoub had two wives before me and outlived them both. We were married three years ago."

"A pleasure to meet you, milady."

"Mister Payne, I would like to visit the quarry after the funeral and was wondering whether you might show me around."

"Of course, milady."

"My husband spoke highly of you. He said you were his supervisor and his best worker."

Payne could not think of how to respond to that.

"You have lost many men at the quarry?"

"Yes, we have. I organize the hauling after the cut is made, and it is dangerous work."

"This is a difficult time, but I have to decide what to do with the quarry now that my husband is dead. You understand?"

"Yes, of course, milady."

Ryder & Meade

The fishing sloop stood off the coast in the moonlight and then sailed in towards an isolated beach in the early morning hours. They had left Cartagena in Spain with a good wind the day before and the plan had been to arrive just before dawn. As the boat came in, Richard Meade jumped into the shallow water near the beach and pulled his pack after him. He was followed into the waves by his friend, John Ryder. They struggled with their packs as they climbed the beach and the steep slope of the cliff overlooking the bay. They no longer looked like the Baltimore fishermen of the past. They wore long beards and were dressed as rich merchants. When they turned to look back, the fishing sloop had already disappeared from view, heading home to Spain.

It had been over two years since the Spanish ship had freed them from a death sentence behind the oar. The Spaniards had treated them like brothers, donating the clothes on their backs and treating them to a riotous night in a bar on their arrival in Malaga. After a dozen pints of *cerveza* and many glasses of *aguardiente*, the inevitable happened. The Englishmen started to wax nostalgic for their homeland.

"Jean-Marc, how will you get home?" asked William Arnold with a drunken stare.

"How do you think?" he replied. "*Je marcherai sur mes jambes*. I'll walk."

"You need a ship," said John Ryder.

"No more ships for me," said Pierre, Jean-Marc's brother.

"What are you going to do, Richard?" asked Ryder.

"I can't go home, John. I ain't got nothing at home," said Meade, pouring himself another glass of *aguardiente*. He looked very sad for a long moment, and then his eyes brightened with a new idea.

"I'm going to return to Algiers and try to find my wife and children."

"No," said Ryder in shock, "you won't go back."

"Yes, I will," insisted Meade, suddenly firm in his decision.

The others looked at Meade as if he were mad. They had endured months of danger and privation together. They owed everything to the Spaniards who had rescued them. They had been given a second chance, and to squander it would be a disgrace. They looked at their friend who wanted to go back to that accursed country and thought he must be off his head.

"You'll never find them, Richard," said Arnold.

"I have three lovely children, William," said Meade. "They are my life. I must try."

Once the idea was out in the open, Meade and Ryder could not leave it alone. John Ryder had a wife and two children in Algiers, and the thought of being reunited with them was hard to ignore. They thought about it constantly day and night.

The two Frenchmen, Pierre and Jean-Marc, were no longer safe in Spain. France was now at war with Spain and they had to be careful not to be arrested as French spies as they planned to travel north through the country. France had avoided direct participation in the Thirty Years' War until May 1635, when it declared war on Spain and the Holy Roman Empire. Pierre and Jean-Marc planned to pass themselves off as Englishmen as they walked north, accompanied by William Arnold, who hoped to catch a ship home from Nantes.

The situation for Meade and Ryder was no less complicated and entailed many risks. If they were going to search for their families in Algiers, they would need papers and money. They were freemen, but penniless, doing odd jobs around the port in Malaga to support themselves. To survive in Algiers, they had to present themselves as men of means, merchants with money to spend.

It wasn't long before the word had gotten out around the docks that the two friends were planning something. There were rumours, almost always accompanied by derisive laughter, about the two mad Englishmen asking questions about the cost of passage to Algiers of all places with no idea that the money they offered was inadequate to the point of insult. The rumours reached the ears of Captain Ignacio Villegas, a seasoned mariner who had been contracted to retrieve the enslaved family members of a wealthy Spanish colonel. He had willingly accepted the money from the colonel but had no idea how to mount a daring foray into Algiers himself. He met the two Englishmen in a Malaga bar. They were not at all what he had expected. They were serious men, not wild-eyed adventurers, and when they spoke of their determination to find their families, he believed them. A deal was struck on the condition that they widen their search to include the Spanish colonel's lost family members.

The Englishmen did not jump at his first offer, something that impressed Villegas rather than discouraged him. They had thought hard about what they had to do and what they would need to do it. Villegas would find them suitable passage to Algiers and would provide them with money, forged papers, weapons, and anything else necessary to carry out their search.

On the coast, Meade and Ryder waited until dawn before taking the road to Algiers. They walked for two days, sleeping in the open and avoiding Turkish military traffic on the road. As they got close to the city, they stopped to buy a hot meal at a roadside kitchen. They were famished, and the food was delicious. They sat in the open air under an awning, eating and drinking as they watched the slaves working in a nearby field. The workers were repairing a washed-out road. It was hard work, digging a drainage ditch and carrying the earth away in baskets. They wore cotton bandannas on their heads and slave clothes as they struggled up the incline in bare feet. Ryder stood up suddenly and advanced to get a better look.

"That's Hugh Pierse," he gasped, pointing at a scrawny, barefoot wretch staggering along under the weight of a heavy basket not more than fifty yards away.

"No," said Meade. "He's way too old, John. You're seeing things."

"I'm not. Bloody hell, look at his friend. That's Richard Lorye, although I'd hardly recognize him in his present state."

"For God's sake, those poor chaps. There's Corent Croffine."

"We better leave," said Ryder, smiling at the cook. "We don't want to attract attention."

They finished their wine and stood up to leave. As they left, Ryder made a remark that disturbed Meade.

"I'd love to free them, Richard. Take them with us when we leave."

"Don't even think about it, John," said Meade, looking at his friend with concern. "Stick to the plan."

The hand of James Frizell trembled as he wrote a letter in his small, tight script. The choice of words showed the depths of his disillusionment.

October 18, 1637

To the Lords of the Privy Council.

The humble petition of James Frizell on behalf of Your Majesty's subjects, now slaves in Algiers.

That I, James Frizell have served in Barbary in most miserable and extraordinary troubles, at great danger to myself, since October 1625. I am now brought so low for want of means to maintain my charge withal that I am in a condition to starve. I do verily believe that never any of his Majesty's ministers hath been so neglected as I am.

Below, I have provided a list of the latest ships captured by the Barbary corsair in Algiers. And of these captives, there is now ransomed one hundred by Mr. Henry Draxer of Leghorn and his Jewish Factor at costs from 150 to 1600 Spanish dollars per head.

I beg for the fruits of clemency for myself and these unfortunate prisoners."

James Frizell, British Consul, Algiers

Frizell stood up and looked out the window overlooking the town. He could see the crowds making their way along Great Market Street and the ships in the harbour in the dazzling sunshine. The people of Algiers were not his people. He liked the town and had many friends, but his people were the poor slaves in the *bagnio*, with little hope of improving their condition.

He was startled by the knock on the door. He did not normally receive visitors, and his first thought was that the landlord had come to badger him again. He didn't respond, just tiptoed to the door and waited. The knock did not come again, and after a few moments, he heard the shuffle of feet on the landing, some murmured voices, and then the footsteps of two men starting down the stairs. Frizell's curiosity overcame his caution. He opened the door and stepped out on the landing.

"Hello," he called. He thought the voices he'd heard were English. He called again: "*Marhaba.*"

"Mister Frizell?" asked a voice from the stairs.

"Yes, can I help you?"

The footsteps resumed, and the men climbed back up the narrow stairs to the Consul's flat. Frizell opened the door to them. They were burly, hard-looking men, and he wondered for a moment if he was making a grave error.

"What can I do for you, gentlemen?"

"We need your help, sir," said Ryder, extending his hand. "We're looking for some people who came here in 1632, and were sold into slavery."

"I see," said Frizell, shaking hands with the men. "Please come in, gentlemen."

The men stepped into his office.

"Wonderful view of the harbour, sir," said Meade, looking out the window.

"Yes, it is. Part of my job is to keep an eye on shipping coming and going into the port," said Frizell.

"We're looking for a Spanish woman and her son," said Ryder.

"When did they arrive?"

"In September 1632, sir."

"What was the name of the ship? Oh, never mind, I have it."

Frizell sat down at his desk and started flipping through the pages of a leather-bound journal filled with his small, cramped handwriting. He waved Ryder and Meade into the chairs facing the desk.

"It's in my notes here somewhere."

"The woman is the sister of Colonel Velazquez of Malaga," said Meade. "He wants her back along with his nephew."

Frizell looked up, his interest piqued, and a glimmer of hope crossed his face. He might earn quite a decent commission from all of this. There was one problem, however, that couldn't be ignored. The colonel could easily negotiate a ransom with the authorities through a third party and could reasonably expect to have his sister and nephew home in perhaps a year or two.

"Why doesn't the colonel simply pay a ransom to get the woman and boy back? A lot of people do."

"A ransom? No, the colonel wants this done quickly and discreetly. He doesn't want to make a public spectacle of his sister and nephew. You understand?"

"Of course."

"We'll pay you for your services," added Ryder, looking at his friend Meade.

"Please let me offer you a drink," said Frizell with a smile. "Where have you come from?"

"Oran, sir."

"Oran. Yes, I like Oran. It's a much more civilized place than Algiers, gentlemen. The Spanish do a good job running the place and trade is booming. Whisky?"

"Please," said Ryder as Meade nodded.

Frizell got up from behind the desk to fetch the glasses and poured the whisky from a bottle of Scotch hidden in a cabinet. He put the glasses in front of the two men and then poured a big one for himself. He sat down and looked across the desk at his guests.

"It won't be easy to find them," said Frizell. "It's been over five years."

Thirty-seven

Payne

The funeral had been a simple affair. The male members of the family carried the corpse wrapped in a cotton shroud on a bier from the road to the gravesite. There were a few Muslim prayers at the grave and then the closest male relatives lowered the body into the hole with the head facing towards Mecca. They piled broad stones on the body and, with spades, filled in the hole with the sandy soil.

Zara Rahmani stood silently at the head of the grave. She was dressed in a *karadou*, a velvet jacket embroidered in gold and silver, and wore a veil and *sarma*, a cone-shaped headdress with gold and silver-coloured ribbons. She was the only woman at the ceremony and was accompanied by the two young sons of her late husband. No other women or girls were allowed at the ceremony.

She looks like a goddess, Payne thought as he observed Zara from a distance, standing near the wagon with the servants. She was holding hands with the boys as she waited for the crowd of about twenty local men to come and pay their respects. The men lingered longer than was necessary, and it was obvious they had taken a fancy to the beautiful widow. Zara knew that she would be solicited by a number of them, even her husband's married brothers would be among them. They would be intent on keeping her inheritance within the family.

After the funeral, the family gathered at the house to mourn the deceased. Payne, dressed in a new cotton *djellaba* and wearing his red *fez*, arrived early with the wagon to collect Zara for the visit to the quarry. He could hear a great deal of commotion and wailing coming from the back of the house. As he came around the back, he saw a dozen country women with blackened faces kneeling on the ground,

278

scratching themselves with their nails and singing incantations for Zara's dead husband. He had been an important man in the community and the family was putting on a big show of sorrow for him.

Payne spotted Zara in the atrium, talking to her cousin Zidan from the funeral. He was an arrogant young man in a turban with a sharp face and jet-black eyes, but what was more remarkable was the scar on his face. It descended from his temple through an eyebrow and cut across his cheek to an ear. It was said that he had earned it in a sword fight and was proud of it. His appearance and reputation scared women and ensured that men gave him a wide berth. He was arguing with Zara, his hands gripping hers, and from the expression on her face, he was hurting her. She pulled free and Zidan raised his hand as if he wanted to strike her, but then thought better of it. He turned away and stormed out of the room. Payne had already started towards them, hoping he wouldn't have to intervene in a family quarrel. He had no idea what they were talking about, and it was not his fight. *Whatever it was,* Payne thought, *there must be some serious tensions within this family.*

Zidan left the kitchen with a sour look and stepped outside to join the family on the terrace. Zara spotted Payne as he stuck his head inside the door. She had tears in her eyes and made an effort to wipe them away as Payne approached. He handed her a handkerchief, and she took it.

"Thomas, give me a few minutes. I can't leave until the women finish their lamentations."

"I'll wait for you out front, milady."

"Thank you," said Zara. She returned to her family and was quickly encircled by her husband's aunts and uncles. Zidan was talking to a young manservant who was holding a tray of fresh lemonade. He avoided looking at Zara.

Ten minutes later, Zara hurried out of the house in her *kurudou* and veil, accompanied by an older woman dressed in black whose presence was necessary to maintain appearances. Zara was happy to get away from cousin Zidan and the immediate family. Payne helped the women up onto the front seat of the wagon and, together, they drove off to the quarry.

"This is Fouzia, Thomas," said Zara. "She is an excellent cook and a very kind, sweet woman."

Fouzia looked up at Payne at the mention of her name and smiled.

"She is smiling because she finds you very handsome," said Zara. "Not to worry. She doesn't understand English."

"I see," said Payne, giving Zara a half-smile.

"I think today is your lucky day, Thomas Payne," said Zara with a secretive look.

"I'm sorry, milady. A lucky day?"

"Don't be sorry, Thomas. Today I have a surprise for you."

"A surprise?"

"How old are you?"

"Thirty-five, but I can't be sure."

"You are still a young man. You have a good future ahead of you."

Payne nodded, unsure as to where this was going.

"You are named after one of Jesus' apostles," said Zara. "That can't be a bad thing."

Payne laughed, and they remained silent for a time until they pulled up under the trees at the quarry. Thomas helped Zara down from the wagon, but Fouzia remained where she was and pulled a drop spindle from her bag. She started turning fibre into yarn as Zara and Payne walked over to the encampment. A huge Swede, blond with a massive chest and arms like tree trunks, appeared from the woods carrying a cloth bag with his washing.

"Hello, Tom. Are we working tomorrow?"

"Yes, I think so — Magnus, this is Zara Rahmani, our new boss. With the passing of her husband, she'll be running the quarry now."

"My condolences, milady," said Magnus quietly. "Your husband was a good man."

Magnus turned and went off through the woods to the creek. It was the lunch hour at the open-air kitchen and several slaves rose respectfully to their feet as they arrived. Payne stopped to introduce Zara to the men.

"This is my friend Abeo," said Payne. "He was with me when I arrived here years ago."

"Good day, milady," said the tall ebony Yoruba tribesman, rising stiffly from the bench. He looked older and his hair was going grey.

They walked over to the quarry. The sun came out from behind a cloud and gleamed off the wall of *marmor bianco*.

"Abeo is getting old, Zara. The work takes a lot out of a man. It is the same for all of us."

"I'm sure you are right, Thomas. You need to take care of your men."

Payne and Zara looked down into the pit. It was an impressive site. Quarried cliff faces covered half the mountain descending down some one hundred and fifty feet below. Payne was careful to maintain a good distance from the unstable rocks on the edge of the cliff.

"Tomorrow," said Zara, "I meet with my husband's brothers and family. We will determine what to do with the quarry."

"Will you keep it going?" asked Payne.

"I hope so. You want to continue working here?"

"I like the work, milady. You have a rich seam of marble with many years left."

"My husband was a rich man, and he owned a lot of land. His brothers will want a piece of the land, but maybe not the quarry."

"Won't you inherit a share?"

"Two-thirds goes to the immediate family, so I will get a share."

"Will you lose the house?"

"I hope not," said Zara, looking for something in her bag. "I have your surprise here."

She pulled a document from the bag. "Do you know what this is, Thomas?"

Payne looked at the document, written in Arabic, and had absolutely no idea. His reading skills were limited even in English, but in Arabic, they were nonexistent. He spotted his name written at the top in Latin script just below the official seal.

"It's your free card, Thomas. My husband admired your work and wanted you to have it."

"I'm a free man, milady?"

"Not yet. It is not signed. My husband never signed it, so it will have to be signed by a member of the family."

Thomas Payne could hardly believe his good luck, but there was still the question of the signature.

"I will get one of the Rahmani brothers to sign it for you."

Amble

Smithing was hard, dangerous work. It was a tough job, working in a dark pit in the oppressive heat of a charcoal-fired forge. You were in a sweat all day long and could never get enough to drink. You felt like a burned-out husk at the end of the day. Smithing meant getting burned, smashing fingers, and living with cuts and lacerations that often wouldn't heal properly. Amble had been at it for a long time and he took care of himself. He liked smithing and was proud of his work, but he knew that a lot of talented men were moved to other jobs after severe burns and infections. When a smith feared getting burned or cut, the boss figured the worker was never going to be productive again.

Amble hated his boss, Amir Nasri, who was always trying to squeeze more work out of the men. Nasri's family came from the south, where they owned and exploited large tracts of land. He had numerous slaves working in his fields in horrific conditions. When a smith was no longer useful in the dark pit, he was sent south or sold to the state. The business was not doing so well due to a change in the supply of metal. The Toledo steel had been replaced with a softer Italian steel, and the work took more time and patience. Nasri had reduced the staff to just three men making blades and one Berber craftsman doing the traditional brass-inlaid decoration. Amble knew that if the shop had to close, he would be sent to work in the fields along with Nasri's other slaves. He had had enough working for a skinflint like Nasri and wanted out. When Nasri came around the shop to check on the production line, he stopped to chat with his oldest and most experienced smith.

"How is the work going, John?"

"Well, sir," said Amble, resenting the interruption. He had been hammering a blade into shape on the anvil, but the blade would not stay hot long enough. "This batch of metal is not so good. It is harder to work and more brittle. Not so good for knives."

"Well," said Nasri, "it is all we can get at the moment."

"Yes, sir."

Amble struck the blade with the hammer and, as if to reinforce his point, the blade broke on the anvil.

"Sorry, sir," said Amble.

Nasri shook his head and returned to his office.

That evening, Amble went to see his old friend Hakim at Vincenzo's in the *souk*. After several glasses of wine and *aguardiente*, Amble told Hakim that Nasri's blacksmith shop was going through a bad patch with the war on between France and Spain, and the lack of Toledo steel.

"Maybe it is time for you to buy the shop and your freedom, John," said Hakim.

"I could make a go of it, Hakim," said Amble. "There are dozens of things that a good smith can make in metal. You'll never find an idle smith in this country."

"I could make him an offer for the shop, John. You think he'd be interested?"

"The timing couldn't be better. Nasri is getting old and doesn't understand a thing about the business."

"Say we go fifty-fifty for the shop, John?"

"No," said Amble, shaking his head.

"I thought you had money," said Hakim surprised.

"I do — enough for my share of the shop, but not enough to buy my freedom, Hakim. You buy my freedom and we have a deal."

The next day, as the shop was closing, Amble went upstairs to have a word with his boss in the office.

"*Salam*, John," said Nasri, turning to look at Amble standing at the door. "You all right?"

"Yes, sir. I mentioned earlier the problem with the steel. We are losing a lot of blades to breakage."

Amble came over and dropped another broken blade on the desk. Nasri picked it up and examined it. The blade had fractured in the middle.

"How many are you talking about, John?"

"Maybe a quarter, sir."

"We better have a talk about this tomorrow."

"By the way, Mister Nasri, there is a man in the *bagnio* who wants to meet you. He says he has an offer for you."

"An offer?" inquired Nasri. "What kind of offer?"

"He says for you to come to Vincenzo's this evening after eight. You know the café in the courtyard?"

"Yes, I do."

"He says you won't regret it."

Nasri appeared interested.

"What does he want, John?"

"I don't know, sir," Amble shrugged, feigning indifference. "They say he's a trader. Maybe he has work for the shop."

"Very well," said Nasri, dismissing him. His expression was impassive, but Amble could sense the speculative gleam in his eye. Amir Nasri loved to make money and who knew what kind of offer was on the table?

Later that evening, Amir Nasri sat down with Hakim Kermali at Vincenzo's in the *souk*. Hakim ordered drinks and Nasri declined the *aguardiente* for a coffee. They talked casually for several minutes before Hakim made his offer. At first, Nasri looked bored and showed very little interest, but soon his interest picked up and the men were chatting amiably.

Amble sat in the back room of a café across the way from Vincenzo's and watched the negotiation. He had no idea how long it would go on and tried not to think about what it would mean for him if Hakim were successful. He wanted the blacksmith shop for himself and Nasri gone, but was it too much to hope for?

After Nasri left the bar, Hakim crossed the street and stood in the doorway before he came over to Amble's table in the corner. He sat down without a word. The suspense was too much for Amble.

"Well?" he asked. "How did it go?"

"I told him I had bought up all the steel supplies in town," said Hakim, smiling. "He didn't like that."

Amble's disappointment was palpable. Hakim leaned across the table.

"He warmed up when I made the offer. It's a good one."

"Did he take it?"

"No," laughed Hakim. "He said he'd think about it. He's going to start worrying about his suppliers and that should lead him to the right decision."

"He could still wait us out."

"You were right about him, John. He's older and I think he's tired of the business, but he's not stupid."

"Good. When will you know?"

"Next week," said Hakim. "When you go back to work, John, don't say a word to the man. He may be second-guessing his decision."

Amble nodded.

On Monday, Nasri came around to see how the men were doing

in the shop. He had a servant check his inventory of metal supplies. Then he went to have a word with Amble, who was banging away on a blade.

"John, what do you know about the trader?"

"Not much, sir. Everybody knows him in the *bagnio*. He is some kind of businessman."

"Yes, but who is he working for?"

"I wouldn't know, sir."

"How is the work going?"

Amble turned to show the batch of broken blades in a box near the forge. Nasri looked concerned and then left the men to their work.

A younger smith came around to have a word with Amble and glanced at the broken blades.

"What are you doing with the broken blades?" he asked.

John raised an eyebrow and smiled at his colleague as he continued to hammer away on the anvil.

The same evening, Hakim met with Amble at Vincenzo's in the *souk*. Hakim had been surprised at how easily the sale had gone.

"How much did you pay for the shop?" asked Amble.

"Less than we agreed upon. I think he's happy to be out of the business."

"That's wonderful. He accepted your offer?"

"Yes, he did. You're free now, John, and you own fifty percent of the shop and the slaves."

"You won't regret it, Hakim."

"Not with you in charge, John."

Hakim finished his drink.

"I don't understand why Nasri was so eager to do the deal, John. The business is still good. There is a constant demand for *bousaadi* utility knives, and I hear the Italian steel is quite good."

"I showed Nasri a lot of broken blades, Hakim."

"Broken blades?"

"You ever hear of quenching a blade in oil, Hakim?"

"No, I don't think so."

"It's an old trick. You can ruin the blade if you don't do it right. You can warp it or fracture the steel."

Thirty-eight

Payne

It all happened very fast. Thomas Payne, dressed in a dark *jabador* and a red *fez*, stepped into the mosque. The mullah received him and he stood with several foreign men waiting for the *Shahada* ceremony to begin. When it was his turn, the mullah asked him to recite the testimony of faith.

"*La ilaha illa Allah, Muhammad rasoolu Allah,*" said Payne with some difficulty, for his Arabic was far from perfect. He had just said the magic words of the Muslim faith—"there is no true God but Allah, and Muhammad is the messenger of God." Once a person had said these words and understood their meaning, he or she was a Muslim. There was no going back.

After a few prayers, the mullah solemnly presented Payne and the other men with a purse of coins and a length of white muslin to make a turban. Payne thanked the mullah and left the mosque. It had taken him less than ten minutes to 'turn Turk'. Payne was not a religious man, although he came from a village of religious zealots. The Baltimore colony was full of Calvinist radicals who had no tolerance at all for the religious rights of others. Payne had never shown any interest in religion, even though his wife had been the daughter of an Anglican minister. He was an ordinary working man trying to provide for his family and had no time for religious debate. He was not judgmental and accepted people as they were.

In Algeria, he had met numerous Muslims who were honest, hard-working and respected in their communities. Old Rahmani was one of them. He had never pressured his Christian slaves to renounce their religion. It was an easy decision for Payne, and he was honest enough to admit that it had as much to do with expedience as religious fervour. He was now officially a Muslim, like more than ninety percent of the population, and if all went well, he would soon be a free man.

Outside the mosque, Zara's old manservant waited for him. He climbed on the wagon and the servant drove him back to the villa to announce the news to Zara. They had planned it so that Payne would become a Muslim before the family met to discuss the inheritance settlement. At that meeting, Zara intended to bring up her late husband's desire to give Payne his freedom. According to Sharia law, the deceased person's property, including his slaves, could be disposed of for up to one-third of the value of the estate before the remaining assets went to the family. The fact that Payne had become a Muslim would increase his chances that the family would endorse their brother's decision to free him.

The remaining assets would be divided up among the family members after payment of the funeral costs and any outstanding debts. As a widow without children — the Rahmani children were from a previous marriage — Zara would receive 1/4 of the estate while the two boys would each get 1/6, with their sister a miserly 1/12, before any contingent beneficiaries such as uncles, aunts and others got their share.

In the short time since the funeral, Zara had received several demands in marriage from local men and an urgent one from her cousin Zidan. She had been betrothed to Zidan before her marriage to Ayoub, but she had refused to go ahead with the marriage after she had learned how violent he was. For an unmarried woman, it was not unknown for a family to force her into an arranged marriage and take custody of her husband's children. Zara was fond of the children and had no desire to be separated from them. She hoped to keep the quarry for herself and pressure the Rahmani brothers to respect her right to inherit. She knew she would have to give away some of her husband's land to his brothers, uncles, and cousins to make it happen.

The quarry had always been Ayoub's passion, but his brothers did not share the same interests. They were mostly farmers and were always looking to increase their holdings. Zara had made an arrangement with one of the brothers to exchange her share of the fertile land to the west of the house for a larger share in the quarry. With his support, she hoped to hold on to the quarry and win custody of the children.

The meeting was held in the parlour of the house. The Rahmani brothers sat in silence near a low table with the oldest brother, the executor, sitting apart. Payne sat a little behind the men at the table while Zara and the aunts remained standing in the corner of the room after serving tea to their menfolk. The brothers knew something was up when cousin Zidan arrived and appeared to be openly hostile to Payne. *It was outrageous*, Zidan thought, *for a foreigner and an infidel slave to attend a meeting of the family.* There was a palpable air of tension in the room as they waited for the executor to bring the meeting to order. Moments later, the man raised his eyes and noticed Payne at the table.

"Mister Payne, I hear that you are now a Muslim," said the executor with a smile.

"Yes, sir," said Payne in Arabic.

"*Alhamdulillah,*" said the executor. "Praise be to God."

"*Alhamdulillah,*" repeated the brothers, and the women murmured their approval in the background. Everyone appeared to react favourably, mollified by the fact that the man they thought was an *infidel* actually shared their faith.

"I hear you are the supervisor at the quarry."

"Yes, sir."

"Zara tells me that my brother spoke highly of you. He desired that you be granted your freedom."

Payne nodded, and the executor asked the assembly to raise their hands if they agreed to the provision for Payne. Everyone agreed, except for cousin Zidan, whose long face said it all. Payne smiled with relief at Zara. She did not meet his eye. At first, he was disappointed until he realized that in such a public setting, it would not be appropriate for her to acknowledge him.

The executor launched into a long list of Ayoub Rahmani's assets in Arabic and explained painstakingly how Sharia rules of inheritance applied. Payne understood next to nothing of what was said. Cousin Zidan interrupted the reading of the assets and seemed to argue with the executor about a point of the law. This went on for a long time and Payne sensed that it had to do with Zara's share of the property. It was a tense moment and after Zidan had finished, the executor demanded that the brothers raise their hands if they agreed with their cousin, but no one raised their hand. The executor moved on as Zidan stalked out of the room, clearly unhappy with his share as a male cousin. No one spoke as the executor shuffled his papers and looked around the room for further comments. The room remained silent, so he called the meeting to a close and the family filed out.

The executor came over to shake Payne's hand and to sign the papers for his release from slavery. Zara invited him to join them for the midday meal, but he declined because he had a business meeting to attend. After he left, Payne sat down with Zara.

"Are you happy, Thomas?"

"Very much so, milady," replied Payne, smiling.

"You are free now. You can call me Zara and I'll call you Thomas."

"Thank you, Zara. Thank you for everything. I don't know whether I feel any different, slave or freeman."

"Well, you should. You are your own man now."

"What was all that about with your cousin?"

"Zidan has always been a troublemaker. He's not a nice man. He wants me to marry him, and I have refused several times."

Payne realized that Zara was under immense pressure as an unmarried woman in a patriarchal society. Women had no rights and men could easily exploit them. Zidan would continue to ask for her hand and Zara might have to concede to his wishes under pressure from the family.

"I'm going to be your new boss," said Zara, smiling mischievously. "Does that make you nervous?"

"Not at all."

"I will have to pay you now, for your services."

"Yes, you will, but don't worry, I won't charge you much."

Zara smiled at Payne, who was already under her spell, and she knew it. For Payne, Zara was charming, vivacious, and endlessly entertaining. He was happy just to be around her and couldn't keep his eyes off her. He tried to remember how many times since leaving the *bagnio* he had actually spoken with a woman. *I can count them*, he thought ruefully, *on the fingers of one hand*. The country people were admittedly worse than those in the city with regard to the relationships between men and women. A man was not permitted to speak one word to his betrothed before the marriage. It was absurd.

For her part, and even before she met him, Zara had been intrigued by the English slave her husband praised so generously and seemed to rely on so much. Ayoub Rahmani was not known to be effusive with his praise, yet he had often remarked how clever Payne was when he watched the men working at the cliff face. Payne seemed to have a knack for equally distributing the weight of the huge blocks of marble among his crew as they descended them with their ropes to the road below. He had saved the lives of many slaves by maintaining strict security measures during the transport. This was enough to make him a valuable prize in her eyes. He was a handsome man, even though he was at least ten years older than her. The more time they spent together, the more attractive he seemed to become.

After all the Rahmani family members had gone, Zara introduced the children to Payne. There were the two boys, Sami and Hassan, six and ten years old, and their sister, Laila, who was only four. When Payne looked at them, he realized just how much he missed his own children. Zara was soon called to the kitchen and, since it was too hot to go outside, Payne sat down in the dining room with the children and played *mancala*, an old board game. The children placed their seeds in holes around the board and moved them counterclockwise. The winner was the player with the most seeds at the end of the game. The boys were experts at the game and easily thrashed Payne, whose mock protests and cries of anguish provoked gales of hysterical laughter from the children.

After the children had gone to bed, Payne went for a walk with Zara along the cliff overlooking the sandy beach.

"Do you miss your family, Thomas?" asked Zara.

"Yes, very much so. I try to avoid thinking about them because there is nothing I can do to change anything."

"You're free now. You could return to your home."

"It's been over six years, Zara. There is nothing for me at home. My boys were sold in the slave market, along with my wife. They are young men now, and my wife — well, last I heard, she had moved to Tunis and remarried."

"I'm sorry, Thomas. Life moves on."

"Yes, it does. All we have are our memories, Zara."

They walked on in silence for a time.

"Have you ever thought of returning to Oran?" asked Payne, surprising himself with the question.

For a very long time, he had ceased to show any interest in the lives of others. As a slave in a diminished state, there had been no hope of improving his lot in life. Now, he was a free man and everything suddenly seemed possible, even his obsession with his new boss.

"No, I'm happy here with the house and children."

From the cliff, they could see small boats fishing off the coast in the failing light.

"You must wonder why a woman my age would marry a man old enough to be my grandfather?"

Payne watched Zara from the corner of his eye.

"It was an arranged marriage. I was only eighteen, but I was older than my sisters when they married. You know he never touched me once during all those years."

Payne looked at her and could hardly believe such a thing was possible — she was a lovely woman.

"We faked our marriage night," she giggled at the memory. "When the women entered the bed-chamber, I expressed great joy and sang with them so that all our neighbours could hear. After that night together, we slept in separate bedrooms. I was a virgin queen."

Zara and Payne turned down a path towards the beach among the sand dunes and were soon invisible to any observer at the house.

"My husband was a good man, Thomas. I cannot complain. He never beat me and was good to his children."

"The children are a blessing, Zara."

"His second wife died in childbirth, giving birth to little Laila."

"She's a lovely child."

"Yes, she is. I love them all dearly."

Thomas felt her fingertips on his own as she reached for him, bringing his hand up and pressing it against her breast. Thomas pulled her closer, and they kissed, collapsing together into a sandy hollow in the dunes. He could feel her urgently pulling at his underclothes, and almost before he knew what was happening, they were having rough sex in the dunes.

They remained in the dune for a time, silently enjoying each other, touching and embracing, and were soon going at it again, but slower this time.

Thomas sat alone in the garden in the dark while Zara had gone to look in on the children. It was a warm night with an abundance of stars and Thomas was savouring a wonderful feeling of post-coital bliss. He had gone years with no feminine presence in his life and he had missed it terribly. He knew he was hopelessly in love with Zara and that it might end badly, both for him and for her, but he had to try.

A young servant appeared with a tea tray containing a pot of mint tea and two glasses and put it on the wooden table near his chair.

"*Shukran*," said Payne, thanking the young man.

He nodded shyly and withdrew. Moments later, Payne heard footsteps and a voice coming from the house.

"I thought you might like some mint tea," said Zara. "English people in Oran like it."

"It's very nice, Zara. Thank you."

Zara served the tea, and then boldly took Payne's hand in hers, looking him in the eye.

"You're a lovely man, Thomas. You don't know how much I needed that, but we'll have to abstain for a time. I have a family and servants and at any hint of scandal, I will have the Rahmani brothers coming after me and taking away the children and the quarry."

"I understand. I will try to ignore you, my sweeting, but it will not be easy."

"It will be harder for me," she said, "because I am surrounded by a house full of women. They notice these things."

"I'd better go," Payne said, although that was the last thing he wanted to do. "I need to get an early start on the morrow."

He finished his tea, and Zara followed him around the dark perimeter of the house to his wagon. She slipped an arm around him and kissed him in the dark shadow of the house. After releasing him, she stood near the wagon while he climbed on board.

"With my newfound freedom, Zara," he said with an expression of mock solemnity. "I will need to visit you more often — to talk business, of course."

"Of course," she said, grinning. "I would like that, Thomas."

"Good night, dearest heart," said Payne, driving off.

As Payne was approaching the quarry, he was suddenly confronted by five thugs brandishing long knives. He tried to whip the mule to go faster, but one man seized the animal's bridle and held on to it while the others surrounded the wagon. By the look of them, they were a hard breed of men, mainly local youths and paid assassins, doing the dirty work of rich landowners in the lawless western regions of Algeria. Payne had seen their kind before lazily watching the Rahmani wagons hauling slabs of marble to town.

Zara's cousin Zidan stepped out from behind a tree and levelled a pistol at him.

"Mister Payne," said Zidan in Sabir. "You are a free man today, but you will be a dead man tomorrow if you do not leave this place for Algiers right away."

"But I have work to do at the quarry," Payne replied, trying to remain calm.

"That is over, finished. We no longer need your services. You were seen with my cousin Zara, so you can no longer remain here. You must leave immediately."

The thugs grabbed Payne and pulled him off the wagon. He spotted Zara's young manservant in the shadows as he was dragged on his knees towards Zidan. A man held a knife to his throat as Zidan put the pistol muzzle to his head.

"If you agree, my men will take you to Algiers," said Zidan, "but you must never return."

Payne remained calm and reflected on his situation. Landowners like Zidan ran the country and made the law. He had heard terrible things about slaves being tortured and murdered in regional backwaters across the country. There was no security for the oppressed and the Turkish militias posted in the major ports never investigated the suspicious death of a slave or a *renegado*. If he refused, they would kill him on the spot and not even bother to hide the body.

"Of course," he said resignedly. "I will go, but I need to get my things at the camp."

"We will take you there."

The men allowed Payne to get back on the wagon and he set off for the encampment with several of Zidan's thugs riding beside him in the wagon to prevent him from changing his mind. Zidan and the manservant talked briefly together before Zidan left to accompany the wagon.

Thirty-nine

Ryder & Meade

The sun reflecting off the white stone of the building dazzled James Frizell as he crossed the courtyard to the palace. There were gardeners working in the beds of red oleander near the lemon trees. Frizell hurried into the side entrance reserved for merchants and low-level bureaucrats. After an hour, he reappeared and left the palace gates, turning onto Grand Market Street.

In a café in the *souk*, Richard Meade and John Ryder were drinking coffee as Frizell arrived.

"Gentlemen, it went well. I'll have the information for you tomorrow," said Frizell.

"Mister Frizell, sir," said Meade, looking worried. "We need to know where they are and whether they are together."

"Very good. I should have that information too."

"Have you heard about the Baltimore slaves, Mister Frizell?" asked Meade. "What became of them?"

"A very sad affair, gentlemen," said Frizell, as a waiter brought him coffee. "There seems to be no hope of ransoming those poor souls."

"What happened to the women and children?" asked Ryder.

"The men are all over, some are galley slaves, others are in farming and construction. I think most of the women are probably still here in the city. There are a lot of domestic jobs for women slaves here. I have no idea what has happened to the children."

"What about the king, hasn't he shown any interest in ransoming them?"

"The answer, my friend, is no. The crown has shown no interest in returning those people to their homes."

After Frizell had left for urgent business in the harbour, the two Englishmen went to the *bagnio* and sat in a bar, hoping to spot some of their compatriots. It was unlikely they would be recognized, but they couldn't take the chance. They sat in the darkest of stalls and hid their faces as best they could. They hoped to see a face or two that they recognized, but they saw no one. Meade noticed two Arab men talking in the street and both men had deep scars on their arms.

"You see them scars, John?" asked Meade.

"Yes, I do. It looks like the devil's work," said Ryder.

"It's self-mutilation. I've heard that men with scars like that are pederasts. They call them signs of love."

"Signs of love, my arse."

"Want some more wine, my friend?"

Ryder nodded and felt a growing sense of outrage.

"If I showed cuts like that back home, they'd string me up to the nearest tree. Bleedin' pederasts."

Before returning to their rooming house, they took a turn past the shops on Grand Market Street and walked past the bakery, where they spotted young Geoffrey Gunter in the alley playing with a ball. He was fourteen years old and a tall lad. He had grown up since they last saw him in Baltimore. He was unmistakably a Gunter. *What was Geoffrey doing behind the bakery?* thought Ryder. *Maybe his mother worked there?*

As Meade kept watch outside, Ryder stepped into the shop and bought a sweet *kalb el louz* pastry from the woman at the counter.

"Is Sally Gunter here today?" asked Ryder.

"No, sir," said the woman. "She's not in, but she'll be back later tonight."

He nodded at the woman and felt encouraged as he left the shop. Sally Gunter had been allowed to keep her boys. She might know something about the other women.

It was after midnight when Ryder and Meade returned to the bakery. They knew that the bakery worked through the night and there would be more people in the early morning hours. There was a lot of movement and noise coming from inside the building. They went up the stairs and pushed open the door into a large room where some twenty women were working the dough on long tables lit by tallow candles. Sally was not among them.

A young woman came over to ask them about their business and directed them to a small office in the back. Ryder knocked on the door and stepped inside. Sally was writing in a ledger by the light of a candle, and her eyes widened in surprise.

"My God!" exclaimed Sally. "John. John Ryder. Is that you?"

"Yes, Sally, it's me," said Ryder, gesturing towards his friend Richard. "You remember Richard?"

"Of course I do," said Sally, plainly delighted to see them. "What on earth are you doing here?"

"It's a long story, Sally," said Ryder.

"I hardly recognized you with those beards."

"We're looking for our wives and children, Sally. We've come a long way from Spain to find them."

Sally's face showed her dilemma. If she encouraged these poor fellows to look for their women and children, she would be doing them a disservice. If she discouraged them and told them the truth about how hopeless the task was, they might not believe her, but she would not be lying to them.

"It's been six years, John."

"We know," said Ryder, "but we think that we can find them."

"Anything you can tell us, Sally?" asked Meade.

"You don't understand," said Sally, taking a deep breath. "Your women are gone. They both worked for me here at the bakery before they remarried."

The two men stared at her, shell-shocked. They hadn't in their worst nightmares imagined that their women would remarry. Finally, Richard managed to speak.

"Are you sure?"

"Yes, I'm sure. I never met the men, but I think they married *renegadoes* they met at the *bagnio*. I heard one was a German man, and the other might have been a Spaniard."

There was a very long silence while John and Richard tried to come to grips with what they had just heard. They felt betrayed. Their hopes of ever finding their families were dashed.

"What about our children?" Ryder asked, his voice barely audible.

"Your children were sold, John," said Sally, "the same way we all were. No one knows where they are."

She saw the shattered, stunned looks on their faces.

"Your wives had no choice. They moved on with their lives. I'm sure they are free now. A lot of women marry in the hope of being free one day."

After meeting Sally, Ryder and Meade had returned to their hotel where they finished off a bottle of *aguardiente* in the early morning hours as they tried to bury their sorrow and forget how hopeless their situation was. Regardless of how they looked at it, their women were gone and weren't coming back. Their only hope was to try to find their children.

The following morning, they were still hung over as they made their way through the *souk* to a tailor's shop, where a dozen women were busy cutting fabric and sewing it together. The two Englishmen were ignored by the women as they entered the office where James Frizell was drinking coffee with the tailor, a fat, bearded man. Frizell stood up and made the presentations.

"John Ryder, Richard Meade — this is Joseph Penn. Joseph is the owner of this establishment and has lived in Algiers most of his life."

Frizell allowed himself a smile.

"He knows everyone, and he can help us."

The men shook hands and Penn showed two chairs for his guests. As the servant girl brought in mint tea for the men, Penn occupied himself, tamping down the tobacco in his pipe. The girl served the tea and then lit Penn's pipe with an ember from the fire. No one spoke until she had left the room.

"James here has told me you are looking for a Spanish woman and a child by the name of Velazquez," said Penn.

"Yes, sir," replied Ryder.

"James has given me the name of the dealer who handled the sale. I know this man. He can be bought."

"This needs to be handled discreetly," Frizell cautioned.

"Of course," said Penn, who raised an eyebrow. "I'll go see the dealer this evening, gentlemen. Perhaps I will have a name for you tomorrow."

"Very good," said Meade.

"If I'm successful, you can then approach the buyer and make your offer."

"There is something else," said Ryder, shifting in his chair. "I have a further request. It concerns the children of two women captured in Baltimore."

Frizell and Penn looked at each other and thought the same thing. Their fees had just gone up by a significant margin.

"When did this happen?" Penn asked.

"They arrived a year earlier," said Meade, "in July 1631."

"There are people I can ask, but it will not be easy to find slave children after six years," replied Penn, puffing on his pipe. "A lot of Christian boys end up working in rich houses after they convert to Islam. The girls are even harder to find working as scullery maids and servants."

"I've seen a number of Christian boys at the palace," said Frizell.

"The pasha's men have a thing for Christian boys, I'm afraid," added Penn with a look of disgust. "I'm sure you've seen the pederasts around town with the cuts on their arms."

Meade and Ryder nodded.

"As I'm sure you're aware, gentlemen," Frizell said, "in the Mahometan faith, it is not a sin for older men to bed young boys."

"Bleedin' pederasts," growled Ryder. "No codding, Richard. This is a heathen town, just like bloody Sodom and Gomorrah."

Penn exchanged a look with Frizell and then put down his pipe. He leaned forward, fixing Ryder with a stern look.

"You need to be very careful where you poke your nose, gentlemen. There are a lot of very powerful families in this town."

"Don't worry, sir," said Meade. "We'll be careful."

Ryder acknowledged the warning with a sheepish nod of his head and let Meade do the talking.

"There's a house off Grand Market Street," said Penn, "where you'll find a lot of these pretty boys. You might have a look there."

"Thank you," said Ryder.

"Don't mention my name, please," said Penn, "nor that of my friend James here."

"Of course, sir. We won't mention any names."

In the afternoon, Meade and Ryder walked past the address of the house on a narrow street. It was an ordinary building in a quiet neighbourhood near the Dey's palace. It would not do to make a mistake, so they kept watch for some time before they saw a muscular black man, undoubtedly the house pimp, step out the door and head for the shops on Grand Market Street.

Meade left Ryder as a lookout and went into the house to have a look. He climbed to the second floor, where he found himself in a long corridor crowded with a lot of fair-haired boys, ages six to twelve, milling about, waiting for clients to arrive. There was a hard edge to these pretty boys. Gone was the guileless innocence and playfulness of ordinary boys. The boys quickly identified Meade as a client and jostled each other for his attention. One of the older boys made short work of the competition and seized Meade's hand, leading him down the hall as he jabbered away in Arabic. Meade understood none of it, but he used the opportunity to have a look at the boys in each room they passed.

Suddenly, he froze as he spotted a strikingly handsome young boy standing in a nearby doorway watching him. There was no sign of recognition on his face, but Meade knew instantly who he was. His green eyes and blond hair gave him away. Meade let go of the hand of the first boy and headed towards the familiar face. The blond boy looked to be about eight years old. He took Meade's hand and led him into a tiny room, shutting the door. Meade quickly sat the boy down on the edge of the straw bed.

"It's me, Elias," he said in English. "My name is Richard Meade. I'm a friend of your father's. I'm from Baltimore."

"Baltimore?" said the boy, who looked annoyed. There was no sign he had understood any of it.

"Elias is not my name, sir," he said in halting English. "My name is Hamid."

"No, son. You listen to me. Your name is Elias Ryder. Your father is John Ryder."

"No," stammered the boy. "My name is Hamid."

Meade was quickly losing patience with the boy.

"I've come a long way to take you home, to your family."

"My family? My family is gone."

"Your father is downstairs, son. Please come along."

He stretched out an arm to help the boy up, but Elias pushed him away and threw himself on the bed. He screamed. He had waited too long to be free and the emotional stress was too much for him. He only wanted to be Hamid, the good Muslim boy who avoided the beatings. Now this man from his past had arrived and would compromise his future.

Meade swore and was reaching for the boy when he heard the chatter of voices in the corridor, replaced a moment later by the harsh, guttural sounds of a man's voice in Arabic. The black pimp stood in the doorway and looked menacingly at Meade. *I'm the boss here,* thought the pimp. *I make the rules. I'll get this man to pay double the usual rate if he wants the boy.* He shouted something in Arabic and when Meade said nothing, he grabbed his arm to remove him from the premises. Meade pulled free, and the enraged pimp struck Meade hard across the face and shoulders with a whip.

Meade exploded. He was immensely strong after his time as an oarsman on the Dey's galleys. He seized the pimp by the throat and lifted him up off the floor with one hand, crushing his windpipe. Then he pulled out his knife and stabbed the pimp through the heart. It happened so fast, young Elias could hardly believe it when he saw the pimp lying on the floor in a pool of blood. He was stunned by the violence of the act and tears coursed down his cheeks as he sat silently on the bed.

Meade wasted no time. His anger was gone, and he was thinking about how he would get the boy out of the house without incident. He quickly rolled the pimp up in several prayer mats and hid the body behind the bed. He then squatted down near Elias to get his attention.

"You need to come with me," said Meade. "We will go quietly. You will go first and wait for me at the door."

"You killed that man," said Elias, astonished.

"He can't hurt you anymore, Elias. He was a bad man. You will go quietly and not make a fuss, do you understand?"

Elias nodded and stood up, grabbing a cotton bag with his only possessions from under the bed.

"Go on now. Speak to no one."

Elias slipped out of the room and disappeared down the hall. Meade followed and found the hallway empty. All the boys were hiding in their rooms, fearing a whipping from the pimp. Meade and Elias headed for the stairs.

John Ryder knew something had gone wrong. He had heard a shrill scream from the house just before the pimp had arrived from the market. There was nothing for it but to go in after his friend. Ryder crossed the street and was about to open the door when Meade rushed out with a small boy in tow. Ryder didn't recognize the boy at first as they crossed the road and turned the corner into Grand Market Street. Ryder suddenly recognized Elias as the boy turned to look at him. Before he could embrace his son, Meade pulled him aside and whispered in his ear.

"Don't say a bleedin' word, John. We need to get away fast."

Elias ignored his father as Meade led them to a quiet café in the *souk,* where they could sit down and talk.

"Elias, it's me. You remember me," said Ryder as they sat down. "I'm your father."

Elias started to cry again, perched on the edge of his chair.

"Give him time, John," Meade told his friend as a waiter came over.

Meade ordered coffee for Ryder and himself, and a chocolate drink for Elias.

"He calls himself Hamid now," said Meade. "He was upset. He didn't want to come with me."

"Have you seen your sister?" probed Ryder in a whisper.

"No," replied Elias. "She's gone."

Elias shook his head to stop the questions.

"Have you seen my children, Elias?" asked Meade. "You remember Tommy, Joyce and Eileen."

Elias' memories were hurtful, so the effort to think about Meade's children set him off again. Meade drank his coffee and stood up.

"Stay with him, don't move. I'll be back after I've seen Penn."

Ryder nodded and looked at his son as the boy sipped from the chocolate drink.

Forty

Amble

Hakim Kermali was a man of many parts. He was a rich merchant who traded in everything: cloth, metal, timber, tobacco and wine. He would buy a load of stolen merchandise off a ship at a bargain price, stock it in his warehouse and resell it a week or a month later at a profit. He had no qualms about buying stolen goods and would regularly visit corsair ships arriving in the port.

John Amble knew all this, but he felt he owed the man a great deal. He was a full partner in the blacksmith shop with Hakim, so he felt it was time to get to know him better. Amble willingly accepted a dinner invitation and travelled by dogcart to Rouiba, east of Algiers. The dogcart dropped him off at the gate and he entered a lovely garden of blue flag irises and red oleander to discover his host chatting with a gardener. After a tour of the property, Hakim ushered him into the dining room, where a low table had already been set for the evening meal. The two men relaxed on cushions and Hakim took his time opening a bottle of whisky for his guest. They drank to their new business venture together.

"My wife is away for a few days, John," said Hakim, looking up at a slim, attractive woman with dark hair who brought in a large dish of lamb stew and put it in the middle of the table. "This is my sister, Samia. She is taking care of us while my wife is away."

Samia picked up some elaborately embroidered napkins, giving one to Amble and the other to her brother.

"Thank you, Samia," Amble said, nodding at the woman. She glanced at him shyly, surprised. Algerian men rarely deigned to speak to the women serving them.

"John is a Christian, Samia," said Hakim with a smile. "He talks to everyone, don't you John?"

"Well, I try to."

"That is the English way, is it not?"

"Yes, I suppose it is."

"Samia, say a few words in English for John."

Samia had learned some words from her brother.

"Hello," she said haltingly. "Good day, John."

"Very good," said Amble as Samia dipped her head, embarrassed, and fled into the kitchen.

"She is not herself," said Hakim, shaking his head sadly. "Her husband was killed a few weeks ago. He was a janissary on one of the Dey's ships."

"I'm sorry to hear that."

"It's not easy for her. She has a daughter who is three years old, but the Dey doesn't care much about his janissaries and even less about their families."

This is dangerous talk, thought Amble, who was flattered that Hakim trusted him enough to say such things.

"Do they live with you now?" asked Amble in an attempt to change the subject.

"No," said Hakim. "They live nearby. Her husband was a good man, John."

"A janissary's life is not an easy one, I think."

"No, it isn't. I have known many janissaries and they all complain about the leadership. The Dey appoints their commanding officers for political reasons. The agas have no military training and are often incompetent. The janissaries pay for it with their lives."

The men dipped their fingers into the lamb stew as Samia brought in the couscous and wine.

The next two weeks were uneventful. As the new owner, Amble had kept on the Berber craftsman and the two *bagnio* smithies. The shop was still making knives, but had branched out into a new, shorter sabre designed by Amble himself that seemed to be popular with the local janissaries. They had found some new supplies of Toledo steel, so the sabre blades were of very high quality.

Amble's usual practice was to work in the forge during the day and do his bookkeeping in the small office upstairs in the evening. He was just sitting down at his ledger when his Berber craftsman came to the door.

"There is a woman downstairs to see you," said the young man.

"Send her up."

The shop did not get many female visitors, and Amble swore under his breath as he looked at the disarray in his office. He could already hear soft footsteps on the stairs, so there was nothing he could do about the appearance of the office. The mystery woman turned out to be Hakim's sister, Samia. As soon as he saw her, he knew something was wrong.

"Hello, Samia," said Amble in greeting. "What is it? Is everything all right?"

"I'm fine, John," said Samia in her halting English, "but Hakim is not so fine." There was fear in her voice.

"Please sit down," said Amble. "Can I get you a cup of tea?"

"No, no, thank you, John. I need to tell you something, something important."

She looked on the verge of collapse, and Amble helped her into the chair.

"My brother is in trouble, John. My late husband owed some gambling debts to his aga. Now he wants Hakim to pay him back."

"Why?" Amble asked. "Your husband is dead. That doesn't make sense."

Even as he said it, he knew how stupid he sounded. This was Algiers. Of course, it did not have to make any sense.

"Hakim is rich," said Samia. "Everybody knows he has a lot of money."

That was true. Amble had heard about Hakim long before he met him. He had quite a reputation.

"So Hakim is going to pay this man?"

"No, he refuses," said Samia, exasperated. "You know how he is. He's stubborn. It is not a lot of money, but he has refused to pay the aga. He said that he can't let this man threaten him because all his clients would do the same if they were unhappy with a sale."

"Well, I don't know what I can do for him, Samia."

"He got a message today. He has to bring the money tonight or they will kill him."

"He has to pay them, Samia."

"I told him that, but he won't listen."

Amble figured that his friend Hakim was a dead man. The janissaries were powerful people in Algiers. They were brutal and commanded their own private armies with men who would follow orders without question. They answered only to the *Dey*, a man who did not concern himself with gambling debts or how they were resolved. The aga would beat Hakim to death and dump his body in the sea if he didn't bring the money.

"Do you want me to talk to him?" Amble asked.

"It's too late for that," said Samia, shaking her head. "In two days he is to meet with the aga on his boat in the harbour. He thinks he can talk him down to a more reasonable amount. I told him that the aga is not a reasonable man. He wants his money."

The trouble with Hakim, thought Amble, *was that he thought everything in life was a negotiation. And why wouldn't he? For him, it had always been that way.* Hakim had been too rich and too clever for too long and he had forgotten what men like the aga were capable of.

Samia had been watching him and reading his mind.

"My brother is a fool," she said with resignation as tears welled up in her eyes.

Ryder & Meade

It had taken Ryder the better part of an hour to bring the boy to the realization that he was safe with his father again. He knew that it would take time for his son to fully return to him. He had tried to embrace him, but the boy did not want to be touched. For now, Ryder was just thankful to have him back.

Meade had gone to see Frizell, who had some information for him from Penn. He paid an extravagant fee for their services, but now he had the name and address of Elena's *patron* in a nearby town. He hurried back to the *souk* to fetch Ryder and Elias. The city gates closed three hours after dusk, so they had to hurry to leave the city in time. They didn't want to be found within the city walls in the morning when the body of the pimp was discovered.

Meade and Ryder were freemen, bearded and dressed as affluent Algerian traders. The city gate was a busy place and, if the Turkish garrison was looking for anyone at this point, it would be a missing infidel boy, not the small veiled woman who sat on the mule led by

Ryder. Meade had provided the veil that he had purchased in the *souk* on his way to collect his friends.

They set off on foot for the town of Blida about twenty-five miles distant with the mule carrying Elias, their bags and provisions for the journey. After two or three hours on the road, the boy was falling asleep on the mule and risked falling off, so they made camp near a copse of trees. Ryder helped his son down and laid him on the soft ground. The boy was soon asleep while Meade and Ryder shared a bottle of whisky.

"I want to thank you, Richard," Ryder said, shaking his head. "You saved him. He ain't himself yet. Maybe he ne'er will be, but you saved him."

"We saved him, John," Meade told him, "but we're not done yet."

"We came for your kids and we leave with one of mine," said Ryder.

"It don't matter none, John," said Meade. "We did our best. We were damned lucky to find the boy. I just pray that my sweet children are all right."

The next morning, they woke Elias and told him it was safe for him to shed his disguise. The boy actually managed a smile of sorts, and after a breakfast of bread, cheese and figs, they set off again. He seemed to warm to his father as they chatted together on the road.

By late afternoon, they were in Blida, a lovely Algerian town on the Oued-el-Kebir river. It was very hot, so they stopped at the river for a wash before going further. It touched the hearts of both men to see the wonder on Elias' face as he gazed up at the nearby mountain and its idyllic surroundings. The water was cool and refreshing, flowing as it did out of the Chiffa gorge. The boy had come from a world of moral depravity and human squalor and he seemed to be transformed by the beauty of the land and its purity. They rested on the grassy bank and listened to the rill of the water falling on stones in the river. Soon, all three of them were fast asleep on the riverbank.

Elias woke up first and went for a dip in the river. He threw off his clothes and plunged into the cool depths. Meade awoke and watched the boy for a while before he started filling their goatskins with fresh water and loading them on the mule. A short time later, they left the river and trudged along a tree-lined road, stopping for a meal at a roadside kitchen. After putting food in their bellies, they passed through the town square dominated by a mosque and ringed by shops and houses. From there, they went looking for a certain farmhouse on the outskirts. It was getting late by the time they arrived at a stone building near a gristmill. They knocked on the door and a woman appeared on the threshold. She was rake thin and carried a wooden pail with her washing.

"*Señora Velazquez?*" asked Meade.

The woman stared open-mouthed at the two Englishmen and the boy. For a moment, she looked like she was going to faint, but then managed to recover herself.

"*Señora Elena Velazquez?* asked Ryder. "Your brother, the colonel, sent us to find you."

"You are English?" asked the woman.

"Yes, we've come from Malaga."

"Malaga?"

"We've come to buy your freedom. *Su libertad,*" said Ryder with a smile. The woman's air changed immediately.

"Who is this?" asked Elena, smiling at Elias.

"He's my son," said Ryder, resisting an urge to put his arm around the boy. "His name is Elias."

"*Señora,* where is your son? *Su hijo?*" asked Meade.

She was about to reply when a large Arab man appeared in the doorway, scratching his belly and looking about suspiciously.

"Good day, sir," said Meade. "*Maa alsalam.*"

"*Maa alsalam,*" said the man with an indifferent air.

Elena started talking rapidly to her *patron* in Arabic. He listened, but his eyes flicked between Ryder and Meade as he tried to size them up. Suddenly he held up his hand to stem Elena's flow of words and waved the Englishmen inside.

They followed the man into the living area near a large fireplace where a meat stew was cooking in a pot. The man sat down on some cushions at a low table and motioned for the men to join him. There was an awkward silence while Elena prepared the tea. After the tea was served, the negotiations began.

"We are here to buy Elena and Esteban's freedom, sir," explained Meade. "You paid ninety Spanish dollars for Elena and her son six years ago. We offer you the same."

Standing near the stove, Elena repeated Meade's offer in Arabic. The *patron* said nothing for a long time. He drank his tea and waited patiently to see whether these rich foreigners would offer more.

Ryder had witnessed this negotiating ploy a hundred times at the *bagnio. Be patient, hold your tongue and the offer always goes up.*

"Where is the boy?" asked Meade.

"Esteban is working in the field," said Elena. "He will be back soon."

Ryder and Meade exchanged a glance, confirming their thoughts. *We can play this game too.* They drank their tea in silence. The standoff continued for a time until Ryder made a show of getting up.

"*Shukran,*" he said, looking directly at his host. "Thank you, but we must go."

Elena hastily told the *patron* the men were leaving. He smiled at the Englishmen and appeared to warm to their offer. He waved them back, muttering something to Elena in Arabic.

"He says ninety dollars for the woman, not the boy," said Elena, translating. "The boy is more expensive."

"One hundred dollars for both of them," countered Meade.

The man listened to Elena and shook his head dismissively. He muttered something angrily to her in Arabic.

"He says the boy is worth more now that he has learned to work in the fields," Elena told the men.

"All right," said Meade, throwing up his hands in frustration. "Sixty dollars for the woman. Ninety dollars for the boy."

The *patron* shook his head and spat on the ground. The boy was more important to him than the mother.

"Sixty dollars for the woman alone," said Meade, hoping to provoke a counteroffer. "No offer on the boy."

Elena stared at him, horrified. It was clear that she couldn't stand the thought of being separated from her son.

The *patron* nodded. Meade handed him sixty Spanish dollars in coins from a small purse.

"Please," whispered Elena to Meade, her eyes pleading. "Wait for my son to arrive."

As Elena poured them more tea, her *patron* counted his money and appeared more relaxed as he savoured his win in the negotiation. After a few minutes, a tall lad about sixteen years old, wearing a wide-brim hat, appeared in the doorway, covered in bits of hay and dirt from the field. His eyes widened when he saw the two foreigners at the table.

"*Qué pasa?*" he asked his mother.

Esteban came in and removed his hat. His face fell when Elena told him that the men had bought her freedom, but the *patron* had refused to release him. He threw his arms around his mother, and for a tearful moment, they just clung to each other. Then she gently pushed the boy towards the door.

"Wait for me outside, please," said Elena to the two Englishmen. "I will talk to him and get him to release the boy."

The men stepped outside with Esteban. Elias was sitting under a tree waiting for them. Ryder went to the mule and pulled a pistol from his pack.

"I'm going to teach that son of a bitch," said Ryder.

"Wait a moment," said Meade. "Let's see whether we can talk him up."

"He ain't gonna give up the boy, Richard," said Ryder.

"Stay here with Elias," said Meade. "I'll go see—"

A scream was heard coming from the house. Elena appeared in the doorway with blood on her hands and apron. She took a single step and collapsed on the ground before they could reach her.

Esteban rushed to his mother's side while Meade ran into the house to find the *patron* lying on the floor in a pool of blood. It looked like the man had been sitting at the table when Elena had asked him to release her son. When he refused, she must have slipped behind him and with an ordinary kitchen knife slashed his throat. The bloody knife lay on the floor beside the dead man.

Meade picked up the gold coins from the table before he joined the others outside. They stared at him as he approached Esteban, who was supporting his sobbing mother.

"Esteban, my boy," said Meade, "you are going home with your mother."

Esteban had no idea what Meade had said.

"*Te vas a casa,*" said Ryder to the boy, who understood and smiled at the men.

Forty-one

"Guarda per ti, et non andar mirar mugeros de los Moros;
nous autros pillar multo phantasia de questo conto."
A warning to all male slaves in Sabir.
(Watch yourself, and don't look at the wives of the Moors;
we are very particular in this matter.)

Payne

P ayne had already become a fixture at the *bagnio* café as he tried
to make sense of his new life. He couldn't return to Kleber and
the quarry now that Zara's cousin Zidan was running things.
Renegadoes were often warned by their *patrons* that Algerine women
were off limits and any infraction would result in harsh punishment.
If he returned, he would put his own life and that of Zara at risk.

So Payne spent his days in low spirits at the same table, drinking
coffee and *aguardiente,* and hoping that some new opportunity would
find him. He sat alone for hours on end, often pulling his free card
from his *fez* to examine it and to convince himself that he was truly
free. He could go anywhere he wanted now that he was free, but
where would he go? He had lost his wife and boys in the slave market
and he knew no one at the *bagnio*. He spent hours trying to get a grip
on his new situation, but his mind kept returning to one person: Zara.
She was everything he had ever wanted in a woman, but now that
chapter of his life was over. There was no way he could ever go back.

"There you are, Tom. I've been lookin' for you."

Thomas looked up to see Abeo, his old Yoruba tribesman friend,
towering over his table and drinking thirstily from a glass of goat's
milk.

"Abeo!" thundered Payne, standing up to embrace his friend.
"How did you get here?"

"Zara sent me, Tom." The big African's smile disappeared. "She needs your help."

"I can't go back," said Payne. "Her cousin will kill me."

"She gave me this," said Abeo, reaching into his pocket and carefully putting a gold necklace on the table. "She said you would recognize it."

Payne was astonished. It was the same necklace she had worn on their night of frantic love-making in the sand dunes. It had fallen from her neck and he had found it later in the sand.

"She says it's urgent, Tom," said Abeo, handing him a sealed letter.

Payne opened it and read the slanted handwriting:

DEAREST HEART, I NEED YOUR HELP. MY COUSIN ZIDAN HAS TAKEN THE CHILDREN AWAY. I BEG OF YOU, PLEASE COME.

"They've taken her children," said Payne in shock as he smelled Zara's perfume on the folded letter. "How could that sick bastard do it?"

"Zidan has a bad reputation with women, Tom. Everyone knows it."

"She says we are to spare no expense," said Abeo. "She gave me money, Tom."

Abeo put two gold doubloons on the table, enough money to finance a small war in a village like Kleber.

Payne grabbed his bag from a chair and stood up.

"Have you eaten, Abeo?"

"Not yet."

"We'll eat before we go."

Two hours later, they left the walled city and took the western road to Kleber. Payne had bought pistols and swords in the *souk* and a horse for himself. They rode their horses hard over hill and vale, hoping to reach the quarry in the early hours of the following day. Payne wanted to move fast and hit Zidan before he would have time to react.

They arrived at Zara's villa just as the servants were waking up with the dawn. Payne rushed inside to find Zara coming out of her bedroom.

"Thomas, you're here," she exclaimed happily. "Abeo found you and you came."

"We rode all night, we're knackered," said Payne, who wanted to hold her in his arms, but remembered her warning about the watchful eyes of the servants. "Are you all right?"

"I'm fine, but I miss the children," she told him. "You must be hungry. We'll talk after you've eaten."

Payne nodded and held her hand before Zara led him into the kitchen, where Fouzia was making tea and preparing food with two other women.

"Abeo is waiting in the yard, Zara."

"Good, I'll send someone to get him."

They moved into the dining room and the women brought in the tea along with bread and cheese.

Abeo appeared in the doorway, towering over Zara's old manservant. As he came in and sat down at the table, Payne got a glimpse of a young man in the hallway. He looked familiar.

"That's the boy!" said Payne, keeping his voice low.

"Which boy?" asked Zara.

Payne jumped up and ran into the hallway. He rounded the corner just as the boy came out of the kitchen. He was carrying some plates, and his eyes went wide as he saw Payne coming at him. He dropped the plates and tried to run, but Payne was already on him, his right forearm around the boy's windpipe and his left hand twisting his arm up behind his back. The boy struggled, but Payne was far too strong for him. He frogmarched the boy into the dining room, shoving him into the chair next to Abeo. The boy tried to squirm away, but Abeo laid one massive arm across his shoulders and held him in place.

"This is Malek, Fouzia's son," said Zara, looking at Payne as if he had gone mad.

"I don't care whose son he is. This boy is a spy, Zara. He was with Zidan on the night they grabbed me."

Payne shot Zara a look and waited for her to seize the gravity of her situation.

"He knows, Zara. He knows where Zidan has taken your children."

Zara went white with rage. She couldn't believe her own kitchen staff were working against her. She yelled an order in Arabic to her old manservant and moments later, Fouzia appeared, wiping her hands on a towel. Fouzia listened quietly, her face a mask, as Zara told her of the accusations against her son. The young man interrupted once, denying everything, but Fouzia silenced him with a look of real loathing. She walked over to her son and slapped him. Malek sat there, humiliated and stunned, and by the time he had recovered to yell insults at his mother, she had turned her back on him and left the room.

Zara stood up and approached the boy.

"How much did he pay you, Malek?" asked Zara in a voice full of contempt.

The boy said nothing. He was a proud young man and had no respect for women. He was about to shout insults at Zara when Abeo seized him by the neck and the blood drained from his face.

"He knows," said Payne, looking at Zara. "Abeo, take him outside."

The big man grinned and picked up the kid, throwing him over his shoulder like a sack of grain.

"Don't worry, Zara," said Payne as they heard Malek's shouts in the courtyard. "We'll get to the truth and find your children."

Zara nodded, and Payne followed his friend outside.

Amble

Late in the evening, a caravel was moored near the mole in the port of Algiers and a celebration was going on in a cabin below decks. There were a dozen janissaries having a party on board when a dogcart deposited Amble and Samia on the dock a hundred yards from the ship.

Amble had first gone looking for Hakim at his home, but soon realized he was in hiding when the servant told him he had taken his wife and children and left town for an unknown destination. Amble had then gone to his warehouse and his other places of business in town to see whether anybody knew where he had gone, but no one had seen him. Luckily, Samia had known where the aga's ship was docked and they had arrived early, hoping to prevent Hakim from boarding the vessel.

Ten minutes later, the party broke up and most of the janissaries left the ship for the bars and bordellos in town. The three men remaining on deck appeared to be waiting for someone. The flamboyantly dressed, corpulent one in the middle had to be the aga, but he was flanked by two muscular men in full janissary uniform. They looked fearless as they awaited their prey.

"That one," Samia whispered, indicating a tough-looking man of medium height, "is the adjutant. The big fellow is the corporal."

Amble had no plan. He had hoped to grab Hakim in town and talk some sense into him. When that failed, he thought they might intercept him on the docks before he boarded the ship, but that was not going to work. Suddenly, a dogcart pulled up near the ship and Hakim stepped down. He climbed over the gunwale of the caravel as the cart sped away. Hakim shook hands with the men on the deck who seemed to be friendly enough and then the aga invited him below for a drink. The huge corporal remained behind, watching the dock.

Maybe Hakim was right to negotiate with the aga, argued the voice in Amble's head. *The exchange on deck looked amicable enough. Hakim was a great negotiator. He could always share the profits from some future venture and avoid paying the debt in blood.* But Amble didn't buy it. He figured his friend had bitten off more than he could chew. His worst fears were confirmed when he and Samia approached the stern in the shadows and heard angry voices coming from inside the ship. The aga was furious that Hakim had not brought the money with him and instead had the temerity to try to negotiate a deal.

Amble sighed as he realized nothing was going to satisfy Hakim's enemies. He had to do something fast or his friend was a dead man. He sent Samia along the dock to get the attention of the corporal while he climbed over the gunwale in the stern, heading forward to where the corporal stood amidships. The corporal was a big man, and he knew his only chance was to take him by surprise. Samia flirted outrageously with the man, who was so bemused by her attention that he wasn't aware of Amble's approach until it was too late. Amble moved silently along the deck and came at the corporal from behind. He wasted no time slitting his throat with a very sharp *bousaadi* knife. Samia stifled a scream as the corporal bled out on the deck.

"Stay here," said Amble to Samia. "Let me have a look below."

It had been a long time since Amble had been in a real fight and he fought to control his nerves as he stepped into the ship. He went down the stairs to the lower deck and stood silently in the companionway while he removed a sabre from his cloak. It was one of the short, razor-sharp sabres he had designed and made himself. He remembered a janissary telling him only days ago how deadly it was in close combat. He hoped the man was right.

One way or the other, he was soon to find out. He was about to start down the corridor when he heard a movement behind him and whirled around, raising the sabre. It was only Samia who had been following him in the hope of finding her brother.

In the captain's cabin, Hakim cursed his own stupidity.

"I have the money," he pleaded desperately with the aga.

"Then why is it not in my hand?" the man roared.

The tragedy was that Hakim was immensely rich. He had a lot of money, but he just did not have it on him. He knew better than to carry money into a nest full of vipers. Better to negotiate terms and work out something beneficial to both parties. That was how he had become rich in the first place, playing on the greed of other men. He had not counted on a man as brutal as the aga. He nodded at his adjutant, who clubbed Hakim to the floor as casually as swatting a fly.

"I'm a simple man," the aga growled, leaning over and seizing Hakim by the beard. Despite his portly size and soft appearance, the man's eyes were hard as flint.

"If you owe me money, you pay me, trader," he said. "No talk, no promises, no ideas about making me rich. I am already rich, almost as rich as you. You are not as smart as you think. You have forgotten one thing. I do not need you alive to collect my due."

He slammed Hakim's head on the floor and stood up.

"After I kill you, the money will still be there. Your wife and family will inherit it and I will kill all of them unless they pay me, you understand?"

Hakim tried to raise his head, but the room spun. His vision blurred as he fought for consciousness. He saw the adjutant stand over him, raising his sword. *He had placed his whole family in danger,* thought Hakim. *His sister had warned him, but he hadn't listened. Even now, he could hear her voice scolding him.*

Amble stood in a room just off the corridor that led to the captain's cabin. The door was open and he could hear Samia shouting out a bogus warning about a fire on a neighbouring ship. It was all they could think of for drawing out the adjutant.

Unlike Hakim, Amble had a realistic view of his own abilities. Attacking two men in a small room — even if one of them was a fat, middle-aged aga — was way too risky. One opponent at a time was quite enough for a man like Amble. He only hoped the ruse would work.

Samia was shouting all kinds of nonsense, trying to get the attention of the men in the cabin. Amble heard the aga bark an order, followed by heavy footsteps as the adjutant opened the door and hurried down the corridor towards Samia.

He never got there. Amble waited until the adjutant was passing his door and quickly stepped out into his path with the short sabre held low. He gutted the man with the blade and then used his knife to stab him in the heart. Amble stood up and pulled the sabre clear of the body, but Samia would not wait. She had already run past him in a headlong rush to reach her brother.

Inside the cabin, the aga was finishing a glass of *aguardiente* as he watched Hakim writhing in pain on the floor. He had just about given up on the trader, who was bleeding from a head wound and suffering from several broken ribs. He figured it would be good to send a clear message to the family. They must come up with the money or else they would die like Hakim.

Suddenly, the door burst open and Samia flew at the aga, screaming and clawing at his face. The attack happened so fast and was so unexpected that all he managed to do was throw the woman against the cabin wall. He was turning around to confront the second assailant when he was nearly decapitated by a roundhouse slash of Amble's sabre.

It took Amble a moment to regain his senses. Samia was on the floor with her dazed brother. Hakim was conscious and smiled at his sister and friend come to his rescue. Amble took a moment to rifle through the aga's bloody clothes and then did the same with the drawers of the ornate desk. There was nothing he could see that mentioned Hakim's name or a debt of any kind. There was a journal sitting on the desk that might have belonged to the aga, but he had no time to thumb through it, so he simply stuffed it inside his cloak.

"What are you doing?" Samia asked.

"What do you think? I'm removing any evidence that your brother was here."

Samia nodded as she stumbled towards the door, holding her brother upright. Amble came to her aid, grabbing Hakim under the shoulders and helping him up the stairs to the deck. The port and mole were quiet as they emerged on deck. They climbed over the gunwale and headed towards the old town.

"Look at you," said Samia, peering at the blood splatter on Amble's cloak in the light of a boat.

"Damn," said Amble, pulling off his cloak.

"Give it here," said Samia. "I'll wash it when we get home."

"See, John," croaked Hakim, "Samia is a good woman."

Samia gave her brother a dressing down in Arabic, which got him laughing and, at the same time, crying in pain.

"We'll get you a dogcart in town, Hakim," said Amble. "You'll be home soon."

"I told you Samia was a good woman," said Hakim.

"Yes, she is. She just saved your life."

Forty-two

Payne

It had not taken them long to get the lad to confess. Payne had been hesitant to punish him since he was only fifteen years old, but he needed him to talk. In the garden, Abeo had kicked the boy's legs out from under him, then hauled him up by the feet so he was upside down. Zara's old manservant provided the lash and Payne gave the boy a *bastinado* that he would remember for a long time. Five lashes were quite enough to get him talking. He was ready to confess to anything, and Payne suspected the little wretch would have turned in his own mother if he thought it would stop the pain.

A short time later, Payne, Abeo, and Zara left the compound in a wagon heading north. They drove to an isolated farmhouse belonging to Zidan's family. It was not hard to find. A woman was in the kitchen preparing food accompanied by a young man, who once he had looked at Abeo, made no effort to stop them. Zara talked to the woman briefly in Arabic, and she led them to the barn to see the children. Young Sami was throwing a wooden ball to his older brother Hassan while their sister Laila watched from a bale of hay. The kids were happy to see Zara but didn't appear at all stressed by their experience. Payne and Abeo watched as Zara was smothered with hugs and kisses from Laila and the two boys.

Payne and Abeo exchanged a puzzled look. There was no sign at all that the children had been mistreated in any way, and neither the woman, nor the young man objected when Zara gathered up the children and shepherded them out of the house. After Payne and Zara had helped the children climb on board the wagon, the cook arrived with a tray of baked treats for the children in case they got hungry on their ride home. The young man stood in the doorway and watched them drive off. It had been simpler than Payne had expected. Maybe

Zara had over reacted and this cousin of hers was not such a threat after all.

"What do you think?" Abeo asked, still puzzled as they drove away.

"I don't think Zidan was expecting a visit," said Payne with a worried look. "He certainly won't be happy when he learns we've taken them back."

The two men fell into a companionable silence as Zara and the children chatted happily in the back of the wagon, but Payne could not stop thinking about how easy it had been. *Muslims worshipped their children*, thought Payne. *If Zidan had hurt them, Zara would never forgive him and never give herself to him. She would die first.* The man was an idiot. He had no hope for a life with Zara, much less love. He had played his last hand with the children and he had lost. Now he would lash out, and this time it would be to the death.

Payne had a good reason to change course. They took the precaution of returning by way of the quarry encampment instead of going directly to the villa. There were men in the camp who could help, and they already knew about Zidan and what he had done. Zara had told everybody when she had gone to the camp in a state of almost hysterical agitation and demanded that Abeo go to Algiers to fetch Payne.

The quarrymen and their kitchen staff had been anxiously awaiting news, and they crowded around the wagon as it pulled into camp. They had been outraged when Zidan had taken the children and now they had their chance to fuss over them. The Berber women sat the children down in the kitchen and gave them a hot chocolate drink. Everyone wanted to help in any way they could.

After an hour's rest, Payne felt it would be best to leave the children at the camp while Zidan was on the rampage. He left them in Abeo's charge and borrowed two horses for himself and Zara. They rode west to check on the villa. He said little to Zara on the road, while his mind was absorbed in hatching a plan to rid them of cousin Zidan. When they arrived near the villa, Payne dismounted and left his horse with Zara as he approached on foot to get a look at the building from afar. Everything appeared normal and there was no sign of Zidan or his men in the courtyard. He waved an all-clear to Zara, who rode on towards the house. She dismounted and ran into the building. A few minutes later, she reappeared with her old manservant carrying a canvas bag. Zara mounted her horse and rode out of the compound with the bag.

"Any news?" asked Payne.

"Nothing. There's no news, except that Malek has run off. He won't get far walking on those painful feet of his."

"Good."

"I've got the children's things. It can be cold at night."

The light was failing as Magnus left in the wagon with Zara and the children. It would take them a good half hour to make it to the wooden shelter at the bottom of the quarry. The road went the long way around the pit and was a rutted track in bad shape. Payne thought Zara and the children would be safer at the shelter and Zidan's thugs would never think of going there.

Payne was confident that Zidan and his men would come to ambush them at night and knew he would need all the men he could muster to fight them. After Magnus returned with the wagon, Payne assembled his men in the open-air kitchen and sent the Berber women home with strict orders not to say a word to anyone. The quarry slaves remained and were as heteroclite a group of men as you could find anywhere in North Africa. Some were European, some were from the Middle East, and others were from the African subcontinent, but they had one thing in common. They liked and respected the man who stood in front of them. Thomas Payne had been their supervisor for a long time and had never asked them to do anything that he would not have done himself. The quarry was a very dangerous place, and every man there could recall the times when Payne's diligent attention to their welfare had prevented a crippling accident or even saved a man's life.

They were ready for the fight. They held their improvised weapons — knives, sledgehammers, wicked-looking work tools of every description — and waited for Payne to speak. The men had been expecting a rousing call to arms and were disappointed when Payne told them his plan. They were to descend into the pit after it got dark and hide themselves while Payne waited in the camp for Zidan's men to arrive. There was a puzzled silence as they thought their supervisor was mad or soft in the head. This didn't seem like any kind of sensible plan they had ever heard of.

"Don't go all the way down into the pit," said Payne. "Just space yourselves out along the trail and wait."

The silence was replaced by a low, unhappy murmur of voices.

"While we are all hiding like little children afraid of the dark, Tom, where are you going to be?" asked Abeo, clearly unhappy with the plan.

"I'll be right here," Payne said confidently.

"You are going to kill Zidan and his men all by yourself?" Magnus asked.

The big Swede had never dared to speak to Payne this way before, but he was angry. What Payne was proposing was suicide.

"What do you need us for?" asked another man.

"I'll need you, all right."

"When?" Magnus demanded.

"Trust me, my friends —you will know when," said Payne in a voice that brooked no argument.

Ryder & Meade

Time was running out. They had less than forty-eight hours to get to Tipaza on the coast to catch the Spanish boat out of Malaga. Tipaza was not so far, so they decided to rest up for a day before leaving. It would not do to get there too early.

The night of the murder, they had dumped the body of the *patron* near the edge of the wood and returned to the house to clean up the kitchen. Ryder and Esteban had burned the rug and the cushions stained by the blood in the fireplace. Elena had recovered from the shock of killing her boss and was in a cheerful mood as she finished preparing the evening meal for her son and her honoured guests.

"What was he like, your *patron*?" asked Meade.

"*Un cerdo*, he was a pig," said Elena as she chopped vegetables on a wooden tray. "His wife ran away and went back to her family. All he had were his slaves, me and my son."

She poured the olive oil and cooked the vegetables over the fire, turning them over in the pan.

"You came for us, Mister Richard, but you were ready to leave without my son?"

"I thought if we bought you, the man would make a counteroffer for your son, but he never did. We would not have left without Esteban, Elena."

"You would have killed him if necessary?"

"John wanted to kill the bastard as soon as we saw him, but we thought it better to try to negotiate a price."

"I have no regrets, Mister Richard. I could never leave without my son. It was me or him."

"You are a courageous woman," said Meade, sitting next to Elias with a glass of wine.

After it got dark, Ryder and Esteban returned to the body and dug a shallow grave for the *patron*. It took them several hours to dig the hole in the hard ground and roll the body into the shallow grave. Meanwhile, Meade put the mule in the barn and fed the animals.

The following day, Elena's guests were up early except for Elias, who was exhausted and slept late. Esteban returned to the fields so that the neighbours were not surprised by his absence. Ryder and Meade examined the *patron*'s wagon in the barn and loaded it with sacks of grain for the journey to the coast. If they were stopped by the Turkish militia, the grain would give the appearance of a trip to buy supplies for the farm. Ryder found a musket in the house and put it in the wagon with powder and ball. Meade stored their bags in a corner and removed the pistols which he loaded. He hid the pistols and a short sword behind the sacks of grain. They loaded a water barrel, along with an old mattress and several pots and pans from the kitchen that Elena provided.

After some debate, Meade and Ryder decided to take the *patron's* mule and their own. If anyone came around, it would look like the *patron* had gone away to get supplies and taken his wagon. Elena provided her *patron's* working clothes and several wide-brimmed hats for the men, who needed to change their appearance to look more like farm labourers than rich merchants from the city.

After Elias was up, Elena prepared a special breakfast for the lad. He ate a *tostada* with tomatoes, meat, and cheese and drank tea. He was hungry and seemed at peace with himself in the presence of Elena.

"We must leave tonight," said Meade to Elena. "We have a boat waiting for us in Tipaza."

"Tipaza is not too far. I dream of my family and our return to Malaga," said Elena with a joyful air. "We'll be home soon."

She looked ten years younger now that she was returning to her family. She put an arm around Elias and made jokes with Esteban. She sang a melancholic song for the two boys, dancing around the kitchen as the boys laughed.

After their midday meal and several glasses of the *patron's* red wine, they napped for a few hours and were up as the light was fading in the west. They shut up the house and left in the wagon with Esteban driving. Meade sat beside him, the *patron's* musket within easy reach, while Elias, Ryder and Elena remained out of sight in the back. There was always the possibility that a Turkish patrol might stop them outside Blida, but once they were out in the country, no one would bother them.

Elena's motherly attentions seemed to calm Elias and spared Ryder from difficult conversations with his son. They had hardly exchanged a word since they escaped from Algiers. Ryder had no idea how to broach Elias' experience as a male prostitute, so he let it lie. Meade had warned him to go easy on the lad or run the risk of upsetting him further by asking about the past that he would be better off forgetting.

It was a cool night in the wagon as the *patron*'s mule plodded along the road with the second mule bringing up the rear. Ryder and Elias fell asleep while Elena watched the road filled with nervous energy. *Was it possible,* she thought, *that she would be reunited with her family in a few days*? She felt no regrets for killing the *patron*. She had been raped repeatedly by that horrible man during her first year as a slave when he had threatened to kill her son if she objected. After the first few years of abuse, she had put a stop to it by concealing a knife on her body, which she told the *patron* she planned to use to cut off his balls. The rapes stopped, and the man left her alone.

In the morning, it got to be terribly hot under the white tarp stretched across the wagon. Meade had replaced Esteban during the long night, and Ryder had replaced his friend in the early morning hours. Esteban, Meade and Elias were fast asleep on the mattress in the back. Elena had not slept a wink since they departed. She was exhausted, but she managed to cook a copious meal for the men when they stopped to eat at midday. They had no idea when they would eat again, so Elena slaughtered a chicken and cooked it over an open fire by the side of the road. As they waited for the meat to cook, Esteban distributed bread and cheese to the men and opened several bottles of wine. It was going to be a very long, tiring day.

Their destination was Tipaza, an old Punic trading post on the coast, that the Roman Emperor Claudius had turned into a fort. The *cardo maximus* was the main street and its columns ran all the way down to the sea. It was easily visible from boats way out in the bay and a convenient rendezvous for contraband and pirates. It was here that the Spanish boat would come for them in the early morning hours.

The timing of their arrival was critical. They were fugitives, and they did not want to arrive in broad daylight. They planned to travel at a slow, unobtrusive pace and arrive late in the evening. They arrived around midnight and descended the *cardo* to the sea. It had been an uneventful trip, and they had not seen any Turkish patrols. Ryder spotted a copse of trees near the shoreline that offered a semblance of concealment. They drove the wagon under the trees and waited. From time to time, they heard the voices of young men enjoying a night out or engaged in illicit affairs under the columns, and Turkish janissaries patrolling the *cardo* and calling out to people.

As Elias and Esteban slept in the wagon, Elena and the two Englishmen watched the sea for signs of the Spanish fishing sloop. Meade and Ryder knew that the boat would only make one attempt to collect them. They had agreed to this plan, knowing the risks involved. If the boat didn't come tonight, it wouldn't come at all.

"What if the boat doesn't come?" asked Ryder

"Don't worry, John. Captain Villegas won't let us down," said Meade. "The colonel will have his hide if he doesn't send the boat."

"What did Penn say about Oran?"

"He gave me the name of a fellow who can get us through the Turkish patrols."

"I hope it doesn't come to that."

"Me too, John. We'll wait here until an hour before dawn."

"We can't stay here with the Turk patrols in broad daylight."

"Don't worry, we'll take the road back to Blida, then go west."

After two o'clock, the noise from the *cardo* diminished, and all they could hear were bird calls and stray dogs sniffing around in the refuse. Ryder went to check on any Turkish patrols in the area. As he descended among the Roman columns towards the beach, he heard voices coming from behind a column and hid in the shadows. There were three Turkish guards sitting on the ground with their backs to the column. They were drinking *aguardiente* and watching for movement in the bay.

What were they doing there? Ryder asked himself, as he returned to join the others. The bay was close enough to Algiers to be an excellent site for smuggling contraband alcohol, tobacco, and other cargo. The smugglers could unload on the beach and hide the stuff in the hills for pickup later by wagon.

"There's a Turkish patrol watching the beach," said Ryder when he returned to the wagon.

"How many are they?" asked Meade.

"Three of them. I would think they're on the lookout for smugglers."

"If there are only three of them, we could kill the bastards."

"We could," said Ryder, but then thought better of it. They would only be adding more risk to an already risky venture. "For now, let's keep an eye on them and wait for the boat."

At around four o'clock, Ryder returned to the *cardo* to have another look. One man was asleep while the other two were huddled in conversation while they finished off the bottle of *aguardiente*. There was still no sign of a light on the horizon. Sunrise would be in two hours and the window for their escape was closing fast.

Forty-three

Payne

It was just after midnight and quite dark when Zidan and his men thundered into the camp on horseback. They were surprised to find no one around, even after they dismounted and ransacked the place, thrusting their knives and sabres into any space a man could possibly hide. Zidan barked an order in Arabic and the men spread out, warily searching through the trees and boulders on the camp's perimeter.

Payne stayed very still, watching as one of the thugs, braver than the rest, edged closer to where he had crouched in the darkness. The man was only a few feet away, aimlessly probing the sparse bushes with desultory swipes of his sabre. After he had passed by, Payne came out of hiding and attacked the man, stabbing him through the heart. *This won't do*, he thought. *It's taking too long and there are too many of them.* He waited for a second assailant to approach and raised one of his pistols, listening intently. A moment later, he heard another man moving only a few yards away. There was a muffled curse in Arabic as he tripped over a rock outcropping. Payne jumped up and fired at the man before he ran off in the direction of the quarry.

The loud report of the gun, coupled with its muzzle flash, attracted the attention of Zidan and his men who ran after him. They were fearless. They would thrash the life out of this *renegado*, cut off his balls and slit his throat. They had killed slaves before, and this one stood no chance against them. But first, they had to catch him, and Payne knew where he was going. They could see next to nothing in the camp under the trees, and their lurid threats transformed into howls of pain and furious curses as they tripped over obstacles. They were seconds behind Payne when he reached the edge of the pit and fired his second pistol at the closest man before he disappeared from view down the rabbit trail.

"That's him," yelled Zidan, who recognized Payne in the muzzle flash. "That's him. Get after him."

It was even darker in the pit, with the moon low in the sky. This was not a problem for Payne, who knew the trail like the back of his hand. He had descended and climbed the same trail hundreds of times. This wasn't the case for the thugs who were blindly pursuing him. The first two who descended into the pitch-black hole missed the trail entirely and ran headlong over the sheer drop. Payne heard their screams as their feet found only empty air, followed by the sickening crunch as their bodies hit the rocks two hundred feet below.

Zidan's men were more careful after that. They descended one by one, going slowly as the trail zigzagged both left and right. The trail was very steep in some places, nonexistent in others, and a wrong turn could be fatal. They were moving from ledge to ledge in near-total darkness. One of them lost his footing in the scree of a rock face and plummeted past Payne, who had tucked himself into a niche part way down. He could hear Zidan vainly raging at his men to move faster, but they were completely out of their element. They spent as much time trying not to fall as they did trying to engage in combat.

Deadly, unseen fights were breaking out all over the trail. To his left, Payne heard a brief scuffle and shouts as Abeo shoved two thugs off the ledge into the pit. To his right, he heard Magnus swearing in Swedish as he slammed another man off the trail. It was easy pickings for the quarrymen, who were hidden along the rock face and only had to jump out at Zidan's men and push them off the trail.

Above him, Payne heard a pistol shot, followed by a long silence. Payne suspected it might be Zidan, who had fired the weapon since most of the quarrymen were armed only with knives and tools from the camp. He moved slowly, going up the trail as silently as he could. He climbed onto a ledge to the spot he thought he had heard the sound coming from, but there was no one there. He turned and started to leave when he heard a voice behind his back.

"Mister Payne, you should not have come back," said the voice from the shadows. It had to be Zidan, and unlike his men, he sounded supremely confident. "I warned you not to come back, now you must die."

Thomas turned to face the man, his eyes searching the shadows. All he could see was a dark silhouette and the faintest suggestion of movement as Zidan raised his pistol.

"Stand near the edge, Payne, where I can see you."

Payne moved closer to the edge in the moonlight and then threw himself on the ground just as Zidan's ball passed over his head. He squinted in the darkness and realized that Zidan thought he had hit him. The bastard was taking his time, casually putting the pistol away and unsheathing his sabre to administer the *coup de grâce*. Payne lay motionless on the narrow ledge, his arms outstretched, and let his enemy get closer. He could hear Zidan laughing. He was a man who enjoyed killing.

"I'm surprised, Payne," said the voice with a sneer. "You thought we would accept a slave and an infidel like yourself into our family. You must be very stupid."

Zidan stepped closer. He was starting to raise his sword when Payne reached low and ran his *bousaadi* blade through Zidan's foot. He cried out in pain as he attempted to bring down the sword on Payne's head, but was again surprised by a stab wound to the femoral artery in his leg. Zidan landed hard on his back as his sword spun harmlessly off the cliff into the night. Payne pounced on the man and grabbed him by the neck before he hurled him over the edge with all his force.

Payne stood up and realized the battle was almost over. Abeo was calling to him from his left.

"Tom, I heard a gunshot. Are you all right?"

"I'm fine. How are you?"

"We got five of them."

Other voices started calling from Payne's right and left, providing information about the number of Zidan's assailants who had gone into the pit.

Payne stood on a ledge and counted heads as he mustered the quarrymen on the trail. The pit was littered with the bodies of Zidan and his men, some of them horribly mangled by their fall on the rocks, but Payne had not lost a single man. They were all accounted for.

There was still a lot of work to do, but it could wait until the morning. The fighting had been brutal, and while he doubted there were any survivors, it would be best to look for them in daylight.

They too, would have to be executed and thrown in the pit, along with the rest. They could not allow any of Zidan's men to survive to tell the tale — the rebellion of the quarry slaves against their Arab masters. They would have to destroy any sign that a battle had taken place or the Dey's janissaries would hunt them down to the ends of the earth for challenging the natural order of things.

The immediate mission was to return to camp and look for the raiders' horses. It would not do for riderless horses to be discovered wandering around the countryside or, worse yet, finding their way back to the homes of their late owners. While the men searched for the horses, Payne sent Magnus with the wagon to fetch Zara and the children and drive them home.

After all the horses were accounted for, the men gathered in the open-air kitchen and broke out the *aguardiente* to celebrate their victory. They felt triumphant and exhilarated from the fight. Payne's plan had worked. It had been an unequal contest, and while they were all nursing minor scrapes, they were otherwise unscathed. They were ecstatic, having enjoyed every moment of the confrontation. They were proud of what they had done and were confident they had killed most, if not all, of Zidan's men. They told each other stories about their heroic exploits, toasted their brilliant leader, and drank as much as they could. An hour later, they were too drunk to continue and took to their hammocks, falling asleep.

Payne was exhausted after forty-eight hours without sleep, but he still had the energy to mount his horse and ride out to the Roman villa to check on Zara and the children. He gave instructions to Abeo to collect all the dead men in the morning and to execute the survivors. They would need to find a deep hole in the pit to hide all the bodies. Later, they would take Zidan's horses to Algiers and sell them in the market. It would mean a clean slate for the quarrymen, since he doubted any of Zidan's men would be missed.

The sun penetrated the parlour and flooded it with light. Payne was fast asleep on some cushions near a low table and only heard movement at his side when young Laila arrived, holding a cup of tea in her trembling hands.

"Payne," she said in a whisper. "Payne—"

Payne woke up and wondered where he was. He had arrived very late last night and completely lost his sense of time. *It must now be close to noon*, he thought, as he smiled at the child.

"Laila, my dear," said Payne in Arabic as he took the cup from her. "Thank you."

He looked up and saw Zara watching him from the doorway.

"Thomas," said Zara in English, "you look much better. You fell asleep last night while I was talking to you."

"I did. I'm very sorry, Zara. What did I say?"

"Not much. You said there were no witnesses, so the battle at the quarry had never happened."

Zidan would not be missed, thought Payne, as he drank his tea. *He had vanished into thin air. No one would be the wiser.*

"You said we were safe now that my cousin has gone."

"Yes, that's true," said Payne as Laila pulled him by the hand. "You look very lovely this morning, Zara."

She smiled at him as he got up and followed Laila into the kitchen where food was waiting for him.

Forty-four

Felix & Caleb

Much had changed in the lives of the Gunter boys. Captain Murad had managed to escape from his Maltese prison, returning to Algiers in ill health but hailed as a hero. The boys had not seen him again after he was appointed governor of the great fortress of Oualidia, near Safi in Morocco.

Time had passed, and the boys had become accomplished sailors after Captain Marcellus had taken them under his wing. They were veterans of numerous voyages out of Algiers and Tunis, sometimes on the same ship and sometimes apart. They had risen quickly, the result not only of the high casualty rate among their corsair brethren but also because of their own abilities and experience. The corsair business was a promotion-rich business for European *renegadoes*.

Felix was Captain Felix Gunter now, albeit of a relatively small xebec with a crew of only ten. Nevertheless, he commanded a shipboard force of thirty janissaries and served at the pleasure of the Dey as Murad had before him. His ship had a shallow draught and was used for flushing out enemy ships from the bays along the coast. His mission was to stop the seemingly endless procession of vessels from Spanish Oran, Tangier and elsewhere trying to smuggle goods into the country without paying import duties.

As they sailed west in the early morning, they spotted a polacre, slipping into a bay near Tipaza. The polacre had reduced sail in the shallow water and was no match for Felix's xebec. Felix raced towards the ship and his janissaries boarded it. They searched the hold for contraband and after finding a large quantity of Spanish wine, Felix ordered his janissaries to seize the contraband and arrest the crew. His brother Caleb was to take command of the ship and follow him back to Algiers. The sailors on the polacre would be arrested and held until the duty on the cargo was paid in full.

That had been little more than an hour ago. It had taken some time for Caleb to get their prize sorted out, and he had just signalled to Felix that they were ready to fall in behind him for the return trip. Felix gave his orders to his crew, and as he turned away from the tillerman, he noticed a fishing sloop on its way into Tipaza Bay, presumably after a night of fishing. Felix glanced at his brother and waved a dismissive hand. They would ignore the sloop and maintain their course east for Algiers. Fishing boats were of limited interest to Felix and his brother, who were after illicit goods on cargo vessels.

Ryder & Meade

An hour later, the eastern sky was getting brighter, and Meade worried it would soon be time to leave Tipaza to avoid the patrols. He could hear the dawn chorus of birdsong as he observed the dark band of sea and sky. He thought it would be wise to turn the wagon around and prepare Elena and her son for the inevitable deception that no boat was coming for them from Malaga. They needed to get back on the road and head west for Oran. He was about to give the order to pack it up when suddenly he spotted a light far off in the bay. He warned Elena, who jumped up and lit the wick of the oil lamp with her tinderbox. The oil burned brightly and Elena turned it up so the flame was even brighter. She wordlessly handed it to Meade and went to wake the boys.

Meade held the lamp high over his head until he got an answering signal from the boat. Then Ryder and Meade grabbed their bags and pistols and followed Elena and the boys down to the beach. They waited in the shadows of the *cardo* as the Spanish boat approached slowly from afar. It was heading straight towards them and the Turks waiting in the shadows.

From the shore, they could just see the Dey's xebec with a polacre in tow, heading east. They didn't think the small fishing sloop would be troubled by any patrol vessels in the bay, but danger certainly lurked in the shadows of the *cardo*. Ryder knew the Turks would be alerted as soon as they stepped out onto the beach. He told Elena and the boys to wait for them in the sand dunes near the beach and to stay out of sight. He left with Meade, armed with pistols and a sword. They followed a circuitous route through the *cardo maximus* to come up on the Turks from behind. They stepped silently from behind a column with their pistols raised and saw that two of the Turks were fast asleep on the ground and snoring loudly. The third man seemed to have disappeared. They looked around and finally found him peeing on a sand dune a hundred yards away as he watched the fishing sloop close on the shore.

Ryder and Meade waved to Elena and the boys to run for it while they fixed their attention on the Turk in the dunes. The Turk rubbed his eyes and was surprised to see a fishing boat coming in on the waves. As he turned, he saw Ryder and Meade coming at him with pistols raised. He dropped to his knees and raised his hands, throwing up the *aguardiente* he had consumed over a long night of drinking.

Elena and the boys ran into the waves as the sloop struck the sandy bottom. A crewman lifted the boys, one after the other, to the deck and then took Elena's bag and helped her grab onto the railing of the boat. Ryder and Meade didn't hesitate a moment and ran on past the astonished Turk, heading for the boat. They raced into the waves and quickly shoved the boat off the bottom, scrambling on board with their packs.

The fishing sloop quickly turned around and heeled to the leeward as its lateen sail caught the wind. It headed out of the bay to the northwest at a good clip. Twenty minutes later, the sloop was gone. It had disappeared beyond the horizon.

PART THREE

RANSOMED

Forty-five

"I thought to have taken away the better sort of people first, and the rest afterwards, the which I understood to be the command given to me, but it pleases God to order that I must take away those I could have for cloth, and leave the rest until afterwards... I beseech your Honours not to think that this redemption may be part one year, and part another. And I desire your people may go home in summer, for I do assure you, their clothes be thin. I think two good ships and a pinnace will be fit to fetch away the rest of the slaves." Edmund Cason, 1646

September 21, 1646
Algiers

The English gentleman Edmund Cason stood on the deck of the *Charles* and gazed raptly at the white diamond of Algiers against the greenery of the Sahel hills. He could scarcely believe he had made it, yet here he was. He had tried several times to sail to Algiers, and each time had failed. His efforts had begun six years earlier when, in 1640, the Long Parliament had charged him with securing the release of hundreds of English and Irish slaves in Algiers. His plans had been frustrated by events, chief among them the outbreak of the English civil war in 1642 between the Royalists and the Parliamentarians.

Cason's first attempt to sail to Algiers had been in the summer of 1645 after Oliver Cromwell's New Model Army had won the Battle of Naseby for the Parliamentarians. The battle marked the beginning of the end for Charles I. Cason had set sail on the *Honour*, but only got as far as Gibraltar before the ship burned at anchor in a bay near the Straits. The voyage was a complete disaster and Cason lost all the ransom money. He returned to England penniless and discouraged, but only a year later he was on his way again on the *Charles*. Now he had arrived and his mandate was to ransom as many slaves as possible and negotiate a permanent peace.

It would not be easy. It had been fifteen years since the raid on Baltimore, and many things had changed. A new Dey ruled the kingdom. Cason was granted an audience with Yusuf II, who entertained him at the palace and agreed immediately to a peace treaty, but was far less enthusiastic about giving up English slaves. He told Cason that the slaves had been bought in good faith and their owners could not be expected to part with them without payment.

Frustrated, Cason requested an audience with the Diwan, the senior council of janissaries, so that he could present his offer directly to them. The Diwan was the real power behind the state. It was the Diwan that made the laws, while the Dey played a more or less ceremonial role in government. The Diwan quickly agreed to both the proposal for peace and the end to English slavery. Henceforth, any Englishman who was brought to Algiers as a slave would be immediately released and both sides would avoid interfering with each other's shipping.

Cason tried to negotiate a fixed price for every slave, but was forced to accept the fact that he would have to negotiate prices with every slave owner. He set up shop in Algiers and then went looking for the slaves and their owners. He noted their names, their prices, and their places of origin. There were some 25,000 slaves in Algiers at the time, but only a fraction of them were English or Irish. Most of the women and children worked in the houses of the well-to-do as maids or servants doing household chores. The men worked on the docks, on building sites, on farms and as galley slaves for the Dey. Some of the men had acquired shops of their own in the *souk*, selling tobacco and wine, and all manner of other goods.

News of the arrival of an English gentleman in Algiers to ransom slaves spread like wildfire. After five weeks, Cason had put together a list of over 650 men, women, and children from England, Ireland, Scotland, and Wales. Fifty percent of them were from the West Country and around thirty percent from London, while the rest originated from virtually every corner of the British Isles. A hundred English slaves were away at the time of Cason's visit with the Turkish fleet at Crete, sweating at their oars in the long and bloody Ottoman campaign to take the Venetian citadel at Heraklion. Many of the slaves had converted to Islam or had moved to other ports in the east. Their names were immediately expunged from the lists. To 'turn Turk' was apostasy, and it was presumed that none of these people would have any interest in returning to their Christian homeland.

The logistics of ransoming so many men and women was a huge task. Cason had brought with him a limited amount of funds and a large consignment of cloth, which he could exchange as barter for slaves or sell to the highest bidder. The price per slave varied enormously. It all depended on the person's age, status, and skills, and the slave owners drove a hard bargain. Men with skills such as carpenters, coopers, sail-makers, tailors, and others were in high demand in Algiers and were ransomed at a higher price. Cason paid the amount of £7 for one Edmond Francis of Dorset, while he spent well over £80 to ransom Elizabeth Alwin of London. The average price was just under £30 per captive, the usual rate for ransoming ordinary mariners and boys. The Baltimore slave Joane Broadbrook was ransomed for £32 while Ellen Hawkins went for £19. He could not save them all, but Cason eventually ended up ransoming a total of some two hundred and forty-five slaves.

Joane Broadbrook and Ellen Hawkins were the only slaves from Baltimore who chose to return. They embarked on the *Charles* for the return voyage. The great majority of the Baltimore slaves remained in Algiers and were happy to carry on with their lives there. Maria Bouziane had brought the children along to see their mother off. There was the youngest, Evelyn, and the two boys, Malcolm and Liam, now full-grown Muslim men with their own wives and families. Liam had recently married a lovely Algerian woman who was expecting a baby, while Malcolm already had two children.

Ellen Hawkins, the Irish maid with the missing finger, had never really integrated Algerian society. She had remained faithful to her Christian upbringing and refused to 'turn Turk'. She had worked for a time sorting tobacco leaves with Emma Pierse and had moved on to other menial jobs. Her *patron* was happy to ransom her and he made a nice bonus in addition to the revenue she had earned for him over fifteen years of service.

The families stood on the dock and watched the ship shake off its moorings and head out of the bay. Joane stood on the deck in tears, waving to her children. She had long ago accepted the fact that she would never see her children again if she dared to return. Her children had been a source of immense joy in her life, but also of frustration. They had 'turned Turk' against her will and, most painful of all, had accepted Maria as their surrogate mother. That had been the end for her since she no longer felt she had a place in the their home. There was nothing left for her but to return to her roots in Baltimore and the comfort of her religious beliefs.

March 15, 1647
Baltimore, West Cork

It had been a long, tiring journey home. Joane had taken the coach from Castlehaven to Roaring Water Bay with frequent stops at villages along the way. Rain clouds were threatening in the southeast as she finally disembarked opposite the coach house and livery stable in Baltimore. There were a few people about, but beyond the coach house, the village looked empty. She found a dogcart to take her down to the cove. A boy harnessed a horse to a two-wheeled cart and off they went, driving down the steep road towards the cove.

A lot had changed in the village, and she didn't expect to recognize any faces after so many years. Her memories would have to suffice. The line of broken cottages was visible even before they reached the shoreline. Many had fractured walls and roofs that had collapsed, and the surrounding sand was strewn with refuse of all kinds. The wooden beams had been scavenged for use in new dwellings along with anything else of value.

There was no sign of life. The cove lay abandoned these fifteen years. The survivors of the attack were long gone. She climbed down from the cart and went to have a look. Her cottage had been the third from the end. She stepped through the broken door and stepped back fifteen years in time. Much of the structure was intact, but it was painful to see what had happened to the cottage. Masonry was broken, cupboards were smashed, and broken glass littered the floor. She went into the bedroom and sat down on a wooden stool to get her bearings. She took out her most prized possession, her book of hours, and studied the magnificent drawings of pastoral scenes. She started to pray, almost silently and then louder, as the words reverberated against the stone walls.

"Our Father which art in heaven, Hallowed be thy name. Thy kingdom come, Thy will be done in earth, as it is in heaven—"

Suddenly, she stopped. She felt something, a presence, in the room with her. It was strange. The house was empty and abandoned, but someone had been living here after she and the boys had been taken. *It must be Stephen*, she thought as she got up and walked around nervously. She ran her fingers over the only intact wall left in the cottage and found the false brick. She stopped to pry it loose. It had been her husband's secret cache of money and papers. She peered inside the niche and saw a faint glint of metal in the dusty interior.

It was her wedding ring, a simple gold ring on a chain. She pulled it free and held it up. It was the ring she often couldn't wear during her pregnancy because her fingers were too swollen. She touched her lips to the ring and thought about Stephen.

He waited here, she thought. *He didn't give up. He prayed for our return.* Her eyes glistened over with tears. He must have remained in the house for a time, hoping that his family would return. The memories came flooding back — the wonderful summer day before the attack and the simple joys of life in the cottage. She remembered the times she had nursed the boys as she watched the fishing boats bobbing at anchor in the cove at the end of a day. She remembered the moments at the kitchen table when she and Stephen shared a laugh with the boys. The laughter would always start with Liam trying to repress a silly giggle followed by Malcolm's jeering snicker, and soon the boys had them all in stitches.

Joane forced herself to move. *If she didn't leave now*, she thought, *she would never leave*. There was nothing left for her in Baltimore, but those wonderful memories. She left the house and walked down to the sandy beach, looking up at the darkening sky. A moment later, the downpour struck, and she ran for the dogcart to avoid the rain.

EPILOGUE

The Barbary slave trade was enormously profitable for the city-states of Algiers, Tunis and Tripoli. In 1641, Charles I appointed a committee to look into the matter called the 'Committee for the Captives of Algiers'. They reported that there were five thousand English slaves in Algiers and Tunis, and a fleet of thirty corsairs was to be expected off the English coast during the summer months of the same year. In the summer of 1645, while Edmund Cason was preparing to leave on his first attempt to get to Algiers, a Turkish raiding party landed on the Cornish coast and kidnapped 240 men, women, and children. There was no stopping the tidal wave of Christian captives and pirated vessels arriving in the ports of North Africa.

As remarkable as Cason's achievements had been, there were still some four hundred slaves who desired to return and had been left behind. Cason wrote to Parliament to request two good ships and a pinnace to bring them home, but his request was ignored. He didn't give up, however, and remained in Algiers to continue his work to free the slaves and to ensure that any English man or woman who arrived aboard a corsair vessel would be freed and returned home. In the 1640s, Parliament dispatched a new consul, Humphrey Oneby, to replace James Frizell. Oneby stayed in Cason's house in Algiers, and over the next few years helped him secure the release of a number of slaves as they found money to ransom them and pay for their journey home.

The peace treaty brokered by Cason lasted well into the 1650s and no English ships were captured by Algerian corsairs over the period. As a result, the merchants of every nation in Europe endeavoured to pass off their ships as English merchantmen carrying English passengers to avoid being attacked by the Algerian corsairs. Cason never saw England again. After rescuing so many men, women and children, he died in Algiers in 1654.

HISTORICAL NOTES

This novel is an imaginative re-creation of a true story. We know a lot about the Baltimore slaves. We know the raid occurred on June 20, 1631, and the raiders arrived in Algiers, as recorded by James

Frizell on July 28. The voyage took exactly 38 days to complete. This surprised me at first. The distance by sea is around 1600 nautical miles and at 10 knots, they could have completed the voyage within a week with a good wind. So Captain Murad must have had some very good reasons for taking his time sailing south along the coast of France, Spain and Portugal.

I believe the main reason was that his ships were not designed to take on the Atlantic gales along the French and Spanish coasts. He had to hug the coast as he sailed south and this only increased the danger of attack from French and Spanish naval vessels. Furthermore, he needed fresh water and food to feed the people on board his two ships: 230 janissaries, 150 captives and 20 crew members. It takes a lot of fresh meat to feed 400 people. The foraging expeditions along the coast would have provoked confrontations with the locals who feared being enslaved by the corsairs.

Although various victim accounts mention being locked up in the hold of ships for long periods of time, you cannot keep men, women, and children locked up below decks in the heat of summer without putting their lives at risk. The hold of a ship is a humid environment with bilge water, lice and rats. It is no place for young children and remember, there were over fifty children on board the ships. To maintain the health of his captives, Captain Murad would have had to stop every few days to air out the hold and allow the captives to walk about on the deck in the fresh air. If this is the case, and I'm convinced it is, then it explains the time it took to get to Algiers.

I have tried not to embellish or exaggerate the events of the voyage. The escape from Algiers by William Okeley in a canvas boat is well documented and quite remarkable. I hope I have done justice to the slave market of Algiers. It really was a terrible place. I have tried to imagine the lives of the Baltimore slaves after they arrived in Algiers — how they adapted to their new lives, how some improved their lives while others failed.

I have described the heroic work of James Frizell and Edmund Cason, who worked to ransom the English slaves with little or no help from the English Parliament. I have tried to bring all of this to the novel in an honest and satisfying way. I have allowed myself several bits of fictional fancy, including the capture of the young Jean-Marie de Bancalis de Maurel, son of the Duke of Quimperlé, and the parade of the wife of the Duke of Lucca in the port of Algiers. These characters are entirely fictional, as are the Baltimore slave characters that I have described.

The American historian Robert Davis has estimated that there were over a million, primarily white Christians forced into captivity in the Barbary States of North Africa between 1530 and 1780. Of course, this number pales compared to the over ten million black slaves involved in the Atlantic slave trade that came later. The slaves in Barbary were European and mainly white, but the corsair raiders had no hesitation in enslaving black and brown captives. Slaves were Catholic, Protestant, Orthodox, Jewish and Muslim. No one's racial or religious background excluded them from being captured and sold as slaves.

The Catholic Church had acted shamelessly for centuries against Jews and Muslims alike, starting with the Inquisition in France in the 12th century. The Spanish church forced the Sephardic Jews to convert to Christianity in 1492 and ten years later, forced Muslims to do the same. Between 1609 and 1614, Spain deported 300,000 Moriscos or Spanish Muslims by loading them on ships for North Africa and the Middle East. The Moriscos were welcomed in towns across North Africa. People took them in and helped them set up shop. It was a huge opportunity for local economies and brought with it an army of skilled artisans and labourers.

The Catholic church throughout its history has demonized the Muslims of North Africa and the Ottoman Empire. Islam was the enemy. The Moors were barbarians, both in the sense that they were Berbers and that they came from beyond the boundaries of Christian civilization. *Renegadoes* were apostates who had deserted their religion and handed over their immortal soul to the enemy. This was the ultimate betrayal, worse even than robbery and murder.

It is not surprising that Catholic clerics exaggerated the violence done to Christians by Muslim corsairs. Congregations were shown pictures reminiscent of Dante's Inferno with captives strung up, beaten or burned into submission. Slaves who had been ransomed by the Church were expected to help in the collection of funds by travelling the countryside and telling tall tales of their imprisonment at the hands of their Muslim jailers.

In 1634, Father Pierre Dan estimated that there were 32,000 slaves in Algiers and Tunis. Francis Knight, who had been a slave in Barbary for seven years, gave a number twice as high. Father Dan estimated the number of slaves in Algiers at 25,000, with some 8,000 having 'turned Turk'. I suspect this figure is too low. It was extremely easy for a Christian to become a Muslim in North Africa, and instantly the doors of commerce and society would open up for the ambitious *renegado*.

In 1641, the English Parliamentary 'Committee for the Captives in Algiers' estimated the number of English slaves in Algiers and Tunis at 5,000. This figure is probably a good estimate. Frizell noted the arrival of some 340 English slaves between July 1629 and July 1631. So over thirty years, we can estimate the influx of English slaves in Algiers alone would be around 5,000 individuals. This influx would certainly be enough to top up the English slave population and maintain it at 5,000 individuals. If only 650 English slaves were eager to be ransomed by Edmund Cason, this means that only about 13% of the English slaves in Algiers were interested in going home. The other 87% had either 'turned Turk' or had adapted to their new lives in Algiers.

The Baltimore slave story testifies to the immense adaptability of humans. After fifteen years in Algiers, most of the Baltimore captives had moved on with their lives. For them, North Africa was a land of opportunity. The Mediterranean basin stretching from the Straits of Gibraltar to the Holy Land was the greatest marketplace in the world with some thirty kingdoms, republics, sultanates, duchies, and principalities trading with one another. Algiers with its many connections to the east was a vibrant, cosmopolitan and technically advanced city, while England was a backward country at war with itself, its poverty and human misery often unspeakable. The average post-infancy life expectancy in Algiers was around sixty years old and the city was a model of cleanliness and industry. There was clean running water, piped sewage, and an abundance of flowers and fruit trees in the parks. There would have been little interest among the Baltimore slaves to return to the drudgery of life at the fish palace in rainy, windswept Ireland.

Of course, not everyone was happy with their new lives. There were many slaves who suffered terribly and others who tried to escape. The Spanish slave Miguel de Cervantes made four daring escape attempts during his five years of captivity in Algiers and later wrote his famous novel *Don Quixote*. The English merchant Francis Knight spent seven years in captivity before he escaped during Ali

Bitchin's catastrophic raid against the Venetians. Captain John Smith, who was destined to become the leader of the Jamestown colony, was enslaved in Constantinople and later escaped to England.

The corsair raid on Baltimore was one of the most shocking ever recorded in the 17th century. Today, in the cool interior of the Anglican Church of the Holy Trinity in Algiers, there is a marble slab dedicated to the memory of the Baltimore slaves.

1631 ✝ Two Algerine Pirates landed in Ireland sacked BALTIMORE and carried off its inhabitants to slavery in Algiers

ACKNOWLEDGEMENTS

I would like to thank my wife Andrée Tousignant, son Thomas Kinsey, my editor Doug Sutherland, consultant Clare Dyer, my daughters Eve and Josée Kinsey, and everyone else who believed in this adventure and provided assistance.

PICTURE CREDITS

1- Engraving: *Ein Janitschar* by Christoph Weigel the Elder & Caspar Luyken, Neu-eröftnete Welt-Galleria, Nuremberg, 1703

2- Engraving: Barbary Galley, *Histoire de Barbarie et de ses Corsairs*, author Pierre Dan published in 1684

3- Drawing of Spanish Xebec

4- Engraving: *"De Stad Haven En Mouillie Van Algiers Neven Desselfs Kasteelen"* (the city, the port, the mole d'Algiers) by Gerard van Keulen circa 1690, Nederlands Scheepvaartmuseum Amsterdam

5- Engraving of Slave Market in Algiers: *"Mannier Hoe de Gevange Kriften Slaven tot Algiers verkoft worden"* by L.Luyken circa 1650

6- Engraving of men paddling small boat, *Histoire de Barbarie et de ses Corsairs*, author Pierre Dan published in 1684

7- Engraving: "Fathers of Redemption", *Histoire de Barbarie et de ses Corsairs*, author Pierre Dan published in 1684

8- Photograph of a marble slab, Anglican Church of the Holy Trinity in Algiers

OTHER BOOKS BY THE AUTHOR

Playing Rudolf Hess (2016)

An Absolute Secret (2017)

Shipwrecked Lives (2018)

Remembrance Man (2020)

See the author's blog: www.nicholaskinsey.com

One of the greatest mysteries of WWII

A Cinegrafica / Booklocker paperback and ebook, 2016

ISBN: 978-0-9952921-0-9

After parachuting into Scotland in 1941, the German Reichsminister Rudolf Hess is revealed to be an imposter. MI5 puts together a team of intelligence officers led by Paul Cummings and his German wife Claudia to investigate the Hess double. They are sent to Camp Z where Hess is being held in relative comfort following Churchill's orders. The team soon starts to uncover the imposter's secrets involving the shadowy Herr Oberst and his secret training by the SS. But the British government decides to bury the truth and it is only in 1973 that a British doctor confronts the imposter during a medical examination in Berlin and discovers the truth.

"Makes history come alive like a thriller"

"Must read, forgotten WWII story"

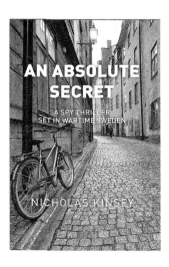

A spy thriller set in wartime Sweden

A Cinegrafica / Booklocker paperback and ebook, 2017

ISBN 978-0-9952921-2-3

A spy thriller set in wartime Sweden when Stockholm was a bourse for foreign intelligence and German war booty. British SIS officer Peter Faye is sent to Stockholm in 1943 to spy on German Intelligence Officer Karl-Heinz Kramer. With the help of his assistant, Faye recruits an Austrian maid working for the Kramer household who manages to sneak out secret documents held by Kramer in a locked drawer. The documents are so sensitive that they cause a commotion in London. With the help of Swedish journalist Anders Berger, Faye discovers a network of Soviet moles working in British Intelligence. The novel is richly evocative, skilfully paced and a real page-turner. Kinsey's meticulously crafted second novel is based on true wartime stories with their heroes and villains.

"A great war time spy thriller"

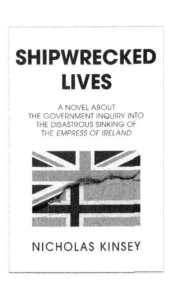

A novel about the *Empress of Ireland* disaster

A Cinegrafica / Booklocker paperback and ebook, 2018

ISBN 978-0-9952921-4-7

The *Empress of Ireland* passenger liner collided with the Norwegian collier *Storstad* in the St. Lawrence River on a foggy night in May 1914, sinking in 14 minutes and claiming the lives of 1,012 people. This is the story of the survivors and the government inquiry into Canada's worst maritime disaster. It is based on the actual testimony of witnesses at the *Commission of Inquiry*, which was presided over by Lord Mersey, the gruff and opinionated British jurist and politician.

"From the very first lines, Kinsey skillfully crafts this novel. We are drawn into the lives of the individuals on the *Empress*, passengers confused and frightened when loud blasts of the ship's whistle sound and the ship begins to list, then rapidly sink. He weaves the story between the disaster itself and what follows with the survivors in a courtroom as lawyers and witnesses try to unravel the cause of the collision. Kinsey has written a historical novel that is impossible to put down. I found that the transitions from survivor story to courtroom events held my interest from start to finish." Rosalie Grosch, www.norwegianamerican.com

Fear and despair during the 1832 cholera epidemic

A Cinegrafica / Booklocker paperback and ebook, 2020

ISBN 978-0-9952921-6-1

During the 1832 cholera epidemic, Paolo works for his uncle as a gravedigger in Western Ontario. At night he earns a bonus from wealthy clients as a 'remembrance man' whose job is to watch over selected graves for signs of the undead. He discovers a young woman who has been buried alive and is drawn into a terrifying story of revenge and insanity. This is a tale of murder, greed and deceit, and the breakdown of society. Family members turn against family members, friends against friends, and soon everyone is out for themselves. Cholera victims are simply abandoned on the roads, and wagons are sent around to collect the bodies and bury them in cholera pits. During these dark days, stories spread about reopening coffins in which the dead had apparently revived after burial, only to die in a futile attempt to escape. No one wanted to bury a loved one who might still be alive, which led to the habit of keeping corpses around so that the families could be sure the person had really died.

"Rarely has a novelist managed to convey more vividly the breakdown of society during a cholera epidemic."

Printed in Great Britain
by Amazon

24918618R00212